# The Silent Cradle

# The Silent Cradle

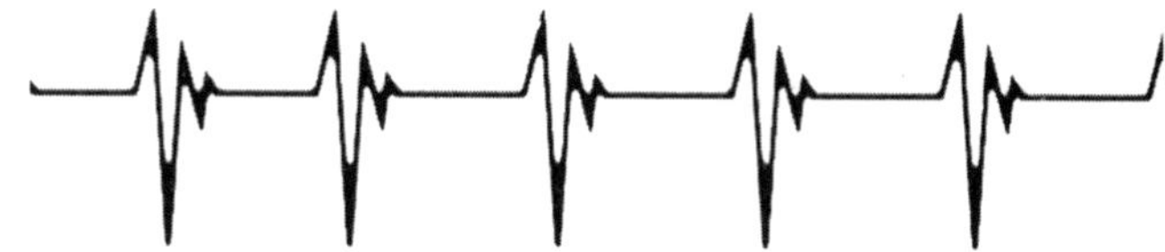

Margaret Cuthbert

SIMON & SCHUSTER

First published in Great Britain by Simon & Schuster, 1998
A Viacom Company



Simon & Schuster Ltd
West Garden Place
Kendal Street
London
W2 2AQ

Simon & Schuster Australia
Sydney

A CIP catalogue record for this book is available from the British Library.

ISBN Hardback 0-684-84044-8
ISBN Trade Paperback 0-684-82152-4

1 3 5 7 9 10 8 6 4 2

Printed and bound in Great Britain by
Butler & Tanner Ltd, Frome and London

This book, along with my heart and love,
is dedicated to my husband, Ronald A. Dritz, M.D.

# Acknowledgments

I would like to thank my patients for teaching me about courage. I am also grateful for the undergraduate creative-writing program at Stanford University, the novel-writing program at the UC Berkeley Extension, and the fiction writers program given by the Squaw Valley Community of Writers.

Now, on to individuals. Hugs and kisses to the literary professionals who assisted me in my transformation from doctor to novelist; novelist Donna Levin, who read my first draft and still kept me in her writing class; novelist and mentor James N. Frey, who was going to drill the path of the hero's journey into my thick skull even if it killed me; Mill Valley novelist Susan Trott, who knew when my first forty pages were good enough to show to an agent, so she did; world's greatest literary agent Theresa Park, who, believing in me and my protagonist, launched my professional writing career with a single phone call; world's greatest editor Emily Bestler, who made rewriting so exciting I was sad when she said we were done, and who, along with Gina Centrello, most wonderful publisher, decided to buy the book and make my lifelong dream come true.

Many thanks to the medical types who shared their knowledge and expertise in order to make me look good: Krishnamoorthy Yogam, M.D.; Tracy Flanagan, M.D.; Edward Blumenstock, M.D.; Michael Katz, M.D.; Stuart Lovett, M.D.; Gil Duritz, M.D.; Evangeline "Dinky" Augustin, R.N.; Gary Goldman, M.D.; Gregory Kelly, M.D.; Larry Caldwell, M.D.; Larry Siegel, M.D.; Clifford Schultz, M.D.; Coyness Ennix, M.D.; Leigh Iverson, M.D.; Frank Snell, C.R.N.A.; Larry Shots, C.R.N.A.; Beth Ilog, C.R.N.A.; Brian Richardson, M.D.;

Richard Dailey, Ph.D.; Nancy Levine-Jordano, L.C.S.W.; David Henderson, L.V.N.; and the staff of American Medical Response Ambulance Company. Thanks to the CEOs and administrative folks who took time from their busy schedules to answer my questions: John Loden, Al Green, Wayne Moon, Anthony Wagner, Craig Sullivan, Gary Depolo, Jan Long, Ed Berger, Ron Marshall, Alan Fox, Susan Whiting, Gerald Saunders, Kristen Jones, Janelle McDonald, and Annabelle Reeve. Special thanks to law enforcement's finest: Sergeant Stephen Odum, Sergeant Michael Holland, police officer Joe Anderson, and to fellow writers: Susan Domingos, Elaine Avila, David Wimsett, Valerie Perry, Deb Cooksey, Diane Holt, Barbara McHugh, Eric Roher, Marilyn Day, Heather King, John Meeker, Leon Tsao, Paul Diebels, Carl Gonser, Stephen Linsley, Annagret Ogden, Donna Gillespie, Donal Brown, Bruce Hartford, Bob Hunt, Brad Newsham and Leigh Anne Varney. Cheers to friends who advised and encouraged me from the time the story was in diapers to the present: Penny Mullinex, Veronica Bhonsle, Kathryn Torres, Nancy O'Donnell-Souza, Diane Walden, David Wendel, Judy Wendel, Hilary Schultz, Marilyn Loden, Mia Kelly, Carol Caldwell, M.D., Eric Kelly, Val Kelly, Ann Braunstein, Roya Maroof and Karen Russo.

Most of all, I want to thank my husband and *plot-meister,* Ron Dritz, for his knowledge, patience, advice, and love as we traveled this long journey together, one page at a time.

# The Silent Cradle

# Prologue

"I CARRY THE LORD'S BABY IN MY BELLY!" BELLOWED NOLA Payne. "My destiny belongs to Him!"

"That's really swell, Miss Payne," said the paramedic, Theodore McHenry, as he and his twin brother grabbed the sides of Nola's gurney. "And don't you worry. We're Hillstar's superstars. It's our job to get you safely from the Birth Center and over to Berkeley Hills Hospital for your C-section."

"Hey, keep moving," Leonard McHenry grumbled.

Theodore smiled down at Nola. "I hear your baby's breech. Smart kid. Who wouldn't want to enter the world landing on his feet?"

Nola was beyond answering this question, so as they struggled to shift her five-feet-one, 267-pound frame into the ambulance, she just kissed the yellow Day-Glo crucifix suspended from her shoestring necklace. After all, her faith was in God, not man.

And sure enough, as if on cue, God lifted the gurney into the air—closer to Heaven, she thought. God could do anything. All one had to do was to believe.

Theodore stayed with her inside the back cabin where her gurney was secured to the floor. Leonard, clad in the same navy-blue jumpsuit as his brother, jumped back onto the ground and slammed the doors shut.

Immediately Nola's coal-black eyes darted back and forth. Such a small room, she noted, and so stark. No pictures of angelic babies frolicking across the ceiling, or the sound of sweet violin music coming from salmon-colored walls. The ivy-laced Birth Center had both, not to mention the cherry candy—Nola's favorite—on the bedside table. Instead, the ambulance had blue bins filled with plastic-wrapped packages, and rows of bright lights that made her squint.

But the smell was nice. Clean. Like rubbing alcohol. She had rubbed alcohol on her stomach for the past nine months. She wanted to birth the cleanest baby ever born. Cleanliness was next to godliness, and she lived to be close to God.

She heard the engine kick over and felt the lurch of the ambulance as it took off. Theodore, his smoky gray eyes still smiling at her, gently strapped a green plastic mask over her face before turning a valve on the wall to his right. The blast of funny-smelling air made Nola turn up her nose and try to push the mask away.

"It's the plastic," Theodore apologized, replacing the mask. Over the top of the mask Nola saw his bald round head glisten under the lights, and a face full of freckles over a fiery red mustache. He looked exactly like his brother, except that he was not quite as bulky.

"Oxygen has no smell, Miss Payne," Theodore explained. "So just breathe normally. It's good for the baby."

From one of the overhead bins he removed a new IV bag. "This your first?" he asked, as he tore off the bag's plastic wrapping.

He pulled the tubing out from the bottom of the Birth Center's empty IV bag and stuck its arrow-tip end into the new bag that he had retrieved from the blue bin. Next he twisted a plastic screw attached to the tubing. Salt water dripped in like water from a leaky faucet.

"I've got a couple of kids myself," he went on to say, as he crumpled the plastic wrapping and stuffed it into a hole in the wall next to him.

"You've got a couple of begging midgets," yelled Leonard from the driver's seat. "Nothing but gimme, gimme, gimme, all day long."

Theodore chuckled as he turned the oxygen valve again. The air blew even more harshly against her face. She still hated the smell, but she breathed in and out deeply, for the baby's sake.

"That's the ticket," Theodore said. He lifted her lime-green gown and placed a smaller version of the Birth Center's hockey puck against her belly. "Okay now. Hold very still. It's time to check out your little man—"

"No, siree, no kids for me!" Leonard sang.

"Hey, pipe down a minute!" Theodore said. He listened again, his eyes closed.

As he pressed the machine hard against her, Nola moved it to the spot where Jenny, the Birth Center nurse, had found the "perfect heartbeat" only minutes before.

Suddenly, she pushed his hands away altogether. From out of nowhere came a horrible, ripping agony. The pain stretched from one side of her belly to the other, and just as fast, it dove down between her legs.

She grabbed her crucifix, but the pain worsened. Dropping it, she reached down to her pelvis instead, but the pain changed direction, and burned a path straight to her chest. Nola clutched her breastplate, but again, the pain had moved. It now fanned out across her entire belly like twenty flaming arrows shot straight from Hell. Then came the nausea, and a cold, drenching sweat. She tried that cleansing breath she had heard about on TV, but to no avail.

She slapped at Theodore's hands. "The pain! The pain!" But her words only got as far as the plastic mask. She shouted louder, but Theodore just kept sliding the hockey puck over her body. His bald head had erupted into a maze of tiny rivers. His eyes looked panicked.

Finally, she ripped the mask from her face. All this time she had not heard the baby's heartbeat. "What's happening? My baby boy!"

"Hey, what's going on back there?" Leonard asked.

"Breathe!" Theodore ordered, mashing the mask back on her face. "Your baby needs this—more than ever!"

"No!"

An uppercut from her right elbow slammed against his jaw. He fell back and crashed against the interior wall of the ambulance. She tore the mask off and flung it behind her. "Save my baby!"

"Theo," Leonard yelled, "what the hell are you guys doing? Is the baby coming already?"

"Oh, my God!" Theodore cried. "This can't be happening! Not again."

"Please, save my baby boy! My sweet Baby Je—!"

"Theo? What the hell are you talking about?"

"The baby's heartbeat, you damn fool! I can't find the baby's heartbeat!"

"No way! Another one?"

"Stick it, Leo!"

"Save us all, Lord Jesus!" Nola screamed, grabbing her belly. "Oh, it hurts! It hurts! It hurts!"

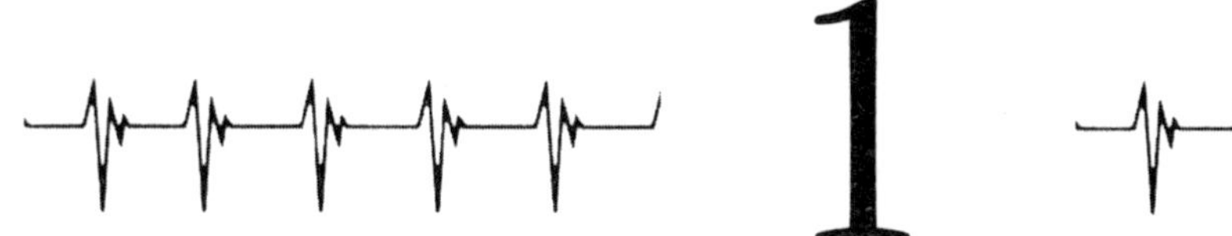

# 1

"PUSH!" SAID DR. RAE DUPREY, TO HER PATIENT, ANGEL Lloyd.

"Just take it out—take it OUT!" Angel screamed.

"Hunker down now, honey," said Angel's husband, Max.

"You hunker down if you think it's so easy, Mr. Lamaze!"

Rae chuckled as she sat on a stool between Angel's pale thighs. She moved in closer, using sterile gauze to wipe flecks of blood from Angel's perineum. The baby was crowning beautifully. Another contraction was starting.

"That's right, just ease it on out, nice and slow now," she coaxed.

"Aaiieee!" Angel shouted. "Please, Rae, pull it out! Don't just sit there! Give me a cesarean—do something!"

"I told you to have that epidural, honey," Max said, wiping his wet brow.

"Shut up. And stop calling me honey!"

But then the back of the baby's head emerged, covered with wet black hair; and as the neck extended upward, out came a pink and wrinkly face.

Rae stared back at the two large slate-blue eyes that gazed questioningly up at her. With the tip of her gloved finger, she touched the tip of the baby's nose. Then she cleaned out both nose and mouth with a tiny blue suction bulb. "Rough trip, eh?" she said to the little face.

Thirty minutes later, Rae had showered and wrapped a towel

around herself. She was a petite woman, barely five feet three, 105 pounds, with the lithe body of a dancer. Her light brown eyes, spaced widely apart and almond shaped like a Serengeti leopard's, stared straight ahead at the stark white walls. Sighing, she closed them for a few seconds and thought about the two babies that had kept her up all night. A smile crept across her face. Sure she felt tired, but mothers and babies had done well. And that, she thought to herself in this quiet predawn hour, was all that mattered.

She sat on the locker room's sleek wooden bench. In her hand she held a Dictaphone, into which she began reading her grocery list. Not that she had much time to shop. Being the vice-chair of Berkeley Hills Hospital's prestigious OB/GYN department left her little time for a personal life. So when she did shop, she wanted to get in and out in a hurry.

There would be even less time when she became chair of the department—the long-awaited goal of her professional life. That would happen in January, she recalled happily, which was now less than three months away. She would not only be the hospital's first *woman* chair, she would be its first *black* woman chair. The fight to get there had been a tough one, and, as far as she was concerned, worth every sacrifice she had made.

"And some steak bones for Leopold," she said into the Dictaphone, ending her list. Leopold was her black Labrador retriever.

The locker room smelled of soap, deodorant, and Rae's cologne, and the mist from her hot shower still hung in the air. On the other side of the door she suddenly heard the whirl of a vacuum cleaner. The sound grew louder, and when Rae looked up, she saw that the door had opened and Bernice Brown, veteran maternity nurse and Rae's best friend, had entered the room.

"Good Lord, what a night!" Bernie exclaimed. "And that Angel, like an outtake from *The Exorcist.*" The door clicked shut behind her. She had changed in the nurses' locker room, but as usual, was stopping off to visit with Rae before going home.

"Why don't you tell me how you really feel, Bernie?" Rae teased. She spoke with the singsong quality of her mother's New Orleans voice: soft, sweet, and melodic. Only inside an operating room did she bark orders like a drill sergeant having a bad day. "But leave the 'good Lord' out of it," she added more seriously.

Rae's mother had bled to death giving birth to a stillborn baby boy in the back of an ambulance. At thirteen years old, she had witnessed the whole thing, and at the funeral, she had made two decisions. One, that she would become the world's greatest obstetrician so that no woman would ever have to go through what her mother did. And two, that God was not on her side anymore, for how could he be on her side if he let her mother die the way she did?

From that day on, she was no longer a little girl. At her mother's funeral, her stern father forbade her to cry. Not a single tear, he warned. So she had swallowed her grief and buried her feelings deep in her soul. Then, methodically and meticulously, she went about pursuing her own ambition. And she had never looked back. Not once.

Bernie stared down at Rae from her height of six feet. "Come on, Rae. I know you feel the same way. Angel was a bit much, even for you." Bernie adjusted a four-generation-old nursing hat she always wore inside the hospital, even when she was dressed in her jeans and blue parka, as she was now. "Admit it. You're getting too old for these all-nighters."

Rae raised her slim arms above her head and yawned. "I never get tired," she said. "Who gets tired at thirty-eight?"

"We do," Bernie said.

Rae hated admitting how old she was, even to Bernie. Her mother was thirty-eight when she died. She changed the subject quickly. "Wasn't Angel's baby a cute little thing?" she asked. "Did you see those buggy eyes staring at us, saying, 'Hi. I'm Angel's baby. Who the heck are you?' How could I be tired after something like that?"

"I actually don't know how much longer I'll be doing these night shifts," Bernie interrupted, changing the subject back.

"Why, I feel as spry as a new baby, Bernie," Rae said. "I feel as springy as a new chick."

She waited for her friend to finish the ditty.

"I don't feel like singing," Bernie said instead. "And I'm sick to death of that song."

Rae crossed one bare leg over the other. "Oh?" she asked. She knew Bernie's moods, but she also knew that Bernie always got as much of a kick out of a nice delivery as she did. "You've never complained before."

Bernie leaned against the locker and crossed her arms over her chest. "I might be out of a job," she said.

Rae dangled her Dictaphone like a socialite holding a cigarette. She sighed loudly. "Not this again, Bernie," she said. "You really shouldn't listen to rumors. That's all they are."

Bernie plopped down next to Rae. "Indeed." She reached inside her parka and pulled out a piece of paper. "So what's this?" she asked, handing the paper to Rae.

The letterhead belonged to their hospital. Rae read the memo out loud. "Due to declining revenues, Berkeley Hills Hospital will need to cut each department's budget by fifteen percent. Management will make every effort to avoid cutting necessary personnel. We will keep you informed."

"But they won't cut this department," Rae said, handing the notice back to Bernie, who stuffed it back into her pocket.

"Get your head out of the sandbox, will you, darlin'?" she retorted. "If there's any department that's in trouble, it's ours. The Birth Center's killing us. Maybe we ought to follow suit and bring in some nice music and stick flowers in every room, and get rid of these white walls and computers . . ."

Rae stared at her. "The Birth Center's all smoke and mirrors, Bernie."

"Smoke and mirrors I can handle. But that place is hitting us where we live. And if you had any sense, you'd change your mind and apply for privileges over there yourself—"

"Never!"

"We—the nurses," Bernie continued, holding her thumb and index finger an inch apart, "are about this far from a pink slip. You read the memo. They're not whistling Dixie, honey."

Rae tapped her Dictaphone against her forehead. "But they can't even do C-sections over there, Bernie."

Bernie snatched the Dictaphone from Rae's hand and said into the mike, "Delivering babies is a job, sugar, not a calling from God."

Rae snatched it back. "I never said it was."

"And your little hoedown with the board of trustees this morning isn't going to change anything," Bernie added.

"The board's not stupid," Rae said. "Obstetrics built this hospital. By the time the meeting's over, we'll be *hiring,* not firing, more nurses. Nobody, and I mean nobody, is going to lay off people around here. Not if I have anything to do with it!"

"That's not what Bo said—"

"Who cares what Bo said—you've been talking to Bo?" Rae stopped pointing her Dictaphone at Bernie. Her body stiffened involuntarily. Bo Michaels was the medical director of the Birth Center, the chairman of the hospital's obstetrical department, and Rae's ex-boyfriend.

"You better believe I've been talking to him," Bernie said. "We all have. He's offering us day shifts, for a lot more ducats."

"You're just pulling my leg—"

"And full medical benefits from day one," Bernie added.

Rae rolled her eyes. "I don't believe you've been talking to anybody. Especially to Bo. He's the reason why your job's on the line now. He's the one who started the Birth Center and did everything he could to lure business away—"

"How come whenever we start talking about Bo, we always wind up arguing about Bo?" Bernie interrupted.

Rae tossed the Dictaphone into her locker. She felt her good mood dissipating quickly, like the mist from her shower.

She shook her head, as if trying to shake Bo from her thoughts. "Well, it doesn't matter. I don't believe you'd have anything to do with him."

"For what he's offering, you better believe it," Bernie said.

All of this talk about Bo Michaels made Rae feel uncomfortable. She started to change the topic, but Bernie spoke first. "Look, honey, the person who *needs* to talk to him is you. It's time to kiss and make up and admit you were wrong about what Bo's trying to do with that place. Remember how we both thought the Birth Center was a joke a year ago? Well, darlin', the joke's on us now. The Birth Center is now the Mecca of obstetrics, not Berkeley Hills Hospital—hey, what's with the long face, Rae? Don't look at me that way. You two used to be partners. For heaven's sake, you used to live with the man!"

"But I wasn't on his payroll!"

Bernie opened her mouth, started to say something, but let out a long whistle instead. Crossing her arms over her chest she said, "I'm going to let that one float right on down the river, honey. I said you were tired. Maybe you ought to skip the meeting and get some sleep."

"I'll only have nightmares about you and Bo working together."

"Suit yourself." Bernie started to walk away.

"Hey," Rae said, grabbing Bernie's parka. "I'm sorry." She shrugged. "It's just that a year later, I still let him get to me."

"It's called love," Bernie said. "L-O-V-E."

Rae sighed. "Not anymore. Maybe not ever. At least that's my conclusion after a few weeks of spilling my guts to a shrink."

"Ah, so you took my suggestion after all," Bernie said, raising an eyebrow.

Rae leaned forward to remove a pair of stockings from her locker. She wanted to get off the subject of Bo and back to the matter at hand. "What about the fact that they can't do a C-section over there, Bernie?" she asked. "What about the fact that they have to rely on ambulance transports? You can't even stand it when one of our patients has to labor in room seventeen. And why? Because room seventeen is the farthest from the operating room. Every time we have to rush a patient out of there and down the hall for a stat section, all you do is scream about how we're not pushing the gurney fast enough! So why are you talking about going to work at the Birth Center? Room seventeen's only a few yards away from the operating table. That damn Birth Center is way the hell across the street."

"Have you ever been to the Birth Center, Rae? It's beautiful, and they do a good job over there." She pretended to study her blood-red fingernails.

"No, but—"

Bernie held up her index fingers in the sign of the cross. "Okay, okay, darling. How about we let this go for now? I'm tired. You're tired. And I'm not going to let you yell at me when the person you really want to yell at is Bo."

"I thought we were done talking about him."

Bernie patted Rae's bare shoulder. "Maybe one day you'll tell me *exactly* what cut the cord between you two."

"I told you everything."

"So you've said a zillion times."

"Believe me," Rae said, patting Bernie's hand, "you don't want to know—"

"Yes, I do, Rae," Bernie said, raising her voice. "We used to laugh and giggle and paint our toenails like there was no tomorrow. But now all we do is argue, and in the middle of every argument is Bo. So what the hell is it? What is so terrible that you can't tell me?"

"Okay, okay!" Rae barked. She waved off Bernie. "Give me a second, will you?"

She had never wanted to tell anyone the cause of her breakup with Bo. But Bernie was right again: holding back was poisoning their friendship.

She cast her eyes downward. "How about I dictate you a letter, Bernie?"

"How about I beat it out of you instead?"

Rae paused again, and listened to the whirl of the vacuum cleaner. "Do you hear that?"

"What?"

"Just listen, damn it!"

"Okay, okay," Bernie replied. She closed her eyes and feigned deep concentration. "Sounds just like a vacuum cleaner."

"I heard that sound in my head every day for a year," Rae said. "It drove me crazy. It took everything I had to make it stop."

Bernie's eyes narrowed. "You heard a vacuum cleaner in your therapist's office?"

"In a way."

"Hell, I'm lost," Bernie said. "What's a vacuum cleaner got to do with you and Bo?"

"I had a miscarriage," Rae said quietly.

The sound of the vacuum cleaner faded. Rae hated the silence that it left. She could almost hear the sound of her heart pounding inside her head. No one but Bo, and a nurse and a gynecologist in another town, knew of Rae's pregnancy.

"Well, say something," Rae said.

"Why didn't you tell me?"

"That's why Bo left me."

"Bo left you because you miscarried?"

"I missed a pill, Bernie," Rae continued. "I never planned to have children, you know that. But it happened, and I told Bo, and he went crazy—"

"But Bo doesn't want children," Bernie said, slumping down next to Rae.

Rae looked down at the floor and sighed. "Bo was the one who changed his mind about having children. We fought about it everyday. I was confused about everything. Suddenly I couldn't decide. It's different when you're pregnant. He finally gave me an ultimatum . . .

"Then I started to bleed. A sonogram showed a blighted ovum. Bo blamed me for the miscarriage. He said I never bothered to slow down . . . anyway, I never had to make a decision. Still, it took me half a dozen sessions with a therapist to sort things out."

Bernie looked at Rae incredulously. "So you had a D and C, and you did it all alone?"

"Afterward, Bo said he was sorry. He wanted to make another go of it. But we were having problems before the pregnancy, Bernie. Bo had become more of an entrepreneur than a doctor. The Birth Center proves that. Sure, the money he makes from it allows him to donate a ton to the March of Dimes and anybody else doing research on birth defects. But his philanthropy is for strangers, not for the people in his life. And when it comes to living with him, well, let's just say that our hearts didn't speak to each other. I do what I do because I love it. He does what he does because of the return on his investment . . .

"Anyway, that's in the past. All I want to do now is become chairman of our department and make sure things are done right around here. I wish you'd reconsider about applying for a job at the Birth Center. At least until after I meet with the board of trustees this morning and try to talk some sense into them."

Bernie leaned over and hugged Rae. Rae felt she could have held on to her forever. "No more secrets, okay, Rae?"

Rae nodded into her friend's shoulder. "No, no more secrets," she said.

"Well," Bernie said tiredly, "I guess I should go home now. Call me tonight, okay? No, call and leave a message on my machine after the board meeting. The first thing I want to know when I wake up is whether or not I still have a job."

Rae patted the back of Bernie's hand, which still rested on her shoulder.

"Now you know why Bo ignores me when he sees me," Rae said.

Bernie smiled weakly. "Now I know why he looks like he can't live without you," she said.

After Bernie left, Rae let herself feel the full extent of her exhaustion. Yawning, she looked at the overhead clock. It was 6:55 A.M. She'd been up all night. She'd better hurry if she wanted to get dressed, get something to eat, and meet with the hospital's board of trustees by eight o'clock. She pulled on her stockings and then reached for a navy-blue dress. She always kept several changes of work clothes at the hospital just in case she couldn't make it home to change after a night on call.

"Dr. Duprey! Are you still there?"

It was a voice from the intercom. Rae recognized it immediately. "Sorry, Trish," she said jokingly to the intercom. "Dr. Duprey left ten minutes ago."

"Dr. Duprey, we can't find Dr. Michaels!"

"I'm sure you can find him at the Birth—" Rae started to say.

"—and one of his patients just arrived by ambulance from the Birth Center! The baby's heart rate's in the sixties, and it's not coming back up! She's only one centimeter dilated!"

Rae snatched the towel from her body, and from a glass wall cabinet grabbed a clean set of white surgical scrubs. "Is she on the table?"

"She needs a cesarean—are you coming?"

"Get her on the table!" Rae barked. "And see if you can find Bernie," she added quickly. She knew that there would be good nurses available on the day shift, but Bernie was the unit's best nurse, day or night.

The intercom had clicked dead. Rae didn't know if Trish had heard her request to hunt down Bernie. But in less than thirty seconds, she was dressed and speeding down the stark white hallway to the operating suite.

Forget the war between the Birth Center and the hospital. She had a baby to save.

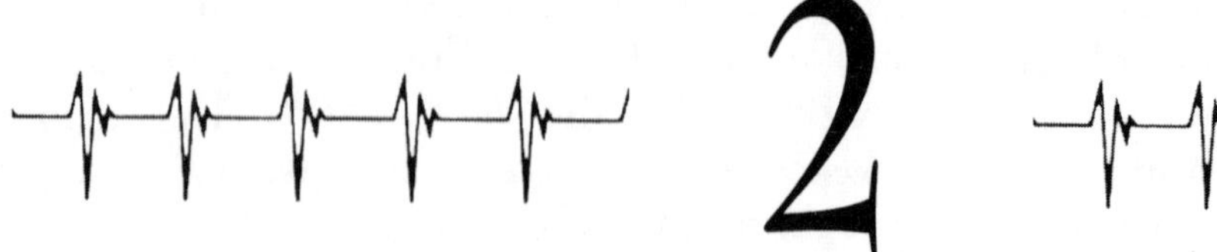

# 2

RAE KNEW HER WAY AROUND THE U-SHAPED MATERNITY UNIT of Berkeley Hills Hospital better than she knew her way around her own home. But as always, she took the corners too fast, and at the first right, she crashed into a cleaning cart being pushed by Claudia, the day shift cleaning lady.

"Sorry!" Rae shouted as she regained her balance and kept running.

"I want a girl this time!" Claudia yelled after her.

Rae ran on sheer adrenaline. She had not eaten anything since the day before. Within another sixty seconds she had scrubbed, donned gown and gloves, and was standing on a lift next to the operating table upon which the anesthetized patient lay unconscious. As soon as the women was intubated, Rae could start the case.

Her slender fingers held the blue handle of a scalpel as lightly as she held the bow of her beloved violin at home. She lowered its shiny silver blade to exactly one centimeter above the patient's belly. An iodine solution had been splashed across her skin, which now glowed like a pumpkin.

Already she could imagine the predictable hues of the tissue layers under the epidermis. People looked so different on the outside, she mused. But inside, they were all the same color.

"You can't cut yet," said her assistant, Eva Major, a young scrub nurse who had married only four months earlier. Eva swung around the overhead lights to the exact spot where Rae would make her incision. Four maternity nurses and two pediatric nurses hurried about, hooking up the suction, counting lap sponges and packages of sutures, and resetting dials on the newborn resuscitation cart.

"Oh yeah? Watch me."

"But, Dr. Duprey—"

Rae turned her head to read 7:04 A.M. on the wall's digital clock. She had no intention of cutting the patient until the anesthesiologist completed the intubation.

"What's the heart rate now?" she shouted above the commotion.

"It's still in the sixties!" a voice called back.

"Has Bo made it to the party?"

"Haven't seen him yet!"

Being the only obstetrician didn't bother her, but waiting for the anesthesiologist to intubate the patient did. "Come on, Charley!" she yelled. Dr. Charley Grant worked the night shift, and Rae could see the top of his blue surgical cap on the other side of the drape. "I can't cut without you—"

"The name's Hartman. Sam Hartman," came the reply. "Sorry. Charley left."

"You forgot about the change of shift," Eva whispered.

"Sam Hartman?" she whispered back. "Who the hell is he?"

Eva shrugged.

"That's fine, Dr. Hartman," she said, feeling the seconds speed past, "but we still need to get this little number going—"

"Five more seconds."

"We don't have one—"

No, hurrying him would only make him nervous, she told herself, tapping her tennis shoe impatiently. She looked up at the clock. 7:05. Charley's shift had ended at seven.

Sam Hartman? Sam Hartman? Then she remembered. He was the new chief of cardiac anesthesia recruited from Harvard to work in the hospital's expanding cardiac surgery program. That was another reason for the rumors about proposed layoffs in labor and delivery. Cardiac surgery had suddenly become the hospital's newest darling.

But what in the world was a *heart* anesthesiologist doing in maternity? And why the hell couldn't *Charley* have stayed on?

"How long's the heart rate been down?" she asked the nurse.

"It was down when she got here."

"How long ago was that?"

"Seven minutes ago—no! Make that eight!"

"Shit," Rae mumbled. "Shit, shit, shit!"

By now the adrenaline that had carried her legs from the locker room to the operating room was doing a number on her cardiac muscle. Her heart hammered against her chest. Her breathing came shallow and fast. All she could think was that it was the job of the obstetrician to save the life of the mother and the baby. *Save the life! Save the life!* That was her mantra, her reason for living.

Her impatience flared higher. She had a baby to save and time was running out. She felt confident that once she got started, she could deliver the baby in record time. Thirty seconds, tops.

No, make that sixty seconds, she thought, palpating the patient's belly. Operating on big women always took longer. More fat and tissue to cut through and retract out of the way. And more blood everywhere.

She also knew that the patient's size was the reason why this Harvard transplant was taking forever. Just getting a big person's neck flexed back was a major feat. But despite her understanding, she couldn't help how she felt. She had to do something other than hold the shiny Bard-Parker scalpel in her hand.

"Your five seconds are up, Dr. Hartman," she barked.

But Sam Hartman didn't answer. This infuriated her more. Quickly she stole another look at the clock. Still 7:05, but thirty more seconds had passed!

Hating to keep her eyes off of the patient's belly for too much longer, she peered back over the drape. She was about to goad him again, but finally she saw the plastic breathing tube disappear past the woman's teeth. Then his right hand slid down to the breathing bag, and he gave it a squeeze. The patient's chest rose and fell under Rae's free hand, letting her know that the tube was finally in.

"Go!" he shouted, but she had already made the first cut. She sliced the skin horizontally between the patient's hip bones. With her second swipe she split the five inches of fat. Her third cut split the sheetlike fascial layer, all shiny and white, where the muscles converged.

"Here," she said to Eva, handing back the scalpel. The body's underlying tissues were as soft as butter. Ripping them with her fingertips would be faster than cutting them with the blade, and in an emergency situation, just as safe.

With both of her small hands pulling in opposite directions, she tore the white fascia off of the rectus muscles, first side to side, and then up and down. She saw the thin tissue between the muscle bellies and she ripped it apart. Next she stuck her index fingers into the transparent cover of the abdominal cavity, tore it open, and pushed the wormy mass of intestines out of her way.

"Pull a little harder on that retractor, Eva," Rae said. "We're working in a very deep hole here."

Her fingers cramped and her neck muscles burned to the bone. Globules of fat melted across the back of her gloves, making everything slippery. Now she could see the deep pink muscle of the uterus. With her index finger she poked a hole in it, and then tore it open from side to side, careful not to burst open the bed of puffy purple blood vessels coursing along the edges. A deluge of brownish-green amniotic fluid poured out and spread across the operating field. The color told her that the baby, under stress, had dumped its first bowel movement into the water bag. If any of the noxious fluid got into the baby's lungs, it could lead to a terrible chemical pneumonia, and from there, to death.

"Great, meconium was all we needed," she said, hoping that the baby had not already inhaled the deadly fluid into its lungs.

Suddenly she found herself teetering. Under her feet, the uneven corners of the lift began to rock. A wave of dizziness swept over her, most likely from dehydration, for she had had little to drink all night. Rae inhaled deeply, as if sucking more air into her lungs would make up for the lack of sleep and water and food.

"Somebody tell me what time it is!" she cried, hoping no one would notice how she felt. She reached inside the patient's uterus, and began to search for the baby's head.

"It's seven-oh-six!" she heard back.

Another minute! Rae thought. A full sixty seconds more!

The operating field was drowning in a sea of blood and meconium. For some reason, Eva—the unit's best scrub nurse, next to Bernie—wasn't doing a very good job at wiping up the mess. "Don't be afraid to move a little faster, Eva," she said.

"She smells kind of funny," Eva whispered.

Rae wondered if anyone outside of medicine knew that surgeons and nurses often spoke of topics other than the surgery during a case. But she wasn't in the mood to talk at all just then.

"It reminds me of rubbing alcohol. A lot of rubbing alcohol," Eva said queasily.

The odor was getting to Rae, too. "How'd they say this baby was coming down?" she asked as she reached up toward the top of the womb.

"Didn't Trish tell you?" Eva asked. "She's breech."

"She probably tried to, but I cut her off on the intercom," Rae said. "So, where are the feet?"

She reached in higher, and fished around more urgently.

"I'm really feeling sick, Dr. Duprey—"

"Get the bandage scissors ready. We should have the baby out in ten seconds or less."

"I've been meaning to tell you—"

"And get the Mayo clamps ready too—"

"I'm sorry, Dr. Duprey, but I'm not feeling well—"

"Neither am I, Eva—"

"Please, Dr. Duprey! I'm two months pregnant!"

"Damn it!" Rae said.

She had finally found the baby's feet inside the womb, high up on the right, under the liver. The head floated to the left, just under the spleen.

"Look, Eva. See? The baby's coming down as a back-down, transverse lie. That's the worst, damn it. The absolute worst."

Her heart pulsed faster than ever. *Stay calm, Rae,* she told herself. *Stay calm!*

"I think I need to lie down—"

"In a minute, okay? Just moisten one of those towels. We'll turn it around and deliver it as a breech anyway."

She felt sorry for Eva, but for now, all she could think about was the baby's health. She rummaged around until her fingers found the tiny spine, and then she followed the spine down to the leg until she found a foot. "Now we're cookin'," she said.

She moved her fingers back up half an inch and grabbed the baby's ankle. Or what she thought was an ankle.

"Damn it!"

"Isn't that the hand?" Eva whispered.

"I know, I know!"

Cursing softly to herself, she stuffed the baby's fingers back into the womb. Only obstetricians knew how much alike hands and feet felt during a cesarean birth. She reached in higher. The alcohol vapors made tears well up along her lower eyelids.

"Come on, little baby," she said. "Help me out here. You don't know it yet, but we're in this thing together."

By now her arm was so far inside the patient's body that she could have fallen right in. She fished around again, and this time there was no mistake when she pulled out an ankle. She found the other foot and snatched it out too.

With her right hand she grabbed both ankles. She pulled until she had the baby's buttocks and back exposed. She kept pulling until she saw the next important landmark of a breech delivery, the scapulas.

"Looks like a boy," Sam said matter-of-factly, peering over the drape.

"Right," Rae said. A real genius, she thought.

Taking the moistened blue towel from Eva, she wrapped it around the baby's hips. She twisted him to one side, and when she saw his armpit, she used her right index finger to gently pull out the arm and hand. She twirled the baby 180 degrees, and repeated the maneuver with the other side.

"Just a couple more seconds—"

She looked at the clock. 7:08. Already another two minutes had passed.

*Faster!* she thought. She had to work faster! A baby with a heart rate in the sixties could not survive inside the womb for much longer. By now she had the baby's body out up to the level of his shoulders. But when she went to deliver the head, she saw that the womb had clamped down around his neck as tight as a hangman's noose.

"Eva," she said, pointing to the area just under the patient's left breast, "keep the head flexed by pressing here."

"Dr. Duprey, I—"

"No, not there. Here!"

But Eva's hand slid away in the opposite direction. Looking up, Rae saw the nurse getting shorter and shorter by the millisecond until she disappeared completely somewhere on the opposite side of the drape.

"Eva! " she cried out, lunging for her.

"She's out cold!" one of the other nurses said.

Then the sterile drape started to slide off of the table, and the instrument stand began to topple back.

"She's caught!" Rae shouted.

She tried to snatch the stand back toward her. But it and most of its instruments crashed to the floor. She only managed to grab a couple of clamps, as well as the bandage scissors used for cutting the cord.

But she wasn't ready to cut the cord! she thought. She hadn't even delivered the head yet!

"Somebody take care of Eva."

"I've got her!" Sam called out.

"—and somebody else needs to scrub in!"

She looked at the clock and felt a wave of panic wash over her, an emotion completely unfamiliar to her inside an operating room. 7:09. Another minute gone. She could almost hear the baby inside the womb, crying out to her, "Save me! Save me!"

Now sweat soaked her armpits and her back. Worse, she couldn't see if anybody was slipping on a surgical gown.

"I said I need somebody else to scrub in!"

She knew that someone must be in the process of doing just that, and she hated herself for yelling. But she couldn't help it. She cared about one thing and one thing only. The baby. The seconds were ticking past, and each one was a needle prick on the back of her neck. Her fingers cramped terribly. Her upper back and shoulders burned worse than before. She found the tiny space between the baby's face and the uterus, even though the baby's head was still trapped inside. Carefully she slipped her fingers into his mouth. Pressing her index finger against his delicate palate she tried another time-honored breech maneuver and pulled. Nothing happened. The head was still trapped.

"Need some help here, Doctor?"

The voice belonged to Bernie, who was already gowned and gloved.

"Big time," Rae said as Bernie stepped up to the side of the table where Eva had fainted only minutes before.

"I *almost* had a clean getaway," Bernie said wryly.

"Hold open the uterus and press right here," Rae said as if her friend had been there all along.

As Bernie got into position, Rae quickly reassessed the situation at hand. She looked down at the baby's body. His white arms and legs were draped across his mother's thighs. His neck stretched tightly from the uterine incision and his head was hidden inside the pink muscle of the womb. A few flecks of meconium, like green ants, dotted the exposed parts of his body.

Rae readjusted her stiff fingers one more time. Pain shot up from her hand to her elbow. "Gently," she coaxed herself confidently. "Steady now. Keep the head flexed."

She pulled carefully, yet with all the determination and conviction she could muster. Skillfully she toed the line between pulling too hard and too softly.

"Why don't you T the incision?" Bernie asked.

"No, we've got the room," she insisted.

And sure enough, out popped the baby's chin, lips, nose, eyes, and finally, his forehead. Quickly she unwound the three loops of umbilical cord that had wrapped themselves around the baby's neck. She suctioned out the meconium from his nose and mouth.

"Bandage scissors!"

She cut the cord with the thick blades of the bandage scissors, and then scooped the enormous baby boy into her slim arms. His huge head thumped sickly against her chest. His legs and arms hung slack. Worse, his eyelids were half open, and behind them, two dull pupils rolled around aimlessly, like a child's marbles.

She rushed him across the seven feet separating the operating table from the resuscitation cart. Nurses, all awaiting the final verdict, moved out of her way. No one said anything. The only sounds were the bleeping of the mother's heart monitor, and the harsh swishing of her breathing machine.

Completely drenched in sweat, she lowered the baby onto the cart's white mattress. Then she looked at the clock. 7:10 A.M.! The time hit her between the eyes like a mallet.

She had entered the operating room at 7:03. Her first cut had been at 7:05. Thirty to sixty seconds tops to operate, she had promised herself. Now she saw that what should have taken her one minute at the most to do had taken her five. And she knew that every minute the baby was inside the womb with a heart rate in the sixties diminished his chances of being a normal child by the time he was ready for kindergarten.

For the pediatrician and the nurses who prepared the baby for resuscitation, Rae kept an air of confidence and calm. But inside she was pleading silently: Come on, little baby. Remember, you and me, together. We've come this far. We can do it. We can do it!

As she watched her colleagues work, Rae crossed her arms over the front of her gown, which was covered with blood and meconium. The warmth of both fluids seeped through her scrub shirt. She wanted to reach out and touch the baby, whose skin had turned as gray as winter's dusk. She held back though, because the person now in charge of the resuscitation was pediatrician Dr. Arnie Driver. Damn it, she thought, why did it have to be Arnie? He may have been his department's best diagnostician, but he was also the most technically incompetent pediatrician on staff.

Driver was a mountain of a man, whose wispy blond hair now curled along the edges of his blue surgical cap. He not only was a full-time pediatrician, but also the president of the hospital's medical staff. Golf and cigars were his true passions though. And he detested women doctors.

Rae nervously drummed her fingertips along her biceps as Arnie slid a seven-inch-long breathing tube down the baby's throat. But instead of connecting the tube to the breathing bag in front of the resuscitation cart, Arnie muttered to himself and pulled it back out. His thick brow furrowed. He tried slipping in the tube again.

It was obvious to Rae that the tube was in the baby's esophagus, not the windpipe. She turned to face the staff behind her. "Call the neonatologist!" she said sharply. "Tell her we need some help in here!"

"I can do this!" Arnie said. He turned to Jessica Howe, the nursery nurse, whose right thumb and index finger tapped together in rhythm with the baby's heartbeat. "Well, is the heart rate up or not?" Arnie barked.

Rae ripped off her bloody gloves and fanned her fingers across the baby's rib cage. His skin felt warm, dry, and doughy. Through the tiny bones she felt the slow beat of the baby's heart.

Jessica's fingers tapped slower and slower. "Still in the sixties."

Rae looked around the room for the neonatologist. But Dr. Catherine Drake was not in the room.

"Damn it, Arnie, get it in!" Rae said.

Arnie ignored her and kept fumbling with the tube. She felt like snatching the short piece of plastic from his oversize hands and sticking it down the baby's throat herself. Had she known how, she would have done it in a minute. But that special skill belonged to the pediatricians.

The overhead clock read 7:11 A.M. Rae gave a sigh of relief when Arnie's hand slid down to the gray Ambu bag. Obviously, she thought, he had finally placed the tube in the baby's trachea. But when he squeezed the bag, nothing happened. The baby's chest failed to rise.

"You're still in the esophagus!" she exclaimed.

Jessica's counting slowed. "Sixty-two. Sixty. Forty-eight . . ."

Rae pushed Arnie out of the way. "Start CPR, now!" she ordered. "Jessica, use the mask to ventilate the baby. I'll compress his heart—"

"Hey—!" Arnie shouted.

But Rae ignored him, and pushed in closer to the cart. She may not have known how to intubate a baby, but she did know how to give basic life support. This baby's heart had to pump faster if they wanted to keep him alive.

"What the hell are you doing?" Arnie asked.

The first two fingers of her right hand pressed against the baby's sternum, indenting it like it was a plastic doll. She pumped at a rate of 120 compressions a minute. The little breastplate bridging the ribs felt as if it would break at any moment.

"What's it look like I'm doing?" she snapped back.

Her eyes were glued to the baby's chest. "One-and-two-and-three-and—" she counted to herself, trying to keep the rhythm and pace correct. Then to Arnie she said, "Find me somebody who knows how to get this damn tube in the right place."

Arnie pushed Jessica out of the way before the nurse could cover the baby's face with the mask. He stuck the tube back down the baby's throat and again squeezed the breathing bag. "I'm in now!"

But the baby's chest still did not move.

"Bullshit!" Rae said.

"Doctor?"

"What, Bernie!"

"Our patient here . . ."

Shit! Rae thought. She had forgotten all about the mother! "Isn't Bo here yet?"

"No."

"Then call him again! And let me know if she starts to bleed!"

Rae knew that as long as the patient wasn't bleeding much, she could afford to stay where she was. Bernie was a top-notch labor and surgical nurse. If the patient showed any signs of trouble, she would call Rae immediately.

"I'm still not hearing any breath sounds, Dr. Driver," Jessica said, as she pressed the tiny silver bell of a pediatric stethoscope against the baby's chest.

"Give me that!" he said angrily.

Sweat from Arnie's forehead dripped onto Rae's arm as he snatched the pediatric stethoscope from Jessica's hands. He mashed the bell against the baby's chest and stuck the plastic plugs into his ears. "Damn it, I've got to be in!"

"The neonatologist can't be here for another five minutes!" someone shouted.

"Then call the nurse anesthetist!" Rae shouted back.

"Can't! Frank's tied up with a vacuum delivery in Room Seventeen!"

"We wouldn't be in this mess if you hadn't taken your sweet time—"

"You've got your own problems, Arnie," Rae retorted.

"Jesus Christ," Arnie said, trying again, "I can't get this damn thing in."

Rae was thinking of what to do next. And then she remembered. The new guy from Harvard. He had been trained to intubate adults. She could only hope he knew how to intubate a newborn baby.

"Hey, Hartman!" she shouted. "Get over here!"

Immediately his body was pressing hard and lean against hers as he sandwiched himself between the others ringing the resuscitation cart.

"Keep listening," he said, nodding at Jessica, and taking the breathing tube from Arnie's hand. "And keep pumping, Dr. Duprey. Go down one-half to three-quarter inches. No more. No less. Keep a steady rate at one hundred twenty per minute. And whatever you do, don't take your fingers off that chest."

Rae didn't need to be told what to do, but she kept her thoughts to herself.

"I'm telling you, I couldn't see a damn thing!" Arnie repeated, stepping out of the way.

Rae watched, holding her breath, as Sam tried to slip the breathing tube down the baby's throat. "Well?" she asked. The baby's lips grew duskier and duskier at the tips of his fingers. They were almost the color of black pearls, instead of the sweet hue of summer strawberries.

She also hated to see, as she kept compressing the baby's sternum, that the rest of his body was just as blue. His eyelids were still only half open, and behind them, a vapid stare. Compressing his chest forever was worthless unless somebody got some oxygen to his brain.

Damn it! she thought. At the beginning of this resuscitation, she had worried how the baby would be at age five. Now all she could think about was that he might not make it to tomorrow.

"What you have here is a bad case of laryngospasm," Sam said in his matter-of-fact voice. Rae appreciated his calmness after all the yelling that had gone on between Arnie and her.

"Dr. Driver, is the oxygen turned up all the way?" Sam asked.

"It's blasting," Arnie said.

Sam rolled the plastic breathing tube between his fingers like a toy baton. "Exactly what kind of tube is this?"

"What kind of tube is—a damn inner tube!" Arnie shouted. "For God's sakes, man! The kid's as big as a moose! I used a Number 3.5 French—!"

Rae peered down upon the mattress pad and saw the torn plastic wrapping that had once belonged to the breathing tube now in the baby's throat. "God damn it, Arnie, can't you read? A Number 3.5 my ass. You stuck a Number *4.5* down the kid!"

"No wonder it wouldn't fit," Sam said. "And that also explains the spasm."

He pulled out the tube and placed an oxygen mask over the baby's face. He squeezed the breathing bag and the baby's chest rose and fell, but only slightly. "This is better than nothing, but the right size tube would do the trick."

Arnie snatched the plastic wrapping from the mattress. "Don't tell me—"

"Somebody get Dr. Hartman a Number 3.5 French pediatric endotracheal tube!" Rae shouted.

"I'll get it!" said Hannah Brokonsky, a frail, bleached blond nurse, who was known to flit constantly, like a hummingbird.

Hannah ran to the far side of the room and swayed back and forth in front of the computerized floor-to-ceiling metal cabinets. All she had to do was punch the name of the requested item across a keyboard, and the door to the appropriate bin would automatically rise.

"What size?" Hannah asked.

"Three-point-five!" Rae shouted along with everybody else.

Hannah's fingers sped across the buttons. A bin opened in a second. She reached in. Rae watched her every move and ignored the muscles in her fingers that had gone into a spasm of their own against the baby's chest.

But Hannah fumbled as she felt around for the right package. She turned toward the resuscitation cart with bulging eyes. "We're out! "

"Oh, for the love of God!" Arnie cried.

"Jessica, take over for me," Rae said, pushing past Arnie.

Quickly she punched in a set of new letters. She spent so much time at Berkeley Hills Hospital that she knew it inside out. Lately, restocking the cabinets had been a problem. Mistakes were common. As reimbursements to the hospital from insurance companies declined, so had staffing. Supplies were often not where they belonged. But that would all change, she thought, as soon as she became head of the department.

Rae's hunch had been that the tube was merely in the wrong cabinet. And sure enough, there, in the bin for the Number 4.5 endotracheal tubes, was the Number 3.5 tube that Sam needed to save the baby boy. She tore off the package's plastic wrapping as she raced back to the cart. Handing the correct-size tube to Sam, she pushed Arnie out of the way, and resumed the job of compressing the baby's chest. Arnie had performed the task during her absence.

Sam removed the mask from the baby boy's face and slipped the laryngoscope down his throat. The smaller tube immediately disappeared past the vocal cords. Rae watched with grave intensity. Through the clear plastic of Sam's face shield she could see the lines of his face. A few around the eyes, fewer along his forehead. The lines relaxed—he was apparently satisfied with the tube's placement.

But when he squeezed the bag, the baby's chest did not move.

Rae's eyes widened in disbelief. "You've got to be in!"

"Just a minute," Sam mumbled.

He repositioned the tube. Rae held her breath. Breathing might suck in the precious air that she knew the baby so desperately needed. Sam squeezed the bag again. This time the baby's chest rose and fell, and it kept rising and falling as he pumped. She looked at Sam's face for a reassuring nod. But his pale blue eyes never left the baby's face. He just kept squeezing the bag, as if he were using it to fill his own lungs.

"I hear something now!" Jessica said, as she repositioned her stethoscope on top of the baby's chest. Her thumb and index finger tapped together much faster than before.

"Keep listening," Sam said.

Rae kept compressing the baby's sternum. She waited for him to show some sign of life. A twitch of his cheek. A brief flick of his toe. But the baby just lay there as if he were part of the resuscitation cart.

"The heart rate's up to one hundred!" Jessica said. Her fingers tapped faster than Rae had seen them since the resuscitation began.

"Hold off on those compressions, Dr. Duprey," Sam said.

Rae stopped pumping but she kept her fingertips on the baby's chest.

"That's it, baby," Jessica said. She pressed the ends of the stethoscope deeper into her ears. "Come to mama, honey—"

Heavy silence hung in the air. Seconds passed like individual lifetimes.

And then, just when Rae thought the baby's heart rate had plummeted again, Jessica's eyes widened and she shouted, "God Almighty! He's back!"

"Good," Sam said.

"Are you sure?" Rae asked.

"Here, listen for yourself."

Greedily, Rae grabbed the stethoscope. She mashed the plugs into her ears. "How fast?"

Jessica smiled. "He's a-cruisin' at a hundred fifty-two miles per hour."

And sure enough, Rae heard the baby's heart galloping like a pony, and the rush of air in his lungs. Suddenly, she felt boneless, like a jellyfish. To hold herself steady, she tightened her grip on the side of the cart.

It didn't matter to her that Sam still had to squeeze the Ambu bag in order to fill the baby's lungs, or that, once inside the nursery, he would be hooked up to a mechanical ventilator, for a few hours at least. All she knew was that the tiny heart was beating on its own, and that now, any oxygen delivered by man, or by machine, would not only fill his lungs, but fuel his brain.

And his sweet soul, she thought.

The soul. Not the kind spoken about in the Bible, or by some priest giving last rites. But the soul that makes one person different from another, on this earth, in this lifetime. The soul gave hope, and hope gave life. Save the life! Her hope—her life—depended on it.

Arnie wiped his beefy brow. "I'll call the nursery, tell them we're coming over." But with his first step, he bumped into Hannah, who was hovering at Rae's side. "Next time, Hannah, just give me what I ask for."

"I gave you what you asked me for *this* time, Dr. Driver!"

"Dr. Duprey," Bernie called.

"Coming."

She took one last look at the baby boy. Sam had crisscrossed two pieces of tape over the plastic breathing tube to hold it in the baby's mouth. She reached over and touched his tiny hand, as if the life from her own body would flow through her fingertips and into his. Then she turned away and hurried back to the operating table.

She pulled on a new gown and a new pair of gloves and looked at the clock. 7:15 A.M. The baby was born at 7:10. Five minutes used up in resuscitating the baby, added to the five minutes she had used to operate—that meant ten minutes in total. And ten minutes was the maximum amount of time a baby could go without oxygen to his brain—No, she thought. She wouldn't think about it now. She still had a case to finish. She stepped back up onto the lift.

Bernie had cleaned up some of the blood and meconium and placed ring clamps on bleeders along the torn edges of the womb.

Rae raised her eyes and looked at Bernie. Bernie looked back with quiet understanding. They had worked together for ten years. Now their deepest thoughts were the ones left unspoken. "Thank you," Rae said simply.

"My pleasure," Bernie answered with a smile.

Having her best friend so close felt comforting. Rae took in a deep breath and then exhaled quickly to clear her mind of everything except the surgery. She reached inside the womb to extract the placenta. But the womb was empty. Obviously, Bernie had already delivered the afterbirth. She lifted the empty uterus up through the incision, stretching the eight or so ligaments anchoring it to the pelvic floor. The uterus looked like a shiny, pink bald head, with white ovaries sticking out like ears on either side.

"What do you think happened?" Bernie asked, handing Rae a needle holder.

"Whatever it was, I'm sure those three loops of cord around his neck didn't help," Rae replied. And then she started stitching.

Not a single motion was wasted. She was her department's premier obstetrical surgeon. For every one stitch completed by her colleagues, she completed four. For every six minutes they used up in the operating room, she accomplished the same things in two. She stitched and tied and cut so quickly that the layers of the patient's womb and abdominal wall fell together as if they had willed themselves to close.

Bernie handed her the staple gun, and she rifled in fifteen silver staples to close the skin. Next she applied pressure to the belly to push out of the vagina any clots still trapped inside the womb. Then came the dressing, made of gauze pads and white surgical tape.

"We could have gotten her on the table a lot sooner if she had been here all along," Rae said, not bothering to hide the anger in her voice.

"Maybe the baby's heart rate bottomed out at home," Bernie said.

"I mean it, Bernie. If the Birth Center can't do their own cesareans in their own building, then they shouldn't be delivering babies at all."

"Okay, Rae, okay. But if I get laid off, you're supporting me and the lifestyle to which I've grown accustomed, understand? You'll have Leopold and yours truly to worry about the next time you make out your grocery list."

"Oh no," Rae groaned. "I forgot all about the meeting—what time is it?"

"Seven-nineteen."

"Your patient's waking up, doctor," Sam said.

Rae was still standing on the lift. She peered over the drape to see the face of the woman whose body she had just stapled shut. A crucifix hung from her neck, from what appeared to Rae to be a necklace made from a tennis shoe string.

Such a peaceful face, she thought. Cherubic. Dark eyelashes that looked like tiny slivers of charcoal pressed against fleshy pink cheeks.

"What's her name, Dr. Hartman?" she asked.

"Isn't she *your* patient?" Sam asked back.

Just then the woman's eyes opened. They darted about until they came to rest on Rae's face.

"Hi. I'm Dr. Rae Du—"

"Hi, Dr. Rae. I'm Nola Payne, the Blessed Mother."

Rae heard Sam chuckle. She glared at him, and he smiled back.

"Sorry," he said.

His eyes were filled with the same compassion and quiet understanding that Bernie's eyes had shown only minutes before. Sam was a stranger. Yet, he seemed to understand what she understood, and to have the same worry for Nola's baby as she had, despite his chuckle.

"That's okay, Dr. Hartman. No need to apologize."

"Sam. Call me Sam."

Rae felt a warm hand on the back of hers. She looked down, and saw Nola's pudgy fingers covering hers. Nola lifted her blond head and looked around the room. "Dr. Rae, how is my Baby Jesus? How is my baby boy?"

Rae felt a lump welling up at the top of her esophagus. "Your baby boy was born ten minutes ago. He's with the doctors in our special baby unit, getting some extra care. Let's get you to the recovery room. You can see him later, as soon as you're stable."

But Nola had drifted off to sleep again.

Rae took a step to leave, but she had forgotten that she had been standing on the lift. There was no ground under her. She felt herself falling. Sam grabbed her elbow. She tried to pull away, but he held her firmly until she was safely balanced on both feet.

Embarrassed, she straightened up. "I'm fine, I'm fine."

She tore off her gown and gloves, and helped move Nola to the gurney. Then she jotted down a few orders in the chart. "Thanks, everybody," she called out to the staff, as they wheeled Nola out of the room.

Now Rae was all alone. She looked around slowly, as if seeing the room for the first time. It looked like a battlefield. There was blood and meconium on the floor, and gauze sponges and plastic wrappings strewn about all over the place. The room still smelled of blood, amniotic fluid, and human sweat. But neither the sights nor the smells bothered Rae. What bothered her was the quiet. For at no point before, during, or after the surgery had the room's four walls echoed with the lusty cry of the newborn baby boy.

The operating room doors opened, and Claudia, the elderly black cleaning lady whom Rae had crashed into only minutes before, came shuffling in with her cart and mop. Claudia was dressed in a white scrub dress, covered by a blue surgical gown, the same kind of gown that Rae had just operated in.

"How'd we do, honey?" Claudia asked. As usual, her old gray eyes were soft and cheery. "You got me that girl I asked you for, right?"

Rae placed her hand on Claudia's shoulder. "Not exactly."

Claudia shook her head and clucked her tongue against her teeth. "Next time, give me a girl next time."

Rae padded out of the operating suite and headed toward the locker room. There she planned to shower again, and change into her street clothes, and if anyone at the board meeting even hinted at laying off one person in her department, she was prepared to kick his ass from there to kingdom come.

# 3

The board of trustees was Berkeley Hills Hospital's highest governing body. It was composed of more lay people than physicians and represented a not-for-profit hospital responsible for the health of many of Berkeley's 120,000 residents. Rae, in turn, represented the obstetricians of her department, all forty-five of them, two thirds of whom were male, and the majority having privileges at both the hospital and the Birth Center.

The hospital itself was a seven-story, 350-bed glass and concrete building, whose roof-top garden boasted a 360-degree view of the entire San Francisco Bay area. But it had been built high in the north Berkeley hills as a testament to cutting-edge medicine, not for the panoramic vistas. For this reason, Rae had chosen its third-floor maternity unit for delivering her babies in—over Stanford and UCSF where she had trained, over Harvard and the Mayo Clinic, who wanted her when her training was completed.

But the cost of cutting-edge medicine had outgrown the money supply in the 1980s, and "managed care," the catch-all phrase for taking care of people for less money, hit in the 1990s. As a result, most hospitals' bottom lines, including Berkeley Hills's, took a downward spiral. Technology, which everybody wanted if it meant the difference between life and death, had outpaced pocketbooks.

Certainly Rae understood this, as well as the tough budgetary decisions the board had to make. Like cutting back on hospital supplies and cafeteria hours, and tightening the belt on surgical instruments that Rae and her colleagues used in the operating room. But the hospital was still losing money.

So the board had begun to decrease salaries and cut the payroll for nonnursing personnel. Layoffs started with workers in housekeeping and dietary, followed by orderlies, ward clerks, and middle management. But the big employers told the health plans that premiums for health insurance were still too high. Not wanting to take cuts in their own bottom lines, the health plans, such as Perfect Health, which Rae detested, decreased their premiums to the employers—the purchasers of health care—by further cutting payments to doctors and hospitals. The health plans justified the cuts by claiming that doctors and hospitals made medicine's slice of the gross domestic product soar to a whopping 17 percent.

That meant, essentially, that for every six dollars spent on anything in the country, one of those six dollars was spent on health care. So the board had no choice but to make more cuts. And next in line to be cut were not just the salaries of the nurses, but, as Bernie and others feared, the nurses' jobs. Rae wasn't going to let that happen, she thought determinedly as she changed her clothes for the board meeting.

Her work wardrobe consisted of simple dresses—straight affairs with zippers in the back that made changing easy. Like the one she stepped into now, a black wool gabardine number with a high neck and long sleeves, and a matching black jacket. Her pearl earrings were still in place from the day before. She spent a minute or two applying her makeup and then slipped on a pair of black suede pumps. Finally, she brushed back her short cropped black hair, grabbed her purse from her locker, stuffed her soiled scrubs into the bin, and headed out for the board room.

She hurried down three flights of stairs. Coming up the stairs—slowly—was Dr. Mattie Henshaw, an obstetrician who ran a full-time practice and who was now eight months pregnant with her third child.

"Are the elevators out again or are you just a glutton for punishment?" Rae teased. She stopped to give Mattie a friendly tap on her belly and felt the baby kick under Mattie's white doctor's coat.

"Both," Mattie said with a grin. "I'm on my way to do a section. Got triplets waiting for me. All I need—besides a trip to the ladies' room—is for the OR to be ready. But with all the nurses going over to the Birth Center, it's a miracle we've got enough staff left to get the job done at all."

"It's not that bad, yet," Rae said.

Mattie grabbed the rail and continued her ascent. "The operative word here is *yet,*" she said. "I heard about the cutbacks."

"I'm on my way to discuss that very issue with the board," Rae said.

"Knock 'em dead, Rae. If anybody can, it's you."

Rae smiled to herself as she exited the stairwell and entered the lobby of the hospital. It was nice to get a vote of confidence from her colleague. The lobby of Berkeley Hills Hospital, like its third-floor maternity suite, had been built to take everyone into the twenty-first century. The furniture was all glass and chrome. The carpet resembled a huge checkerboard made of black and silver squares. The futuristic look may have lacked warmth but it certainly represented the confidence of a hospital that knew it had some of the state's top doctors and nurses, and the best lifesaving equipment on the face of the earth.

Until recently, those top doctors and nurses had been well paid for their services. But as incomes dropped for medical personnel—just as they dropped for educators, bankers, and air traffic controllers—the best doctors and nurses were threatening to leave, and applications to fill empty positions had plummeted.

Floor-to-ceiling windows served as walls for the lobby. More glass filled in the part of the ceiling that projected out past the second story. On the days that Rae never made it out of the hospital, the sunlight streaming in through the lobby's ceiling and walls was as good as it got. But this morning all she could see outside was thick, gray fog.

Doctors and nurses walked purposefully by, most dressed in white coats and uniforms, or, for those just coming to work or about to leave the hospital, in thick sweaters, gloves, and overcoats. Women pushed strollers here and there, while inside, babies slept peacefully. There were white people and black people, Asians and Hispanics. There were poor people and rich people, and everyone in between. Rae loved the diversity of cultures and language and incomes that proved that sometimes, all sorts of people could work together under the same roof.

She greeted everybody she recognized with a friendly smile. Rae had worked hard for her reputation. Many people knew and respected her. Whether they liked her or not was not as important, but it certainly made work more pleasant. As she passed by a food cart, the aroma of coffee made her mouth water. She longed to stop for a cup. But her watch said six minutes to eight. Besides, there would be coffee at the meeting. She hurried on.

"Say, Dr. Duprey, whatcha doing for Halloween this year?" shouted Tim Puck, a gift shop volunteer, as he stood inside the doorway next to a window display of porcelain pumpkins and designer chocolate candies.

"A night off would be nice," Rae said with a laugh as she waved back to him.

Finally she reached the end of the lobby. A private marble hallway led to the board room on her right. She made the turn, and found herself alone once again. But she was not alone, really. Try as she might not to think about it, the memory of Nola's baby pressed against the back of her brain like an anvil. How was he doing? she wondered. Had he started to breathe on his own yet?

"I've been trying to reach you, Rae."

Rae did not have to turn around to know who had spoken to her. The deep voice belonged to Walker. Walker Stuart, chief executive officer of Berkeley Hills Hospital.

"I've been upstairs all night. What's up?" Rae said as she waited for Walker to catch up with her.

Just seeing Walker made Rae feel better. She smiled and patted him on his back. Walker, who was fifty-two years old, was her friend and mentor. He had been vice president at her training hospital, and CEO of Berkeley Hills Hospital for the past five years. He was not a physician, but he cared about patients as much as she did.

"No wonder you didn't call me back," he said. "I left a message on your home machine."

At six feet four, Walker towered over her. She had to take one and a half steps for every one he took. His penetrating forest-green eyes stared straight ahead as they walked. Every strand of his silver hair was immaculately brushed back, his white beard neatly trimmed. As usual, he was dressed to kill in a navy-blue Italian suit, crisp white shirt, navy and burgundy silk tie, and shiny black wing tips.

Walker lived in a grand Tudor home in the upscale neighboring town of Piedmont. He had been married for twenty-seven years and raised two daughters, the older of whom had a six-month-old child named Agatha, whom Rae had delivered.

Rae patted her purse. "I do carry a beeper," she said. "What was so important?"

She wanted to tell Walker about Nola's C-section. The misplaced endotracheal tube bothered her a great deal. It would bother Walker too, if he knew about it. Quality patient care was his top priority. But the strained look on his face made her hesitate to tell him about Nola's surgery. Obviously, he had enough problems of his own this morning.

So she waited for him to speak his mind. They stood in the middle of the marble hallway that led to the board room, the inner sanctuary of the hospital. Of course, some people thought Walker had gone overboard when, five years ago, he took the helm as the hospital's chief executive officer and spent money on "spiffing things up." But money was plentiful then, and Rae rationalized that if nice surroundings made the board of trustees a better decision-making entity, then so be it. Although the board did not have to think on its feet, as Rae often had to do inside the operating room, its decisions were just as important, and the consequences of those decisions were just as grave.

"Listen," he said, "I couldn't chance calling your answering service last night or this morning. I'm not supposed to tell you this now. I could lose my job over it."

He paused to look around. Rae saw that the hallway was empty, except for the two of them.

Concerned, Rae said, "I'm listening."

"Look," Walker said, "I heard about what happened to you and that patient in the OR this morning—at least one version of it."

Rae didn't need Walker to explain what he meant. Hospital rumors spread fast.

"That can't be what you wanted to talk to me about since the section was this morning and you were looking for me last night," Rae said.

"It's all related," Walker said. "At least it could be."

Rae recited a thirty-second version of Nola Payne's C-section and of the resuscitation done by the staff.

"Thank God you were on call," he said. "And believe me, if I have to stock those bins myself, those endotracheal tubes—or whatever you called them—will be where they're supposed to be."

"Nola should have been in our hospital from the start," Rae said. "You should have seen her. Low-risk? Yeah, right. How a patient like that ever got into the Birth Center in the first place is something I plan to find out. And now the board wants to lay off our nurses—"

"That's not the half of it," Walker said. "That's why I was trying to find you."

Rae's eyes narrowed. Walker's voice had taken on an ominous edge. "Meaning?" she asked.

"Last night, there was a meeting with the board's Finance Committee. An emergency meeting. You see—"

But before Walker could continue, Rae heard, "Ah, Walker, could I have a quick word with you?"

Rae followed Walker's stare to Heidi O'Neil, the chairman of the board. Walker spoke in a low tone to Rae as Heidi, dressed in a tailored red business suit and white silk blouse, walked toward them. "About Nola—that was the name of your patient wasn't it?"

Rae nodded as she watched Heidi approach.

"Walker, please," Heidi said. "I've got to talk to you before the meeting."

"Is that story something," Walker said quietly, "that you could tell the board?"

"What do you mean?" Rae asked, trying to read Walker's mind.

"I might need you to tell them about Nola in case things get out of hand."

Rae did not like his tone, or the nervous look in his eyes. "I couldn't mention her by name," Rae said slowly.

"But you could tell the story?"

"Walker, what's this all about? What might get out of hand?"

But Walker had no chance to respond, for by then, Heidi had joined them and had grabbed Walker's arm. "I'm not used to coming to get my men," she said with a smile.

"Good morning to the world's greatest banker," Walker said. "And what can I do for you?"

"You don't mind if I steal him for a while, do you, Rae?" Heidi asked.

Rae shot Walker a nervous glance. Heidi, as chairman of the board, was his boss. Rae had to be careful. The last thing she wanted to do was to get him in trouble when it was Walker who was trying to help her.

"Just return me to my good friend Dr. Duprey in one piece, Heidi," Walker said as he let Heidi lead him to the twelve-foot-high silver door of the board room. Rae watched the two of them walk away. What did he want to tell her? And what, she wondered, did it have to do with Nola Payne?

Rae had come to the board meeting worried about Bernie's future, and the future of the rest of the maternity nurses. She had been counting on Walker to help her fight for them. But now she wondered if he needed her more than she needed him. Feeling uncharacteristically off balance, and not at all like the prepared negotiator she thought she would be, she entered the board room. As the door clicked shut behind her, she suddenly felt certain that saving Bernie's job would turn out to be the least of her problems.

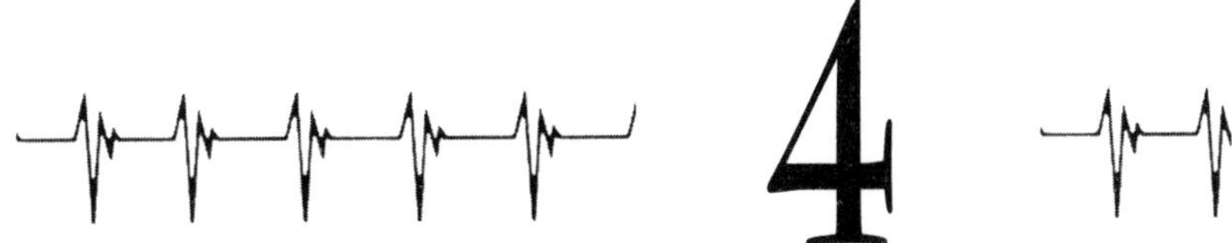

# 4

INSIDE THE BOARD ROOM STOOD A LONG, RECTANGULAR GLASS table surrounded by thirty upholstered chairs. Lining the walls were framed black-and-white photos of past board presidents. Not surprisingly, all of the photos were of white males, average age fifty-five.

The big room smelled of coffee and freshly baked muffins. Walker had finished speaking with Heidi, and had taken his seat. Whatever Heidi had said appeared to have shaken him. His fingernails rapped nervously across the glass. He removed a small leather-bound book from his suit coat and, frowning, made a few notes in it.

Concerned, Rae watched Walker from her seat at the far end of the room. She tried to force herself to relax and settle back in her chair. The chair's cushion felt good against her legs and back, so good, in fact, that had she not been surrounded by board members she might have given in to her exhaustion and fallen asleep.

A wiry, twitchy little man, dressed in a tight business suit, plopped down in the seat next to her. "Good morning," Rae said.

"Is it?" he snapped back.

He opened his briefcase, pulled out a medicine bottle, and popped a pill. Then, just as quickly, he pulled out a stack of papers and proceeded to read them. Rae sighed. Probably took an antacid for heartburn, she thought. Serves him right.

In front of her was a pot of coffee. She sat back up and poured herself a cup. Perhaps she should pour one for the man next to her. On the other hand, maybe it would be better to leave him alone. She was new to the board. Only recently had the board asked the vice-chair of the obstetrics department to attend the meetings—and then just as a supplier of information, not as a voting member.

And where was Bo? she thought, looking around. Although Bo was the medical director of the Birth Center, he was also the chair of the hospital's obstetrics department. Rae knew that once she was chairman of the department, she would change its bylaws to prohibit any director of the Birth Center from holding an office in the department. The conflict of interest was too great.

She sipped the coffee, but it was lukewarm at best. Not having hot coffee made her irritable, and now she wished she had stopped off for a hot cup from the cart in the lobby. She nibbled on a muffin served on a tiny china plate and inspected the other board members, many of whom were already in their seats.

The nonphysician board members were mostly people who owned their own businesses. Members were not paid for serving on the board. Yet here they were, at five minutes past eight on a Friday morning, helping to solve the problems of the hospital.

There were no other black people in the room. Rae was used to this. Ever since she left the public schools of Los Angeles, she was often the "only one," the "only black." Now, being the one and only was second nature to her, like breathing. An advantage—she now understood. Being different had taught her to be tough, resourceful, and self-reliant. People—including herself at one point—were wrong to view being a black woman in America these days as a liability.

Last to enter the board room was a man dressed in a blue surgical gown over white scrubs. Rae immediately recognized the flamboyant Dr. Marco Donavelli. Marco was chief of cardiac surgery of Berkeley Hills Hospital, and known affectionately to his friends as Marco the Magnificent or simply, Il Magnifico. Rae suspected that Heidi had been waiting for him before starting the meeting. After all, Marco's cardiac program made millions of dollars for the hospital.

Walker, in need of someone to kick the heart program into gear, had been the one to recruit Marco to Berkeley Hills Hospital. Having heard about Marco's research and exceptional skills at Harvard he had written Marco and promised him the job of chief of cardiac surgery, with nearly free rein over the department. Marco had not disappointed Walker. He performed the primary cases that the other heart surgeons were too afraid of, and the "redo" cases for which his colleagues didn't even want to serve as *assistant* surgeons.

Postoperatively, Marco's patients did better than patients operated on by other heart surgeons. This was the fact that pleased Rae most. Since joining the staff of Berkeley Hills Hospital, he had turned a little known program into the bay area's finest—almost single-handedly. If you disputed that claim, all you had to do was to ask Marco himself.

The other reason why he was called Il Magnifico was because of his reputation with the nurses. No one hopped in and out of bed with more of them than Marco did. It was not just his looks that made him so desirable, although he was handsome enough with his thick blond hair, deep-set green eyes, and fine Tuscan features.

What drove most nurses to his bed was his skill in the operating room. Rumor had it that he devoted the same amount of attention to pleasing his lovers as to fixing an ailing heart. Rae had often noticed that operating rooms were breeding grounds for affairs. Being so close to death all the time made you want to reach out and touch someone else, perhaps just to prove that life goes on, somehow, somewhere.

Although Marco would be the first one to claim responsibility for the success of the hospital's cardiac surgery program, he vehemently denied his sexual trysts with the nursing staff. He had to deny it. After all, he was forty-eight years old, and a married man with four children. And his wife was no dummy—she would sue him for everything he had if he gave her reason to.

Enough about Marco's private life, Rae thought, giving herself a mental shake. Now that he had arrived, why hadn't Heidi started the meeting? She looked at the clock. Ten after eight. Could Heidi be waiting for somebody else? Then another thought crossed her mind. Why *had* Marco been invited to the board meeting? The person who should have been there was not the chief of cardiac surgery, but the chief of *general* surgery, who, like Rae, was a non-voting member of the board.

Then came a knock at the door. Everyone looked up curiously. No board member ever knocked before entering the board room. Heidi rose and opened the door. Walker had placed his notebook back inside his coat pocket.

"Ah, Dr. Hartman, I was afraid that you might not be able to make it," Heidi said.

"Me too," said Sam Hartman.

Rae sat up in her chair. Now what was *he* doing here?

"Sam, over here," Marco said, waving Sam to an empty seat as if the two of them were at a baseball game.

Sam sat in the seat next to Marco as the surgeon poured some coffee for him. Catching Rae's eye, he raised his cup to her. She turned away, embarrassed that he had seen her staring.

"Ladies and gentlemen," said Heidi O'Neil, "I now call the meeting to order."

*Settle down, Rae. Get ready.*

She looked at Walker. He nodded at her, and sipped his coffee.

There were the usual reports, then Heidi quickly moved to the matter at hand. "Now, ladies and gentlemen," Heidi said, "the board's Finance Committee met last night. There it was proposed that, despite our number one ranking in the state of California, we can no longer afford to deliver babies here at Berkeley Hills Hospital. So starting January 1, Berkeley Hills Hospital will close down its maternity unit and focus on expanding this hospital's department of cardiac surgery. Now, is there a motion?"

"What?" Rae blurted out.

But at the same time Rae asked her question, someone from the opposite end of the room said, "I move we close down OB in January."

"Is there a second?"

"Second," said the man sitting next to Rae.

"Hey!" Rae said.

"All those in favor," Heidi said, as if Rae had not spoken, "please raise your right hand. Remember, this applies to voting members only."

"Excuse me!"

Rae slammed her palms against the glass as hands went up all around her. She stood up quickly, knocking over her coffee cup in the process.

"Dr. Duprey, please sit—"

"What the hell is going on here?" Rae cried. She swiped at the coffee spill with a napkin as she stared angrily around the room.

When she looked back down, the coffee had wound its way to the twitchy man sitting next to her. He snatched his briefcase out of the way.

"Sorry," Rae said to the man, and then looked again at Heidi. "What do you mean we can't deliver babies here? Here where?"

"Here," Heidi said. "At Berkeley Hills Hospital. On the third floor. The Finance Committee has already met and voted on this issue. This vote is just a formality—"

Rae waved Heidi off. "What issue?" she asked. "What vote? *Who* voted for *what?"*

Rae was beside herself. Surely this was some huge joke. Had she heard right? Was there actually a proposal on the table to close down obstetrics at Berkeley Hills Hospital? Didn't Heidi mean that they wanted to cut a couple of nursing positions at the very most?

She turned to Walker. He was standing now. "Walker? Is this true?" So this was what he wanted to tell her, she thought. And he *would* have told her had Heidi not interrupted him before the meeting.

"It's not the full story, Rae," Walker said.

"Then somebody tell me what is—" Rae began.

But someone else cleared his throat before Rae could continue. She whipped her head around to Marco. "Point of order, Madam Chairman," he said. "Perhaps Dr. Duprey is simply trying to point out that a call for the vote went out before the call for discussion."

Heidi's head jerked back as if Marco had slapped her, which was exactly what Rae wanted to do. "Is there any discussion?" Heidi asked wearily.

Rae was incredulous. Any discussion? she thought. She had a lot to discuss, but she was so upset—so utterly shocked—that she could barely speak. In fact, for the next few seconds, she could do little else than study the faces of the other board members. Most had already raised their hands in support of Heidi's proposal, but now, when they saw her looking at them, their hands dropped like lead pipes.

"You people are not serious?" Rae began.

Heidi tugged at her suit jacket. "Didn't Dr. Donavelli tell you?"

Rae looked at Marco again. Marco crossed his hands together as calmly as a priest. "Why don't you return your messages sometime?" he asked. "I must have called you ten times."

Rae was incensed. "I called you back every time," she said coldly. "It was you who was too busy to talk to me."

Marco raised his hand and Heidi recognized him as the next speaker. "Just for the record," Marco said, "I was able to speak with the *chairman* of the obstetrics department, and Dr. Bo Michaels is fully aware of the need to close down this hospital's obstetrical unit. In fact, he understands the need completely. He respects the board for the tough decision it had to make."

"Bo!" Rae shouted.

She was beside herself with rage.

"This is crazy—" she started to say.

"Dr. Donavelli still has the floor," Heidi interrupted.

"Not anymore!" Rae said. "You people are insane! You can't just shut down my maternity ward! And Bo, he can go to hell for all I care. Don't you see? He's selling us out for his damn Birth Center!"

"May I remind you that you are not a voting member, Dr. Duprey," Heidi said. "You are here to provide information—"

"What the hell do you think I'm doing? I'm informing you that you've all gone nuts."

She paused to look at Marco, who was still sitting there with that damn grin on his face. Had he been planning on this the entire time? Was Bo involved? But then it occurred to her that he couldn't be. The Birth Center *needed* the hospital as a place to do cesarean sections.

"You are out of order, Dr. Duprey," Heidi said.

Rae forced herself to settle down. If she was going to get anywhere, she'd have to control her emotions. "May I have the floor?" she asked.

Heidi looked at the little man sitting next to Rae, and Rae saw him shaking his head from side. "Perhaps it would be better if we moved along," Heidi began.

"Please?" Rae said. "I just need a point of clarification!"

Heidi looked at the man again, but he was busy popping another pill, and wiping his brow with his hand.

"Well, what is it?" Heidi said, turning away from him with exasperation.

Rae knew she had only one chance to change the board's mind about its preposterous proposal. She took a deep breath—

"We don't have all day," Heidi added.

"With all due respect to my colleague, Dr. Donavelli," Rae began, "it seems to me he must be mistaken about the sentiment of our chairman, Dr. Bo Michaels."

Rae couldn't believe she was defending Bo. Wait until she got her hands on him, she thought.

"Oh, I don't think so," Marco said.

"I have the floor, damn it," Rae said.

She looked at Heidi for confirmation. Heidi had her head in her hands. "Go on," Heidi said. "Go on."

"The reason why Dr. Donavelli may have his information mixed up is because Dr. Michaels needs our unit to do his cesarean sections. I'm sure you are all aware that the Birth Center is only licensed to do vaginal births—"

Now Marco stood up. "Madam Chairman, if I might save the board time, and clarify a point for Dr. Duprey—"

"Dr. Donavelli has the floor," Heidi said.

"But—" Rae began.

"Dr. Donavelli has the floor!" Heidi shouted.

Rae sat down. Sam Hartman, sitting to Marco's right, was staring at her with a look of compassion. But what good was compassion when the life of her department was on the line?

"Apparently the chair and vice-chair of the OB department don't communicate in a professional manner," Marco said. "For if they had, Dr. Duprey would know that Dr. Michaels has taken care of that little detail, and that the Birth Center will use Berkeley City Hospital as its backup—"

"Berkeley City Hospital? That dump?" Rae cried.

"It's a reputable hospital," Marco said.

"But it's three miles from the Birth Center!" Rae said. "And I didn't see you deliver any of your kids there, Marco! It's too far away to use as a backup! You can't subject patients to that kind of delay. One in every five labor patients gets transferred out of the Birth Center! What, are you planning to do emergency sections in the back of the ambulance along the way?"

"The staff at the Birth Center doesn't seem to share your concerns," Marco said.

"The staff at the Birth Center!" Rae exclaimed. "I've seen no evidence that they care at all about what happens to their patients!"

"That's enough, Dr. Duprey!" Heidi said. "Sit down and be quiet, or you will be asked to leave—"

"I will not sit down or shut up! If you want me to leave, you'll have to throw me out! I am not going to let you shut down my department!"

There was a gentle cough, and Rae looked in Walker's direction. "May I have the floor?" he asked.

Rae tried to settle down. Surely Walker would take care of this. He had told Rae things might get out of hand, that he might need her to tell the story about Nola—

"Mr. Stuart has the floor," Heidi said. "This is your last warning, Dr. Duprey. "

A beeper went off just then, and Marco rose. "Excuse me," he said. "I have a page to answer."

"As the CEO of this hospital," Walker began, "I wear two hats. The board," and he nodded at Heidi, "is my employer. I must make the board happy if I am to keep my job. On the other hand," and he nodded to Rae, "I have a responsibility to the doctors and nurses who work here. Sometimes, what the board wants and what the medical staff wants are two different things. But above all, both parties need to do what is in the best interest of the patients—"

"And that is to make sure that they get the care they need right away," Rae interrupted.

"Dr. Duprey—" Heidi began.

"Let her finish, Heidi," Walker said. "We've all had the benefit of hearing the news last night. Give her a chance to state her case. The least we can do is hear her out."

All eyes turned to Rae. Walker, Rae understood, had given her his cue to tell the board about Nola Payne. She walked to the front of the room, her heart pounding, her mind flooded with memories of Nola's C-section, and standing next to Walker, she began. "A woman was transferred from the Birth Center this morning. Now I don't know exactly what happened over there, but I can tell you that had she been here, in our unit, her baby would be cradled in her arms now, instead of inside an incubator, with a tube down his throat, fighting for his life in our neonatal ICU. His mother had to be transferred from her bed inside the Birth Center—after *waiting* for an ambulance to arrive—then placed on an ambulance gurney, rolled down the Birth Center hallway, pushed out the door, loaded into the back of the ambulance, and driven across the street to our emergency room. Once here, she had to wait for the elevator, be transported in our elevator to the third floor, pushed down our hallway, wheeled into our operating room, placed on our operating table, and finally, operated on by our staff, who didn't know a thing about her but who, at the same time, were supposed to save her baby's life.

"Now, I don't know how many steps I've just listed, but if that patient had been here at Berkeley Hills Hospital in the first place, she would have been transferred only one time—from her labor bed to our operating room table. That, ladies and gentlemen, only involves two steps. But here you people are, proposing to add *three miles* on to the transfer. Well, go and tell that to the little baby upstairs. Go and tell that to his mother, who keeps asking how he is. If you can live with it, then go ahead and vote to shut down this hospital's obstetrical department. Just be sure to tell that little baby upstairs why it's such a good idea."

The room had become completely silent, and Rae feared that the board members could hear the pounding inside her chest. She looked at the faces around the table. Still, no one spoke. When her eyes reached Sam's face, he smiled and gave her the thumbs-up sign. "For the record, I agree with Dr. Duprey," Sam said.

"Well, I sure as hell don't!"

It was the little man who sat beside her. He slammed his briefcase shut.

"Leave this to me, John," Heidi said.

"Enough melodrama," the man said. He pulled at his tie irritably, as if he were having trouble getting air, and then looked up at the rest of the board.

"I'm not going to let some sentimental obstetrician let this hospital go belly up," he began.

"Sentimental obstetrician?" Rae interrupted. "And who are you?"

"John Vincent's the chairman of the Finance Committee," Walker said. "John, this is Dr. Rae Duprey."

"I know who she is."

"I told you that Dr. Duprey would fight tooth and nail to save her department," Walker said. "And after listening to the case she just presented, who can blame her?"

"And you," John said, pointing his finger at Walker, "you said you'd back us if she tried. Traitor. Liar." He looked at Heidi. "I told you we couldn't trust him."

"John, please!" Heidi said.

What the hell was going on here? Rae asked herself with amazement.

"I never said that. I said we should look at all of the options. Now, if you'd just listen—"

"I'm tired of listening! You're going to double-cross us again, you son of a bitch!"

John slammed his fist against the glass. "We agreed last night, remember? You went along then! And now you've lost your nerve! The Birth Center's eating us alive. Let's cut our losses and stop this hemorrhaging! And quit letting some idealistic vice-chair get in the way!"

"Are you referring to me?" Rae challenged.

"I certainly am!"

"Then speak to me directly. I'm standing right here."

"May I finish?" Walker asked.

"No!" John said. "We've already decided—"

"Let him finish," Rae said. "There are options, and I'm not going to let you railroad this committee into shutting down my department."

Everyone began speaking at one time. Heidi called for order. Rae walked back to her chair and sat down. "Walker has the floor," Heidi said.

"Thank you," Walker said. "Now, as I said, I represent both sides. What I have to say is for Dr. Duprey and all of those in this room who may agree with her. John Vincent has a very good reason for proposing that we stop delivering babies here at Berkeley Hills Hospital."

"Walker!" Rae blurted out.

"Now listen to me, Rae," Walker said. "I couldn't agree with you more. But at some point we've got to deal with reality here. Your obstetrical unit's just not making it. We've taken money from other departments just to keep yours in operation. But your department is ruining the overall financial health of this hospital. What do you want, Rae? Do you want the whole ship to sink trying to save your department from drowning?"

Rae shook her head miserably. She felt trapped. What Walker said made sense. But what she had said about Nola Payne made sense too.

She raised her head and looked Walker straight in the eye. "What I want," she said, her voice now calm, "is not to let what happened to Nola Payne's baby happen to somebody else."

Again no one spoke for a few seconds. Rae, having spoken her heart, had nothing more to say.

"No!"

John Vincent opened the first button of his shirt. "Don't listen to her! Can't you see what she's doing? She's working on your sympathy, not your intellect. You all have a fiscal responsibility to the city of Berkeley. You keep the maternity unit open at this hospital, and within six months, we're history! You can close down obstetrics and build up cardiac surgery, or keep obstetrics open, and close down the hospital. Those are your choices!"

Suddenly John stopped talking. His face turned ashen gray and he scrabbled at his chest with his hands.

"John!" Heidi shouted.

She pushed Walker out of her way and ran toward Rae's end of the table. But John had already slumped down onto the glass. Rae turned him over. His lips were slate blue and vomit trickled out the corner of his mouth.

Sam was somehow at Rae's side, helping her.

"Call the operator!" shouted Rae, feeling John's neck. She felt no pulse coursing through his carotid artery. John Vincent didn't have heartburn. He was having a heart attack! "We've got a cardiac arrest here!" she said.

*"No!"* Heidi shouted.

"Give us room!" Sam barked.

As the members of the board pushed back their chairs, Rae helped Sam lower John to the carpet. Sam wiped the vomit out of his mouth and Rae dropped to her hands and knees and hovered over his chest. With the heel of one palm over the other, she pumped against his heart, while Sam held John's head back and pressed his lips together.

Sam placed his lips over John's mouth, and blew in a mouthful of air. Rae pumped and counted out loud. "One one thousand, two one thousand—"

But all she could think about, as she felt the sternum compress under the weight of her hands, was that John Vincent wanted to shut down her department. And now, here she was, trying to save his life.

# 5

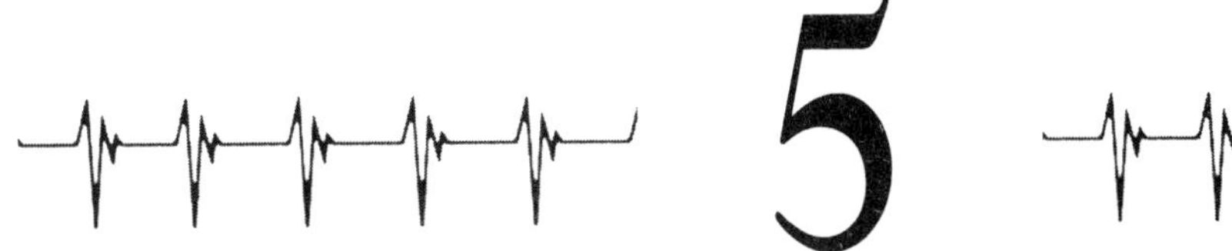

Some thirty minutes later, Rae sat across from Walker inside his office. It was an immaculate, simply designed room, with a glass desk, comfortable leather chairs, computer, pearl-white carpet, and glass display cabinet. Unlike many of the other administrative offices, Walker's had no loose papers lying about, no unsharpened pencils, no opened books. Everything was neat and tidy. Everything had its place. The only framed picture on his desk was of his grandchild, Agatha, now six months old.

But for once, Rae felt completely out of place in the tidy office. After the morning's events—from Nola's baby to John Vincent's cardiac arrest—she felt there was nothing tidy about life at all.

Inside her hand she held a tiny red satin cradle, a present she had given to Walker on behalf of her department six months ago. As CEO, Walker had purchased sophisticated fetal heart machines, central monitoring, and advanced computer systems. He added more LDRs—labor-delivery-recovery rooms—and hired the best nurses in the state. He refurbished all the locker rooms and the lounge. He added more private rooms for postpartum care, and installed a video library for new parents. He increased the number of ward clerks and maintenance people and hired more certified registered nurse anesthetists. And most amazing of all, he had done it all in five years.

The bottom of the cradle contained a small compartment with a music box where Rae had placed a tiny note card that read "Thank you" and was signed, "The Babies." The compartment was locked, but Rae didn't mind since she was in no mood to wind it up and listen to any music. Funny, she thought, as her fingertips stroked the soft satin, it was the music that had drawn her to the cradle in the first place. Brahms's Lullaby was the tune. So sweet, so soft, so safe—

But nothing in life was safe.

Intellectually she understood why Walker had to point out both sides of the argument at the board meeting. Emotionally, she wished he could have supported her position 100 percent. "I ought to take this back," she griped as she placed the cradle back on Walker's desk. But he was still on the phone with a nurse in the cardiac unit, checking on the status of John Vincent.

"Thank you, thank you very much," Walker said before hanging up.

He sat behind his desk across from Rae and said, "Sorry, I didn't hear you."

Rae nodded at the cradle. She could not take back a present that he had earned in the days before managed care. "I said, I can't remember the last time you took this out of your cabinet."

"Me either. I don't even know why it's out now."

He rose from his seat and, taking it from her, walked toward the opposite end of his office to a glass display cabinet. After placing the cradle on the middle shelf, he removed a key from his coat pocket and locked the door.

"There now," he said, "back where you belong." He turned to Rae and smiled. "By the way, John's going to be just fine. Congratulations. You saved his life."

Rae let out a deep breath. "I didn't want to ask. I was afraid—"

"That he wouldn't make it . . ."

"Or maybe that he might," she said miserably.

She leaned her elbow on the armrest and cradled her chin in her palm. "I know that sounds horrible," she apologized, "but at some level, I mean it. John wants to shut down our maternity unit, Walker. Like all of those little figures he crunches out everyday tell him something. And you support him."

Walker returned to his chair. "Now you're being childish," Walker said.

Walker was right, of course, but the future of her department was at stake. So what was he going to do now? What was she going to do?

"I suppose," Rae continued, "I'm glad to hear he's going to make it. But my department—he wants to shut down my department, Walker, and expand Marco's. That's not exactly the kind of CPR I had in mind."

Walker folded his arms across his chest. "But, Rae, listen—" he began.

"Delivering babies is my life, Walker," Rae interrupted. She felt her anger growing again, but kept her voice calm.

Inside, though, she didn't feel calm at all. She stood up and began pacing the floor. Stopping to look at her palms she said, "I can still feel his ribs against my hands, Walker. Thin, breakable ribs. I thought I would crush him. I wanted to crush him."

Walker laughed. "You're nuts, you know that?"

"I mean it, Walker."

Walker massaged his beard and ran his hands through his hair. "No you don't. It's not your style." He paused, then said, "Look, I know what delivering babies means to you, Rae—"

"I want my department kept open, Walker. I really don't want to hear about anything else. Even the Birth Center needs us to stay in business." She paused to rub the tight muscles in the back of her neck. "I can't believe I'm saying that."

"I'm sure you and I weren't the only two people at that table who want to keep delivering babies here."

Rae paced back and forth across the floor. Her fight was not with Walker. But what about the patients and the babies? Who spoke for them? She could not let the board close down the number one unit in the state. She couldn't let the women of the Birth Center be forced to endure a three-mile ambulance ride to City Hospital for a C-section.

Walker pointed to the chair. "Sit down," he said. "I want to tell you something."

Rae made herself perch on the edge of the chair.

"I presented the Finance Committee's position for one reason. And that reason was to buy time. The time I need to solve this mess."

Rae sat up straighter. "I'm listening," she said. It was Walker's confident tone that got her attention more than what he said.

"But first," he continued, "let me explain something else." He strolled back to the display cabinet. "Remember when you gave me this?" he asked, rapping his knuckles against the glass in front of the cradle. "No other gift—other than my children—has ever meant more to me."

He sat down in a chair next to Rae's. Her chin rested in her hand, and she stared out the window. She could see the Birth Center directly across the street. "How could a place like that close down our maternity unit?"

"For the moment, Rae, forget what the board will do to me if OB stays open. I told you this hospital was my empire. You're not the only one who believes in what this hospital stands for. Women are safer here than they are anywhere else on the planet. I never told you this, Rae, but remember how you watched your mother die in the back of that godforsaken ambulance?"

"We don't talk about that, Walker."

"Nonetheless—do you think, for a moment, that I want the women of Berkeley to have to suffer like she did? Like the woman this morning—what was her name?"

"Nola Payne," Rae said, sitting up. Her anger was returning, with a vengeance.

"Yes, Nola Payne. Anyway, I know what it's like to deliver at some mediocre hospital, to have mediocre doctors and nurses working on the ones you love. You know that I wanted to be a doctor. Hell, what hospital CEO didn't? I took chemistry, and physics, and math. But then came biology, and, well, let's just say blood is not my specialty. So, I thought, how else could I make decisions that affect people's health? That's when I decided I'd become a hospital administrator."

"I know all of this, Walker—"

"But what you don't know, Rae," he said, "is about my first wife. I've never told you about her. Her name was Florence. I was only twenty-one, and so was she."

"You were married, before Denise?" Rae asked, taken aback.

"Denise doesn't even know."

Walker had risen again, and was looking out the window. He stood with his back to Rae. "Florence was beautiful. I loved her. When she got pregnant, I married her right away. But well, we were just kids, really. What did we know about doctors, and hospitals? She was poor, I was poor. Our parents—well, let's just say neither pair showed up for the wedding.

"Anyway, halfway through her pregnancy, she started to bleed. Not a lot, but there was definitely blood. And like I said, blood is not my specialty, but even I knew a pregnant woman shouldn't bleed in her fifth month.

"It was almost winter. A cold day, like today. I knew we couldn't afford the private hospital. We had both just finished college and neither of us had any health insurance. So, I rushed her to the county hospital. A little rinky-dink thing, whose emergency room—filled with drunks—smelled like an outhouse. And we sat in that damn waiting room for six hours before they called us, and then waited in a freezing exam room before Florence was seen.

"By then it was too late. She had, we found out later, an incompetent cervix. The doctor, who was way overworked, even admitted that had Florence been seen right away, and had a stitch put in her cervix, she would have kept the baby. But, well, neither happened. She wasn't seen early, and the stitch never got placed. So the baby just slipped right out, right there in that wretched room."

"I'm sorry, Walker—"

"Of course, the baby died right away. The marriage died two years later. I was devastated. I felt desperate to right a wrong. And desperate people do desperate things, Rae. Anyway, I decided then and there that one day I would run the number one hospital in the state of California. I would make the policies. I would decide how long a patient would have to wait and where she would have to wait."

Walker sighed, then turned to face Rae directly. "But even *I've* got to face the facts, Rae," he continued. "Even I may have to give up my dreams for the world's greatest maternity unit. Don't you see, Rae? The health of my entire hospital has got to come first. I've got to remember obstetrics is only one department in this hospital. Besides, if the whole place goes under, you're out of a job too."

"I could always start another practice, deliver someplace else," Rae said.

"Yes, I suppose you could," Walker said, rubbing his beard. "But then, someplace else wouldn't be Berkeley Hills Hospital."

Rae stood up and walked over to sit on the end of Walker's desk.

Her pumps dangled above the floor. Outside the window, the fog had lifted, and weak sunlight spilled in through the glass.

"There has to be another way," Rae said.

"There always is," Walker said. "The worst case scenario is that OB closes, Marco's department expands and makes a ton of money, and we open OB again."

The clock in Walker's office chimed nine. Otherwise the room was as silent as the toy cradle in the glass cabinet.

Rae hugged her shoulders. "I suppose you've already tried to buy the Birth Center from Bo?" she asked.

"Three times," Walker said.

"And I suppose you tried to buy out the other doctors?"

"Of course," Walker agreed.

"Hmm." Rae thought for a few more seconds, then suddenly, she sat up straight. She had a plan.

"Well then," she said, "I suppose we've got to—"

But before she could finish her sentence, there was a knock at the door.

"Come in," Walker called out.

In walked Heidi O'Neil. Rae jumped off of Walker's desk and returned to her chair.

Heidi's eyes were red and puffy.

"Good Lord, Heidi," Walker said. "Here, take a seat."

"John is dead," Heidi said. She wiped tears from her eyes.

"But Walker just called the unit," Rae said.

"I don't care if he made a person-to-person call to God himself! John is dead, do you hear me? D-E-A-D. Dead. He had another heart attack."

Rae slumped back in her chair. "But—"

"But what? You don't care! You're the reason he had the heart attack in the first place."

"Me?"

"What are you talking about, Heidi?" Walker asked.

"And you're just as much to blame as she is!" Angrily Heidi reached into her briefcase and pulled out a Kleenex, then raised her hand to cut off Walker, who was just about to say something. "Close down maternity, you said that too, Walker," Heidi continued. "Put our money into cardiac surgery. Why, it was even your idea to invite Dr. Donavelli and Dr. Hartman to the meeting, as a show of good faith."

"I'm sorry about John, Heidi," Walker said. "I didn't even know he had any heart problems."

"Nobody did," Heidi said. She blew her nose. "Nobody," she continued, "but his doctor and me. But John wouldn't listen to either of us. Now I wonder how many more lives we're going to lose dealing with this OB bullshit."

Heidi held her Kleenex to her lips and turned her face away from Rae and Walker.

"I'm sorry too, Heidi," Rae said. She *was* sorry, she thought, but she was also interested in the relationship between Heidi and John Vincent outside of the board room. Obviously the two of them discussed more than the hospital's future. And if they had, the odds were stacked against Rae getting Heidi to keep open the hospital's maternity unit.

"Oh, what difference does any of it make now?" Heidi retorted, shooing away Rae with her Kleenex.

No one spoke for a few seconds. Outside the window, the sky clouded over again.

Rae rose, walked over to Heidi, and placed her hand on her shoulder.

"I really am sorry about John," she said. "And I'm sorry if I played a part in upsetting him. But Heidi, please. When things settle down, let's talk some more. This isn't the best time now, but I'm sure later we can talk about a way to get my colleagues to stop delivering at the Birth Center and start delivering all of their patients here."

"I don't give a rat's ass about your colleagues," Heidi said.

Rae, knowing that patients faced with terrible news will say just about anything, continued.

"But you do care, Heidi. You care like you've never cared for anything in your life. I've seen you speak so proudly about this hospital's maternity unit. Your son's wife delivered here, didn't she? And your mother was operated on by one of our gynecologists, isn't that right? You, of all people, Heidi, as chair of this hospital's board of trustees, know the far-reaching value of having the world's best and safest maternity unit. That is why I deliver my patients here. That is why Walker is this hospital's CEO. And that is why, Heidi, you chair our hospital's board, our highest governing body. There is no way, Heidi, that you are going to let anything shut down our third floor."

Rae waited for Heidi to say something. But her eyes were closed, as if she had fallen asleep. "Heidi?" Rae asked.

"Are you finished?" Heidi replied, her eyes still shut.

"I guess I am," Rae said.

Heidi's eyes opened. "And just how," she said, "am I supposed to keep your precious little department open, without shutting down everything else?"

Rae exhaled slowly. She had to be careful. This was her big chance.

She sat on the edge of her chair. "This is, without a doubt, the best place for a woman to have a baby. We can do everything here, Heidi, everything a woman needs to deliver safely. That is why we are here. The health of the community is our responsibility. If we don't insure that, who will? The public depends on us—"

"The public," Heidi said with a laugh. "Yeah right."

"Listen, Heidi," Rae said. "People care about babies. The public may disagree about education, religion, or who will make the best president. But everybody agrees that the only kind of babies we want are healthy babies. A new mother wants a good baby, not a bad baby—like the one I told you about in the meeting."

Rae paused to see if any of what she said was getting to Heidi.

"Go on, go on," Heidi said.

"Maybe the public doesn't understand how important it is to deliver in a place where cesareans can be done on site," Rae said. "Maybe the average woman doesn't see that she has a risk of having a C-section and that she might even have an emergency C-section where every minutes counts. So if we can educate women that our outcomes are better than the Birth Center's, they'll make up their own minds and come back here."

"Don't you think we talked about that?" Heidi asked. "Don't you think I asked John the same thing? But the truth is, the Birth Center has excellent outcomes. Babies born over there are just as healthy as ours."

"So how do you explain Nola's baby?" Rae asked, her voice rising.

"One baby doesn't mean the whole place is a disaster," Heidi said.

"But if she had been here, if she didn't have to wait for an ambulance to bring her over—"

"Enough!" Heidi said. "We've been through all of this before."

"But you don't understand!" Rae cried. "An ambulance ride means minutes lost, lifesaving minutes."

Walker rose. "I think," he said, "Dr. Duprey is only asking for a little more time, Heidi. Besides, after this morning, I think everyone needs to settle down before you call for another vote. You're going to need time too, Heidi. John meant a lot to you. He meant a lot to all of us."

Rae felt grateful that Walker had spoken for her. Looking at Heidi, she suddenly understood what having power was. Maybe one day she might try to become chair of the hospital's board of trustees if it meant she'd be in a better position to protect the lives of women and babies. But for now, she had to await the decision of the current chair. Rae could only hope that Heidi put babies before dollars. Running a hospital was not like running a bank.

"How much time do you need?" Heidi asked. Her eyes had dried, and she sat up in her chair.

"Three months," Rae said. "Give me three months."

Heidi stuffed her Kleenex back in her purse. She rose from her chair and tugged on her suit coat. "You've got two weeks," Heidi announced. "John said we'd be out of business in six months unless we changed our course. I'd hate to see him die for nothing."

"But that's impossible," Rae said. "There's no way . . ."

Heidi sighed. "Then forget it," she said.

"It's the best offer we've had all morning," Walker interjected.

"But—" Rae began.

"God damn it, Rae, Heidi's offering you another chance. And you don't have to start from scratch. You've already got Nola Payne."

Rae's mind raced wildly. Two weeks to convince her colleagues to deliver all of their patients at the hospital? Ridiculous! On the other hand, Walker was right. Two weeks was better than nothing.

"Okay, Heidi," Rae said. "Two weeks, and we're back in business."

"And if not," Heidi said sternly, "I call for the vote. And there will be no discussion."

"We're grateful," Walker said.

"Thank you, Heidi," Rae said.

"I'm sorry about some of the things I said earlier," Heidi apologized. "And, well, I'm sorry for what John said about you too. Thank you, and thank Dr. Hartman the next time you see him, for trying to save John's life. At least I got to speak to him before . . ."

Rae nodded. "Forget it," she said.

After Heidi left, Walker and Rae sat for a while in silence. Finally, Rae rose from the chair. "Walker, is there anything else you haven't told me? About my department, I mean?"

"God forbid," he said. "I don't think my nerves could take it." He paused and then added, "You know the odds are against you."

"And so they've been most of my life," Rae replied.

"Just be careful, okay? There are plenty of people who won't agree with what you're doing."

"I've got the babies on my side," Rae said. "That's all I need."

Walker chuckled. "Go on. Get out of here. I pity the poor sucker who tries to fight you."

Rae left the room, thinking that Walker was right. The odds were against her, but what other choice did she have?

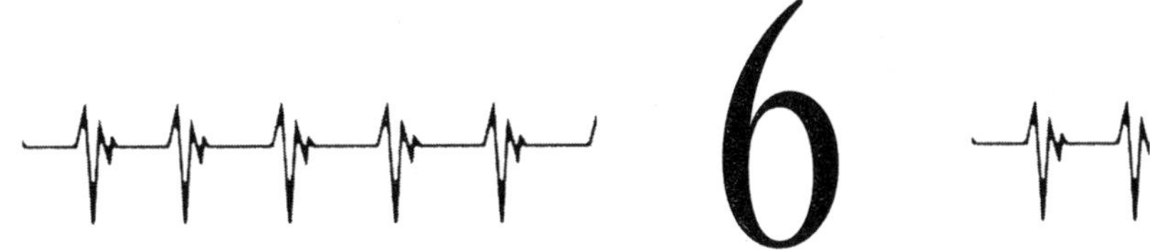

# 6

BERKELEY HILLS HOSPITAL HAD THE TOP NEONATAL INTENSIVE care unit in the state. Rae had hoped to take solace in this fact as she hovered over Nola's baby. But despite its expertise, the nursery had failed to make the baby move his finger, or flick his toe, or twitch an eyelid. He just lay there, his chest rising and falling with each heave of the ventilator pump.

The infant lay prostrate on top of a floral mattress inside his incubator. His chubby arms and legs were tied down by Velcro straps. Spaghetti-size tubes snaked out of the severed stump of his umbilical cord. A similar-size tube sprang from a vein along his scalp. A small piece of red aluminum foil shaped like a heart was pasted to his chest to monitor body temperature.

The baby looked more like a laboratory experiment than a patient, Rae thought sadly. "No one should have to start life this way," she said, touching the warm skin of one of his tiny fingers.

"What's that, Rae?" asked Dr. Catherine Drake, the neonatologist, as she peered over black-rimmed reading glasses to adjust the ventilator settings. Next to her was Jessica Howe, the nursery nurse who had assisted at the initial resuscitation. They were surrounded by other incubators, with other little sick babies.

"I said what a way to end a week."

"And how," Catherine agreed.

"So, what do you think?" Rae asked, referring to the baby's prognosis.

"You never know with these kinds of cases," Catherine said. "We might not know anything for weeks—excuse me, Rae—Jessica, are those blood gases back yet?"

Jessica crossed the room and punched a few buttons on a computer keyboard. Immediately a printer crunched out a report.

"I've been tied up with meetings all morning," Rae said. "Have you heard anything about what happened to the mother before she arrived here?"

Catherine shook her head. "We're always the last to get the full story," she said. "Too bad the babies can't talk to us."

"I was thinking the same thing."

"Anyway," Catherine continued, "if he can just hold his own for a while, we should know more about how he's doing in seventy-two hours." Wearily she pushed her glasses back onto the bridge of her nose as Jessica returned with the printout.

Seventy-two hours? Rae thought, anxiously rapping her fingertips against the metal frame of the incubator. Seventy-two hours was way too long. That would mean she wouldn't know anything until Monday. She wanted to know *now* that the baby had a chance.

Catherine read the report, pulled her mouth into a tight line, and massaged her eyelids. "Like you said," she began, handing the printout to Rae, "what a way to end the week."

Rae scanned down the page, hoping to find a pH value over 7.10 to let her know that the baby hadn't suffered a dangerous degree of oxygen deprivation to his brain. But her hopes vanished when she read the report. "Six point eight?" she asked out loud.

Immediately her pulse quickened. Her normally steady hands shook perceptibly. No, she thought. That poor baby. She reread the report. But the same values stared back at her. The oxygen level was way too low, the carbon dioxide value was way too high—each was exactly the opposite of what it should have been.

Then she glanced at the values depicting the base excess. Her heart sank even further when she realized that the prolonged anoxia had caused a severe metabolic acidosis as well. She rubbed her eyes hard as she imagined how the baby might look some ten years later: eyes blank, head rolling aimlessly, hands pulled back like claws against his chest.

She sighed and handed the paper back to Catherine. "I had hoped for better news than this. I still have to talk to the mother."

"He's alive, you can tell her that," Catherine said as she passed the report on to Jessica. She leaned over to realign tubes coming out of the cut umbilical cord.

"Just *barely,*" Jessica said, filing the report into the baby's metal chart clipped to the side of the incubator. "He didn't have a chance in hell. His heart rate was in the toilet when they moved him out of the Birth Center—"

"It was not," another nurse said.

Rae turned and saw Eileen Tan strolling over to join their conversation. Eileen was only an inch taller than Rae. She had a bobbed haircut and deep dimples. "The baby's heart rate was just fine in the ambulance," Eileen added.

"That's not how I heard it," Jessica said.

Rae looked from one nurse to the other. Each seemed convinced of what she had heard. "Who'd you talk to, Jessica?"

"Sylvia, who else?"

"Sylvia?" Rae's mind raced through the names of all the nurses on the maternity and nursery staffs.

"Of course you know Sylvia, Dr. Duprey," Jessica said. "Sylvia Height. She's the charge nurse on days for the ER."

"Oh, that Sylvia."

"Well, she's wrong," Eileen said. "I spoke with—"

"Jessica," Catherine interrupted, "call down to CT and order a scan for first thing Monday morning. And try to get that EEG to follow." She snapped off her gloves. "I'll call you later, Rae, if things change."

"Call me even if they don't."

She watched as Catherine Drake limped out of the room. Only six months ago, she had shattered her hip in a biking accident and had an artificial hip put in. Rae had always admired her. Even her own infirmities didn't stop her from taking care of the hospital's sickest babies.

At least, she thought, she could tell Nola Payne that her baby was literally in the best of hands. That was something. Maybe not a whole lot, given the baby's current condition, but it was so much better than the dismal blood gas report.

She turned to Eileen as Jessica used a nearby phone to schedule the tests that Catherine had ordered. "You were saying?"

"I know Leo better than anybody," Eileen said. "He wouldn't lie to me. I don't care what Sally, or whatever her name is, told Jessica. The twins told me this baby was fine when they left the center—"

"The twins?"

"The twins are the paramedics. Leo and Theo—Leonard and Theodore, I mean. They were in the ambulance that brought the patient over."

"And one of them said that the baby's heart rate was fine when they left the Birth Center?"

"That's right."

"Oh, *those* paramedics," Jessica said, hanging up the phone. "No wonder you're sticking up for them."

Jessica jerked her thumb at Eileen. "Leo's her boyfriend, Dr. Duprey. She'd believe anything he said."

"Just what is that supposed to mean?" Eileen said.

"Jessica," Catherine Drake called out.

Rae turned and saw the neonatologist poking her head back into the room.

"Sorry to break up the party, ladies," Catherine announced, "but I need Jessica down in the transition nursery."

"That baby was in trouble long before he got here," Jessica hissed, walking toward the door. She paused to make sure that her stethoscope was around her neck. "Just ask Sylvia. She'll tell you how things went down."

After Jessica left, Rae felt Eileen's hand on her shoulder. "So what if Leo is my boyfriend?" Eileen said. "That doesn't make him a liar."

"Nobody said anything about anybody lying."

"I mean it, Dr. Duprey. Leo's a very good paramedic—"

"I'm sure he is, Eileen."

"He would never lie to me. He told me the baby's heart rate was perfectly normal when they dropped the patient off in our ER—"

"Eileen, if you keep defending him, I'm going to start to believe Jessica."

"You can't believe Jessica!" Eileen knitted her brow and sighed deeply. "Look," she continued, dropping her voice, and looking around the room to see if anyone else was listening, "Jessica's still all bent out of shape because she was dating Leo's brother until she found out he was married. I ought to know. The four of us double-dated. Theo even has two kids."

The last thing Rae needed was an update on the latest bed-hopping practices of the nursing staff. "My concern is that somebody was taking care of the baby—regardless of when the baby got into trouble." She paused to consider the conflicting stories. Either Eileen or Jessica was right, but not both.

"I'll tell you what. Why don't I talk to the nurses at the Birth Center, you know, the ones responsible for transferring the patient, and then I'll talk to Leo and his brother—what did you say his name was?"

"Theodore. Theo for short. Leo and Theo McHenry. And Theo's the oldest."

"And they were both in the ambulance?" Her stomach growled. She had to get something to eat, she thought.

"Theo was in the back, with the patient," Eileen continued. "He's always in the back—hey, are you okay, Dr. Duprey?"

Rae had suddenly reached for the side of the incubator to steady herself as fatigue and light-headedness swept over her. She knocked the metal chart off the incubator, and it clanged when it hit the floor.

"I just need to put something in my stomach," she said, stooping down.

Chart notes had scattered all over the floor. Eileen bent over to help her retrieve them. "Here," she said, singling out a form among all of the rest.

Rae stuffed the others inside the chart and then studied the one Eileen held in her hand. She saw that it was an ambulance report.

"See?" Eileen said, pointing to one of several boxes. "It says so right here. The baby's heart rate was normal during the ambulance ride. A hundred fifty-two beats per minute."

"Yes, it does say that." Rae studied the numbers again. She shook her head, stood back up, and waited a second or two for the dizziness to pass. Then she studied the paramedic's signature. It resembled two copulating caterpillars. "Is that your boyfriend's handwriting, Eileen? It's terrible. Worse than mine."

Eileen blushed. "I'd know that signature anywhere," she said proudly.

"How about writing down his name for me—legibly? And his brother's. I can't make this out. And put down their last names too."

As Eileen scribbled the information on a nearby pad, Rae scanned through the rest of the chart notes. There was a form from the Birth Center that the nurse had filled out. Rae had to take a couple of seconds to orient herself to the different format. But by the time she finished, she deduced that everything about Nola Payne's care at the Birth Center appeared appropriate.

Except for two things.

First, in the box labeled Presentation, the word *breech* had been written, although Rae had found the baby to be in the transverse position during the cesarean. Second, the box labeled Fetal Heart Rate was empty. There was nothing written down. Not even a question mark. But Rae had a huge question mark in her own mind. Why wouldn't a nurse write down the baby's heart rate? That was standard procedure. That was the first thing one did. Unless . . .

Rae read the signature at the bottom of the page, next to the letters *R.N.* She squinted and turned the page this way and that before she could make out the writing. Jenny, she finally decided, was the first name of the signature. Rae studied it for a few more seconds before finally giving up on trying to make out the rest of it. For now, Jenny's last name remained indecipherable.

Hopefully, Rae thought, there was only one Jenny who worked at the Birth Center. She would call as soon as she could. Just then the door to the nursery opened, and Bernie strolled into the room. Rae thought Bernie had left long ago. But now, she was glad to see her.

"How's he looking?" Bernie asked, now standing next to Rae and Nola's baby. "Did they say—hey, Rae, the baby looks better than you do."

"Thanks," Rae said, rubbing the tired muscles in the back of her neck. "So I've been told. Say, Bernie, do you know—"

"Here," Eileen said, interrupting to hand Rae a piece of paper. "I mean it, Dr. Duprey, Leo is—"

"Yes, yes, yes," Rae said wearily. "A very good paramedic."

Eileen smiled sheepishly. Her dimples deepened. "I guess I did kind of overdo it," she said. "But thank you, Dr. Duprey, for listening to me. I'm around if you have more questions."

"What was that all about?" Bernie asked as Eileen crossed to the other side of the room.

Rae read the names on the paper Eileen had given her. Leonard and Theodore McHenry. "That's exactly what I plan to find out," she said, folding the paper twice before stuffing it into the pocket of her scrub shirt.

"How's our baby?" Bernie asked.

"We won't know anything until at least Monday. He stays on the ventilator for now. A CT scan and an EEG will be done then too."

"At least he's a pink little cutie," Bernie said, rubbing the baby's fingers in one hand, and giving the thumbs-up sign with the other.

"And alive." Just seeing Bernie looking hopeful made Rae feel hopeful too. As Catherine Drake had said, if the baby could just hold his own . . .

Rae was about to ask Bernie if she knew Jenny, but the door to the nursery opened again. In walked the tall, handsome figure of Bo Michaels, Rae's former partner in private practice, her former partner in life, and currently her department chief and medical director of the Birth Center.

The same Birth Center, Rae thought, where, according to Eileen's paramedic boyfriend, Nola's baby had a normal heart rate, and where, according to Sylvia, he didn't. And where a nurse named Jenny had not written down the fetal heart rate at all.

"Uh-oh," Bernie whispered, "I don't like how Bo's looking at us."

Rae sighed. Seeing Bo always filled her with mixed emotions. She knew she no longer loved him, but she definitely still had strong feelings for him. That was evident from her conversation with Bernie earlier that morning. What bothered her now was the promise she had made to Heidi, to do whatever she could to get the doctors to stop delivering at the Birth Center.

Bo's Birth Center. He started it, he owned it, he got the other doctors to join in. The only doctor he couldn't get to deliver over there was Rae. And now, here she was, about to launch an all-out attack against it, the place he also referred to as his baby.

On the other hand, what else could she do? His Birth Center was the reason that the board wanted to close down her department. There was no way in hell she would let that happen without a fight—without a damn good fight. In her heart she knew that women were safer delivering inside her hospital. Depending upon ambulance transport was simply too dangerous. It certainly hadn't worked for her mother.

As Bo walked toward them, Rae felt the muscles along the back of her shoulders tighten. Bo's large brown eyes stared directly at her. His mouth—the same one that used to kiss her with such tenderness—was drawn into a straight line. He headed toward her, almost bumping into a nurse who didn't get out of the way fast enough.

Rae inhaled deeply, patted Bernie on the back, and said, "Do you still think Bo looks like he can't live without me?"

"More than ever," Bernie replied.

"I'm really sorry I missed the C-section, Rae," Bo said as he walked up to her. He was dressed in a navy-blue blazer, light-blue shirt, and camel-colored slacks. Perhaps he had lost a few pounds since their breakup, Rae thought, which only accentuated his sharp features and deep-set eyes.

Feeling uncomfortable, Rae walked around to the other side of the incubator. Looking down at the newborn, she said, "We won't know how he's going to do for a while yet."

Bo stood opposite Rae and spent a few seconds studying the baby. "I was at home—in the shower—when they paged me," he said. "Unfortunately, I didn't hear a thing. Usually they phone—well, anyway, I just came to thank you for doing your best."

Rae's eyes narrowed. Her best, she thought?

Suddenly Bo looked up at Rae. "Got a minute?" he asked. Then, looking at Bernie, he said, "Would you mind if I spoke to her in private?"

"I don't have much time, Bo," Rae said before Bernie could answer.

"No one knows that more than I do." He gave her a half smile.

"Why don't I meet you in the recovery room, Rae?" Bernie asked.

After Bernie left, Rae pointed to a small conference room separated from the main nursery by a glass wall. "Fine," Bo said.

Inside was a round glass table, surrounded by six sleek metal chairs, a phone, a bookcase filled with pediatric journals, and an upholstered sofa. Rae plopped down on the sofa, as Bo turned to face her. She could see his mind working, as if weighing each thought before speaking.

His brown skin was as smooth as a caramel-coated apple. His body was lean and fit, and he had an air of perpetual motion about him. At forty-three years old, five years older than she was, he showed few signs of aging. An occasional gray strand of hair; perhaps one or two wrinkles at the corner of each eye.

"I didn't want to say anything in front of Bernie," Bo said finally. "But, well, based on what I was told, I hear I might have a—well, hell, Rae, my Birth Center sent over a normal baby, and now I hear we have a vegetable on our hands."

"I'm trying to figure out what happened too, Bo," Rae said. Her hands smoothed out the creases in her dress. She crossed one leg over the other. "There seems to be a discrepancy over when the baby's heart rate bottomed out."

"I really am grateful for how you tried to help us out," Bo said as if Rae had not spoken. "But, well, my staff's very concerned and I need to know. Did you really take out a hand instead of a foot? Did you ignore Eva when she told you how sick she was? And the baby's head—I heard you could have made more room by T-ing the incision—"

"Who told you this?" Rae interrupted.

But Bo didn't answer.

"Instead of worrying about my technique, why don't you send your patients over sooner?" she asked sarcastically, rising from the couch. "Better yet, why don't you limit your deliveries to low-risk patients?" She headed for the door.

"I'm not done yet," Bo said.

"Oh, I think I know where this conversation's going," Rae said coolly. "Call me when you want to hear my version of the case."

Bo walked toward her and placed his arm against the door. They stood so close that she could detect the faint scent of his cologne, triggering unwanted memories. She stepped back. She felt safer with more distance between them.

Finally Bo sighed and shook his head. "I'm sorry, Rae. This is not how I wanted things to go."

Rae waited.

"I'm not referring to Nola, not now," Bo said. "You know how people talk around here. I want to protect you. I've always wanted to protect you. It's just that sometimes you make it so difficult."

He walked to the sofa and sat down. "I mean, sure, I'm upset about it," Bo said, "but I had something else I wanted to talk to you about. That was the real reason why I wanted to find you this morning. But then I heard about what happened in the OR—"

"You haven't heard my version," Rae interrupted. "Would you like to hear it now?"

When he didn't answer, she headed for the door again. "I didn't think so," she said.

"God damn it, Rae! Won't you ever listen?"

"You're not making any sense, Bo," she said. "I told you at the beginning I didn't have much time. I still have to find out what happened to Nola before she got here."

"Please, Rae," Bo said. "Let's take off our doctor's hats for a moment, okay?"

Rae crossed her arms over her chest.

"I got up," Bo continued, "after not sleeping all night, planning to hunt you down first thing. No wonder I didn't hear my beeper go off. I was thinking of what I had to say to you. I have something important to say, but you always make things so hard—"

"You've made some pretty hard statements already—"

"Would you just quit being *Doctor* Duprey for two seconds, please?"

Rae sighed. Even though Bo worked seventy to eighty hours a week, he had a habit of accusing Rae of always behaving like a doctor, never a "person." Like there was a difference, she thought wryly.

"I came—" Bo started, and then hesitated, as if searching for his next words. "I came to ask you to make another go of it."

"Another go of what—"

"Will you just let me finish? I want to know, I need to know, if . . . if you and I—if we could try to be together, like in the old days."

"You want to go into practice together?" Rae shook her head in disbelief.

"I want us to be together, to live together, like we did until who knows what happened to bust everything up."

"Live together?" Rae whispered.

"There, I've said it. And I'm glad I said it—please, don't look at me like that . . . "

Rae stared at him, her eyes wide with incredulity.

"This is hard enough, Rae. I was wrong, okay? It's not a baby I want. It's you."

She couldn't remember when she had felt so confused. What in the world was he talking about? They had broken up a year ago, and since then, he had only spoken with her out of necessity, in words that were always curt.

"Say something, please."

She rubbed her forehead. "I'm tired, Bo. And you're not making any sense."

"I mean it, Rae. So we don't agree on everything—children, the Birth Center, linen versus flannel sheets. But you've got to agree with me on this: you're lonely. I'm lonely. You still need me. And I need you. I miss you."

"Enough—"

"And I know you miss me."

"I don't miss—" Rae stopped herself. She had never lied to Bo and there was no reason to start now. "Okay, so I miss being with somebody, Bo. So I sleep by myself. But I've moved on—you should move on."

Just then the conference room door opened and a delivery man poked his head inside. "Flowers for Dr. Duprey," he said.

He handed Rae a bouquet of red and yellow roses. "From a Dr. Bo Michaels," the man said cheerily. "Have a nice day."

"Bo," Rae began. The flowers were beautiful and full of sweet fragrance. But the butter-yellow roses mixed in with the blood-red ones made Rae feel nauseous. She closed her eyes and for one awful moment she was thirteen again—and using the yellow sweater her mother had knitted for her to mop up the blood inside the ambulance.

Rae opened her eyes and tried to hand the bouquet to Bo. "Thank you, but I can't accept this."

Bo shook his head. "They're just flowers from a friend," he protested.

Rae walked over to the glass table and set the flowers on top. Before letting go, she pricked her finger on one of the thorns. Blood welled up before she placed the cut fingertip into her mouth.

"I really have to go, Bo." Suddenly the conference room was way too small to contain the emotions washing over her.

Bo walked over to her and lifted her chin in his hand. "Please," he whispered. His voice was softer and kinder than she had ever heard it before. "We can do this, Rae. Please, at least think about it. I may not be so willing to give you another chance—"

Ah, so there it was, Rae thought. Bo setting the terms again.

She pulled away. "You left me, Bo, remember?"

"I was confused," he replied.

She sucked on her finger, and seeing that the bleeding had stopped, she raised her right hand to the back of her neck. The muscles had knotted up all the way across her shoulders.

"Let's not start this discussion all over again, Bo," she said. "Why don't we just let things be?"

"You said you missed having someone in your life," Bo said. "That's enough reason to start over, isn't it? Being a doctor—it'll never be enough for you. You need a man in your life. You need *me*."

She remembered her father having the same argument with her mother, an argument about "need." Her father had convinced Rae's mother that she "needed" to have a son to make the family complete. Six daughters had apparently not been good enough. Her mother had lost that argument, and look where it got her. Dead, in the back of an ambulance. And a dead baby buried with her.

"I've got to go," Rae said.

"Don't turn me down again," Bo said. His arms were crossed over his chest, his feet spread apart solidly on the ground.

"You shouldn't have asked in the first place," Rae said, more quietly now. Suddenly, she missed her mother. She had missed her for years. And now here was Bo, using the fact that Rae missed him to win her back. Well, she thought, no amount of missing her mother would bring back her mother and no amount of missing Bo would bring back what they once had—

"Then maybe I shouldn't have defended you," Bo said. "There's talk that you deliberately tried to kill that kid—"

"What?" she asked him, incredulously.

"I was told everything was fine until you got hold of him."

Rae threw up her hands in disgust. "Now you're accusing me of trying to kill somebody! You hypocrite! That baby was almost dead when he got here!"

She was angry at herself more than she was at Bo. She should have seen it coming. But she had let her feelings for him lower her defense, a defense she'd have to stick to until Bo Michaels was completely out of her system, like waiting for the last molecule of chemotherapy to clear the bloodstream before feeling whole again.

"All I know is that my nurses said that baby was perfect!" Bo shouted angrily. "And no matter what happens, I'm not going to let you make my business look bad for something you did!"

She took a deep breath, trying to calm herself. His business. His bottom line. They always came first for Bo, she thought.

"I wonder," she said with barely restrained fury, "how this little conversation would have gone if I had dropped to my knees when you said you loved me? I wonder what would have happened if I had said, 'Yes, Bo, darling, I've been dreaming of the day when you would ask me back'? But now I see that this whole thing has nothing to do with me or Nola or her baby or anybody. All you care about is getting what you want, and if you can't get what you want, you start attacking everything around you. Whether I come back to you or not is not the issue. Whether that baby turns out to be a 'vegetable' or a vegetarian is not your concern. But damn it, Bo, it is mine!"

"Stop it, Rae."

She raised her hand to cut him off. "Now, it's my turn to ask the questions. First of all, why was such a high-risk patient ever allowed inside the Birth Center? The center's for low-risk women only, if I recall. Second, why did your staff say the baby was coming down breech, when it was transverse? And why didn't your staff send over another doctor if they couldn't find you? Our unit only promised to back your little operation if one of you comes over here to operate."

"I told you. They thought I got the message on my pager."

"Shouldn't they wait to hear back from you before assuming anything?"

"Even if I had gotten the message, there would not have been any rush."

"No rush? Are you crazy? That baby had a heartbeat in the sixties when it hit the door, and you say there was no rush? What in the hell do you think would have happened if I hadn't been here? You think you have a vegetable on your hands now? You'd have a damn corpse if everybody had waited for you to show up!"

It was getting harder and harder for her to speak. Of all her emotions, she wished she could control her anger. Anger made her words stick painfully to the back of her throat.

"I better leave," she said, collecting herself, "before I say something else I wish I hadn't."

"So you won't even consider—"

"Consider what?" she snapped.

"You and me, getting back together?"

She shook her head in absolute bewilderment. This time when she grabbed the doorknob, she turned it.

"Please, Rae—"

But she was out the door before he could finish his sentence.

Outside the conference room, Bernie, who apparently had not left the nursery after all, walked up to Rae. "That looked like a seven point nine on the Richter scale," she said.

"I thought you were going to meet me in the recovery room," Rae replied. She could see Bo sitting in one of metal chairs, his head in his hands, his elbows on the table. She turned away, rubbed the tight muscles in her neck, and then noticed that all of the other nurses in the neonatal intensive care unit had also been watching the morning drama. Now they quickly averted their eyes from hers and resumed their tasks as she and Bernie strolled out into the hallway.

"The good news," Rae said, wanting to get change subjects, "is that you still have a job."

Bernie patted Rae's shoulder. "Good work, Doc. Maybe one day you'll be the chairman of the board."

"Bernie, do you know a nurse named Jenny who works at the Birth Center?"

Bernie adjusted her nursing cap. "Jenny who?"

"Have you heard anything about a couple of twin ambulance drivers?"

"That would be Leo and Theo."

"Yes."

"No, not much." She smiled and poked Rae in the ribs. "I know that they're new, and breaking a lot of hearts around here."

"New?"

"Yeah. They only started with Hillstar this year."

"Hillstar?"

"You really ought to get out more, Rae. Hillstar's the name of their ambulance company. We have a contract with them for a dedicated rig to bring the Birth Center's patients over here. Though the twins aren't my type, they certainly are handsome."

"Will you do me a favor, Bernie? Before you leave, could you find out what you can about them? I've got to see Nola in the recovery room. But when I'm done there, I'll need to call—what did you say the name of the company was?"

"Hillstar."

"I'll need to call Hillstar, and ask them a few things. And if you have the time, can you get the last name of this Jenny person at the Birth Center? She was the one who took care of Nola—"

"Sure, I can do that," Bernie said. "Hey—why are you asking about the twins?"

"Something about this whole episode with Nola doesn't sit right with me."

"The Blessed Mother? She did call herself that when she woke up from surgery?"

"That's right."

"But you thought the baby got into trouble because of those three loops of cord around his neck," Bernie said, looking confused.

"I said the nuchal cord didn't help. Now listen, Bernie, and keep this between us for now, okay? There seems to be some discrepancy over just when the baby's heart rate bottomed out."

"I heard it was fine when Nola left the center—"

"And I heard it wasn't. See what I mean?"

They were coming up on a stairwell of the back hall. Bernie made a quick left and started up the stairs.

"Hey, where are you going?" Rae called after her.

"You're the one who wants me to get the lowdown on the twins," she answered. "And for that, I'm going to need some caffeine. Everyone knows the coffee's much better on Four Northeast."

Before Rae could say anything, Bernie was halfway up the stairs.

With Bernie gone, Rae's thoughts floated back to her conversation with Bo. She wondered who had told Bo about Nola Payne's surgery. Although his conclusions were wrong, he knew as much as if he had been at the operating table, and at the resuscitation cart, right along with her.

The list of possibilities raced through her mind as she proceeded down the back hallway. Quickly she eliminated Bernie, even though it had been she who had suggested Rae T the uterine incision. There was no way Bernie would have spoken to Bo about the surgery. So, who else could have told Bo about the events of the surgery?

By now, Rae was coming up on two service elevators on her right. Perhaps it had been Eva, but Eva had fainted before the surgery was over. Was it Jessica, the nursery nurse, who had helped with the resuscitation? No, Rae thought, Jessica liked Rae. And Jessica hated the Birth Center for luring so much of the hospital's business away.

Hannah? No, too shy. Nola? Yeah, right.

All of the other nurses who had been inside the operating room were now just a blur in Rae's mind, like a terribly out-of-focus photograph. Besides, there had been so many people running around, all hell-bent on trying to save Nola's baby.

Perhaps it had been Marco? Marco and Bo were good friends. And now, with the board threatening to shut down Rae's department and dump money into Marco's heart program—why wouldn't Marco have placed a quick call to Bo, and told him about Nola's surgery?

Someone close to Marco, who had been present at Nola's surgery, could have gotten back to him with the report. Was it one of the nurses having an affair with him? Or was it . . .

Yes, the new anesthesiologist, Rae thought. Sam Harter, or something like that. No, Sam Hartman. How appropriate, she thought. Dr. Hartman did hearts, of all things. But he was a cardiac anesthesiologist. Marco had recruited Sam himself. So what was a heart anesthesiologist doing with a pregnant patient in labor and delivery? Heart cases were done down in the basement, in the main operating room.

Sam could have told Marco what happened during the surgery, and Marco could have been the one to tell Bo. Or Sam could have told Bo himself. But, Rae remembered, Sam seemed to be on Rae's side. In fact, he was the only one at the board meeting who supported her opposition to closing down the maternity unit.

Rae shook her head. She was confused, tired, and frustrated. Why was she worrying so much about who told Bo anyway? The point was, Bo knew. And now he was intending to use Nola's case as an example of Rae's incompetence, when she had planned to use it to show that *Bo* ran an incompetent Birth Center. Keeping her promise to Heidi wasn't going to be easy. Perhaps that was why Walker had warned her to be careful. Okay, so she was warned. And "easy" was something she did not expect from life. All she expected was to keep delivering babies at Berkeley Hills Hospital.

She thought of another person who could have told Bo about Nola's surgery. Arnie Driver, the pediatrician—what about him? After all, Rae had shown him up more than once during the resuscitation of Nola's baby. Rae hoped it wasn't Arnie who had told Bo. He would happily use Bo to get at Rae or any woman doctor for that matter. With Arnie, everything was always so personal. Playing by the rules didn't matter to him. What did matter was revenge.

Please, don't let it be Arnie, Rae thought, as she padded by a double set of elevators. She preferred a fair fight, but if she had to, she could get as down and dirty as the next person. Even Arnie Driver.

Two steps past the elevators, Rae stopped suddenly. She thought she heard a noise coming from behind the doors. She backed up and stood between them, trying to decipher where the sound was coming from. Finally, she pressed her ear to the door on the left. But the sound now seemed to originate from the one on her right. She moved over and listened again. The sounds became clearer. Somebody was screaming.

Suddenly, the elevator door banged opened. Two paramedics—the twins, Rae noticed—and the emergency room nurse, Sylvia Height, flanked an ambulance gurney. Upon the gurney lay a pregnant woman with raven-black hair plastered to her tear-streaked face. The woman's thighs were spread apart, and between them, Rae saw the head of a baby only partially born.

"Keep pushing, Meredith!" Sylvia said.

"I can't *stop* pushing!" the patient cried.

The twins pushed the gurney out into the hallway.

"Sylvia!" Rae shouted above the commotion.

Sylvia turned toward Rae. Her eyes were wide with terror, her heart-shaped face filled with confusion. "She wasn't even crowning in the emergency room!" she explained rapidly. "And then all of a sudden, the head comes blasting out, and now the shoulders are stuck, damn it!"

A shoulder dystocia! Rae thought. It was an obstetrician's worst nightmare.

"Wait for the next contraction," Rae said as she ran alongside the gurney. Quickly she calculated in her mind that the delivery deck was still some fifty yards away. If they hurried—

"You don't understand!" Sylvia said. "It's like she's having one, long, continuous contraction!"

The paramedics had suddenly stopped pushing the gurney, as if they thought that was what Rae wanted them to do. She didn't want them to stop at all. She had no choice but to try to deliver the baby immediately. Every second counted. But she wanted to be close to an oxygen source once she got the baby out. At the very least, the baby would need oxygen.

"Keep moving!" she shouted.

On the gurney, the woman, turning her head violently from side to side, was crying uncontrollably. "My baby, my baby!" she sobbed. "Please, help my little girl!"

Rae grabbed the sides of the gurney as it sped down the hallway, and hoisted herself up onto the mattress pad. Only when she felt a draft on the back of her legs did she remember she was still wearing her black dress. She knelt down next to the patient. Meredith, Rae thought. That was what Sylvia had called her.

Rae grabbed Meredith's knees, then looked her directly in the eye. She had only a couple of seconds to establish the rapport that would get them through this safely. "I'm Dr. Duprey," she said soothingly. "You're going to be fine, okay? Just pull your legs way back—yes, that's it."

"Something's wrong," Meredith moaned.

Flexing Meredith's thighs was the first maneuver to overcome a shoulder dystocia. "I know it's scary," Rae said, "but just keep your legs way back."

Satisfied that Meredith was following her instructions, Rae asked Sylvia, "How long's the head been out?"

"Three minutes at least!" Sylvia said as she walked swiftly alongside the gurney.

That meant three minutes that blood had not been flowing through the umbilical cord, Rae thought. Three minutes without oxygen getting to the baby's brain. Too much more time, and the baby would die.

Now that she had Meredith's legs all the way back, Rae pulled on the baby's head. Nothing happened. The shoulders remained impacted behind the pubic bone.

"Hang in there, little girl," Rae said, holding on to the baby's head with one hand and looking at a pair of scissors dangling from the side of Sylvia's white pants.

"Give me those scissors, Sylvia," she said as calmly as she could. "I'm going to need more room. I need to cut an episiotomy."

The gurney swung around a tight corner, almost hurling Rae to the floor. She let go of the baby's head just long enough to hold on to the side rail.

"You can't cut her without an anesthetic!" Sylvia protested.

"You let me worry about that. The scissors! Please!"

"But—"

"Give her the goddamn scissors!" one of the paramedics said.

Rae could feel the seconds ticking by as she pinched Meredith's tender flesh with her fingertips, an old trick taught to her by one of her professors during her residency at UC. A time would come, he said, when Rae would have to perform an episiotomy without anything for pain except the distracting pressure from her fingers.

Still on her knees, Rae lifted the baby's head—a head even bigger than Nola's baby's—in order to expose the skin that she needed to cut. Quickly she opened the thick silver blades of Sylvia's scissors and then sliced the soft, almost purple-pink tissue from the opening of the vagina, down to within a centimeter of where it bulged over the anus. Immediately blood splashed onto her hands and knees, her dress and her stockings. Meredith had begun screaming again, but Rae knew the screams were from the relentless contractions, and not from the cut she had made.

"I'm so sorry, Meredith," she said. "Just work with me now." She kept her voice as soothing as possible, the kind a mother would use to calm a young child.

Satisfied that she had more room, she placed her bare palms on either side of the baby's face. She pulled on the head again, careful not to damage the delicate nerves of the brachial plexus that stretched from the spinal cord to the neck. But despite the extra room and her careful tugging, she still could not get the baby's shoulders out.

"Shit!" she hissed under her breath.

By now the gurney had sped through the double doors of labor and delivery. When it reached the nursing station, more nurses joined in to help. A young couple carrying a suitcase jumped out of the way.

"Is this the patient from the Birth Center?" someone asked from behind the desk.

"Yes!" Sylvia answered.

The Birth Center? Rae thought. Unbelievable! Not again!

"It hurts, it hurts, it hurts!" Meredith screamed.

"We need a delivery room!" Rae said. "Which one is open?"

"Three active patients just showed up!" someone shouted back. "There aren't any empty rooms, and the ORs are tied up with triplets and a postpartum tubal! And the east wing's still closed for construction."

Rae jumped off the gurney and onto the floor. She could feel Meredith's hot blood all sticky and wet under her dress and against her skin. "Then we'll take her into the recovery room," she said, grasping the end of the gurney and changing the direction in which they had been heading.

A cesarean section was not an option. At this late stage, one could not push the baby's head back in. Since getting the patient's legs all the way back and then cutting an episiotomy had both failed, she would next try to deliver the baby's posterior shoulder.

For that, she would need to get Meredith onto a delivery table, or at least move her over the end of the gurney in order to have a clear space below the head. If that didn't work, then she'd be forced to break one of the baby's clavicles, even if that meant the arm would be permanently damaged.

"Over here!" she shouted, once she was inside the recovery room. She directed the paramedics to push the gurney to an empty spot just past the door. Not only was the space empty, but wall oxygen was available. Perfect!

"Dr. Rae! Dr. Rae! Where is my Baby Jesus? My Baby Jesus, Dr. Rae! Where is my little boy?"

The voice belonged to Nola Payne. But Rae couldn't stop to answer her. And then she remembered. Nola was from the Birth Center. Meredith was from the Birth Center. Damn it, she thought, as she set the brake on the gurney. And damn Bo!

With both of her hands, she grasped Meredith's bare buttocks. Meredith, eyes shut tightly, held back her knees and bore down.

"Let's get her down to the end of the gurney!" Rae barked.

"Hurry up with the $O_2$! And get somebody in here from the nursery!"

"Dr. Rae! Dr. Rae!" Nola called out again.

Rae pushed her right hand into Meredith, and forced it deep inside. There was little room to work with. The baby was wedged in the pelvis as solidly as a cork in a bottle.

And the uterus kept contracting as if it were going to explode. Which, Rae realized, was exactly what would happen if she didn't deliver the baby's shoulders first. Pressure was building up behind the baby. Too much pressure and the uterus could, and would, burst. A ruptured uterus could easily kill both the mother and the baby. Rae could not let that happen. "Save the life! Save the life!" Rae whispered to herself, almost as if she were chanting in some ritualistic dream.

Now her fingertips found the baby's rib cage, and plastered against it, the baby's arm. She grabbed hold, and tried to sweep the elbow down and out. That should have delivered the baby's posterior shoulder, and once that happened, the rest of the body would fall out. But the arm didn't budge. The shoulder stayed trapped. There simply was not enough room. Now she had no choice. She'd have to break the baby's clavicle.

Quickly she followed the same elbow up to the shoulder. She held her breath, and closed her eyes. Then, between her two fingers, she snapped the tiny bone. She felt, and heard, it break. Both sensations nauseated her.

But the arm could now be moved in any direction she wanted. She grabbed it, and swept it across the baby's chest. The little elbow came out first, followed by a tiny hand, and finally the entire arm. It just hung there, by the baby's head, all akimbo.

Again she grasped both sides of the baby's head. The face had gone from pink to blue. She pulled. Immediately she saw the posterior shoulder pop free. And then the top shoulder. And then the rest of the body shot out. A cheer rose up from the nursing staff. The patient fell back onto the gurney, gasping.

"It's a girl!" shouted the man with the suitcase.

"Get him out of here!" Rae said.

She grabbed the baby, and turned to Frank, the nurse anesthetist, a tall black Englishman, who had arrived in the recovery room only seconds before with the resuscitation cart. Her hands trembled as she lowered the baby onto the mattress. She couldn't celebrate until she knew the baby would be all right. Immediately Frank put the oxygen mask over the baby's face. Rae expected to see a rehash of what had happened to Nola's baby.

But to her surprise and relief, she saw the baby girl pink up as soon as Frank gave her a few whiffs of oxygen from the mask. Then came her sweet cry. "Ah wah! Ah wah!" she wailed, although the sound was muffled under the mask. Her chubby legs kicked violently in the air. In fact, all of her parts thrashed about, all except for her little left arm.

"She's a cutie," Frank said in his strong British accent. "In time, she'll be turning somersaults with the best of them."

Rae gave Frank her most brilliant smile. What a high! Delivering a healthy baby was what her life was all about. She started to pat Frank on the back, but stopped when she saw her bloody hand. "That's the best news I've heard all morning," she said, wiping her hand on the mattress pad.

"Dr. Rae! Hurry, Dr. Rae, for Jesus shall rise in three days. Let me rise with him, for he is my Master!"

Rae looked over and saw Nola propped up on her elbows on a gurney at the far side of the room. Then she looked at the overhead clock. Just shy of ten o'clock. Certainly all of this had not happened in just under three hours, she thought, studying the clock again. Two Birth Center patients. Two potentially bad babies. Both births involving fetal distress. Her exhilaration of a moment ago was gone.

"Just a minute, Nola," she said, slumping down into a nearby chair.

She opened her eyes when she smelled the strong scent of coffee. In front of her was a Styrofoam cup. She followed the muscular arm that held it, and kept her gaze going until it reached a man's face.

"Here, you look like you could use this," Sam Hartman said.

She reached out. Her fingertips touched his as she grasped the cup. "Actually, I could use some answers," she said. "Someone needs to explain what the hell's going on around here."

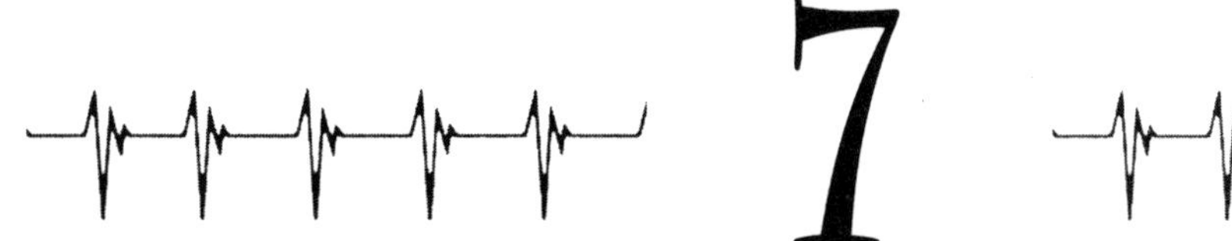

# 7

RAE GULPED DOWN THE COFFEE IN A COUPLE OF SWALLOWS. "I hate vending machine coffee," she said.

"Here, try this," Sam said, handing her half of a glazed donut.

"I better wash off some of this blood first."

After using the recovery room's sink to clean her hands and legs, Rae plopped down in a chair behind a desk used for writing orders.

Sam handed her the donut. She was so hungry she almost swallowed it whole. "This'll do, but I like chocolate donuts better," she teased.

"Hmm," Sam said.

Rae wiped her mouth with the back of her hand. She was about to ask him what he was doing back in labor and delivery when she heard, "Dr. Rae! Dr. Rae!"

It was Nola. Again.

"You're being summoned," Sam said, looking in Nola's direction. "Don't worry, I just checked on her. As you can see, she's alive and yelling."

Rae waved at Nola and Nola waved back. "I wish I had something good to tell her."

She started to walk away, but then she turned and looked at Sam, who was strolling in the opposite direction as if he had not a care in the world. "Hey, Hartman," she said.

He turned to face her.

"Sorry. I just wanted to thank you for the coffee—and for the donut. I do feel better, now."

He smiled back. "That's all that matters."

"Oh, so there you are!"

Marco Donavelli sailed into the recovery room. He was dressed in scrubs. Rae still had not forgiven him for showing her up at the board meeting, and for supporting the closure of her department.

"Lost, Marco?" she asked.

"Looks to me like my main man has something that interests him on the old maternity floor," Marco said, grinning broadly at Sam.

"Just checking on my patient," Sam replied.

"As a good doctor should," Marco agreed. He patted Sam's back. "This here, Dr. Duprey, is Dr. Sam Hartman. Best gas passer west of the Dolomites. He ain't cheap, but hey, what's a few lire between friends?

"Anyway, I heard, my good Sammy," he said, slipping his arm under Sam's elbow, "you were up here checking on a case. Sorry about that. But not to worry. We didn't ask you to head cardiac anesthesia just to stick you on the maternity floor with a bunch of screaming ladies. But Dr. Duprey's unit *is* a little understaffed, and we do believe in helping out our greedy—I mean, needy—colleagues, regardless of what department they're in. Isn't that right, my sweet Dr. Duprey?"

Marco was staring and smiling at Rae now. She reached up and patted his chest with mock tenderness. "They ought to make you a saint, Marco," she said.

The grin on Marco's face cracked briefly, but then he smiled even more broadly than before. "Okay, okay, so you're still pissed at me. Fine, I apologize. Is that better? But I tried to track you down. I considered Western Union, but that seemed a little excessive, don't you think?

"Anyway, show me I'm forgiven and come to a little soiree I'm throwing at my house tonight. Sammy here is coming. Just think, he's giving up his Friday night for me. What do you say?"

Marco's face, a deep, sandy brown from Berkeley's tanning salons, was all smiles. But his eyes, as dark as emeralds, told Rae that the invitation was not a friendly one. What kind of trap did he have in store for her? What more damage could he do to her department?

Sam coughed gently. "I would like you to come," he said.

"See, that settles it then," Marco said.

"She hasn't said if she would or not," Sam interrupted.

"Sure she did," Marco boomed. "Didn't you, Rae?"

Rae had attended several of Marco's parties in the past, but always with Bo. They were extravagant affairs, usually sit-down dinners for ten or twelve people. Everyone knew that some of the most important networking between physicians took place between sips of Marco's fine French burgundies. And now that the board had essentially pitted her obstetrics department against Marco's cardiac surgery department, Rae owed it to the future of her staff, and to her future as the new chair, not only to attend Marco's party, but to rub elbows with everybody there.

"Wouldn't miss it," Rae said. Now she spoke with enthusiasm. Perhaps, she thought, the sugar from Sam's donut and the caffeine from his coffee had kicked in. "What time would you like me to show up?"

Marco wagged his index finger in the air. "Drinks with Marco the Magnificent are at eight," he said.

He laughed heartily, as if no one appreciated making fun of himself more than he did.

"Don't make me change my mind, Marco," Rae said. "I've waded through enough shit this morning. Just be sure to set another place setting."

"I'll even pull out the high chair for you."

"Hah, hah," she said flatly, and turned to walk away.

"Rae, wait."

It was Sam. He approached her quickly. "I'm glad you're coming tonight. I'd like to take you, if I could."

At first Rae didn't answer. She just looked at him, as if she hadn't heard right. Was he asking her on a date? Well, yes, that was obvious. But he just met her that morning. Barely a hundred words had passed between them.

"Oh," Rae began, "I think—"

"I can pick you up at seven forty-five."

"Sounds like you know where I live," Rae said skeptically. "I don't know if I should be flattered or concerned."

Rae had to admit, she did like Sam's forthrightness. Most men were intimidated by the fact that she was a doctor, and those who were not still seemed to hem and haw before getting to the point of asking her out. Sam Hartman, on the other hand, seemed to be a man who knew what he wanted and went after it. And there was something appealing, as well as sensual, about him. Perhaps it was his half smile, the way he looked at her as if they shared a delicious secret. Perhaps it was the way he seemed to see straight into her soul, she thought, flashing back to that moment of perfect understanding in the OR after Nola's C-section.

"I figure you can't live far from here," Sam said. "I heard what you said at the board meeting. I bet you live close to the hospital so you don't have to worry about missing any deliveries."

So he was intuitive too.

She found herself smiling. "That's why I have a fast car," she said. "Zero to sixty in four point three seconds."

"The faster the better," Sam said.

Rae smiled again. "I'll see you at quarter to eight, Dr. Hartman."

Rae told Sam her address and phone number. "Aren't you going to write them down?" she asked.

Sam tapped his forehead. "It would be hard to forget these numbers," he said.

She watched him as he walked away.

But just as Sam walked out of the door, Bo Michaels walked in. He came directly at her, and judging from his business-like expression, she knew he had not come to talk about their private lives.

"I came to ask you a few questions," he said.

"And I have a few questions for you," she said. "But right now, I have a couple of patients who need my attention."

"That's *two* babies you screwed up on."

Rae looked around to see who else was in the room with them. In one corner was Nola, and in the opposite corner was Meredith. Betty Green, a recovery room nurse, was changing Meredith's IV bag. Other than that, she and Bo were by themselves. Still, she kept her voice low so that only he could hear her.

"Goddamn it, Bo," she said, "what the hell is going on over there? Two patients were sent from the Birth Center this morning for routine C-sections. One arrives with a heart rate in the toilet, and the other arrives screaming bloody murder because she can't push her baby's shoulders out. And you come in here saying you want to ask me some questions! I suggest you go back and review what happened at your place. Because I sure am, and I'm going to check out every detail until I'm satisfied that you and that little center of yours did nothing to harm those patients."

"I see," Bo said.

Rae did not like the tone of his voice. "You see what?" she asked.

"I see that I heard right about what happened at the board meeting. I see that you couldn't wait to get your hands on another Birth Center patient. What do you do, Rae? Hang outside the emergency room door and wait for our ambulance to show up? Does being the next department chairman mean that much to you? Your ambition has always shown, Rae. But I never thought you would take it this far. I just finished talking with Arnie Driver. He's the one who told me about your section this morning. He advised that we hold a formal hearing."

"A what?" Rae blurted out.

"A formal hearing," Bo continued, "to have you thrown off the staff."

"On what grounds?" Rae asked disbelievingly.

"On the grounds that you'll do anything to close down the Birth Center, if it means keeping your own department alive."

"Anything like what?" she demanded.

Bo turned calmly to his left and nodded at Nola, and then to his right and nodded at Meredith. And then he left. Rae started to go after him, but she knew trying to talk to him when he was acting like an ass was useless. Instead, she walked over to see to Meredith.

Meredith held her daughter close to her chest. Frank had swaddled the baby in a pink blanket before he left the recovery room. Good old Frank, Rae thought. He was her hospital's most skilled nurse anesthetist.

Rae smiled at the look of awe and wonder in the big black eyes of the baby as she stared at her mother's face. Just like Meredith's, the baby's lashes were long and dark. Meredith cradled the baby in her arms and held her there as if no one else existed in the world. Rae knew of no other bond as precious as the one between a mother and her newborn. For this reason she stood patiently at the foot of the gurney, not wanting to violate the serenity of the moment. It was only when Meredith finally looked up that Rae said, "Hi, I'm Dr. Duprey. I was the one who delivered your daughter."

Meredith smiled at Rae and then looked again upon her daughter's face. "I hope she's going to be all right," she said.

Rae took a deep breath. Knowing what she had to tell this patient made her feel bad. But there was no getting around it. Being honest was always best.

"I'm sorry," Rae began, "but I had to break your daughter's arm. You see, she had what we call a shoulder dystocia and—"

"I know what you did," Meredith said.

"I tried everything I could first—"

"And I'm grateful. Very grateful."

Rae raised an eyebrow. "Something tells me you know what a shoulder dystocia is."

"I know all too well," Meredith said. "Scariest thing in obstetrics."

"Are you a doc?" Rae asked.

Meredith swept her black hair off her face and gave an airy laugh. "Better," she said. "I'm an L and D nurse at City Hospital. I know what the outcome would have been if you hadn't gotten my baby out. This is my second baby, Dr. Duprey. I never expected something like a shoulder dystocia to happen to me. But then, my friends all kept saying this one looked twice as big as my son."

Meredith moved the baby up and down in her arms as if weighing a sack of potatoes. "Looks like they were right," she said.

Rae felt relieved. Although she believed that honesty with her patients was always best, she never knew what their reactions would be. And now she was free to pursue her questions about what had happened to Meredith before she arrived at the hospital. The fact that she already had a medical background would make it much easier to talk to her.

Rae leaned against the side rail of the gurney. She had the feeling she had known Meredith for a long time. Common knowledge always brought people closer together. It was ignorance, Rae thought, that kept them apart.

"You know, Mrs. Bey—" Rae began.

"Meredith, please."

"Meredith. And please call me Rae. I was scared shi—I was worried about telling you what happened. I was afraid you wouldn't understand why I had to do what I did."

"I knew you were," Meredith said. She laughed again. "But I'm happy. Scary stuff happens in obstetrics all the time. I just never thought it would happen to me. Thank God you were at that elevator."

"Would you mind if I stopped by later today to ask you a few questions?" Rae asked.

"Mind? Of course not! Besides, I'd like a picture of you with my daughter. You'd like that too, wouldn't you, Cynthia?"

"Nice name," Rae said.

"It was my mother's."

"Dr. Rae! Dr. Rae!"

"Is that *your* patient?" Meredith asked. "She's been screaming 'Dr. Rae' all morning."

Rae nodded. "Coming, Nola!" she called across the room.

Rae thanked Meredith again, took one last look at the baby, who was sleeping peacefully, and then walked across the thirty feet of the recovery room to Nola. The woman's tangled blond tresses hung down across her face. She was dressed in a lime-green gown, and Rae recognized it as the one worn by the patients from the Birth Center.

"How's my Baby Jesus?" Nola asked. She swept back her hair and smiled at Rae.

Rae smiled back weakly. As she had done with Meredith, she decided to be up-front with Nola. "Not too well, Miss Payne. In fact, he's very sick right now. His heart rate was very low when he got here. And he's still having trouble breathing. We're keeping him on the ventilator for now."

"But my baby, Dr. Rae? How is my baby boy?"

It was hard enough explaining things to a normal patient, but explaining to a woman like Nola was next to impossible, Rae thought. It was obvious to Rae that Nola was crazy. But hell, they lived in Berserkeley, and the line blurred between the crazy, like Nola, and the crazed, like Rae.

She took a deep breath, and tried again to get Nola to understand. "I'm trying to tell you, Miss Payne. He's in the nursery. He's very sick."

Nola sat all the way up now. She blinked her half-moon eyes at Rae. "Is he going to die?" she asked.

Rae swallowed hard. Who *was* this woman? she thought. Certainly Nola Payne had some sort of mental illness, or a borderline personality at the very least. But as Rae had seen inside the operating room when she first stared into Nola's face, there was something otherworldly about her expression, as if she saw things that no one else did. Not the illusions seen by schizophrenics or someone going through the DTs. But the kind of visions that heroes had in her childhood storybooks, books she read before she was launched into adulthood at the age of thirteen.

Rae forced herself to smile. "I hope not, Miss Payne."

She couldn't go on. Her throat closed like shutters on her words.

Nola reached up and patted Rae's face. Her warm, pudgy hand felt good to Rae. No patient had ever done that before. In fact, no one over the last year had touched her face like that. About as close as she had come to physical contact was the occasional hug from Bernie, and the sloppy licks she got from her black Lab, Leopold.

"Thank you, Miss Payne."

She had come to comfort Nola about her baby. And now, here was Nola, having asked the hardest question a patient could ask, comforting Rae as if it were Rae's child's life on the line. She swallowed hard again, at a complete loss for words.

Nola reached under her lime-green gown and pulled out a Day-Glo crucifix. Rae recognized it from the operating room, where she had seen it hanging from her neck.

Nola kissed the crucifix, and then placed it in Rae's hand. "Fear not," she said, "for my boy is the Baby Jesus, and he shall rise in three days to save the world."

For almost thirty years Rae had not turned to God for her sake or anybody else's. Holding the crucifix now, and seeing how this strange woman's entire belief system hinged on it, did not suddenly inspire her. It made her distinctly uncomfortable. Suddenly she felt very hot. She had to get out of that room.

She handed the crucifix back to Nola. "Rest now," she said. "I'll check on you later."

Nola smiled that ethereal smile and closed her eyes as if she'd just been given a dose of world peace. If only she could feel a millionth of what Nola felt, Rae thought, as she started out the door. If only, if only, if only—

"Pain! Pain!"

Rae swung around.

"Pain! Pain!"

She ran back to Nola. But Nola was bucking wildly on the gurney, and screaming to the Lord to save her from something.

"What is it, Nola?" Rae asked. "Where are you hurting?" Quickly she threw back the sheet covering Nola's body and examined the dressing over her incision.

"Betty, has she gotten anything for pain?" Rae asked the recovery room nurse. The dressing looked fine, Rae thought. Nola's uterus was firm and appropriately at the level of Nola's umbilicus.

"I think she's calling out her last name," Betty said as she approached the gurney with a new IV bag. "I just gave her a shot of morphine five minutes ago."

Nola became even more excited. Her arms flung about and Rae was afraid she would hurt herself on the metal side rails.

"Put that IV bag down and help me," Rae said to Betty as she tried to grab Nola's arms without being struck. Somehow she managed to grab her wrists. They were warm and sweaty. "It's okay, Nola," she said. "Everything's okay."

Suddenly Nola became quiet and fell back against the pillow. She closed her eyes again as if she had fallen asleep. Rae shook her head in bewilderment. She had no idea what was going on with this woman. She and Betty walked away from the gurney and leaned against the desk together.

"You really think she was calling out her last name?" Rae asked.

"Who knows?" Betty replied. "She's been calling out your name and God's name since she got here. P-A-Y-N-E sounds like P-A-I-N to me. I wouldn't put anything past her."

Rae shrugged and looked at her watch. "Well, anyway, I've got an office full of patients waiting for me. Just make sure Nola stays comfortable." She rose from her chair. "If you need anything, page me."

"You mean call you at your office."

Rae glanced at her watch again. She had five minutes before her first appointment. "Right. I've just got to get a little air first before I head over."

"You're pushing yourself too hard," Betty said with concern.

Rae chuckled. "Betty, honey," she said, "that's just standard operating procedure around here these days."

Glancing once more over at the sleeping Nola, Rae walked out of the recovery room.

* * *

After another quick shower and change of clothes, Rae leaned against the balcony of the hospital's seventh-floor garden terrace, overlooking the icy silver-blue waters of San Francisco Bay. The early frost hadn't worn off yet, and the air surrounding the hospital high in the north Berkeley hills still held an attention-grabbing chill. But Rae almost welcomed the numbing of the cold. She needed time to think. The events of the past three hours seemed related. But how?

To the south, she could see the thirty-story high-rise condominium in Emeryville where she had lived for the past year, a building filled with widows and widowers, divorcees, or, as in Rae's case, singles who never got around to marrying or who never planned to marry, ever. She imagined Leopold waiting for her, hoping that any moment she would come through the door. But since Rae often did not come home in the morning, Leopold would have to settle for Harvey Polk, Rae's violin teacher, who lived in the condo across the hall.

She had called her office before coming outside. Luckily, her ten o'clock patient had canceled, so Rae had another fifteen minutes before she had to get back. The sky was just taking on the dull gray of winter, and blowing across it were wisps of stark white clouds. They covered the top of Mt. Tamalpais, and below that, the town of Sausalito, where the north end of the Golden Gate Bridge ended.

She let her eyes rest upon the three-story Birth Center just across the street. It was on behalf of Nola Payne and Meredith Bey that Rae had come to the roof garden. What she wanted to see, from her vantage point seven stories high, was the ambulance dock at the Birth Center, and the route it would take to the hospital. She could see the white ambulance with its gold star trimmed in blue. Hillstar was the name of the company, according to Bernie.

She watched as the ambulance pulled out of the parking lot of the center. She made note of the time on her watch. It was only sixty seconds until it pulled into the entrance of her hospital's emergency room. Sixty seconds. That was all it took. And it wasn't even in a hurry.

"Hey, darlin', you're going to freeze your tushie off up here!"

Rae knew it was Bernie without even having to turn around. With her eyes still on the ambulance, she waved to Bernie.

"Uh-uh," Bernie said from the doorway, "you know I don't go outside past the first floor."

"This is important," Rae said, finally turning around. She waited for a few seconds for Bernie to make up her mind. Finally, she walked cautiously over to Rae, not turning her head at all, but looking straight ahead.

Rae pointed to the ground seven stories below. "Look."

"I will not," Bernie protested, but she cast her eyes down quickly to the Birth Center.

Rae waited for Bernie to read her mind, but when Bernie didn't say anything, Rae pointed again in frustration.

"This is ridiculous," Bernie said. "Are you going to tell me what you see that I'm supposed to see but you know I can't see because I don't want to see what the hell you want me to see down there?"

"The ambulance, Bernie. See, the one with the gold star."

"That's what I came to talk to you about. But I'm not staying out here another second."

"Bernie," Rae said, checking her watch again, "it only took that ambulance sixty seconds to go from the Birth Center to here."

"Good Lord, girl, and just how long did you think it would take?"

Rae turned away from the railing and leaned her back against it. She shivered, but it wasn't from the cold. She did not like what she had seen, or was beginning to suspect. "Sixty seconds," she repeated. "Now what could have changed so dramatically in sixty seconds?"

"You're losing me, hon—"

"Think about it. Two patients were sent here for routine C-sections. 'Routine' means their babies were just fine, that there was no fetal distress—"

"At least, that's what it's supposed to mean," Bernie interrupted.

"But in less than sixty seconds, Nola's baby arrives with his heart rate south of the border, and then another patient—well, you don't know about the shoulder dystocia."

Bernie smiled grimly. "Never underestimate the rumor mill around here."

Rae nodded. "Anyway, according to Sylvia—that's the ER nurse—that baby's heart rate bottomed out just before the shoulders got stuck. It's beginning to seem to me that those patients had serious problems over at the Birth Center, Bernie, *before* they left, before the ambulance even got here."

"Uh-uh, Rae, I don't think so. The Birth Center will ship a patient over to us if she even blinks wrong."

"I'm not so sure of that anymore. I think they may have a reason to try to get more of their patients delivered over there. They have a transfer rate of 20 percent, did you know that, Bernie? Given what I found out this morning at the board meeting, I don't think the Birth Center can afford to send one out of every five patients for much longer. Not if they're going to use City Hospital as a backup."

"A backup for what?"

Rae recalled that she was not allowed to speak about the proposed closure of her department or about the Birth Center's plan to perform C-sections at City Hospital. "I think," she continued, "that the Birth Center is taking a few more chances, letting women in who shouldn't be there, or letting women labor just a little too long in hopes of getting a vaginal delivery. But this morning, they got caught. So we ended up with their disasters, and now they want us to take the blame."

Now Bernie leaned over the railing, but just for a brief second or two. "Sounds like you had one hell of a board meeting this morning," Bernie said. And then she added, "They should have built this rooftop garden on the first floor."

Rae thought of the meeting, and of her conversation in Walker's office afterward. And of John Vincent, who, by now, was probably in a drawer in the hospital's morgue. "The chairman of the board's Finance Committee had a heart attack," Rae said.

"So I've heard," Bernie said. "But that's not going to stop you from reviewing a couple of charts on a couple of Birth Center patients, to see how things went down over there, right, Rae?"

"Exactly," Rae replied.

"I don't understand," Bernie said, trying to keep warm by rubbing her hands together. "You just said you thought the Birth Center took too long in transferring the patients. That should be easy to prove one way or the other."

Rae tapped her watch again. "Well, there's a problem with my theory."

"Now I'm really confused—"

"Meredith said everything was fine until she got here," Rae said.

"They sent her over for a prolonged second stage. She'd been pushing for two hours—longer than her entire first labor."

"But a totally acceptable length of time to allow a woman to push," Bernie said.

"Yeah, but—"

"Besides," Bernie interrupted, "Meredith would know if there was a problem with her baby's heart rate while she was over there."

"I know. But everything's not adding up. I just left Nola—"

"Nola? She's not glued together too tight."

"But in the recovery room—you should have seen her. Something made her go nuts."

"That wouldn't have been too hard to do—"

Rae smiled wryly, then became serious again. She told Bernie about Nola's outburst. "Betty thought she was calling out her last name," Rae said.

"That's a good possibility," Bernie said. "Or maybe she was just hurting."

"No, because at first she was sitting up in bed like she was about to read a good book. Then things changed."

Rae tapped her index finger against her lips. "Looking back on it, Bernie, I'm convinced she was saying P-A-I-N, not PA-Y-N-E. But what I don't understand is *why*. I checked her dressing, examined her fundus. Everything was just fine. Then, suddenly, she was as quiet as a lamb."

"But Nola is crazy."

"I think she knows more than she's letting on, Bernie. Or capable of telling us," she added grimly.

"I don't know why you're going on about Nola when you've got Meredith telling you that everything was just peachy keen until she got here," Bernie said. "That makes *us* look a little strange, not the Birth Center. So, let's just move on, shall we? Anyway, I have something to tell you that might shed some light on this little problem."

Although Bernie was making sense, Rae could not shake the feeling that Nola's outburst meant more than it appeared to. "You mean I shouldn't trust the word of the 'Blessed Mother' over a veteran labor nurse?"

"Now you're catching on, darlin'. Let me tell you what I found out about the mysterious Jenny you asked me to check on."

"She's spanking brand new. Doesn't know breech from a boot—"

"Ah, that would explain a few things."

"And there's more," Bernie continued. "But I'm not going to tell you about it standing out here in the cold. Come on. Let's go inside like two smart people."

"What about the paramedics?" Rae asked, as she walked next to Bernie. "Did you have a chance to check on them?"

"Only if getting an ambulance door slammed in my face qualifies as a 'check.' "

"Oh?" Rae asked, raising an eyebrow.

"Come on, hurry up," Bernie complained as they walked toward the exit. "Not another word until I thaw out my feet."

"The skinny on Miss Jenny," Bernie said as she held open the glass door that led from the rooftop garden to the cardiac ward, "is that she works part-time at the Birth Center *and* part-time at City Hospital. Jenny had a baby recently—delivered by Bo, of course. But she's still new, and everybody at City Hospital's hoping she gets pregnant again just so she can go back on maternity leave."

"Really?" asked Rae, listening carefully. To her right was a set of shiny silver doors marked Coronary Care Unit.

"She's as scattered as beans."

Rae frowned. As much as she wanted to hear that a potentially unskilled nurse had been involved with Nola's care, she had problems believing Bernie's revelation. "Bo wouldn't let somebody like that in the front door of his Birth Center, let alone inside one of his delivery rooms," she said.

"That's the best part," said Bernie, wagging her finger in the air. "Our little Miss Jenny has good old Aunt Freda covering her sweet little tush."

Rae rubbed her eyes. She was tired and this was starting to sound like a soap opera. But Nola's and Meredith's babies weighed heavily on her mind. "Who's Aunt Freda?"

"Freda Austin is Jenny's auntie. A great nurse but a real battle-ax. Jenny's the only real family she has."

Rae's curiosity jolted her onto a higher plane of wakefulness. A pattern was beginning to take shape in her mind. "Don't tell me Freda works at both places too?" Obviously, Rae figured, Bo was counting on the hospital's board of trustees to shut down her unit. In fact, he must have been so sure that he had hired two nurses to act as liaisons for future transfers between the Birth Center and City Hospital.

Like she would let him, she thought. Like she'd let anybody try to shut her place down. Rae quickened her pace across the carpet. She sidestepped a dietary worker pushing an eight-foot-high silver breakfast cart filled with crushed milk cartons and half-eaten muffins.

"You're keeping something from me again, Rae. I can see your thoughts moving inside your head like those EKGs across Dusty's monitors."

"Are you sure Jenny's as bad as you say?" Rae asked. She made a mental note to find out as much as she could about the backgrounds of all of the nurses. No, that would be too arduous a task, she decided. Just how many nurses worked at the Birth Center anyway?

"I mean," Rae continued, "there are other nurses Bo could have hired, right? Didn't you say Bo's trying to get you and the others to come to work for him? I saw Mattie Henshaw this morning. According to her, many of our nurses have already signed on over there."

"Rae, something just occurred to me. Why would Bo use City Hospital when he has us?"

"Hey, I didn't say—"

"Oh, yes you did. Didn't think I noticed that little slip of the tongue up there on that rooftop, did you?"

Rae remained silent.

"Anyway, if Bo's using City Hospital as a backup, he must have a good reason. Did he get a better deal or something from those people? Why would he go three miles down the road when he can send his patients across the street? Come on, Rae. You promised. No more secrets."

Rae's deal with Heidi was confidential. If Heidi found out Rae had told somebody, she might call the whole thing off and ask for the vote the next day.

"Rae?"

But, Rae thought, looking at the furrowed brow of her friend, she needed to trust somebody. What good was having a best friend that you couldn't talk to? And she had placed what turned out to be an unnecessary strain on her relationship by not being up-front with Bernie about why she broke up with Bo. She needed Bernie to help save the babies.

"Okay, okay." After taking a deep breath, she told Bernie about the board meeting, about the board's vote, about John Vincent and his cardiac arrest and her promise to Heidi to find some way to get the obstetricians to bring their low-risk patients back to Berkeley Hills Hospital.

"Two weeks, huh?" Bernie asked. She whistled loudly. "For a short person, you sure aim high."

"So now you see why I asked you about Jenny. And now, after both Nola and Meredith, two bad cases back to back, I want to know everything about the care over there."

Bernie puckered her lips as her expression became serious. "Jenny left a baby in the med room at City Hospital. Then she forgot where she put him, Rae."

"No. She didn't?" Rae didn't know if she should feel shocked or burst out laughing.

"Luckily," said Bernie, her voice even more serious, "Aunt Freda found the baby before things got too wild. The mother never knew anything but all the nurses did. They say Jenny's gotten better since she's had her own baby. But you never know when her amnesiac spells might strike again."

Rae recalled the empty box on Nola's Birth Center encounter form. She relayed the story to Bernie.

"But like you said, Rae, it's going to take more than one nurse screwing up over there to convince those stubborn colleagues of yours to come back."

"It's not about that anymore, Bernie."

Bernie stared at her for a moment and then said, "Are you sure the board wants to close down our whole department? I mean, you were up all night. Maybe your brain died for a few minutes during that board meeting. That memo I showed you only said the hospital was thinking about laying some of us off, not *all* of us, Rae."

Bernie's voice, and her wide-eyed look, told Rae that her words had finally sunk in.

"I don't think one bad nurse is the problem, Bernie," she said. "It's something bigger, and as soon as I can figure out the similarities between Nola's case and Meredith's, I'll know what that something bigger is. So," she said, taking a deep breath and running her hands through her hair, "I'll pay a visit to the Birth Center at lunchtime. Hopefully, Jenny will be there. Care to come with me?"

Bernie, a look of defeat on her face, was staring down at the checkered carpet. "I'm beat. And, I have to work tonight."

"Hey," Rae said, putting her arm around Bernie. "I'm not going to let them shut us down. Bo's crazy for thinking I would. It's bad enough he subjects his patients to an ambulance ride across the street. No way am I going to let his patients—any patients!—travel *three miles* for a cesarean section."

"Now you sound like you're protecting the Birth Center's patients," Bernie said angrily, "and that place is the reason we're going to lose our jobs."

"The babies don't know where they're being delivered, Bernie. But you'll help me, right? You might be the only one who—"

She was suddenly interrupted by the sound of doors banging open. "Get that cart out of my way!" a woman's voice shouted.

Rae turned around toward the CCU and saw an old man lying on a gurney flanked by two nurses and a respiratory therapist. The man had an oxygen mask on his face. His body was covered by a white sheet. Plastic IV tubing ran from his neck and arms and legs.

The doors banged open again. Standing there, about twenty feet from Rae, was Sam Hartman. He turned his head in Dusty's direction and yelled, "Tell the OR we're coming and tell the pump tech to get ready!"

"Isn't that—?"

"My date for tonight," Rae said.

Bernie's eyes widened. Rae watched as the nurses rushed the gurney to the service elevators and Sam Hartman disappeared down the adjoining stairwell.

"So, cavorting with the enemy?" Bernie said.

"Marco invited me to his annual elbow-rubbing dinner," Rae explained. "Sam offered to take me, that's all. It's strictly business. I can't do it alone, Bernie. I need to talk some sense into some of the cardiac surgeons. I have to get the other obstetricians to bring their patients back here, and I have to convince the cardiologists that they need us as much as we need them. That's why I'm going to the party. Who do you think Marco's guests will be? The only reason he invited me was for appearances. He pissed me off at the board meeting. So he's trying to be the nice guy. Well, while he's doing that, I'll talk to a few of his buddies and get some of them on my side. Why not start with Sam? From what I saw this morning, he and Marco are tight but I bet I can pry them apart a little."

"Hmm," Bernie said.

"Don't start in on me, Bernie."

"Hey, get off my case. I can 'Hmm' if I want to 'Hmm.' "

"Well, I don't like it." The truth was, Rae wasn't sure if accepting Sam's invitation to take her to the party was a good idea. It was obvious he was interested in her, and romance was the last thing on her mind despite his attractiveness. But she needed him to get some information. He was a big boy. He could fend for himself. On the other hand, she mused, perhaps she would call him and tell him she'd drive herself to the party. Why make things more complicated than they already were?

"So, how about it, Bernie?" she asked, moving toward the elevator. She'd think about Sam Hartman later. "Will you help me?"

Bernie appeared to be thinking things through again. She stuffed her hands in the side pockets of her parka. She stopped walking and pulled out the memo she had shown Rae that morning.

Rarely did anger cross Bernie's face, but her eyes darkened just then. Her mouth tightened. Bernie nodded her head vehemently. "Count me in. Nobody's taking my job without a good fight."

Rae let out a sigh of relief. And to think, had she not trusted Bernie with the information about the board meeting, she'd be all alone in her quest.

"Rae, did Bo ever say where the hell he was during Nola's section? You say he's going after you. He's the one they ought to run up the flagpole."

The elevator arrived. Rae stepped in, followed by Bernie. "At this point, Bernie, it probably doesn't matter. But I agree. And if Bo tries to mess with me, he's chosen the wrong person."

"He still loves you, you know."

The elevator stopped to pick up more passengers. Rae used the lack of privacy as an excuse to ignore Bernie's statement.

"First I go to my office," she said as she followed Bernie out of the elevator and into the lobby. "In between seeing patients I'll call the Birth Center and arrange for a little tour at noon."

"How about taking a nap first? You look like you're about to drop on your face."

"I'm off this afternoon. I'll sleep after my tour. Besides, I have to be rested for Marco's party. No telling what he'll be up to."

Outside the hospital, the day promised to be even colder than the one before. Still, across the bay, the sun shone on the skyscrapers of downtown San Francisco so that they glistened pearl white against the blue sky.

"Well, call me when you need me, Rae. Just remember to watch your back over there. And whatever you do, don't piss off Freda."

Rae looked across the street to her eight-story concrete office building. Her suite was on the top floor in the northwest corner. Next door stood the Birth Center. Bo's baby.

"Did you hear me, Rae?"

"Freda just better not piss me off," Rae said. "She may be Jenny's auntie, but she's not related to me."

She said good-bye to Bernie and headed for her office.

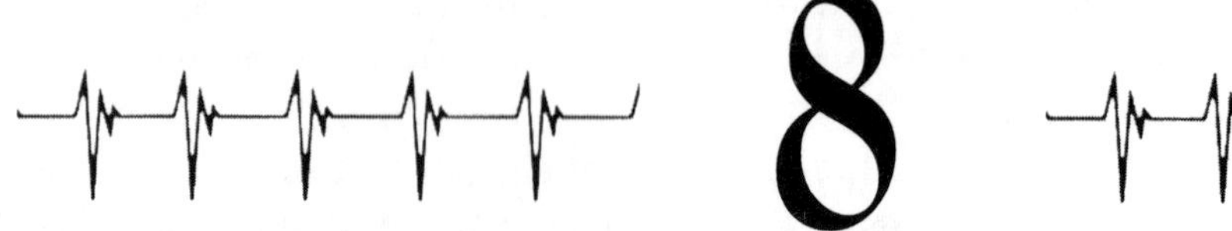

# 8

Getting through her patients after the early morning chaos proved almost impossible. There seemed to be emergencies everywhere. One patient was miscarrying a much-wanted baby; another burst into tears when she found out she was pregnant—for the fourth time. Next there was a woman who yelled at Rae because her period had come—again—after trying for two years to conceive. Then came an expectant—if not downright impatient—mother who was more than a little overdue, followed by a woman who had to be admitted for preterm labor at twenty-six weeks.

Of course, there were the GYN patients too: one had a precancerous condition of the cervix; another's fibroids had doubled in size in a year. And to top it all off, a poor soul who had been married for ten years to a traveling salesman had contracted Trichomonas vaginitis.

"A venereal disease!" the patient exclaimed. Rae spent the next fifteen minutes trying to convince her not to kill her husband.

At five minutes to twelve, Bobbie Cruz, Rae's office manager, poked her head into Rae's consultation room. Rae sat at her desk, finishing a quick lunch of an apple and yogurt between her last office patient and her twelve o'clock appointment with the Birth Center. "You said you didn't want to be late," Bobby said.

Bobbie had worked for Rae for ten years of private practice. She was as much of a fixture as all the others in Rae's thousand-square-feet office suite: the French desk and wingback chairs for the patients, a waiting room that looked like an elegant living room in a fine French home; fresh flowers everywhere and abstract paintings of women and their babies. It was definitely a woman's office.

"If I'm not back by Monday," Rae teased, "call the police."

Bobby's smile vanished and she looked concerned. "Rae," she said, "you know they're talking—"

Rae rose from her chair and grabbed her purse. "My violin teacher told me you should worry only when people *stop* talking about you."

"I know you didn't do anything to hurt those babies," Bobbie said.

Rae felt a catch in her chest. "Have a good weekend, Bobbie." The rumor mill was working overtime, Rae thought, as she made her way out of her office and across the street to the Birth Center.

Jenny King, a twenty-something woman wearing braces and a lime-green jumpsuit, conducted Rae's tour. It began with a walk around the garden, where two patients in early labor sipped tea under an oak tree. "We don't admit them until they're four centimeters," Jenny had said proudly. "That's one way we save money over here."

From there Rae was led up brick steps to the lobby, where the walls were painted in soft salmons and violin music filled the air. There were even babies painted on the ceiling.

"You like?" Jenny asked, as she led Rae to an elevator off the lobby.

Rae thought Jenny was adorable with her cute little braces and her pixie ways. She wanted to dislike her but she couldn't. She also wanted to dislike the Birth Center. The problem was, she could see why a patient would want to deliver there. The Birth Center, unlike her hospital, was warm and inviting. The colors were soft, the music intoxicating. "How long have you worked here?" she asked.

Jenny chattered on about how she joined the staff on a half-time basis a year ago, immediately after finishing nursing school. So, thought Rae, smiling at the young nurse, Bo had been planning on using City Hospital for some time. Obviously he knew he could steal enough business from Rae's hospital and force the board to shut down her department. And the whole time he was their department chairman, using his connections for his own gain. There were no laws saying that a doctor could not run the department and open his own birth center. And no one forced the rest of the obstetricians in Rae's department to deliver their patients at the center either. Still, the whole thing reeked of conflict of interest.

Why hadn't she paid more attention two years ago? It wasn't as if her colleagues began delivering their patients at the Birth Center overnight. The truth was, Rae had underestimated the attraction that it would hold. She thought that patients would not choose the comfort of the Birth Center over the convenience of having a cesarean section room just down the hall. But then, the patients who were allowed to deliver there were low risk; rarely did one of them ever think she would need a cesarean section.

"Ah, here we are," Jenny announced when the elevator came to a halt.

Rae stepped out onto a polished wooden floor, the color of blond ash. Four patients, dressed in lime-green gowns, shuffled to and fro, huffing and puffing, leaning on their partners or on the backs of peach-colored upholstered chairs.

"Freda's in the triage room," Jenny said.

She led Rae past doors marked with names like Camellia and Lilac. From behind one of the doors she heard a baby's cry. She had to smile. The thought of a spanking brand new baby always filled her with joy.

Her face became serious again when she reminded herself of her mission. "Just how many deliveries do you do here in a month?" Despite her fatigue, she tried to notice everything. She saw that everything had been set up for the patient's convenience: comfortable chairs, two phones, well-stacked pantries, and sofas for family members.

"We deliver a lot," Jenny said. "And we're getting busier and busier. Isn't that wonderful?"

"Peachy," Rae replied.

She followed Jenny into the triage room. There was one bed that was empty. Sitting at a desk was a lanky nurse with short blond hair. *Auntie Freda,* Rae thought.

"This is Dr. Duprey, Freda," Jenny said.

Freda's cold black eyes stared Rae up and down. Rae extended her hand. Freda shook it like a man, and then asked gruffly, "Well?"

Rae forced herself to keep smiling. Bernie had warned her about the head nurse, but she thought Freda would wait at least a couple of minutes before she gave Rae a hard time.

"Nice place," Rae said, looking around the room. Pane glass windows. A bowl of cherry candy. A rocking chair in one corner. Halloween decorations everywhere. "May I sit down?"

Freda nodded toward the chair. "I'm here to talk about Nola Payne and Meredith Bey," Rae said.

Freda leaned against the wall. "You're here to shut us down," she said flatly.

Rae tried to keep her composure. Obviously, Bo had spoken to this woman already. She decided there was no use playing cat-and-mouse with this head nurse. "So, what happened to those patients?" she asked.

"It depends on what you did to them," Freda said.

Before the meeting, Rae had asked Eileen Tan, the nursery nurse, to fax over a copy of Nola Payne's record from her stay in the triage room. She pulled it out of her purse and handed it to Jenny. "It seems like there's been an omission. Is that your handwriting?"

Jenny took the paper. "Why yes—"

"Give me that!" Freda said, snatching the paper from Jenny. She studied it and then stared at Rae. "What's your point?"

"The baby was transverse, not breech."

Freda studied the paper again. "Nonsense. I checked her myself. I know feet when I feel them. Do you know feet when *you* feel them, Dr. Duprey?"

Jenny snickered. Rae looked at the young nurse and then back to Freda. Bo had obviously told them about the surgery too. She decided she had to be more careful. Bernie had warned her. Freda was tenacious, not just about protecting Jenny, but about protecting the Birth Center.

"Anything else, Doctor?" Freda said. Her face was as hard as stone. Her eyes bore into Rae's and she didn't blink.

Rae decided on another tactic. Why give Freda something to push against? An animal backed into a corner can only fight its way out. She began to chuckle. Freda arched a thin eyebrow and waited.

"Well, I see I've met my match," Rae said gaily. "Freda, you're legendary. I wish I had someone like you running our delivery suite."

"Trying to get on my good side won't work either, Dr. Duprey,"

Freda said, handing Rae back the report. "I don't have a good side. I know why you're here, so unless you have more questions, let us get on with our work."

But Rae saw that Freda's pale white face had flushed pink. Rae's flattery had touched a soft spot that she knew all good nurses had somewhere, someplace.

She took the triage record back from Freda. "Well, no, I don't really have any more questions. Well, maybe just one. I just wanted to make sure that Jenny doesn't get into any more trouble."

"Jenny?" Freda asked.

"I'm in trouble?" Jenny asked.

Rae finally had Freda's full attention. Slowly she folded the form. "Jenny forgot to write down the baby's heart rate. Normally, that could be a minor detail, but, well, as you know, Nola's baby might not make it."

"Let me see that thing again," Freda said. Rae handed her the form. Freda's face turned red. "Jenny, I specifically told you to write down that fetal heart rate."

Now Jenny stared at the paper. "Oh, I meant to, Auntie, but after I called the drivers, I guess I forgot."

Freda gave the paper back to Rae. "This proves nothing. We have the original fetal heart rate tracing. It documents that Nola's baby was just fine when she left."

"I know that," Rae said. "But, well," and she turned to Jenny, "this isn't your first time forgetting to do something important, now is it?"

Jenny looked frightened.

"Misplacing a baby on the maternity ward is a serious mistake."

"Auntie!" Jenny whimpered helplessly.

"All I want to know is what happened to Nola Payne," Rae said. "And to Meredith Bey."

Freda pointed at Rae. "Then will you leave?"

Rae didn't say yes or no. She knew she had the nurse where she wanted her, and she knew Freda knew too.

"Nola Payne," Freda said, "was not one of our patients, Dr. Duprey. As you know, we only allow low-risk patients here and all patients must have regular prenatal care with a doctor. I doubt if Miss Payne ever saw a doctor her entire pregnancy. She showed up on our doorstep in early labor. You know very well that dumping laws prohibit us from sending away any patient in labor until she is fully evaluated. Why she came here, instead of going to your hospital in the first place, is beyond me. Nonetheless, she showed up, alone, on our doorstep. We had no choice but to take her in."

Rae looked around the room. Such a comforting place, she thought. "It's awfully pretty here."

Freda smiled for the first time. "Thank you. Anyway, Jenny checked her first. She was worried about the baby's presentation. She had me check her too. I swear she was breech."

"And her baby's heart rate was just perfect," Jenny added.

Rae arched a disbelieving eyebrow.

"I mean it, Dr. Duprey," Jenny said. "Of course, the fetal heart rate tracing is on its way to our medical record department, but if it were still here I could show you that Nola's baby had a heart rate of a hundred fifty-two beats per minute."

"Really? You see a lot of patients. How do you remember her baby's heart rate so well?"

"Because she was so strange," Jenny replied.

Rae tapped the toe of her suede pump against the wooden floor. She couldn't argue with that. "Tell me how you guys do things over here."

She listened carefully as Freda explained the Birth Center's policy for labor management. Rae was struck by the meticulous attention to detail. Unfortunately, the more Freda explained, the worse Rae felt. Sure, she was glad to hear that the patients received excellent care, but that didn't help her case with her colleagues. In some areas, the care at the center was superior to her hospital's. Somehow Bo had managed to take good care of his patients for a lot lower cost. The nurses spent more time with each patient. The nurse-to-patient ratio was one to one. Unlike at Berkeley Hills Hospital, where budget cuts had forced one nurse to take care of two active labor patients. The Birth Center also always had an obstetrician in the house. No wonder her colleagues delivered their patients here, she thought.

But *something* had happened to Nola, she reminded herself. And something had happened to Meredith Bey. And things could only get worse during an ambulance ride, especially if that ambulance had to travel three miles to get to the nearest C-section room.

Freda ended by saying, "I hope Nola's baby makes it. In a strange way, I'm very fond of Miss Payne."

Rae rose from the rocking chair. She began to look around the room. "Nola acted very oddly in our recovery room."

"She acted pretty crazy over here too," Jenny said.

"Looking for something in particular, Dr. Duprey?" Freda asked.

If only she were, Rae thought. She tried to remember what had occurred inside the recovery room that caused Nola's outburst. Surely it wasn't Rae's presence: Nola had seen Rae in the operating room and had been fine. Had Betty upset Nola? Could it have been something Betty was doing, or had done? Could that have triggered a memory in Nola's mind about something that had happened inside the Birth Center?

Rae stopped in front of an opened cabinet. Inside, IV bags were neatly stacked. Next to the bags were jars of plastic-wrapped candy. Cherry-flavored.

"How did Nola react when you started her IV?" she asked, removing one of the bags of 5 percent dextrose and lactated Ringer's.

"She was the perfect angel," Jenny said. "I started the IV myself and it didn't bother her a bit."

Rae's eyes narrowed. "Are you sure?"

"She even told the ambulance drivers that the IV was good for her baby," Freda said. "Why, what happened?"

Rae, remembering that she shouldn't trust anybody connected with the Birth Center or her hospital's cardiac unit, decided to keep the details of Nola's outburst a secret. She was tempted to tell Freda and Jenny, because she found herself feeling a grudging respect for these nurses who cared so much about their patients. But she had to keep the big picture in mind.

"Nothing happened, really. You know Nola. She operates on a different plane."

She asked them about Meredith Bey. Freda explained that Meredith had been sent to the hospital for a routine C-section. Meredith had pushed for two hours but it was obvious the baby was not coming out vaginally. "She had delivered her first baby just fine," Freda said. "Who would have thought she'd have any trouble?"

Rae felt she was worse off then than when she had started her tour of the Birth Center. At least at the beginning of her visit she had some honest suspicions that something bad was happening there, or that Freda and Jenny had held on to the patients for too long. But now even those had diminished. Worse, she instinctively liked these two women. How was she suppose to fight against people she liked?

"Who started the IV on Meredith?" Rae asked when Freda finished talking.

"I started Mrs. Bey's IV," Freda said. "Why, was there a problem with it?"

Rae shook her head from side to side. "Just one more question: Is it true—the rumors, I mean—that you all plan to use City Hospital for your C-sections?"

Freda looked at Jenny and Jenny cast her eyes to the floor. "I suggest you speak to Dr. Michaels about that," Freda said.

Rae frowned. "I already have."

Rae looked at the nurses and they looked at her. "Well," said Rae, rubbing her hands together, "I guess I'll be going."

Freda escorted Rae to the door. "You won't say anything to anybody about Jenny?" Freda whispered.

Rae felt conflicted. She would do whatever it took to keep her department open. Yet, she empathized with Freda, whose only family was a young nurse who really hadn't done anything wrong, but whose omission in recording the fetal heart rate value might in the future help Rae's case. So far Rae's case was very weak; for now, a new, incompetent nurse was all she had.

"Can I call on you when I need you? Things might get real ugly and I need to know where you stand."

"I stand for the Birth Center."

"Then I can't promise you anything," Rae said, shaking Freda's hand.

"It's funny how we landed on opposite sides of the fence," Freda said.

Rae felt the sting of Freda's poignant observation as she watched the nurse walk back toward the triage room. After riding the elevator down to the first floor, she used a pay phone to check for messages on her home answering machine. Hopefully Bernie had left the name of a contact person at Hillstar. Just when she dialed the last number, an obviously distraught pregnant woman, escorted by a much younger man, entered the lobby.

"Can I see my doctor?" she asked tremulously. "I think this is about to happen."

Rae hung up the phone and walked quickly over to the patient. But before she reached her, a nurse, dressed in the Birth Center's lime-green jumpsuit, was at the patient's side.

"I've got her, Dr. Duprey," the nurse said.

"Donna?" Rae asked with surprise. Donna Wilson worked nights on Rae's maternity ward. She wore red cat-eye glasses over a pair of sky-blue eyes.

"That's right, now just breathe through it," Donna said to the woman as she escorted her toward the elevator door. She pushed a button and the doors opened immediately. Another nurse stood inside and helped the patient in.

Donna returned to Rae inside the lobby. "You can close your mouth now, Dr. Duprey," Donna said. "Everybody who sees me looks the same way. But when your employer doesn't treat you right, especially after fifteen years of busting your ass, it's time to get the hell out of there."

"But you were the Birth Center's strongest opponent," Rae said, still incredulous that one of the hospital's most respected maternity nurses had jumped ship. "You thought the whole idea of moving labor patients across the street was ridiculous."

"Not as ridiculous as rewarding my fifteen years of service—never missing a night, mind you—with a pink slip. Berkeley Hills Hospital is not my friend anymore, Dr. Duprey. I hope the Birth Center eats them alive."

"You can't mean that—"

Donna waved Rae off. "Now I work days, and here I get six weeks of paid vacation starting with my first year. See you around, Dr. Duprey. Give my best to Trish and all the girls."

"But you haven't been laid off," Rae shouted after her as Donna stepped into the elevator.

"Tell Bernie the coffee's better over here too," Donna shouted, just as the doors closed.

"Damn it," Rae muttered to herself.

She walked over to the phone again and dialed information. "Do you have a listing for Hillstar Ambulance Company?" she asked. The operator gave her the number, but the line was busy. Not her day, she thought.

But it hadn't been a good day for Nola's baby either. And it almost turned out to be a bad day for Meredith's baby as well. She decided to skip the etiquette and pay a personal visit to the ambulance drivers. Maybe they could shed some light on the situation.

Outside the building, Rae shielded her eyes with her hand. To her surprise, the day had warmed a bit since morning. The question now was whether she should go home and fall asleep in the pad of sunshine that would certainly be on her bedspread about now, or hunt down the paramedics. She decided sleep could wait. Perhaps an interview with the paramedics would help her figure out what had really happened to Nola Payne and Meredith Bey.

Rae stepped into the crosswalk on her way to the hospital, still thinking about the mystery of the bad babies. She heard a car horn and the screech of tires. She stood like a deer frozen in front of oncoming headlights as a navy-blue Jaguar headed straight for her.

The Jag stopped two feet away. Arnie Driver, the pediatrician who had failed to properly intubate Nola's baby, sat behind the wheel. He rolled down the passenger window and stuck out his large, blond head. The red skin of his scalp glistened in the sunlight.

"Sorry," he said, pointing a cigar toward the sky. "Too bright to see much of anything."

Rae walked on. She was furious at Arnie for calling the hearing. Worse, she had lost the last remaining shred of respect for him when he almost let Nola's baby die.

"Hey," he called after her, slinking his Jag slowly by, "I hope Bo told you the hearing was his idea."

Rae stopped. This time she looked both ways and then kept on walking. Bo's idea, she thought. Had he lied to her, or was Arnie lying to her now?

"Just wanted you to know," Arnie said. He sped off, and Rae heard his laughter trailing behind him.

Bastard, she thought. But she had more important things on her mind than Arnie Driver. She stood in front of the U-shaped hospital. Directly in front of her was a thirty-foot-high, three-column steel sculpture. It had been built as a testament to the future. Its monolithic columns soared heavenward, as if the sky was the only limitation to man's inventiveness. Until that day, Rae used to like the mighty work of steel. But did expectant mothers like it? she wondered. Or did they find it imposing and intimidating? Perhaps the hospital should think about adding a fountain like the one at the Birth Center. Anything to soften things up a bit.

No, Rae thought, shaking her head and moving forward. Give her a fully equipped maternity unit over the touchy-feely Camellia room any day. The important thing was to have an operating room. But the law was the law. Only a hospital had that privilege.

Rae stopped again. To her right was the Hillstar ambulance parked in front of the hospital's emergency room entrance. The back doors were open, and standing in front was one of the twin attendants who had brought Meredith Bey over, and, according to Eileen Tan, had also transported Nola Payne. Images of her mother's death flooded Rae's memory. She had walked by plenty of ambulances before, of course, but always quickly. If she wanted to ask the driver about Nola and Meredith, she'd have to get a lot closer—for a few minutes at least.

With head held high, Rae walked over to the ambulance. Her gray cashmere dress, which had kept her warm on the rooftop garden, was now making her sweat. Or maybe it was nerves and not the heat? Either way, she wanted to talk to the drivers and get it over with.

"Hi, you brought over the woman with the shoulder dystocia," Rae said, extending her hand. "I'm Dr. Rae Duprey."

The twin, whose badge read LEONARD, shook her hand in his huge palm. Even through the long sleeve of his navy-blue jumpsuit his biceps bulged. "Leonard McHenry," the attendant said.

His eyes shifted left and right, as if expecting someone. Now what? Rae thought. She only wanted to ask him a few questions.

She fanned herself with her hand. "Looks like it's going to heat up after all," she said.

"My brother will be right back," Leonard said. He slid his hands in and out of his pockets and looked around nervously.

"I know you're busy," she said. "I just wanted to ask you a couple of things."

"Hey, hey, hey, it's Dr. Duprey!"

Rae looked up and saw the other twin approaching. His badge read THEODORE. He was noticeably skinnier than his brother, she thought, yet, when she shook his hand, she noted that his grip was just as strong. Fortunately, this twin smiled at her like an old friend.

"I wanted to thank you for helping me with Meredith Bey," she said as she found herself relaxing a little. "Other than a transient shoulder weakness, her baby will be just fine."

"Glad to be of service," Theodore said.

"We've got to get going, Theo," Leonard said.

Rae saw Leonard flash Theodore a warning glance. Probably some secret code between twins, Rae thought.

"My brother," said Theodore, jerking his thumb toward the other twin, "is all work and no play. Say, would you like a tour of our rig? It's Hillstar's finest."

Going inside an ambulance was the last thing Rae wanted. She felt her knees weakening.

"You okay, Dr. Duprey?"

"This looks nice," Rae said. As she pretended to admire the back cabin, she felt a cold sweat breaking out over her skin. Her heart began to race and she felt faint. Even after all the years, the memories were too fresh. Her mother strapped to a gurney. The baby that wouldn't cry. The sight of all that blood. Rae using her yellow sweater to mop it all up, but only managing to cover herself with more blood. Her mother's groans, followed by the screams. And then the silence. The deafening silence.

"Another time," Rae said, crossing her arms over her chest and hoping that the twins did not see the tremor in her hands.

But the narrowing of Theodore's eyes told her he had detected something. Perhaps some of the color had gone out of her face. Whatever it was, she figured it accounted for the inscrutable look Theodore flashed at Leonard, who nodded back. One day, she thought, she'd have to overcome her fear and go inside the ambulance. But not now. For the time being she'd have to find another way to get her questions answered.

"Instead of a tour," Rae said, "would you mind just telling me if anything unusual happened to Nola Payne or Meredith Bey on the way over?"

"Now which one was Nola Payne?" Theodore asked. Again his eyes shifted to Leonard's.

"Nothing happened to nobody," Leonard answered.

"Nola was the one who wore the crucifix," Rae said. Nobody could forget someone like Nola, Rae thought.

"Oh, yes," Theodore said. "The fifty-one fifty. Bona fide psycho. Why do you ask?"

"We've got to get going," Leonard said. "Nothing happened."

"Oh, but it did," Theodore said. "You remember her, Leonard. She was the one who said she was going to give birth to the son of God."

Theodore smiled. Rae had to smile back. She appreciated at least one of the twins being willing to answer her questions. But why all of the secret glances? Unless—unless the suspicions raised by Jessica inside the nursery about when Nola's baby's heart rate bottomed out were founded on fact.

"That's the one," Rae said slowly. "Was there anything else you remember about her, or about Meredith Bey?"

"I remember we have to be at the Birth Center about now," Leonard said.

"Ah, my brother," Theodore said. "Well, you heard him, Dr. Duprey." Theodore slammed shut the door to the ambulance. "I guess we better head on over."

"Are you sure there was nothing unusual? I mean, how much pain were they in on the way over? How fast were the contractions coming?"

Theodore shook his head. "Just that weird crucifix. Otherwise, everything was just fine with both patients. I checked the babies' heart rates myself. They were both normal."

"I didn't say there was a problem with the heart rates," Rae interjected.

"No, but you were going to, right?"

Rae smiled again. "How often did you check them?"

"Once is enough for such a short trip. So, unless you want to raise some Cain between Leo and me," Theodore continued as if Rae had not spoken, "I had better do what he says."

Rae gave each twin her business card. "Just in case you remember anything. Oh—did Nola act funny when you hung the IV?"

"Theo didn't hang any IVs," Leonard said. "They're hung at the Birth Center."

"That's right," Theodore said.

Rae studied one face and then the other. Her interviews with thousands of patients had made her a keen observer of who was lying and who was not. She decided she didn't believe either of them. And she knew that they knew it. But she wanted to keep the lines of communication open. The brothers were obviously very attached and would stick up for each other. "Call me if you remember anything," she said.

Theodore studied her card. "Okey-dokey, Doc."

Rae waited for him to flash Leonard the secret code again, but he didn't. That was when she noted the swelling on his right jaw. It wasn't much, but there was a slight redness and bulge over his otherwise sculpted cheekbone.

"How'd you get that?" she asked.

"Come on, let's go," Leonard barked.

Theodore laughed. "I ran into a patient's fist when I tried to put an oxygen mask on her face. But what can you expect from a fifty-one fifty?"

"Nola hit you?" Rae asked. She recalled Nola's outburst in the recovery room when Betty tried to change her IV bag. When Theodore nodded, Rae said wryly, "I guess she has her way of letting you know when she's not happy."

"You can say that again."

Rae thanked the twins for speaking with her and watched as they drove away. Then she headed for the emergency room, where she was instantly assaulted by the stench of vomit and unwashed bodies. She held her breath for a few seconds until she was back in the lobby and on her way to the third floor. She wished she had had the nerve to snoop around the Hillstar ambulance. Hopefully, Theodore would offer her a tour again.

But what could the paramedics know that would explain what happened to Nola and Meredith? What could happen inside an ambulance? The patients were given oxygen by mask, a little sugar water, and had their babies' heart rates checked. If there had been something else done to or for them, Meredith, at the very least, would have noticed it.

Well, whether the twins knew something pertinent or not was only part of her problem, Rae thought. As much as she hated to admit it, her biggest hurdle would be going inside the ambulance to check things out for herself.

After the morning's chaos, Rae was happy to see that the third-floor maternity suite had quieted down. Only a couple of labor patients' names were listed on the computerized board behind the nursing desk. Rae punched across a computer keyboard to locate Nola's and Meredith's postpartum rooms.

"Are you still here, Dr. Duprey?" asked Trish Barrow, the charge nurse who had first called Rae about Nola. Trish wore red-rimmed glasses and her auburn hair was tied into a tight bun at the back of her neck. She was a little too prissy for Rae's tastes, and very protective of her staff. But she was one hell of a good charge nurse and as far as Rae was concerned, nothing else mattered.

She glanced at the clock. 1:15 P.M.

Waving at Trish, she continued on to the postpartum ward, a unit around the corner from the labor deck. Touches of Walker's vision were everywhere. The corridors were wide and painted in stark white, like everywhere else. The carpet had silver and black squares. The nursing station, with its bank of computer screens, fax machines, and phones, featured the latest designs and the best technology. But, mused Rae, as she approached the rack that held the patients' silver metal record charts, where was the ward clerk? The phones were ringing but no one was answering them. No doubt about it, her department, her hospital, was in deep financial trouble.

"Damn it, will somebody answer the phone!"

Rae turned to her right and saw, hidden behind the file rack, Dr. Marshall White. He was as small as a professional jockey and rarely smiled. Maybe the reason for his dour expression was that at sixty-seven years old, he was still getting up in the middle of the night to deliver babies. Managed care, Rae thought ruefully, had changed retirement plans for many physicians.

Marshall placed his pen next to a chart on the countertop. "This place is going to pot," he said. "Nobody answers the phones anymore. Half the time the patients' call buttons go unanswered."

Rae walked over to the phone. "Marshall," she said as she removed the receiver from its cradle, "you deliver at the Birth Center. Have you noticed any problems with your maternal transports from there lately?"

She put the receiver to her ear but all she got was a dial tone. "Too late," she said.

"No wonder everybody's delivering their patients over there," he said. "At least the Birth Center has staff to answer phones."

"I mean," Rae persisted, setting the phone into the receiver, "have more of your patients been transferred out from the Birth Center because of fetal distress? Have you noticed any increases in your C-section rates?"

"What about my C-section rates?" Marshall snapped.

"Nothing, Marshall," Rae said placatingly. "I want to know about fetal distress cases and the Birth Center."

"How about doctor distress?" And then, looking around, he asked, "Now where in the hell is that ward clerk? I want these orders taken off now, not on the night shift."

The phone rang again. "I'll get it!"

It was finally the ward clerk, Leslie Meyers, a woman in her twenties who wore a diamond in the middle of her tongue.

"Where've you been?" Marshall demanded.

But Leslie only pressed her fingers to her lips as she listened to the receiver. Marshall rolled his eyes and slammed his patient's chart on the counter. "If you ask me, Rae, I'd be better off delivering all of my patients at the Birth Center."

After Marshall stormed off, Leslie hung up the phone and asked, "What was that all about?"

Rae plopped down in a chair next to Leslie and removed Nola's and Meredith's charts from the rack. Her head felt heavy as she thumbed through the pages.

"What gives, Dr. Duprey?"

"That's exactly what I'd like to know," Rae said.

"Say, did you hear about the triplets?" Leslie asked.

"Dr. Henshaw's triplets?"

Leslie beamed. "Three girls. All over five pounds. C-section, of course."

"Don't get me started," Rae said.

Leslie glanced over Rae's shoulder as she studied Nola's chart. "Now that patient is one overcooked potato."

Rae nodded. "Leslie, do you keep a delivery log over here? I could go back to L and D but I don't think I can stand up right now."

"You bet." Leslie punched a few buttons on her computer. A screen popped up with a list of patients' names. "Anybody in particular you're looking for?"

Rae scooted closer. She scrolled up and down. "Don't know yet."

"Cool."

"Can I borrow a piece of paper?" Rae asked.

Leslie gave her a yellow legal pad. "It's on the house."

The computer screen showed the names of the patients who had delivered, the date of delivery, their medical record number, sex of the baby, name of physician, mode of delivery, and the baby's weight and Apgar scores. It also showed how many times a woman had given birth. What it didn't show was whether the subject was a Birth Center patient who had been transferred to Rae's hospital or a woman who had always been a hospital patient. Birth Center patients were often transferred to Rae's unit for labor management, not just for cesarean sections.

"Damn," Rae mumbled.

"Bad news?" Leslie asked.

"Is there any way of telling a Birth Center patient from everybody else?"

"Aren't they all the same once they get here?" Leslie replied.

Rae let out a sigh of exasperation. Then she wrote down the names of patients who had delivered babies with low Apgar scores in the past six months. Apgar scores ranged from 0 to 10. A score of less than 7 meant that the baby needed resuscitation at the time of birth. Like Nola's baby, who had been born with an Apgar score of 1.

Rae counted some thirty babies who had been born with low Apgar scores in the past six months, but many of the babies had been born prematurely and low Apgar scores were expected for them. Rae jotted down the names of the others, about twenty. The reason for their low scores wasn't clear. Now all she'd have to do was to call medical records and request that the charts be pulled for her review. It would be up to her to discover where the patient originated.

She sat back in her chair wearily and rubbed her eyes. Reviewing charts one by one was not a task she looked forward to doing.

"Hey, here it is!" Leslie exclaimed.

Rae opened one eye.

"You were right, Dr. Duprey. There is a special code."

Rae leaned over and looked at Leslie's screen.

"See here?" Leslie said. "There's a little star by the names of those patients who started off in the Birth Center but wound up over here."

"Leslie!" Rae wailed. She didn't know if she should kiss the clerk or kill her. She let her head fall back and closed her eyes. She had just wasted an entire hour. Had she had the strength, she decided, she would have choked Leslie with her bare hands. She opened her eyes and leaned forward to study the screen. "Why didn't you tell me before?"

"But that's what I'm trying to say," Leslie said. Her face beamed, as she pointed to the screen. "This special code was not here two weeks ago. I meant it earlier when I said there was no way to tell the Birth Center patients from everybody else. I guess IT must have added it."

"What's IT?"

"Information technology. You know, the guys who'd rather sleep with their mouses than some of us chicks."

"Let me see that," Rae said.

She began to jot down the starred names. As she wrote, a feeling of foreboding crept over her. There were eight Birth Center patients in the last two months alone who had low Apgar scores, and all of them, according to the computer at least, belonged to Dr. Bo Michaels.

Rae sat back and studied the screen again. When she and Bo had been together, Bo had rarely delivered a sick kid. Now eight in two months? What was going on? Was he spending so much time trying to destroy her department that he wasn't paying attention to his own patients?

There were a few other babies with low Apgar scores, but they were from deliveries further back and all of the doctors were different.

"I hope you found what you were looking for," Leslie said.

"Me too."

Next, she dialed medical records and asked Yvonne Wright, the file clerk, to pull the eight charts. Yvonne promised to have them ready in half an hour.

With time to kill, Rae decided to go back to the cafeteria for another cup of coffee. It was 2:30 P.M. and the cafeteria was emptying out. In the far corner, to her surprise, she saw Sam Hartman speaking with the twin paramedics. They seemed relaxed around him, just the opposite of how their behavior had been with her. Men, she thought. They always stuck together. A team thing, she decided. If they were the ones to give birth, they'd probably deliver inside a huddle.

She continued to watch them. After a few more minutes Rae decided that the interaction between the three men seemed more than a meeting of strangers. Sam was smiling and appeared to be making jokes. The twins smiled back, obviously quite enthralled with whatever he was saying. Then Sam extended his hand and shook each of theirs.

Rae stepped back out of view as Sam walked toward the cash register. He had purchased a cup of coffee and the twins remained behind in the hot food line. They were laughing and piling their trays with French fries. Sam paid for his coffee and walked away.

What was Sam doing with those guys? Ever since Bernie had given her a hard time about cavorting with "the enemy," Rae had planned to cancel Sam's offer to drive her to Marco's party. But now she changed her mind. If Sam knew those paramedics, perhaps she could get him to help her with her inquiry.

She decided to skip coffee and go to medical records. Rae didn't know if it was seeing Sam together with the twins or not, but it suddenly seemed as if she were swimming in much deeper waters than she had previously thought.

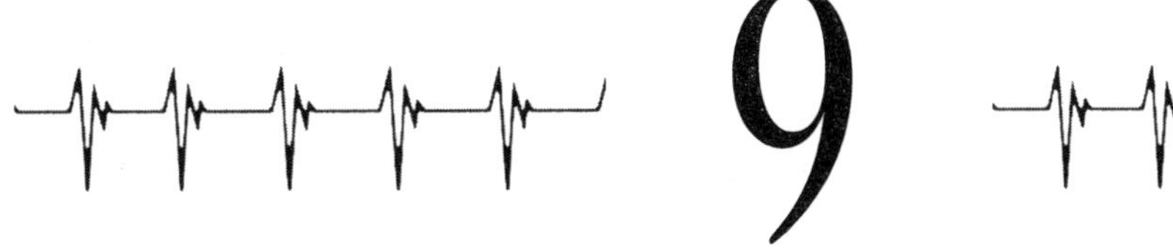

# 9

THE MEDICAL RECORDS DEPARTMENT SPANNED THE NORTHEAST corner of the hospital's north wing. Sitting behind a stack of charts was Yvonne Wright, a laconic woman in her late fifties who had a passion for order and Harley-Davidson motorcycles.

"There're your charts," Yvonne said in her usual deadpan voice. She nodded to a stash in Rae's slot. Each slot was separated from another by a thick, paper file card with the doctor's last name written in bold print along the tab.

Rae checked her watch. "Fifteen minutes since I called, Yvonne. You're fast."

"Hmph," Yvonne said.

Rae carried the thick white folders to a small built-in desk partitioned off from similar desks lining the wall. Unlike the rest of the hospital, the Medical Records Department had not been updated, and for reviewing charts, Rae preferred it that way. It was about the only place where the walls were not painted white and where the furniture had been made for people to actually sit on. In particular, the doctor's file room was painted a soft peach, and the furniture consisted of old-fashioned chairs with real armrests and cushioned bottoms.

Rae counted the charts. There were only four, not eight as she had requested. "What happened to the other ones?"

"Ask Dr. Donavelli. They were last signed out to him."

Rae looked at her askance. "But charts aren't allowed out of the

Medical Records Department unless the patient gets admitted to one of the wards or is being evaluated in the emergency room."

Yvonne rolled her eyes. "Sorry," Rae said, realizing she was preaching to the choir. She stole a glance at Marco's slot. Empty, just as Yvonne had said.

"Are you sure it was Marco Donavelli who requested them, Yvonne?"

"Just what's so important about those charts anyway?" Yvonne asked, narrowing her eyes suspiciously.

Rae wondered the same thing as she sat down in a chair a few feet from Yvonne's desk. She placed the four charts on the counter and opened up the top one. "That's exactly what I plan to find out."

Just then, Bo walked in. He did not seem to see her as he approached Yvonne's desk.

"Yeah?" Yvonne asked him.

Bo handed Yvonne a slip of paper. His back was still to Rae. Yvonne eyed the paper and cut her eyes to where Rae was sitting. "Eight very popular patients," Yvonne said.

Bo turned and followed Yvonne's stare to where Rae sat. "He wants your charts," Yvonne said.

Uh-oh, Rae thought. Now what?

Bo crossed his arms. "Those are Birth Center patients, Rae."

Rae pulled the folders closer to her. "No, these are charts, Bo, and I believe they belong to the hospital." She was curious to find out what he wanted them for.

"Where are the other four?" Bo asked, eyeing the stack.

"Why don't you ask Marco?"

Bo turned to Yvonne. "You heard her," Yvonne said. "And don't bother looking in Dr. Donavelli's chart slot for them. They're gone."

Bo turned angrily back toward Rae. "You ought to be upstairs reviewing Nola's and Meredith's charts, Rae. You'll need to prepare your defense. In case you haven't heard, Arnie scheduled your hearing for two weeks."

Rae pulled out a chair for Bo. When he remained standing, she leaned forward in her chair and looked up at him. In a lowered voice she said, "Listen. Let's just stop arguing for a minute. Why don't we try to figure out why eight low-Apgar-score babies came out of the Birth Center in the last two months."

"Ridiculous," Bo said.

"And all eight babies were *your* babies, Bo. You tell me I have a problem. Eight is four times two, if I remember my math."

"You're not going to drag me into this," Bo said. "And what's Marco got to do with any of this?"

"I should be asking you that question," Rae said coolly. "I learned at this morning's board meeting that you've got Marco convinced that the Birth Center is a good thing. But maybe he's changed his mind. Maybe he's worried that *you* screwed up and that's why he wants to review these charts."

Bo reached down and snatched the charts from Rae before she could grab them. She stood up and tried to snatch them back.

"Hey!" Yvonne yelled out. "You two need to quit acting like children. If the charts mean that much to you, how about I make both of you a copy?"

Feeling foolish for her behavior, Rae replied, "That's a good idea, Yvonne. I'd appreciate you putting them in my box." Then, turning back to Bo, she said, "If there's something in those charts you're hiding, believe me I'm going to find out."

"You'll have plenty of time to look at them," Bo said. "But just for the record, I'm not trying to hide anything from you. I am, however, trying to prevent you from tampering with the charts before copies are made. Why do you think I came down here? What Yvonne just proposed is exactly what I was going to ask her to do."

Incredulously, Rae said, "So now you're accusing me of falsifying records?"

"I don't put anything past you, Rae. Not when it comes to your ambition."

With her still staring at him, Bo carried the charts to the far corner of the room. Fuming, Rae left the file room. It would be some time before Bo finished with the charts and gave them to Yvonne to copy. Perhaps it was better. She was too mad to concentrate.

Even though she wasn't sure where her investigation was headed, the one thing Rae *was* sure of now was that the ante had just been upped. Bo now knew that she suspected *something,* and when Marco heard about the chart fiasco, so would he. Just how many more enemies would she make before this was over? she thought as she headed for the elevator. The numbers seemed to be increasing by the hour.

Rae awoke with a start. For a few seconds, she could not remember where she was. But then the familiar hum of the hospital's ventilation system reminded her that she was in one of the call rooms in L and D. The on-call rooms, which measured some six by ten feet—more like a large closet, really—had been overlooked when Walker refurbished the maternity suite. But for the past hour, this one had been a refuge for Rae.

Turning on the light, she saw her gray dress crumpled in a heap on the floor. She dressed quickly, used the sink to rinse out her mouth, and checked her appearance in the mirror. Her eyes were clear, but the shadows under them had darkened. Oh well, as long as she didn't scare the patients, she could live with the dark circles.

Meredith Bey sat propped up on a thick white pillow at the head of the bed. Like all of the postpartum rooms, Meredith's was spacious and had a panoramic view of the bay. The white walls glistened from the western sun and accentuated the pink glow on Meredith's happy face.

"I hope this is a good time to visit," said Rae as she sat down in a white director's chair next to Meredith's bed. Little Cynthia was swaddled in a pink blanket and was nursing blissfully.

"Sure, what can I help you with?" Meredith asked, looking down to gently readjust the blanket around the baby's head.

"Did you deliver your first baby at the Birth Center?" Rae asked. She had to be careful. She had no proof that something bad had happened to Meredith inside the Birth Center, and she didn't want to raise Meredith's suspicions that something had.

"Heavens no," Meredith said. "My first baby is ten years old. There was no Birth Center then."

And there shouldn't be now, Rae thought. "So why'd you choose it over City Hospital, or over us?"

Meredith's eyes widened. "Haven't you seen it?" she asked. "It's like being at home. My first labor only lasted for two hours. I was the perfect patient to deliver there this time." She paused and patted her baby's bottom. "Except I guess everybody but my friends underestimated how much this little dumpling weighed."

The horrifying memory of the shoulder dystocia sped through Rae's mind. "So everything went well, I mean, over there?"

"I pushed this morning for as long as I was in labor last time," Meredith said. She cocked her head to the side as if a new thought had registered in her mind.

"What?" Rae asked.

"Nothing," Meredith said. "I did my homework before deciding on the Birth Center," Meredith said, shifting the baby to the other breast. "I checked out everything. And it was great. Even the ambulance drivers had it together. As a matter of fact, they were so conscientious that one of them changed my IV bag so that I'd be well hydrated by the time the anesthesiologist started my spinal for the section."

Rae leaned forward in her chair. "The paramedics changed your IV?"

"They most certainly did," Meredith said proudly. "That shows just how good they are."

Meredith leaned back on her pillow. Rae forced a smile while she tried to remember if anything she had read in Meredith's chart mentioned that the paramedics changed the IV bag. Unfortunately, her memory was fuzzy. She'd have to check again. On the other hand, she certainly did remember that the paramedics had told her that they hadn't changed *Nola's* IV bag.

She also remembered that Nola had gone crazy when she saw Betty with a new bag. Was there a connection? If there was a connection, what kind? Neither Freda nor Jenny said anything about the paramedics changing IV bags. Freda had told her that the Birth Center took care of that. But how would the nurses know what the paramedics did inside the ambulance once it left the Birth Center?

"How long did you say you were pushing?" she asked.

"Too long," Meredith said. "At least two hours. Next time, I'm going to have an epidural."

Meredith yawned. Rae rose and fluffed the pillow under her head. She had asked her enough questions for one afternoon.

"Where's your camera?" she asked.

"In that little drawer over there."

Rae brought the camera to Meredith and then lifted Cynthia from her arms. The baby felt warm and wonderful against her body. Rae had held thousands of babies in her life, but never one of her own. Would it feel different? she wondered. Would her heart melt as much as it did now when she stared at the angelic face that now stared back at her with questioning eyes?

"If I ever have a baby," Rae said, "I hope I have one as cute as you, Cynthia." She raised and lowered the baby like a sack of potatoes. "But not as big."

Meredith laughed and clicked the picture. She placed the camera on the side table and Rae handed the baby back to her. "I hope you find out what happened to me after I left the Birth Center," Meredith said.

Rae looked at her with surprise. She had thought she was being subtle.

"Oh, I know what you're thinking," Meredith said. "The problem is, I was wondering the same thing. But the care at the Birth Center was perfect. The care inside the ambulance was perfect too. Everything was perfect! I've been sitting here blaming myself for what happened. If only I hadn't been so hell-bent on a natural delivery when deep in my heart I knew she was too big to come out!"

"I didn't mean to imply—" Rae began to say.

"Dr. Michaels thought I should deliver at the hospital too, but I talked him out of it," Meredith said wistfully. "That's the problem with being an L and D nurse. Not only do we know too much, but we can talk our doctors into taking more chances."

Not this doctor, Rae thought.

Rae thanked Meredith for speaking with her and then advised her to get some rest.

"Next time, I'm delivering here," Meredith said.

Rae smiled at Meredith. "We'll be delighted to have you." She wished Meredith luck with her new daughter. Then she left the room wondering if Berkeley Hills Hospital would still have a maternity unit if Meredith did have another baby.

By the time she passed the nurses' station and headed toward Nola Payne's room, she had decided two things: one, she had to speak with the paramedics about the IV bags. Two, that her department would be there whenever Meredith got pregnant again, and it would be even better. One way or the other, she'd make sure of it.

* * *

Nola's room was located down the hall from Meredith's. Rae looked inside and saw an empty bed.

"She's down in the nursery."

Rae turned and saw the smiling face of the postpartum ward's charge nurse, Marcie Bland. As if to defy her last name, Marcie always wore a headband of purple roses across her blond hair.

"But she just had surgery," Rae said, looking into the room once more.

"Try telling her that," Marcie said. "Try telling her anything."

Inside the nursery, Rae found Nola dressed in a white patient gown and sitting in a chair. The woman seemed to be in a trance. In front of her was the glass hood of the incubator and she was peering through it to study her baby.

Rae strolled over to Jessica, who was busy studying the computer screen. "Should I ask how he's doing?"

Jessica frowned. "We're having a hell of a time keeping his $O_2$ sats up," she said.

Rae shook her head sadly. Even with the baby intubated and on oxygen, the staff was still having difficulty filling up his lungs. Raising her chin in Nola's direction, she asked, "How's she taking it?"

"I think she thinks she's the Virgin Mary," Jessica replied.

Rae walked over to Nola. Nola seemed unaware of Rae's presence, and anyone else's for that matter. Except, of course, for the baby's. He lay flat on his back. His legs and arms were strapped to the mattress pad. He was still hooked up to the monitors and to the ventilator. But next to him was Nola's yellow plastic crucifix, attached to the necklace made of a tennis shoe string.

"I bet he likes that, Miss Payne," Rae said.

Nola remained silent. She didn't even blink at Rae's comment.

Rae pulled up a chair and sat next to her. She wasn't sure how to go about asking Nola about her care in the Birth Center. But she had to give it a shot. She paused to collect her thoughts. How did one speak to the Blessed Mother?

Finally, in a very soft voice, Rae said, "I want to help you, Miss Payne. And I want to help your baby. But I can't do either unless I know what happened this morning."

Nola stared straight ahead, eyes unblinking.

"She hasn't said a word since she came in," Jessica said.

Rae sat back in her chair. She had to get Nola to talk.

"Nola, I'm Dr. Rae," she tried once more. "You remember. I did your surgery."

Again she waited. She was feeling more desperate. Nola might know something about what had happened to her baby. Unless Rae could get her to talk, Rae would be the one who looked crazy if she tried to stir things up. But it was obvious that Nola wasn't talking. She got up and began to walk away, but then stopped, and listened.

"Hillstar," Nola mumbled. "Superstar."

Rae turned and placed her hand on Nola's shoulder. "Hillstar is the name of the ambulance company, Nola," Rae said.

"Hillstar. Superstar. Hillstar. Superstar."

Nola did not blink as she spoke.

"What about Hillstar?" Rae asked. "Did something happen to you inside the Hillstar ambulance, Miss Payne? Did anyone change your IV bag?"

"Salt water. Good for the baby."

It took all that Rae had to control her frustration. She knew that Nola was trying to tell her something, but what?

"Were you calling out your last name in the recovery room?" she asked. "Or were you saying that you were in pain, that something was hurting you?"

"Salt water. Good for the baby. Salt water. Good for the baby."

Rae looked around the room. Jessica was busy attending to another baby, as were the other nurses.

"Why were you so afraid of the bag Betty was hanging in the recovery room, Nola? Did the drivers change it? Did they say something mean to you? Please, tell me what happened. I can't help you, or Baby Jesus—"

Nola turned to her then. "Baby Jesus," she said.

"Yes, Baby Jesus," Rae said. Her mind was racing now. "Baby Jesus wants you to tell me what happened," she said.

"Baby Jesus cannot talk," Nola said. She turned away from Rae and stared at the baby.

Rae slumped back into her chair. She had said the wrong thing and Nola had shut down again. She rose from her chair. She'd have to figure things out without Nola's help. Or would she? she thought, spying the cart loaded with IV bags in the far corner of the room. The bags were much smaller, but they would have to do. She grabbed one and pulled off the plastic wrapping. She returned to where Nola was sitting and held the bag in front of Nola's face.

Nola blinked once, and then again. Suddenly she jumped up from her chair and slammed the bag away. Her eyes filled with terror. She hovered over the bassinet and tried to cover it with her body. "Salt water! Good for the baby! Hillstar! Hillstar! Hillstar!"

"And what about the pain?" Rae asked her desperately.

"Salt water! Salt water!"

"The pain, Nola! The pain!"

"Dr. Duprey, what are you doing to her?" Jessica shouted.

Jessica and the other nurses ran over to Nola.

"Damn it, Nola! Tell me about the pain!"

She was beside herself, wanting to help Nola, and at the same time wanting to shake her silly if that would get her to talk. But Nola was in her own world. The only person who appeared crazy right then was Rae. Clearly the nurses who now circled Nola like a fortress thought so too.

Judging by the bewildered expressions on their faces, Rae knew they were waiting for her to explain herself. "I was just trying to—"

Jessica cut her off with a wave of her hand and at the same time placed a protective arm around Nola's shoulder. "Look, Dr. Duprey, I don't know what's going on with you and that disciplinary hearing, and I don't want to know, but I do think you need to get yourself straightened out, whatever the problem is."

"But—"

"I mean it, Dr. Duprey. I think you better leave. You're upsetting Miss Payne and she already has enough to worry about."

The other nurses looked accusingly at Rae. For her to try to offer an explanation would only make things worse. And the nurses were right, she had done enough damage to Nola, let alone her own reputation, for one day.

"You're absolutely right, Jessica," she said. "I'm sorry, everyone. I'll leave."

She could feel the nurses' eyes on her as she walked out of the room. Her behavior had been inappropriate, but now she knew that something about those IV bags scared Nola to death. And it wasn't just salt water, that was for sure.

# 10

RAE GUNNED THE ENGINE OF HER BLACK PORSCHE 911 AFTER she pulled out of the parking lot and headed for the steep descent down Marin Avenue. It was just before seven and Sam would pick her up at seven forty-five. The sun had already dipped behind the horizon, and the sky was now ablaze in oranges and reds. The bay waters lay absolutely still—not a whitecap in sight.

Rae felt just the opposite of calm. Even the melodious voice of singer Luther Vandross crooning out of her radio speakers did little to soothe her. At this point it would take a general anesthetic to still her racing thoughts.

The smaller streets intersected Marin Avenue every sixty yards or so, then the steep hill would plateau for about twenty yards. Then it would drop off again, like a giant multitiered slide of an amusement park, dipping, leveling out, then dipping again. At the bottom of the hill was a traffic circle. Eight streets fed off the circle like spokes in a wheel. In the middle of the circle was a twelve-foot-high concrete fountain with water spouting from the mouths of four little bears. Rae took the curve around the fountain at forty miles an hour. A leopard-spotted '66 VW honked to her right and she cursed under her breath.

Nothing, she thought, was going to slow her down. She wanted to get home, get dressed, and be ready for Sam Hartman to pick her up. She planned to buttonhole some of the cardiologists at Marco's party and lobby them to support her OB department—just as she would support their heart program. If only she could get them to see that the last thing that should happen was for doctor to fight doctor, for one program to fight another!

Marin Avenue ran into I-80, and at the on-ramp Rae hit the accelerator. To her, the 80 in I-80 meant that she cruised at the same speed. The still gray waters of the bay were a blur in her peripheral vision. In two minutes she was at Ashby Avenue, and in another sixty seconds she had pulled into the gated parking lot of the thirty-story condominium.

"Hey, Doc," said Mack the doorman, whose legs were as long as Rae was tall. "How many babies did you deliver today?"

"Ten," Rae said, although she had delivered only two. "And, Mack, I'm expecting Dr. Sam Hartman at seven forty-five. Ring me when he gets here and I'll come down."

Mack beamed. "A gentleman caller? My, my."

"Don't get too excited. It's just business," Rae said over her shoulder as she headed toward the elevator at the far end of the marble-tiled foyer. Her apartment was at the end of a long carpeted hall on an upper floor. As she removed her keys from her purse, she could hear Leopold panting on the other side of the door.

The door across from hers opened. Standing there, dressed in white shirt, black trousers, and bow tie, was eighty-two-year-old Harvey Polk, her violin teacher. As usual for the evening, Harvey held a brandy snifter. "Down for the count finally?" Harvey asked in a voice as smooth as Rae imagined his drink to be. His gray eyes, more cloudy from age than alcohol, gazed affectionately at Rae.

"Not exactly," Rae said. "Looks like I've got to skip tomorrow's lesson too."

Harvey sipped his cognac. Rae knew how he looked forward to their Saturday morning violin lessons. "Leopold will be very disappointed," Harvey said.

"Just don't teach him more than I know," Rae said. She gave Harvey a half smile and then wished him good-night. How she longed for the day when she could spend every day, not just Saturdays, sitting in front of Harvey's window as he taught her the special secrets of playing the violin.

She opened the door to her unit. First to greet her inside the foyer was Leopold with an enthusiastic round of barks. Next was the sweeping view outside the west window of the San Francisco skyline. The jeweled city was just beginning to come alive, Rae thought. She, on the other hand, felt as if she could sleep for the next century. Hoping to get a second wind soon, she patted the soft black fur of Leopold's head and then flicked on the porcelain lamp that stood on a rectangular table. Next to the lamp sat an opened copy of the month's *American Journal of Obstetrics and Gynecology,* and next to that stood a framed photo taken by Harvey of Rae walking Leopold past the sailboats of the Emeryville Marina. "Did you have a good walk with Harvey today, boy?" she asked her Lab as she rubbed the top of his head again.

Sighing, she stared out the window at the glimmering lights from across the bay. Despite Leopold's presence, she had discovered that nighttime was always the hardest, for at night, loneliness settled in like the dark: quietly, inevitably, and completely.

She sighed again as she walked across the hardwood floors past her study, which was originally a second bedroom. Although the walls of the study were lined with rich mahogany, during the day the light from the two corner windows infused the room with warmth and brightness. But at night, the room became a private sanctuary where she worked out her deepest thoughts and biggest worries. Like the ones she had now, the ones about the babies.

From one of the many bookshelves she removed a leather-bound book on obstetrics written by a British author some thirty years earlier. Although she had much more recent books and the latest obstetrical journals, she preferred this old volume, for the author's greatest skill was in taking the history from a patient. Most diagnoses, in Rae's mind, could be made by just listening to the patient. How had modern science become so dependent on fancy tests often performed before anyone even bothered to ask the patient what happened!

She noted the time on the desk clock. Ten after seven. She was in a hurry but she had to check to make sure she had thought of everything. Quickly she thumbed through the book's chapter entitled, "Shoulder Dystocia." Meredith's baby's head was delivered, and that caused the umbilical cord to be drawn into the pelvis and compressed before Sylvia, the ER nurse, realized that the baby's shoulders could not be delivered.

As she read the list of risk factors associated with shoulder dystocia, Rae leaned wearily against the bookshelf. Leopold wagged his tail as he waited patiently for her to finish. "The incidence of shoulder dystocia for babies weighing under nine pounds, Leopold," she said, "is only sixteen-hundredths percent. But for babies weighing more, the incidence is closer to two percent." She paused as she thought of Meredith's daughter, and then said, "Well, Cynthia certainly weighed more than that."

Still carrying the book, she padded across the carpet and sat down in a comfortable wingback chair in front of the corner windows. A necklace of bright lights spanned the Bay Bridge. She clicked on the lamp. "But for women who push for more than two hours," she said, "and who eventually get delivered by forceps, the incidence of shoulder dystocia climbs to four and a half percent."

Leopold wagged his tail. "No," Rae said. "Meredith never had forceps or a vacuum. She pushed out the baby on her own."

She shook her head in frustration and ran her hands through her hair. "Come on, Leopold," she said.

Rae's bedroom faced west. She stripped off her clothes and spied the sailboats looking for their berths in the Emeryville Marina. How did people have time for such leisure? she thought ruefully.

Usually she would have taken the time to hang up her clothes. She loved a sense of order in her everyday life. Neatness made everything easier, like opening up a woman's belly and packing the bowel away before placing the first clamp on the round ligament at the start of a hysterectomy. But now she let her dress lie in a heap upon the soft peach down comforter of her queen-size bed. Slowly she removed her stockings. She spent a blissful second or two massaging her feet.

Rae's eyes wandered around the bedroom of the condo she had lived in for the past ten years. Out of habit, her gaze settled on the antique nightstand. Upon it sat her old-fashioned clock and a gold-framed photo.

The black-and-white photo was badly faded, yet Rae could make out each detail of the two people in the picture. There was her mother, sitting at the chipped upright piano, her eyes cast down at the keys and a half smile on her lips. Her mother's typically lean face was full in the picture, which Rae understood now was a warning sign of preeclampsia, but which the family had interpreted as normal for a pregnant woman. The doctor, Rae learned later, had warned her mother not to get pregnant again. The risk of a blood pressure complication was way too great. But what did the doctors know? her father had asked.

A lot, Rae thought now. A hell of a lot.

The other person in the photo was thirteen-year-old Rae, her face full of intensity as the fingers of her left hand spread across the neck of her violin. Rae loved the fact that her mother was her violin teacher. It was during Rae's violin lessons that she had her mother all to herself. Otherwise, she had to compete for her mother's attention along with her five older sisters. She sighed and glanced at the alarm clock next to the photo. 7:16 P.M. Next to the nightstand was her violin case. She touched the wood like a lover and then walked naked to the bathroom.

Inside the glass bathroom stall, she showered quickly. The hot water felt good hitting her weary muscles. The day's events had worn her out. The emergency cesarean. The shoulder dystocia. IV bags and missing charts. Bo's crazy accusation that she had tried to kill a baby and injure another.

Why, she asked herself, was she pushing so hard? Why wasn't she as smart as the sleeping Leopold, whose black form she could just barely make out through the steamed-up glass? Surely sleep was what she needed most. She could always speak to the cardiologists later. She lifted her face to the soothing spray and closed her eyes. As long as she felt her patients were in danger, she had no choice but to forge ahead.

Leopold barked when Rae returned to the bedroom. "Leopold," she said as she toweled off, "let me ask you something. Do you think I'm crazy? I mean, something happened to those babies. I don't know what yet, but I'm going to find out."

Leopold stared at her with big, patient brown eyes. "Are you with me, boy?"

Just then the telephone rang. It was Bernie asking Rae what she planned to wear to the party.

"I'm looking in my closet now," Rae said.

"Wear something really sexy."

"I don't want to give Sam the wrong idea."

"Too late for that!" Bernie cackled. "I saw those baby blues of his looking down your gown during Nola's section."

Rae frowned. "This is strictly business," she said.

"How about the one that's cut real low in the back?" Bernie persisted. "That should loosen a lot of tongues, if you get my drift."

Rae was too tired to argue with Bernie about her lack of interest in Sam Hartman. Romantic interest, that was.

"I had quite a time in medical records," Rae said. As they spoke, and despite her comment, she found herself rummaging through her more daring formals. After updating Bernie on the missing charts, she said, "Who knows where they are? I just know that Bo was very nervous. But I'm going back first thing in the morning. Who's to say the four charts Yvonne pulled for me won't suddenly disappear like the others?"

"Leave it to me, girlfriend. I'll get my nose in there before my shift tonight. So, what are you going to wear?"

"It's been a long time since I've been out, Bernie. I think it's too cold to have my back bare."

"But that's exactly the kind of dress one wears to a hoedown at Marco's," Bernie said.

Rae sighed loudly. "Okay, okay. Deal. I'll wear that one and you check the charts. And call me if you find out something."

Rae hung up the phone. Bernie, she thought. What would she do without her? The formal she selected was made of soft satin. It was a simple sleeveless black affair with a low-cut back. Not as low as the one Bernie wanted her to wear, but low enough to get a person's attention.

She held it on a hanger in front of Leopold. "This is safe, isn't it, Leopold?" she asked. He barked twice. "Oh, what do you know? When was the last time *you* had a date?"

Before Leopold could respond, the telephone rang shrilly.

It was Sam.

Immediately Rae knew where he was. The soft but incessant bleeping of an EKG machine carried through the phone line as clearly as if she were in the operating room herself.

"I know this is not the best way to make a good first impression," Sam began.

Rae glanced at the clock. 7:32 P.M. Damn, she thought, he better not say he couldn't make it. But then she remembered she had seen him rushing a patient out of the coronary care unit that afternoon. Heart cases took at least three to four hours, sometimes six to eight. Which meant that he shouldn't have been able to visit the cafeteria where she had seen him speaking with the two paramedics. If he had been tied up with a case, how in the hell could he have been in the cafeteria?

She forced a laugh. "The only person you need to impress is your patient," she said.

"I hope I get the chance," Sam said. "He's an eighty-two-year-old professor who looked like hell when we rolled him in here. He had an infected mitral valve from God knows what, crappy coronaries, and an ejection fraction less than twenty percent. The first time we tried to get him off bypass his pressure bottomed out. We just put him back on and stuck in the balloon. We'll try in a minute to get him off, and with any luck at all, I'll make it to Marco's for the main course. But the way things are looking, I could be here all night."

All night? Rae thought with dismay. She needed to talk to him urgently. Who cared about mitral valves and ejection fractions when she had very sick babies to worry about?

"I'll hold a seat for you," she said, trying to sound relaxed. "Right next to my high chair."

Sam laughed. "Hopefully, I won't be long," he said. "See you—"

"Sam, wait."

"Yes?"

"Perhaps this is none of my business but, well, I saw you speaking with a couple of paramedics this afternoon. Do you have a twin brother too? I mean, how could you be in two places at once?"

There was silence on the phone for a few seconds. "Sam?" Rae asked again.

She heard Sam exhale. "Why do you ask, Rae?"

Because she didn't believe him, Rae thought, but said instead, "Just curious."

Silence again, and finally Sam said, "As it turns out, there was a delay in the case. Believe me, I wasn't happy about it. Anyway, I got some coffee until things were straightened out. If you saw me, I wish you would have come over. I could have used some nice company."

He sounded sincere, Rae thought, but he'd certainly seemed to be having a jolly good time with the boys. "I was in a hurry," Rae said. This time she paused before asking, "Just for the record, what were you and the drivers talking about?"

"Now you've caught me," Sam laughed. "I was asking them for directions to your place. I figure if anyone knows the streets around here, they would."

"They only pick up in Berkeley," Rae said suspiciously. "I live in Emeryville."

"That's exactly what they said," Sam replied.

Rae remained unconvinced. "You could have called the doorman for directions. You could have called me."

"You have a doorman? Now that's impressive. Anyway, don't forget to save that seat."

And then he was gone. The phone clicked dead.

What did she really know about Sam Hartman? she asked herself. He had hesitated before offering his explanation for speaking with those paramedics. He had been vague about how the heart case had been delayed. Judging by the appearance of the patient, it was hard to believe that there would have been any delay at all. She grabbed a black cashmere cape from her closet and wrapped it around her shoulders. Flicking off the lights, she headed out the door. Sam Hartman had better come up with more believable excuses in the future, she thought. Meanwhile, he'd just been added to her growing list of suspects.

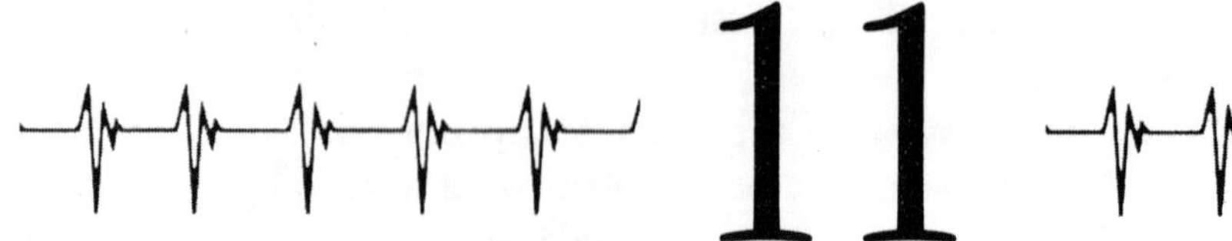

# 11

Rae pulled her Porsche into the redbrick semicircular driveway of Marco's six-bedroom Tudor home located high in the Piedmont hills, some ten miles from the hospital. She wondered how many cardiologists would be present. She was determined to speak with every one of them. "Good evening," said a tuxedo-clad parking attendant as he held open the door.

"That remains to be seen," said Rae as she smiled and handed him her keys.

The friendly man stared at her. Then, pointing his index finger, he said, "Hey, you delivered my sister's baby two years ago. Gladys Tilley, remember?"

Rae remembered the name immediately. She shook the man's extended hand. "How's Elvis?" she asked.

"What can I say? He's two. Is it too late to put him back in?"

Rae laughed and then hurried up the ten brick steps leading to a pair of carved wooden doors where a maid greeted her, took her black cape, and led her into the living room.

The space was massive, with oversized upholstered furniture, an ornate fireplace mantel loaded with framed pictures of Marco and his wife and kids, a grand piano in the far corner, and French windows that led out onto a veranda overlooking the bay.

"There she is!" Marco said jovially as he came up to her. He held a glass of champagne in his hand. "Now the party can begin!" He was dressed in a black wool tuxedo. He leaned down to kiss her cheek. "You're looking marvelous," he whispered into her ear. "And you smell good enough to eat."

"Down, boy, down," said Rae, raising her cheek up to Marco's face as he kissed her. At the same time, she checked out the other guests. There were about twenty in all, mostly male cardiologists and their wives, and two cardiac surgeons. Good, Rae thought. She could handle ten conversations with ten cardiologists in the span of two to three hours.

"Here, this is for you," Marco said, handing Rae the glass.

Rae shook her head. "That'll put me flat on my face," she said. "Where's Marcella?"

"She threw me out of the kitchen ten minutes ago," Marco said. "Did Sammy get hold of you?"

"He hopes to make it here for dessert," she said.

Marco puckered his lips and nodded his head back and forth. "Oh, is that what he's calling it now?" he asked.

"Cut it out, Marco. He only offered me a ride."

Marco raised an eyebrow.

Rae extended her hand toward the champagne glass. "You'd drive any woman to drink," she said.

"Eighty-six Taittinger," Marco said proudly.

Rae had to agree the champagne tasted marvelous.

They were joined immediately by a short man with a goatee.

"Who's *this* exotic creature?" the man asked.

"Peter, you son of a bitch!" Marco exclaimed. "You better let me operate on Mr. Calen or you'll be calling the mortuary for help!"

The short man laughed, but Rae could see the seriousness in his light brown eyes. "I'm Rae Duprey," she said. She extended her hand.

"*Doctor* Rae Duprey," Marco said. "Vice-chair of our OB/GYN department."

"Delighted," the short man said. "I'm Peter Horn, chief of cardiology. I know your name, but I thought the vice-chair was spelled R-A-Y and, well, frankly, I thought you were a man."

"She has balls, if that's what you mean," Marco said.

"Thank you, Marco," Rae said. "I'm sure I could say the same for you."

"Ouch," said Peter, faking a wince. "I like your style, Dr. Duprey."

"You're married, Peter," Marco said.

"A minor complication," Peter Horn said. He smiled at Rae and his eyes bore into hers. "Wouldn't you agree, Dr. Duprey?"

Rae stared challengingly back at him. She had two choices, she thought. She could tell him to get the hell away from her . . . or she could talk to him about supporting her department. She decided upon the latter.

Marco excused himself, and she let Peter Horn make small talk as the maid served them toast with caviar and prosciutto-wrapped asparagus tips from a silver tray. She even smiled back at him as she sipped her champagne. "So, are *you* married, Dr. Duprey?" he asked.

She forced a laugh. "A minor complication," she said.

Peter stared at Rae eye to eye now. "Is that a yes or a no?"

"Enough about me," Rae said. She had Peter's full attention now. "Tell me more about you. I mean, you're chief of cardiology. Don't you think there's enough room in our hospital for both of us—cardiology and OB, I mean?"

"Of course," Peter said. "It's like sleeping in the same bed, so to speak."

"So to speak," Rae repeated. Peter had taken another step toward her. She felt his alcohol-laden breath on her face. She stepped back. Perhaps she had gone too far. Peter Horn, she decided, might be more trouble than he was worth.

"So," Peter said, leaning closer to Rae, "how about I meet you for a drink after dinner?"

"Now *that* could be a major complication," Rae quipped.

But before she could go on, she was interrupted by the sound of a familiar voice coming from the foyer. Standing there, dressed in a elegant tuxedo and handing his black overcoat to the maid, was Bo. But Bo was not looking at the maid. He was gazing at Rae and Peter Horn. He immediately strolled over to them.

"Hey, Bo," Peter said once Bo was within earshot.

"I didn't know you two knew each other," Bo said.

"Hey, I'm trying my darnedest," Peter said. "Oh, before I forget. We've got an eight o'clock tee time tomorrow. Damien says he can be there."

"Who's the fourth?" Bo asked. Although he was addressing Peter, he was staring at Rae as if he expected her to volunteer to complete the foursome.

"Nice tux, Bo," said Rae, hoping to keep their encounter cordial.

Besides, she felt at a disadvantage. Had she known Peter was a golfing buddy of Bo's, she would not have wasted her time talking to him. She felt like a fool. She had to be more careful. But then, political maneuvering was not her forte.

"Arnie Driver," Peter said. "Do you know how to play golf, Dr. Duprey?"

"Since when is knowing *how* to play golf a requirement for playing golf?" Rae asked innocently.

"Dinner is served," Marco announced.

He had donned a white apron and a chef's hat. Rae couldn't help but smile at the spectacle he was making of himself. She was also relieved by the interruption.

"Shall we, gentlemen?" she asked.

Rae walked ahead of the two men and into the formal dining room. Get ready, she told herself. There was no such thing as a free dinner.

In Marco's dining room a glass table that could easily seat thirty guests was set with china and silver and crystal. The centerpiece was a huge bowl of purple grapes whose shiny skins glistened under the lights of a gold chandelier. The glass lights flickered in the gilded gold mirror at the far end of the room. It all looked like some elaborate Hollywood set, Rae thought. Perhaps, she thought again, that was Marco's intention.

Rae's place card was in front of a Wedgewood setting in the middle of the table. Marco had removed his apron and hat and sat at the head. Bo sat next to Peter Horn on the opposite side and to Rae's right. The chair directly to her right was occupied by another cardiologist, David Parks, a quiet man who Rae had heard wrote poetry on the side. She knew little else about him but she preferred what she did know to what she had just found out about Peter Horn. His wife, Peter had said, was home with their two-year-old and expecting their second child in two months.

Also present were the wives of several of the cardiologists. They were dressed in elegant gowns and bedecked with jewelry that reflected the incomes of their husbands. In the past, they rarely spoke much at Marco's dinners. To Rae's left was an empty chair. She read the name *Sam Hartman* on the place card in front of it. The chair across from Sam's was also vacant.

The maid served the first course of sliced tomatoes, basil, and buffalo mozzarella cheese doused in a fine virgin olive oil. Rae made small talk with the quiet David Parks while Peter Horn's voice grew louder and louder as he finished what Rae counted to be his fourth glass of wine.

Bo pretended to listen to Peter, but Rae saw that he seemed more interested in her conversation with David. By the time the second course was taken away, Rae had stated her case and gotten David to agree, in principle at least, that the OB department and the cardiac department should coexist peacefully.

"You just tell me what you need me to do," David said, "and I'll do it."

"Do what?" Marco asked.

Rae turned to Marco. She thought he had not been listening to her conversation with David.

"Hey, just because she's cute, David my man," Marco said, "don't let her talk you into anything that's bad for your health."

Great. The last thing she wanted to do was to get into a fight with Marco at the dinner table. She figured her best strategy for winning support from the cardiologists was to do it one on one, as she had done with David. To take on the cardiologists en masse would be stupid.

"Marco, what's all this about cardiac surgery taking over Rae's maternity unit in the hospital?" David asked. "My wife is due to deliver at Berkeley Hills in December and I'm certainly not going to support anything or anybody that might force her to deliver anyplace else."

"She could always deliver at the Birth Center," Marco said. He looked at Bo, who gave him a look back that was cold enough to freeze the wine in Marco's glass.

"We're not closed yet," Rae said. "Be sure your wife knows that, David."

"We'd be happy to take care of her," Bo said. "As long as she's low risk."

"Yeah, you'll take good care of her," Rae said.

The words just slipped out, or at least that was what she told herself. Maybe the champagne, and now the red wine, had loosened her tongue a bit. She hadn't meant to jump into the argument, but Bo's response ticked her off. Had he "cared" for Nola that morning? Had he "cared" for Meredith? No, she decided, and he didn't seem to care enough about either one of them after they delivered. All he cared about was protecting the reputation of the Birth Center.

Bo started eating again. Rae did the same thing.

"Well, I don't like it, Marco," David said. "Who's running Berkeley Hills Hospital anyway? We're the doctors. We can't have the board deciding our futures for us."

"But that's their job," Marco said.

"Rubbish," David said. "I'm against allowing the board to pit our department against Rae's. Besides, my wife would kill me if she knew I was responsible for making her deliver someplace else. Just like there's room for all of us at this table, there's room for all of us at Berkeley Hills. All we've got to do is stick together as one medical staff."

"I'm all for sticking together," said a very drunk Peter Horn, tilting his glass toward Rae.

As Peter poured himself another glass of wine, Bo said, "Perhaps your wife would be better off at my Birth Center." He glared at Rae and she stopped chewing.

"Leave it alone, Bo." she said.

"I see you're not having much luck with her either," Peter said, slurring a little.

"Did you know about the board's decision, Peter?" David asked. "You're the damn department chief."

"I'm very bored at the present moment," Peter said. "I know that."

Everyone stopped eating but Marco. Peter's insult had not been lost on anyone, Rae thought. But Marco, forever the gracious host, took another couple of bites and then said gaily, "Let's not talk shop tonight, fellas."

David turned to Marco. "Did you know about closing OB?" he persisted.

"I have no beef with OB," Marco said, suddenly serious.

"Just what exactly did Rae tell you, David?" Bo asked.

Plenty, Rae thought, but she only smiled.

"Are we all happy in here?"

The question had been asked by Marcella Donavelli, Marco's wife, who had suddenly appeared in the room. Marcella had fierce blue eyes and jet black, shoulder-length hair. She wore a deep blue dress and a necklace of brilliant diamonds. Tight lines framed the corners of her mouth even though she was smiling at her guests.

"Ah, saved by the bell. Won't you join us, dear?" Marco asked.

Rae knew that Marcella never sat down to dinner with her guests. "No darling, just checking on everyone," Marcella said.

Hearing footsteps, Rae joined the other guests in turning toward the door. Standing there was Sam Hartman and a woman several inches taller. Immediately Rae felt the blood rushing to her face from both humiliation and anger as she watched Sam escort her to her seat.

"I didn't think you'd make it!" Marco said. He stood and walked over to the empty chair across from Rae. "What, did your patient have such cheap insurance you didn't bother to hang around and wake him up?"

The guests all laughed as Sam Hartman waited for the strawberry blonde to take her seat across from Rae. The woman wore a low-cut, flaming-red dress—so low, Rae thought spitefully, that it was a wonder she didn't fall out of it.

"Thank you, Sam darling," the blonde said in a throaty voice.

Sam took his seat next to Rae and placed his white napkin across his lap. "I'm starving," he said. "Thanks for holding my seat."

"No problem," Rae said coolly. The fact that he looked elegant in his tuxedo and he smelled like he had just stepped out of the shower only irritated her more.

"Am I too late for dessert?" Sam asked.

"Obviously not," said Peter Horn as he leaned across the table and openly gawked at the woman's breasts.

Rae wanted to get up and sit at the far end of the table. How dare Sam Hartman ask to drive her to Marco's party and then show up with someone else? Not that it was a real date or anything. But still . . .

Men, she seethed. She had no time for them anyway.

"Sammy," Marco said. He was beaming as he took the woman's hand. "Who's your lovely guest?"

Rae saw Sam flash Marco a look of warning. Rae wanted to know who Sam's "guest" was too. And he had said he was going to be late because he was tied up in surgery. Was that what they called it now? she asked herself.

The blonde batted her eyes at Marco as he kissed her hand. "I'm April," she said in a voice as soft as a whisper.

"Spring is my favorite season," Marco said gallantly as he reached for a bottle of wine.

The maid brought out plates of osso buco. The room filled with the sweet scent of garlic as Marco went around pouring red wine into everyone's glass. When he got to Sam's, he said, "You're just in time, Sammy. David was saying there was no way he'd let his wife deliver at Bo's Birth Center. Imagine that."

"You said you didn't want to talk shop, Marco," Bo said.

"We're talking women's issues here, not shop," Marco said. "I agree with David's wife. All women would be better off delivering at the hospital."

"So why didn't you tell that to the board this morning?" Rae snapped, recalling his position at the meeting.

Marco smiled broadly. "I never said my first choice was to close down your OB program, Rae," Marco said. "But if it means your program closes down and mine stays open—hey, what would you do?"

Just then a pager went off. All of the physicians at the table reached for their beepers, including Rae. "Excuse me," Sam said, holding his in the air.

Right after Sam left, Rae saw that Bo's attention had shifted to her. She knew his jealous stare. He suddenly seemed more interested in the fact that Sam was sitting next to her than he was in Marco's position on the Birth Center. Idiot, Rae thought. Didn't he see Sam come in with the blonde? Besides, Rae was interested in delivering healthy babies, not in a romantic relationship with Sam Hartman.

Bo wiped his lips with a napkin, rose from the table, and walked around to sit in Sam's vacated chair. He leaned to whisper in her ear, and Rae smiled, pretending he was telling her a witty story though she knew something ugly was coming.

"I hate to see you make a fool of yourself in front of these people," he said. "Did it ever occur to you that heading cardiac anesthesia was not all Dr. Hartman was asked to do when he came to Berkeley? When was the last time we had a heart anesthesiologist up in OB, doing a section no less? And he seemed to have taken an inordinate amount of time getting my patient to sleep despite knowing there was fetal distress. He didn't even bother to help out with the baby's resuscitation until you had to call him over, Rae. Now tell me, do you find any of that peculiar? Looks like he's trying to make my Birth Center look bad, if you ask me. Just like you were, Rae."

Bo had definitely had a little too much to drink. But to Rae that didn't excuse his accusations against her and Sam. She was about to give him a piece of her mind, but stopped when she realized that Sam was standing behind her.

"False alarm," he said, patting his pager.

"Thank goodness." Rae smiled as Bo rose and walked back to his chair.

Despite her smile, Rae was disturbed by Bo's questions about Sam Hartman. Yet it still seemed to her that his medical care during Nola's C-section had been outstanding.

Bo spoke up again suddenly, loud enough for all to hear. "I'm surprised Howard Marvin isn't here tonight," he said.

Now what? Rae thought.

April turned from Bo and batted her long lashes at Marco. "Who's Howard Marvin?" she asked.

"He's the CEO of Perfect Health Plan," Bo said. "Isn't he, Marco?"

"And a ruthless son of a bitch," said Marco good-naturedly.

Rae vaguely recalled the name. But then, doctors rarely kept up with the identities of the CEOs of the health plans. The people who ran the health plans were like ghosts: never seen, never heard, even though their decisions affected the lives of millions of people.

"Ruthless, but a moneymaker, right, Marco?" Bo asked. He laughed. It was a derisive laugh, full of spite and anger. "I suppose you and Howard have never discussed trying to buy my Birth Center?"

"We fix hearts. We don't deliver babies, right, Sammy?" Marco asked calmly.

Rae's eyes darted from Bo to Marco to Sam. This felt like new territory.

"One has to be flexible these days, Marco," Sam said. He took another sip of wine.

Marco chuckled and raised his glass in a mock toast to Sam.

Bo returned his empty glass to the table. "Look, fellas, I know that Howard Marvin wants to get his hands on the Birth Center and turn it into a freestanding, mini-heart-hospital—"

"What?" Marco blurted.

"You heard me. A freestanding heart hospital."

"Ridiculous," Marco said.

"In addition to bypass surgeries," Bo continued, "there're millions to be made in the new, minimally invasive surgeries. We all know how advances in laparoscopic surgeries have opened up new markets for surgeons. So, all of you here tonight might as well know that Marco and Howard have a plan to buy me out and open up a new heart center."

Rae turned to Sam. "You know about this?"

"What's Bo talking about, Marco?" David interrupted. A murmur traveled around the table as Marco cleared his throat. "Maybe you ought to take Howard Marvin up on his offer if what you say is true, Bo."

"So you're finally admitting—" Bo began.

"I'm admitting nothing," Marco said. "All I'm saying is that someone like Howard could give you a pretty penny for that center of yours."

Rae leaned across the table to get a better view of Marco. "I thought you wanted my department closed down and the Birth Center left open," she said. "You're not making sense, Marco."

Bo answered first. "Marco wins out either way, Rae. He makes money if the board shuts down your unit and expands his heart program within the hospital. He also makes money if Howard Marvin gets his hands on my Birth Center and turns it into a freestanding, completely self-sufficient mini-heart-hospital. Isn't that right, Marco? No matter what happens to the rest of us, you come out just fine."

"Like I said, I have no plans outside the hospital," Marco said. "I just know a good offer when I see one."

Rae looked from Marco to Bo. Bo's stony expression convinced Rae that he spoke the truth, at least as he understood it. Next she turned to Sam, but he was busy eating his dinner. He appeared to be the only one in the room who was. Either he was starving, as he said, or he was hiding something. No one, she thought, was that unflappable.

"What else do you know about this, Bo?" Rae asked.

Bo sat back in his chair as comfortably as if he owned it. "Like I said," he began, "Howard Marvin has millions to throw at his idea for a dedicated heart hospital. What he doesn't have is the name recognition he'd need for it, or any good heart surgeons to staff the place. So he wants my Birth Center. The location is perfect, the size is right, and it's already been zoned as a medical facility. He wants to kick the pregnant patients out and bring in the heart cases. I don't care what Marco says. It's more than a rumor that Howard wants to partner with the hospital."

"The hospital?" Rae asked. "You mean Walker's in on this too?"

Bo shrugged. "Not that I know of. I don't think Howard has approached him yet. Howard doesn't like to make a move until he's lined up all his ducks. So they're working on me, trying to get me to sell. In the meantime, Howard has gotten Marco to join his team, and since Marco's the chief heart surgeon, Marco will run the thing. Marco gets to bill for his professional services and Howard will split the facility fee with the hospital—that is, if he can get Walker to go in on the deal. What's more, being the quintessential business man, Howard will also direct all of his Perfect Health heart cases—which currently go to other hospitals—to his new facility."

"Nonsense," Marco said. "Who else here has heard this baloney?"

"Is it true?" Rae asked. She wished it were. If Bo sold his Birth Center, all of her problems would be solved. The center would cease to exist, the patients would return to her maternity unit, and the hospital would have enough money to keep both departments open. And no ambulance transports.

"Sammy, will you please tell Bo that you and I have no deal with Howard Marvin?" Marco asked.

"I have no deal with Howard Marvin," Sam said. "But I would like to know how I can get some more of this osso buco."

April giggled. Rae felt a flash of irritation at Sam. Didn't he see how serious things had become? But as much as she wanted to believe Bo, his story raised more questions than it answered.

"Is there really such a thing as a freestanding heart hospital?" she asked. "I've never heard of one."

Bo poured himself another glass of wine.

"Haven't you had enough, Bo?" Marco asked.

"Howard's already partnered up with three other hospitals on the East Coast," Bo said. "Where do you think he's gotten all the money to start a heart center in Berkeley?"

"Marco," Rae said, "a freestanding heart center sounds as bad as a freestanding birth center. Personally, I would like to see you take over the Birth Center. That would take the pressure off of my department. You expand cardiac surgery across the street, leave my unit alone, and the OB patients would come back to Berkeley Hills."

"I see you have it all figured—" Bo began.

"But," Rae continued, "I can't see a cardiologist doing a cardiac cath in a minifacility, and then winding up needing an emergency bypass surgery over at Berkeley Hills. The patient could die of a heart attack during the ambulance transfer." She thought again of Nola's baby.

Marco crossed his fingers together and rested his chin on the back of his hands. "Ah, you weren't listening, Rae," he said. "That's the beauty of Howard's plan, if indeed he has a plan," Marco said. "You see, unlike the Birth Center, which does a good job of glorified home births but can't do C-sections, a freestanding heart center would be prepared to do everything—including open heart surgery—right there on the premises." He cut his green eyes to Bo before continuing. "Howard's freestanding heart center would be on the cutting edge of medicine, not a throwback to medieval times."

Rae turned to Bo. "Maybe you ought to sell Howard Marvin the Birth Center, Bo," she said. "Everybody wins that way. Later, when the laws change and allow you to build an operating room on the premises, you open up another birth center."

"I already have a birth center and it is not for sale," Bo said.

"Why can't you do cesareans in the Birth Center?" Sam interrupted.

"Because that's the law," Marco said. "But," he continued, "if the opportunity to start a freestanding cardiac center did arise, and someone like Howard Marvin made the offer Bo just outlined, I'd be the first to jump at it. And I hope I'd have your vote, Rae."

"Twice," Rae said vehemently.

Bo slammed his empty glass down and rose angrily.

"Please, Bo," Marco said. "Sit back down, will you? I'm sorry. I haven't been a very good host. I invited you all here for a good time. Medicine's got us all a little twitchy. We shouldn't let hospital politics have us going off half-cocked."

"I need some air," Bo said. He tossed his napkin on the table and headed in the direction of the living room.

"Dessert! Everyone to the living room!" Marcella sang. She had entered the room as quietly as a ghost.

Everyone got up from the table except for Rae. She rapped her fingernails on the glass, still reeling from Bo's revelation about Howard Marvin and Perfect Health Plan. Was Bo telling the truth? Was Marco?

She felt a gentle tap on her shoulder. "Please don't jump to any conclusions about April and me until I've had a chance to speak with you in private," Sam said.

Rae stared blankly at him. His date was the last thing on her mind.

"Is Bo telling the truth?" she asked finally. "Did you leave Boston for a reason other than to do cardiac anesthesia at Berkeley Hills Hospital?"

"I sure hope so," Sam said, and then strolled away.

Now what kind of answer was that? she asked herself. Why was he always so elusive? Lost in her thoughts, she drifted to the living room and out onto the balcony. Even the jeweled city was completely hidden in the fog. She didn't feel much like looking at the skyline anyway. She needed time to think.

Minutes later, she heard footsteps behind her. She turned and saw Bo staring at her. He joined her at the railing and stared out into space.

"I was standing here thinking about the dinner conversation," Rae said. "For what it's worth, I believe you, Bo. I believe Howard Marvin made you that offer. Of all the things we've been through, you've never lied to me. I don't see why you'd start lying to me now."

"Do you believe what I said about Marco?" he asked. "Or Sam Hartman?"

Rae sighed and remained silent.

"Frankly, I don't care what you believe," Bo said when she didn't answer. "But I'm not going to let anybody buy me out or kick me out."

Rae turned and faced Bo. "What is that supposed to mean?" she snapped.

"Oh, come on, Rae. You're after my Birth Center. It's all so pathetically obvious." He ran his finger down her bare arm. "Nice dress," he said. "I never counted on you sleeping your way into their camp."

Rae slapped away Bo's hand. "Get out of my sight," she hissed.

"Remember, just leave the Birth Center alone," he said, then turned and walked away.

Marco came out to stand next to Rae. "My, my," Marco said. "Bo didn't look very happy."

"Let me ask you again," Rae said, ignoring his remark, "does Walker know about Howard Marvin wanting to turn the Birth Center into a mini-heart-hospital?"

Marco shook his head.

"Don't lie to me, Marco," Rae warned.

"Not as far as I know, okay?" Marco said. "He's your good buddy, you ask him. But if I were you, I'd concentrate on getting Bo to sell the Birth Center. What with the bad baby thing heating up, Bo's best chance at getting a good price is now."

"It would be easier for one of us to jump off this balcony and fly like Superman," Rae said.

"Then Bo's an idiot," Marco said.

They stood in silence a moment. Finally she said, "You checked out the medical charts on four of Bo's patients."

Marco leaned his arms on the rail. "Isn't this a beautiful night?" he asked.

Rae sighed. "I saw your request for the charts myself," she said flatly.

"I didn't request any charts," Marco insisted. He turned to her. "Who said I did? What charts?"

"Bo's charts," Rae said. "You signed out some of Bo's charts."

"What would I need with charts on pregnant ladies?"

"That's what I want to know," Rae said. "And I'd also like to know what you did with them."

"What I did with four pregnant women?" Marco laughed. "Oh, come on!"

"I want to know where you put those charts," Rae said.

"I said I didn't have any charts, and if you saw a request, then somebody forged my name."

"Like who?"

"Look, Rae," Marco said, "you're going to believe what you want to believe. There is absolutely no reason why I would want any charts on Bo's patients. I have my hands full keeping up with my own patients. And for the record, okay, yes, I've spoken to Howard Marvin. But right now, it's all been just talk, understand. We can't do a thing until Bo sells the Birth Center. But I'm not going to sit on my hands until that happens, okay?"

Finally, Rae thought, Marco was being honest with her.

"And Sam? Is he on this too?"

Marco sighed. "What do you think?" he asked.

Rae turned back toward the bay. Despite the fact that she, too, wanted the Birth Center closed down, she felt saddened by the politics of it all. "So it's babies versus bypass surgeries—the beginning of life against the end of life, is that it?" she asked.

"Honey, come help pour the grappa," Marcella called out.

Marco patted Rae's shoulder. "Let's go inside," he said, pointing toward the living room.

"You know, Marco," Rae commented, "somebody at that table was lying."

"Welcome to the business side of managed care," he replied.

Inside the living room, Marcella offered Rae a dainty dessert plate upon which a rectangular cut of tiramisu had been placed. "Marco says tiramisu now, bypass surgery later," Marcella said lightheartedly.

Rae smiled and thanked her as she accepted her plate, and sat on the piano bench. She didn't feel much like eating dessert, but out of politeness she took a bite of the rich, sweet confection. "I'm surprised Marco doesn't weigh five hundred pounds," she said. "This is good enough to eat every night."

Marcella frowned. "Does April work in your hospital?" she asked suddenly.

"I think I would have seen her if she did," Rae said.

"Are you sure?" Marcella's expression was grave and Rae saw fear behind her dark blue eyes. Did she think that April would be Marco's next conquest? But April had come with Sam. Why did women let men determine their thoughts and feelings? Rae asked herself wearily. Why did everybody substitute fear for love?

"Don't you think she'd be a little hard to miss?" Rae asked.

She saw Marcella's face soften. She smiled. "I guess you're right," she replied.

Just then, Sam strolled up to the piano. "That stuff can kill you," he said. "Forget the grappa. I suggest chasing it down with a shot of Drano."

He lifted Rae's plate from the bench, placed it on a coaster on top of the piano, and sat down next to her. The seat was big enough for three people, but Rae scooted to her right to give Sam more room. "I'd hate to give April the wrong idea," Rae said sweetly.

Two couples were slow dancing across the hardwood floor. A three-piece jazz ensemble played in the far corner.

"Forget about April," Sam said roughly. "Let's dance. I won't step on your feet, promise," he added more gently.

Before Rae could formulate a protest, Sam drew her onto the floor and circled his arms around her. Perhaps she should have pulled back but it had been a long time since a man had held her. She had forgotten how good it felt. Giving herself a mental shake, Rae reminded herself of her plan.

"What's the scuttlebutt on Howard Marvin?" she asked. Even in her heels she was some six inches shorter than Sam, so she had to raise her head to speak to him. She found him gazing down at her with those lake-blue eyes, a half smile on his lips.

"I never heard his name until tonight," Sam said.

"Really? I mean, you and Marco are good friends, right? This thing about a freestanding cardiac unit is a big deal. If one did open, and Marco ran it, it makes sense he would want you to be chief of anesthesia."

"I would hope so," Sam said.

Rae was tiring of Sam's elusiveness. Bluntly she asked, "Does that mean he discussed Howard with you or not?" She felt herself tensing up even as the music grew softer. Marco had turned down the lights so that everybody was framed by a soft glow.

Sam waited a beat and said, "Marco only tells me what he thinks I need to know. But I want *you* to know about April."

"I don't care about April," Rae hissed. "I care about what happened to a couple of babies this morning. I also care about a couple of paramedics who I know weren't straight with me."

Rae stopped dancing and pulled away from Sam. "Did they say anything to you about what happened to Nola this morning?"

"Nola?" Sam asked. He pulled her back to him and resumed the dance.

"The Blessed Mother."

"Ah. No, they didn't say anything. What was there to say about her? She said it all, don't you think?"

He chuckled but Rae didn't feel like laughing. "Then why were they lying?" she asked.

"They were lying?" Sam echoed.

Rae's frustration grew. She had no proof that the paramedics had lied to her. All she had were her suspicions and it would be premature to tell them to Sam. She sighed. "Okay, so tell me about April," she said.

"Why would the paramedics lie to you?" Sam asked.

"So now you don't want to tell me about April?" Rae replied, exasperated.

"Very much so," Sam said. "But there's not a whole lot to tell. She's a clerk in the cardiac cath unit. She started two weeks ago. Already Marco's addicted to her. He had to have her at the party. But he thought it would be better if I brought her and she looked like my date, than if she showed up alone."

Surprisingly, Rae felt relieved that April was another one of Marco's conquests. Even though who Sam took to a party didn't matter to her, he had asked to take her first. It was the principle of the thing, she told herself.

"Marco's the reason why I came to Berkeley," Sam said. "I owe him a few favors." He held Rae closer. "But I'm glad I came," he said.

His hand now rested on the small of her back. The same hand that had given Nola's baby another chance at life. Rae closed her eyes and recalled how Sam had squeezed the breathing bag to infuse air into the baby's lungs. He had restored life to that baby as if his own life depended on it.

Yes, it felt good being held by Sam. Everything in the room had mellowed—the people, the lights, the conversation, and most important, the tension that had been stirred up at the dinner table.

Why not enjoy the end of a slow dance with Sam? He felt good and he smelled good and she loved being held.

"Rae, the song's over," Sam said.

Rae opened her eyes with a start. To her chagrin she realized that she had been leaning against him even though the other couples had left the dance floor. Looking up, she encountered his amused gaze. He took more time than necessary to let her go. "Did I fall asleep?" she asked, too embarrassed to acknowledge what had really happened.

"Do you usually sleep standing up?" Sam asked with a laugh.

"Well, I—" Rae began, feeling her face turn hot. But before she finished her sentence, April marched up to them. By the flushed look on her face she was obviously upset. "Marcella's giving me the evil eye," she said as she took Sam's arm.

"Go on," Rae said, happy for the distraction.

Rae found Marco and thanked him for inviting her to the party. "You and Sammy looked pretty chummy out there on the dance floor," Marco said as he wrapped her cape around her shoulders. "I hear Bo thought the same thing."

Rae tensed. That was all she needed. It was going to be impossible for her to reason with Bo and get him to shut down the Birth Center. When he was in a jealous rage, he had always been impossible, Rae recalled. But for him to act this way about Sam was ridiculous—it had been a full year, for God's sake!

"I hope you told Bo that Sam was just being a nice guy?" she asked. "As you know, he does favors for a lot of his friends—and his friends' girlfriends."

She looked at him challengingly. "Of course," he said, acknowledging her meaning. "We all count on Sammy to do the right thing."

Just then Rae's beeper went off. "There's a phone in the back hall," Marco said.

The page was from Bernie, who said she was in medical records and she thought Rae should review the charts first thing in the morning. There was something in them that had Bernie very worried.

"I'll come down now," Rae said.

Bernie reminded her that the hour was late and that Rae had already missed a night's worth of sleep. She looked at her watch.

"It's only a quarter to eleven," she said. "Besides, I could use the company."

In fact, she felt very alone. Loneliness, she had decided, seemed to have become a permanent visitor in her life. Damn that Sam Hartman, she thought. Why did he have to ask her to dance? All it did was stir up old feelings.

She hung up the phone and headed toward the front door.

Outside, the parking attendant handed Rae the car keys. "Well, did it turn out to be a nice evening?" he asked.

"It's not over yet," she said.

She pushed aside her thoughts about Sam and April and Marco, about Howard Marvin and Perfect Health Plan. Bernie was waiting for her to discuss the charts that might shed some light on Nola's baby. Nothing was more important than that right now.

Still, she was surprised to catch herself wondering as she sped back to the hospital how long it would be until someone held her as tenderly as Sam had.

# 12

"HEY, WAKE UP, SLEEPYHEAD," RAE SAID UPON ENTERING THE physician's file room and seeing Bernie slumped over a pile of charts. Yvonne, the head clerk, had long since gone home and only Rae and Bernie were in the room. The fluorescent lights made the file room appear as bright as it had been during the daytime. That was one of the problems with hospitals, Rae thought. Unless you were by a window, or walked outdoors, you could spend a lifetime inside and never know if it was day or night. But then, illness was a twenty-four-hour business.

Bernie reached up and pretended to straighten out her nursing cap. "It's called meditation, sugar."

Rae plopped down in the chair next to her. "So, what did you find?"

Bernie sat up and stretched her arms over her head. "I think Bo's the one who needs to do the explaining," she said gravely. "These four charts belong to patients who started off in the Birth Center but who got transferred over here. And each patient had Bo for her doctor."

Rae noted that Bernie had the original charts in front of her. "Yvonne was supposed to make copies," Rae said.

"Did you hear me, Rae? Bo was the doctor for all of these cases."

"I know, Bernie," Rae said, stifling a yawn. She'd check her box later for the copies of the charts.

"Then what in the world am I doing here!" Bernie cried.

"But I don't know why the patients were transferred over here," Rae said. "Bo had the charts when I came down here this afternoon. I also don't have a clue what happened to the patients, other than the fact that the babies had low Apgar scores."

"Well, that's more like it," Bernie said, feigning anger. Opening up the first chart, she said, "All patients were transferred over here for a cesarean for CPD. I guess there are lots of big-head babies trying to deliver over there. Most patients only got to four or five centimeters—"

Rae opened her mouth to ask a question but Bernie cut her off. "No, there were no signs of fetal distress in the Birth Center," she said, "if that's what you were thinking."

Rae frowned. "Are you sure?" she asked, thumbing through the charts herself.

"Positivo."

"But what happened when they arrived here—like Nola, like Meredith?" Rae asked.

"Now you're talking, darlin'," Bernie said, her eyes lighting up. " 'Cause maybe I'm going to keep my job in this joint after all."

"Oh?"

Bernie patted the charts tenderly. "Each patient arrived here with a fetal heart rate going south."

"But the heart rates were normal at the Birth Center?"

"At least the last recorded heart rate was. But the way I see it, CPD does not cause low heart rates."

Nodding, Rae was thinking the same thing. "And Bo delivered all of them?" she asked.

"Every last one."

Rae thumbed through the charts. "What about any other shoulder dystocias? Or nuchal cords?"

"No," Bernie answered quickly.

Filled with weariness, Rae ran both hands through her hair. The adrenaline she had felt at the beginning of Marco's party had drained out of her body. Even the knowledge that she had four more cases of babies with normal heart rates in the Birth Center and terrible heart rates in her labor suite was not enough to give her a second wind. She simply could not press on. She felt about as sharp as a doorknob. Her intention had been to give the charts a thorough going over, like a worried mother does when seeing her baby for the very first time. But it would have to wait.

"I'm about to fall on my face," Rae said. She walked over to her file box. It was empty. She turned to Yvonne's desk and noted that Yvonne had written a note to herself to photocopy charts for Dr. Duprey and Dr. Michaels. Rae hesitated, and then said, "I wish I could hide these, but if the patients came into the ER tonight . . ." Her voice trailed off. She had no choice but to place them back on Yvonne's desk for now.

"I'll be back first thing tomorrow morning, Bernie. Who knows, maybe the four other charts will be here too."

"I'll drop back by on my lunch break," Bernie said. "Who knows, maybe the person who stole the charts will start to feel a little guilty in the wee hours of the morning."

Rae could barely keep her eyes open and she still had her drive home. "Let me know if they show up," she said.

"You want me to call you if they do?" Bernie asked.

"I don't think I'll be able to answer the phone," Rae said. "By three o'clock in the morning, I hope to be in a coma."

"Then I'll put them in your box if they show up. Meanwhile, what do you think about Bo being the attending physician for all eight cases? I mean, he's accusing you of screwing up and he's the one who looks like he has some explaining to do."

"I was thinking the same thing," Rae said. "That's why I'm coming back here tomorrow to take a closer look at these charts. I want to review the patients' histories and the ambulance reports and see if there's something else going on—to see if there is some tie-in between what happened to those women and what happened to Nola and Meredith."

"But you haven't even found a tie-in for Nola and Meredith."

"You don't have to remind me," Rae answered.

Bernie smiled. "I'll call you later, Rae."

Rae and Bernie left the file room together and stopped in front of the elevators. "Oh, I almost forgot," Rae began. "Have you heard anything about the heart program wanting to open up a new free-standing heart center? You're pretty tight with Dusty and maybe she said something to you?"

"A what?" Bernie asked. Bernie shook her head back and forth.

"A freestanding heart center? Just how many glasses of vino did they pour down your throat at Marco's?"

Rae smiled as Bernie walked into the elevator. Bernie's expression said clearly she thought Rae had lost her mind. "That was my reaction exactly," Rae said.

"What will they think of next?" Bernie said as the doors closed in front of her.

How about a way to save Nola's baby, thought Rae as she walked across the checkered hallway toward the emergency room exit.

Inside the emergency room, she tried to avoid running into anybody, since it was still Friday night and, as usual, the place was in overdrive. Doctors and nurses rushed here and there attending to patients. A big man with a very pink face complained of chest pains. A frail old woman shook from head to foot and refused to answer the nurse's questions. A teenage girl writhed around on her gurney and complained of stomach pains.

The nurse attending to the girl was Sylvia Height, the same nurse who had attended Meredith Bey. Obviously, like Bernie, Sylvia worked the night shift. She saw Rae at that same time and waved. "How's the baby?" she asked.

Rae gave the thumbs-up sign. She was too tired to do anything else. Sylvia returned the gesture and then focused her attention on the girl.

"Hey, lady, watch out!" a voice called out. Rae saw a large cart filled with IV bags coming toward her. She sidestepped just in time to avoid getting hit.

"Didn't see you there," said a pocked-face orderly.

"No problem." Rae watched as the man pushed the cart to the back of the emergency room until it was out of sight. Seeing the IV bags only reminded her of Nola's outburst and all of the other events of the day. Had she imagined them or had they all happened?

The fog blurred everything outside of the hospital. It was so thick she couldn't see the lights of the city across the bay. She could barely make out the parking lot so she made sure to look both ways before she crossed the street. She had not forgotten how Arnie had almost run her over in broad daylight.

She tightened her cape around her shoulders and wished she had on her more sensible pumps instead of her high heels. Her Porsche was parked near the front of the lot. Ahead of her she saw a man approaching. His confident gait looked familiar. Sam, she thought with surprise.

Still dressed in his tuxedo, he smiled as he approached her.

"What are you doing here?" she asked. She remembered how her face pressed against Sam's chest even after the jazz trio had stopped playing. Now she did her best to hide her embarrassment.

"I came looking for you," he said.

He gazed at her in a straightforward manner. No pretension, no beating around the bush. It was as if they had known each other for years and there was no reason for him to offer an explanation.

He looked behind her. "Is that yours?" he asked, nodding at her Porsche.

She nodded back.

"Marco said you were headed to the hospital," he said.

"I got paged. What's your excuse?"

She didn't mean to sound rude, but she felt distinctly uncomfortable around him. She felt flattered by his attention, but there were too many reasons why an involvement with Sam was a bad idea, not the least of which, she admitted to herself, was that she didn't trust him.

"I didn't mean that," she said when she saw his hurt expression, "but, Sam, although I'm flattered by your interest, my plate is so full right now I barely have time to catch my breath."

Sam was still smiling at her and she felt annoyed. He wasn't taking her seriously. Typical man, she thought.

"I don't think you're paying attention," she said.

"How about joining me for coffee in the morning?"

She shook her head, even though she had to give him an A for effort.

She walked over to her car door. "I've got to be in medical records in the morning," she said.

Again Sam smiled. "I have a few charts waiting for my signature. Maybe we can catch up on a little charting together and then get some breakfast."

Rae sighed loudly. She didn't care if Sam heard her or not. "You would really meet me here at seven o'clock?" she asked.

"Seven's a little early—especially for a Saturday morning," he said. "How about ten? That's much more civilized."

Now Rae felt really annoyed. Did Sam want to meet her or not? "Saturday, Monday, Friday—they're all the same to me. Especially when I've got a bad baby up in the unit."

The smile had left Sam's face. Rae saw that he had removed his bow tie and his dress shirt was opened at the collar. The beginning of an after-five shadow was beginning to show on his face, making him look even more handsome.

"Sounds to me like medicine is a major part of your life," he said.

It was more an of observation than a judgment, yet Rae immediately felt defensive. "Medicine *is* my life," she said.

She made this last statement with a conviction that surprised even her. But she meant it, there was no denying that. To Sam—to anyone—she might have seemed haughty, even self-righteous, but that was Sam's problem, not hers. Her decision had been made twenty-five years ago. And after a day like she had just had, she was not about to change her mind.

Unfortunately, she could not explain any of this to Sam. He seemed more interested in her than in Nola's baby. But being interested in her meant he had to be interested in what had happened to Nola that morning. As far as Rae was concerned, she was connected to all the babies she delivered by a cord of her own.

"So, what did you do with April?" she asked.

"Oh, I dropped her off at her place. Seems the missus found out she worked at the hospital and the two of them got into a little tussle. Marcella asked me to take her home, since I brought her. You weren't there anymore, so I figured why not?"

At her car door Rae said, "One more thing, Sam. I've been wondering about something. Why were you at Nola's surgery? You belong in the basement with the heart cases."

"You make them sound like they're an inferior class of operations," Sam said laughingly as he held the door open for her.

"That's not what I meant—" Rae started to explain.

Sam waved her off. "I know that. Believe me, I haven't done a C-section in ten years. But apparently everybody on OB was busy and I was the only one stuffing my mouth with a jelly donut when the call came down that you all needed some help in your unit."

He paused and then said, "I'm glad I came, Rae. I've never seen anyone do a section as quickly as you did this morning."

"Fast, but not happy," Rae said, starting to close the door.

But Sam held fast and prevented the door from closing. "So, about tomorrow morning, do we have a date?"

"You just don't give up, do you?"

"Not usually," Sam smiled.

Rae turned the key in the ignition. The engine roared. "Seven o'clock sharp," she said.

"Seven o'clock it is," Sam said.

He won't be there, Rae told herself as she watched his reflection grow smaller in her rearview mirror. But she would be. Something was in those charts that would help her. Certainly she didn't need Sam's help in determining what that something was.

At home, she opened her violin case and played for a few restful minutes. The tune was Chopin's "Nocturne in E-flat Major," a melancholy number that was one of her mother's favorites. Once Leopold was breathing heavily at the foot of her bed, she placed her violin back into its case and climbed under the covers.

Her body melted into the mattress. Rae wondered, as the blankets warmed her, if she would ever be able to get up again. But the veil of a deep sleep descended upon her before she could answer the question.

# 13

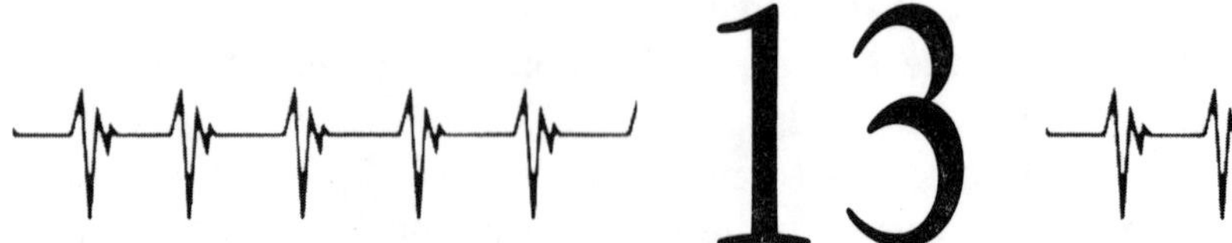

RAE AWOKE WITH A START. SWEAT RINGED HER NECK AND pooled between her breasts. Had she had a bad dream? she wondered.

The nightstand clock read 5 A.M. Outside her window a full moon hovered halfway down the sky and cast a silver streak of light across the black waters of the bay. Leopold breathed noisily at the foot of her bed. But not even Leopold's sentinel position could protect her from a sense of dread that someone—someplace, somehow, somewhere—had intentionally harmed Nola's baby.

She threw off the comforter and within ten minutes was showered and outfitted in jeans, light-blue cashmere turtleneck, and short black leather jacket. "I'll be back by breakfast," she told Leopold on her way out. Her plan was to review the patients' charts before Sam arrived to medical records. This time she wanted to read them without any distractions. The charts, she believed, would shed light on yesterday's disasters.

She gunned down I-80. Since it was early Saturday morning, she practically had the road to herself. Her Porsche roared past the fountain at the Marin Circle and then up the steep ascent to Berkeley Hills Hospital.

The emergency room had emptied out of patients. But Sylvia Height was still there, and she sat on a stool next to a clerk arranging an ambulance transport from a nursing home.

Rae waved to Sylvia as she passed. "You here again, Dr. Duprey?" Sylvia asked.

"Can't get enough of this place," Rae joked.

Inside medical records, she passed by the unmanned reception desk. At that time of the morning, Rae was the only person in the room. The staff would arrive at six. Suddenly, she paused. Something seemed off, she thought. Something *felt* very different. The door to the file room, directly in front of her. Yes, that was it. It was closed. Never, in her ten years at Berkeley Hills Hospital, had she encountered a closed door to the file room.

She opened the door slowly. It took a while for her eyes to adjust to the scene in front of her. Charts were strewn about everywhere. Chairs had been flipped over onto their sides. Phones were off the hook and Yvonne's computer screen was cracked.

Yvonne! Rae thought. But then she remembered: Yvonne and the rest of the staff were off duty at this hour. Still standing at the doorway, she listened carefully, wondering for the first time if she might be in danger. Was the person who had done this still lurking about? But she heard and saw no one and finally took a deep breath. Anger replaced fear.

Quickly she walked over to the phone on Yvonne's desk. She had to call security. She picked up the receiver, and started to dial the hospital's operator. And then she stopped as she felt her heart freeze in place. For on the floor, in the middle of the room, was Bernie's old-fashioned nurse's hat.

Every muscle in Rae's body tightened. Fear prevented her next breath. She dropped the phone in the cradle. She had a view of the entire room except for the far north corner hidden by a file rack. Slowly she made her way over, and stopped when she saw Bernie's body, clad in white surgical scrubs, lying on the floor. She was flat on her back, legs all akimbo.

"Bernie!" Rae shouted. She rushed to Bernie's side and dropped to her knees. Immediately she could see the swollen purple bruises on her friend's face.

Anger propelled her into action. Careful not to move Bernie's head, Rae placed an ear to her nose to listen and feel for any signs of breathing. At the same time she looked at Bernie's chest and waited to see it rise. Satisfied that she was breathing on her own, Rae next felt along her right carotid artery. The pulse was thready but present.

Rae's own breathing pattern came shallowly, and her heart

pounded at a rapid rate. But to give in to her emotions would make her useless. Bernie needed prompt medical care, not a friend's pity. And then she saw the ugly tears and purple bruises around her neck. Only human fingers could have left marks like that.

Her first call was to the emergency room. Sylvia answered. "This is Dr. Duprey," Rae said rapidly. It was a struggle to control her voice, but she had to in order to make sure Sylvia understood her message the first time. "I'm in the physician file room of medical records. Get your team here right away. Bernie's been attacked."

As she spoke, she feared she might break into tears.

"We're on our way," Sylvia said.

Rae next dialed hospital security. Her hands shook so that she had to punch in the numbers twice. The man who answered the phone sounded quite young. He kept asking Rae to spell her last name. "Damn it!" she finally said. "Just get your ass over here!"

At the same time the emergency team exploded into the room. Leading the pack was Sylvia Height, followed by two more nurses and Dr. Everett Lyon, a stocky ER doc who wore battle fatigues to work. Behind Everett, two male orderlies pushed a gurney.

Rae slammed down the phone. "She's over here!" she shouted as she ran to the far corner. She almost tripped over charts along the way.

"Jesus," Sylvia said as she dropped to her knees and quickly wrapped a blood pressure cuff around Bernie's arm. "What happened?"

Dr. Lyon knelt across from Sylvia and lowered his right ear to Bernie's nose. After checking for her carotid pulse, he said to Sylvia, "What you got?" But even before Sylvia answered, he lifted Bernie's eyelids. From his coat pocket he removed a penlight and peered into her pupils.

"There're those marks on her neck," Rae said, worried about the condition of Bernie's brain as well as what she suspected was internal bleeding.

"What the hell happened?" Everett asked as he snapped off the penlight and began to palpate Bernie's abdomen.

"Pressure's sixty over forty," Sylvia announced.

Another nurse had already started a large-bore IV line in Bernie's left arm. "You certainly called it, Rae," Everett said as he helped the staff raise Bernie onto the gurney. "Her belly's soft and I think she's bleeding inside—"

"I'll call the OR," Rae said, rushing to the phone.

"And make sure they find the best goddamn general surgeon and neurosurgeon they can get!" Everett shouted after her.

The OR line rang and rang. "Damn it, somebody answer the phone!" Rae hissed, but just as she was about to hang up and call the operator, she heard someone pick up the line.

"This is Dr. Duprey," Rae said, and she quickly outlined the situation to the nurse.

"You just get her down here to me," said the nurse, "and we'll take care of the rest. Bernie's my walking buddy. I'm not going to let anything happen to her."

"The OR team's waiting," Rae said to Everett when she returned to the gurney. She held on to Bernie's hand, which was cold and clammy. Rae hoped that the liter of normal saline running into her IV line would sustain her until they got her downstairs.

"We'll run her through the CT scanner and find out just how bad that subdural is," Everett said, strapping Bernie onto the gurney. "That'll just take a couple of minutes. She must have put up one hell of a fight. Whoever did this to her had no plans for her to walk out of this hospital."

Rae tried to tune out Everett, but his words broke through her professional defenses. Not Bernie, she thought woefully. This could not be happening to Bernie. She would need a hole drilled into her skull to evacuate the clot pressing against her brain. At the same time, she'd be sliced open from pubic bone to breastbone in order to search for the bleeding internal organ that had caused her blood pressure to bottom out. Hopefully that organ would be her spleen, because a person could live without that. But what injury had her brain sustained? And if she did wake up, would she still be *Bernie?*

"I know she's going to make it," Rae said out loud.

"Better call the blood bank too," Everett said, as if Rae had not spoken. "Tell them to cross-match eight units of packed cells. It looks like she's in for one hell of a morning."

After Bernie was carried out of the room, Rae slumped into a chair and placed her head in her hands. If only she hadn't agreed to let Bernie help her review charts on Bo's patients. If only she hadn't gotten her involved in any of this. Bernie had not made any promises to Heidi. Bernie just wanted to keep her job. And now she was on her way to the operating room.

Rae crossed her arms over her shoulders and rocked back and forth in her chair. She had wanted to accompany Bernie to CT, and then to the OR. But Everett said she had to stay behind to give the report. It had taken every shred of her willpower to let go of Bernie's hand and let them wheel her out of the file room.

She shook her head numbly and finally opened her eyes. On the floor lay her friend's hat. She rose to retrieve it and returned to her chair. Who had done this terrible thing? she asked herself as her eyes scanned the room. And why? Think, Rae, think, she admonished herself. But she felt too stunned to reason clearly.

A sudden wave of anger swept through her. She balled her fists at her sides. Bernie was not only her friend but a friend to a lot of people. Why would someone beat up a nurse reviewing charts in medical records? And beat up Bernie, of all people, who had no enemies.

So why had this happened? Was it a random act, or was it—

She turned her head slowly in the direction of Dr. Marco Donavelli's file box. The day before it had been empty. But it wasn't empty anymore. Even from where she stood she could see the tab of each folder. Four tabs. Four charts. The same four missing charts from the day before?

Inside her purse was the list she had compiled from her visit with Leslie. Her hands shook as she compared the names on her list with the names on the four patient charts. And sure enough, they matched those in Marco's box. Bo's patients.

Her hands no longer shook. For a few seconds she stood there as cold and as lifeless as a statue. There was only one explanation she believed—was willing to believe: the person who returned the charts was the same person who had tried to kill Bernie.

But it couldn't have been Marco, she told herself. Not Marco . . .

Rae removed the four charts from Marco's box. Her own file box was only two feet away. She stuffed them in, next to the other four charts that Yvonne had given her the day before.

"Are you Dr. Rae Duprey?"

Rae turned and faced a young man dressed in the hospital's black security guard uniform. The voice was the same one she had heard on the phone. Although he stood almost seven feet tall, he looked barely old enough to drive a car, let alone protect anyone.

"I hope you didn't move anything?" he asked sternly.

"I thought the security office was only fifty yards away," Rae snapped. "Where were you guys?"

She watched his eyes move slowly over the room's destruction. From the look on his face Rae could tell that he too was overwhelmed by the enormity of the damage. Hospitals were supposed to be safe places, hardly the sites of muggings and beatings.

"Look, my best friend was the one who got beat up here," she said in a more conciliatory tone. "She's on the way to the OR. I want to be there with her."

The guard scratched a few notes across his clipboard. "The police will be here in five minutes," he said. His boyish face darkened into a frown.

"I can be back in two minutes," Rae said. "All I need to do is run down and check on her."

The guard waved her off. "I know what I'm doing," he said.

Rae sighed. She had little tolerance for bravado. But alienating him would only make matters worse. So she slumped down in her chair and gave him a blow-by-blow account of what happened.

"Anything else?" the guard asked.

"What else do you need?" she asked irritably. She'd had enough of his questions. "Someone beat her up—someone tried to *kill* her." Even as she spoke the words, she had a hard time believing them herself. "Can I just go now?"

Just then there was a knock on the door and two policemen walked into the room. They were dressed in navy-blue Berkeley Police Department uniforms.

The older of the two was a black man. His hair was cut close to his head and wisps of gray peppered his mustache. He smiled at Rae as he entered, like a father to a daughter. The other cop, a much shorter white man, had red hair brushed straight back. His square jaw jutted out slightly, his thin lips pursed tight above a thick chin, and he walked way too stiffly for someone who appeared to be in his early thirties.

"I'm Sergeant Lane," said the black cop, offering his hand. His grip was firm and reassuring, the grip of a man comfortable with himself and his ability. "And that quiet fellow there—" He paused to nod in the direction of the younger cop who had already started to look around. "That's Officer Bruce Mailer."

Rae started to extend her hand to Mailer, but obviously, social etiquette was the last thing on his mind.

"You're the doctor who found the victim?" Lane asked.

Rae shook her head numbly. "Her name's Bernie. I found Bernie."

She waited for the sergeant to look around the room. Finally he let out a long whistle. "My kids delivered at this hospital," he said. "But that was way before your time, right, doc?"

"You say she was your friend?" Mailer asked as he stood over Bernie's hat.

Rae cut her eyes to Mailer's thin face. "My *best* friend," she said.

"Well now," Lane said, stuffing his hands in his pockets. Rae noted the thick swollen knuckles of arthritis. "How about we all go out into the main room. I noticed a bunch of empty desks. We can talk there."

"Can I at least call the OR?" Rae asked. "All I want to know is how she's doing."

"It'll be easier if you just cooperate with us now," Mailer replied coldly.

They led her to the reception desk. Sergeant Lane pulled out a chair for her and then took one for himself. As Officer Mailer paced the floor, Lane proceeded to ask Rae some general questions—who she was, how long she had been on staff, how she happened upon Bernie's unconscious body.

"Five-thirty in the morning is awfully early to sign charts," Mailer said.

"So?" she asked defensively.

"Why don't you tell us what happened," Lane said. "From the top—"

"I just told everything to the security guard. He wrote it all down."

"Might be easier just to tell us what happened," Lane said.

It took Rae two minutes to tell her story, down to the detail of picking up Bernie's hat. What she didn't tell them was how she moved the missing charts from Marco's box to her file box.

"Now can I go?" Rae asked when she finished.

Suddenly, there was another burst of activity at the door. Entering the room were five men, some dressed in police uniforms and some in orange jumpsuits. Two of them began to stretch bright yellow tape here and there and others prowled around, pointing and murmuring.

"Well, I don't see why we need to hold you here any longer," Lane said as he rose from his chair. "But if you can think of anything else, call me." He jotted his number down on a piece of paper and handed it to Rae.

She stuffed the paper into the back pocket of her jeans and shook Lane's hand again. Mailer had skipped the good-byes and walked off to join the crime team.

"I still need to review those charts," Rae said. "But they're in there." She pointed to the roped off area.

Lane scratched the back of his neck. "Jesus, we're going to have you doctors going in and out of here all day," he said.

"Probably," Rae said.

Lane pulled at his mustache, then called out to one of the men dressed in an orange jumpsuit. "Let the good doc in," he said. "She's just doing her job."

"And I'm trying to do mine, damn it," the man said. He gave Rae a scornful look. She gave him one right back, then picked up her charts and headed out of the file room.

After returning to the same desk where Lane and Mailer had interviewed her, she set down the eight charts and called the operating room. Bernie, she was told, was just being wheeled in. The nurse with whom Rae spoke advised her not to come visit just then. There were enough people on the scene. Two neurosurgeons, two general surgeons, two vascular surgeons, and of course, a slew of nurses and scrub techs.

Rae thanked the nurse and hung up the phone. She felt devastated, but the nurse was right. The last thing the staff needed was another body getting in the way.

Angrily, she sat down in the chair and began to comb through the eight charts as if her life depended on it. First she reviewed the four she and Bernie had gone over, then the four that had suddenly shown up. But to her dismay, they revealed nothing new. The babies' heart rates were normal at the Birth Center *and* during the ambulance transports. But they were in the toilet by the time the patients arrived at her labor suite. How could that be? Did something happen between the ambulance drop-off and the labor deck? Was Bo right after all? Was everything sheer coincidence?

Well, if there was another explanation, Rae thought, looking at her handwritten notes, the charts certainly did not reveal it. And she had been so sure that they would. Feeling defeated, she closed the last folder and tried to concentrate on her next step. But with Bernie's life on the line, Rae found it hard to think at all.

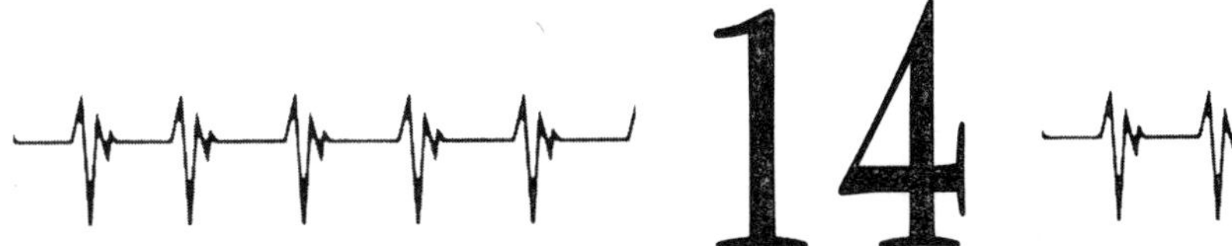

# 14

AT HALF PAST SIX, EXACTLY THIRTY MINUTES BEFORE SAM WAS supposed to meet her, Rae stuffed her notes in her file box and headed for the third floor. It felt good getting away from the policemen, who had been going about their duties of collecting, dusting, and photographing evidence. Members of the medical records staff had come in too. No one asked her any questions.

She had to make rounds on Angel Lloyd as well as the other patient she delivered hours before her. Usually before the change of shift, the nurses would be hunched over their clipboards recording their patients' vital signs. But on this morning, they huddled together, whispering and glancing about, their faces full of concern and fear. In the background, the sound of a patient's call button bleeped softly.

The whispers stopped as soon as the staff saw Rae.

"Good morning," Rae said. "Does anybody plan to answer that?"

Rita Hale, the youngest of the nurses, went to answer the call as Rae reached for Angel's chart from the circular file rack. When Rita returned, she asked tentatively, "We heard you found Bernie, Dr. Duprey. Is that true?"

Rae sat down at the station and opened Angel's chart. Her hands were shaking. "I can't really talk about Bernie right now," she said.

Rita moved as lightly as a ballerina as she slid into the chair next to Rae. The other nurses gathered around. "What do you think happened?'' she asked. ''I mean, Bernie was everybody's friend. Do you think somebody in the hospital did this?''

Rae saw the look of terror in Rita's eyes. ''I'm scared too,'' she said gently. ''But let's worry about Bernie first, okay?''

The nurses murmured among themselves. Rae rose from her chair. ''Now, who's taking care of Angel?'' she asked.

One of the nurses informed Rae that Angel was doing just fine. Another reported that Rae's other patient had no problems either.

''Thank you,'' Rae said. She took a few steps, then, feeling all of the nurses' eyes upon her back, turned to them and said, ''I don't know who did this to Bernie. I can't understand why *anybody* would do such a thing. But believe me, I plan to find out if it's the last thing I do.''

The nurses nodded slowly. Rae walked toward Angel's room. Angel's daughter slept peacefully in a bassinet next to her bed. Just seeing the baby lifted Rae's spirit. To her, a baby meant that the world had another chance at being better than it was the day before.

''So,'' she said near the end of the visit, as she sat next to Angel on the bed, ''do you have any questions for me?'' She forced herself to smile, for Angel's sake.

''Can't I please stay another day, please?'' Angel asked hopefully. ''I know what my insurance says, but you're the doctor!''

Rae reached out and squeezed Angel's hand. ''Let's see, you signed up for Perfect Health Plan. How many days do they give you?''

Angel shrugged. ''I don't know, but next baby, I'm signing on with anybody who lets me stay at least three days. I'll pay more to get more, that's for damn sure.''

Rae chuckled. ''Now that's the American way,'' she said.

''And I'm going to have an epidural next time too,'' Angel said. ''This natural childbirth crap almost killed me.''

Rae chuckled again and reminded Angel that her office would call to make her six-week appointment. ''Are you okay, Rae?'' Angel asked. ''You look like you just lost your best friend.''

Rae shook Angel's hand. ''Close,'' she said. ''My best friend is having an operation this morning.''

Angel nodded sympathetically, then smiled. ''Let's just hope she doesn't have my insurance plan. I bet she could use some recovery time in the hospital.''

Rae wished Angel the best of luck with the baby and headed for the room of Patty West, a black, thirty-two-year-old biology professor whose pregnancy had been complicated by diabetes. Rae had induced Patty's labor and was grateful that after such a difficult pregnancy, Patty had wound up with an easy vaginal birth shortly after midnight. She knocked on the door before she entered.

Inside, the curtain was drawn and the dark room was filled with the fragrance of flowers. Rae could just make out the shapes of at least ten bouquets arranged on the countertop along the far wall.

Rae walked over to Patty, who appeared to be asleep. Her French braids hung down across her shoulder. "Patty?" she said. "It's me, Rae."

No answer. She shook her gently. "Patty?"

Patty stirred. Her eyes opened slowly. "Help me," Patty said weakly, her voice slurred as if she were drunk.

Immediately Rae became alarmed. Then she noticed that the tiny red light was on at the head of Patty's bed. Quickly she felt Patty's forehead. Cold and clammy. She looked at the bedside table. No juice. No graham crackers either.

"Damn it!" Rae shouted as she ran out into the hallway. She had left strict orders that the patient have juice and cookies in the room at all times. Patty was a brittle diabetic and her blood sugar level could bottom out in seconds.

Just outside the door was Georgia Burns, a gregarious nurse who wore a toy baby bottle attached to her stethoscope. "My, you're an early bird—" Georgia started to say.

"Doesn't anybody answer the call buttons around here!" Rae hissed as she ran to the supply room. "Come on! I need an IV and some D-fifty!"

Rita showed up to help. The three of them gathered up a liter of normal saline, an IV catheter and tubing, and an amp of the highly concentrated sugar solution that Rae requested.

Back at Patty's bed, Rae quickly cleaned Patty's right arm with an alcohol wipe while Rita wrapped a rubber tourniquet around her biceps. Georgia handed Rae the IV catheter, and deftly Rae plunged the tip of the catheter into Patty's right antecubital vein. They piggybacked the D-50 into the main line, and when Rae twisted the stopcock to the on position, she saw the sugar solution run freely into Patty's arm.

Within seconds, Patty came around. "Rae?" she asked.

Rae smiled with relief. "Welcome back, sweetie pie," she said.

Back at the nurses' station, Rae was fuming. It was obvious that Patty had called for help, but the nurses had not responded in a timely fashion. Rita came up to her and sat down with a guilty expression on her face.

"It's my fault," Rita began. "I just don't know how I could have missed the call. I'm trying to do my best, Dr. Duprey, but I can't keep up with the workload. With everybody going over to the Birth Center, and with cutbacks in dietary and transportation, those of us left are having do their jobs *and* work this unit, antepartum, and sometimes L and D. Whatever happened to the good old days, Dr. Duprey?"

Rae shook her head wearily. Being a patient in the hospital was boiling down to a crapshoot. Everyone who worked inside the hospital knew that. Sooner or later, the public would figure it out too.

"These are the good old days," Rae said sarcastically. "If things keep going the way they are, we're going to wish we had them back again."

After writing IV orders on Patty and discharge orders on Angel, Rae searched for the charts on Nola and Meredith. When she couldn't find them, she asked Georgia where they were.

"I'm sorry, Dr. Duprey," Georgia Burns said. "But Dr. Michaels instructed me to remind you that those are his patients. He specifically asked that you not be allowed to look at them."

"What?" Rae asked in disbelief. "But I delivered those patients—"

"I'm really sorry, Dr. Duprey, but . . ."

Georgia cast her eyes downward. Rae knew that attacking her for Bo's behavior would solve nothing.

"Okay," Rae said, seething. "Just make sure he rounds on the patients—today."

She started to walk away.

"Dr. Duprey?"

Rae stopped and turned to face Georgia. "Yes?" she asked.

"Is it true what they're saying about you? Are the doctors really going to meet in two weeks to get you thrown off the staff?"

Rae felt her face flush with anger.

"I mean," Georgia went on to say, "I don't believe any of it, but I just thought I could tell a few people where to get off . . ."

Rae tried to calm herself down. Georgia was offering her support, not criticism. "You tell them to take care of their own patients and everything will be just fine," she said.

Georgia smiled and gave Rae the thumbs-up sign.

Rae sighed as she headed back toward medical records. She felt as if her world were caving in around her. Sick babies were coming out of the Birth Center. The staff shortage was beginning to affect the hospital's performance. Her department was at war with the heart program. She was at war with Bo and the Birth Center. A hearing had been called to kick her out. Word of the hearing had spread like cholera throughout the hospital. And her best friend was fighting for her life in the operating room.

Well, she thought stubbornly, straightening her shoulders, she wouldn't give up. But as she passed more nurses coming in to start the day shift, she couldn't help but wonder if they were staring at her. Did they seem a little less friendly, or was it just her imagination?

She hurried on.

Back inside medical records, she retrieved the charts and her notes and tore the top seven pages from her legal pad. The pages contained information gleaned from studying the eight charts. She had drawn lines down the pages that separated the data into columns. What she was looking for were similarities between the cases, with particular emphasis on why the patients had been transferred out of the Birth Center and why the babies' Apgar scores were so low. She was trying to formulate a theory, but she was so worried about Bernie that it was hard to make sense of much of anything. The day before, fatigue had been the obstacle to thinking clearly. Now it was the gut-wrenching fear that Bernie might not make it.

As she poured over them, she heard footsteps approaching the desk. Looking up, she saw Sam Hartman weaving his way toward her. He was dressed in khaki pants, matching polo shirt and a gold cardigan sweater. That confident gait and that never-ending smile. Obviously he had not heard about Bernie.

"Morning," Sam said. "What gives around here?"

Rae clipped the yellow pages together. "I don't think we can meet for breakfast," she said shortly.

Sam raised an eyebrow. Rae decided that since the man had gotten up so early the least she could do was explain herself. "Bernie's been hurt," she said. "Somebody beat her up pretty bad while she was in the file room. She's on the OR table now."

"What? Who's Bernie?" Sam asked.

"My best friend," Rae said. "You met her—you saw her yesterday, in the operating room. She took over for me while we worked on Nola's baby—"

Suddenly she felt very close to losing all semblance of control.

"Whoa, steady there," Sam said. "Take your time. I'm not going anywhere."

She took a breath and explained to Sam all that had happened. His face remained impassive as she spoke. Finally she said, "For the record, do you know if Marco left his house after the party?" She pointed to the stack of charts. "Four of these eight were still missing at midnight. This morning, when I found Bernie, they were back in Marco's box."

Sam's expression remained neutral. "Why don't you ask Marco?" he asked.

Rae shrugged. "I asked him last night if he signed out the charts. He said he didn't."

"So there you are," Sam said evenly.

Rae studied Sam's face. He was so difficult to read! And he had answered her question without having answered it at all, she realized. Not yet, at least. Sooner or later, she decided, he would have to make himself clear.

"Don't you ever just answer a simple question with a simple answer?" she asked. "I asked if Marco left his house after the party."

"I thought I did answer it," Sam said. "Let's see how your friend is doing," he said, picking up the phone. Rae listened as he spoke to the operating room nurse. When he hung up, he said, "Still sounds kind of rocky down there."

Rae's eyes widened in fear. "What else did they say?" she asked.

"They've taken out her spleen," Sam explained. "They've transfused her with six units already. Seems like there's still some pumper they've got to get under control."

Rae raised her open palm in front of Sam. "Let's just think good thoughts," she said, as if repeating a mantra to herself. She took a deep breath, and then pulled the charts toward her and opened the top one. The writing on the pages blurred now. It took her a few seconds before she realized that her hands were shaking and that Sam was staring at them.

Furious, she slammed her fist down on the table. "Damn it, Sam," she said, "quit looking at me like that! If my hands want to shake, let them shake! If I want to sit here and review charts, that's my choice, okay? What do you expect me to do? Fall down on the floor and cry my eyes out?"

"That might be a good place to start," Sam said patiently.

"Tears are useless," Rae said rigidly. "Believe me, I know."

Regaining some semblance of composure, she said to Sam, "Look, you asked if we could do our charts together. So would you get off my case and help me with these?"

"What am I looking for?" Sam asked as Rae handed him a chart.

"See if you agree with this," she said. She explained how she had pored over each chart earlier that morning. What she found was exactly what Bernie had said. All the charts were on patients who had been transferred from the Birth Center. All babies, like Nola's baby, had arrived at Berkeley Hills Hospital showing signs of fetal distress.

"Are you sure?" asked Sam with genuine interest in his voice.

Rae went on to explain that she now was concerned more than ever because all of the babies had low Apgar scores and one of them had even died a week after birth.

Sam shook his head sympathetically.

"And one of the mothers died," Rae added.

"A maternal death?" Sam asked. "That still happens?" He sat up in his chair. "Let me see that chart."

"That's the one I gave you," Rae said.

Now she watched him as he slowly read through the pages. His expression remained placid and Rae, as usual, could not make out his thoughts. Just like a scientist, she thought. Detached, objective, not willing to draw any conclusions until all data were in.

Rae, on the other hand, didn't need all the data. She worked on hunches as much as she worked on fact. There were too many babies in too short a time who had done poorly. And Sam was right. Maternal deaths were almost unheard of. The last time a patient had died from a complication of pregnancy at the hospital was ten years ago, and that patient had a pneumonia that no amount of antibiotics on earth could cure.

"Says here she had a history of chronic hypertension," Sam said in his matter-of-fact tone.

"Nobody dies from a blood pressure of a hundred forty over ninety," Rae said. "And she never developed preeclampsia."

Sam looked at Rae. "Sounds like you pretty much have these charts memorized," he said.

"Something terrible happened to these patients, Sam," she said vehemently. "Just like something terrible happened to the two patients I delivered yesterday morning. I know it, and I'm sure Bo knows it. And if Bo knows it, he's covering something up."

"Like what?" Sam asked. He had closed the chart and leaned back in his chair. He crossed one leg over the other.

"I don't know," Rae said. "But whatever it is, I think that's part of the reason why he's attacking me. He's the one in trouble but he needs me to take the heat."

Rae slumped back in her chair and shook her head. "I just can't believe someone would want to hurt Bernie," she said miserably.

Sam peered around the room. "Oh, I don't think anyone meant to hurt Bernie," he said.

"Oh, so what do you call it when somebody bashes your head in?"

Sam raised his hand. "What I mean is, judging by the mess in there, Bernie probably got caught in the middle of something. Seems to me if someone were out to get Bernie he certainly wouldn't do it in a file room."

"No one's around in the middle of the morning," Rae said.

"And neither is Bernie," Sam said. "She's works L and D and about the only other place she'd be is in the cafeteria."

"But she was helping me out."

"Whatever," Sam said, "but the point is that if someone wanted to get Bernie, he'd get her at her house, or in the parking lot. People come and go here all the time. Besides, if he wanted to kill Bernie, he would have killed her. He would have made it more certain—used a knife or a gun or something."

Rae waved Sam off. She didn't want to hear any grisly descriptions about what could have happened to Bernie.

"Listen, this is my theory," she said, and she told him about the connection she saw between the return of the missing charts and Bernie's attack.

When she finished speaking, Sam shook his head. "I'd say that's pretty far-fetched," he said doubtfully, although Rae could tell by the frown that darkened his brow that he hadn't totally dismissed it.

"But possible," Rae said.

"I suppose."

"So, tell me where you went after I left the parking lot," she said.

"Do you think I actually know something about all of this that I'm not telling?"

"Do you?" Rae asked.

"Do *you?*" Sam asked.

"But why would I hurt Bernie?"

"Why would I?" Sam said patiently. "Besides, remember, Bo was not the one who delivered Nola or Meredith. It was you, Dr. Duprey."

Rae saw how deftly Sam had turned the tables on her. It certainly didn't feel good. "Oh, all right," she said in exasperation.

Sam patted his stomach. "Can we break for breakfast now?" he asked.

"I suppose so," she said, but then something caught her eye.

"What?" Sam asked.

What Rae saw was a signature on the ambulance report. It was the same illegible scrawl that she had seen on the report in Nola's chart. She had not noticed it before.

"Give me those other charts," she said to Sam.

He handed them to her one by one. Each report had the same signature.

"Seems like one of your friendly ambulance drivers was also involved in each case," Rae said.

Sam held the chart this way and that. "It's hard to make out," Rae said, "but the signature looks like it belongs to Theodore McHenry."

"Who's that?" Sam asked.

"Like you don't know," said Rae as she slumped back against her chair. "You only asked Theodore and his brother for directions to my place less than twenty-four hours ago."

She flipped through each chart and then waited for Sam to agree.

"It proves nothing," he said. "I bet you if you look through all of the charts from the Birth Center's transfers, you'd find his handwriting all over the place."

"Why do you keep defending them?" Rae asked.

"I'm not defending anybody," Sam said. "But look. All of these patients were transferred during their shifts. It only makes sense that his name is on the charts. I noticed that one twin seemed to rule the other, so this Theodore is probably the oldest and in charge. So let's not start accusing them just for doing their job."

"This is not just one big coincidence," Rae said.

"You don't even know what 'it' is. So what if all cases involved the same doctor? So what if there was fetal distress? All eight cases could be isolated events. Look here. This patient got transferred over here after being in prodromal labor for three days. This one's blood pressure went south in a hurry and this one developed pre-eclampsia in the second stage. This one had a footling breech and this one showed up with active herpes—what I'm saying, Rae, is that there was a reason—eight different reasons—why the patients wound up over here. Eight bad babies in two months doesn't sound like a lot to me."

"But it does to me," Rae said. "This is Berkeley Hills Hospital. And the reasons you cite don't normally lead to low Apgar scores." She paused. "You've only been here for two months yourself, haven't you, Sam?"

"Maybe you have a need for these not to be coincidences," Sam said.

"Or maybe someone has a thing against the Birth Center," Rae replied. "Maybe someone wants to see it go out of business. That person could have stolen the charts for who knows what reason, then tried to return them when he knew nobody would be around. But Bernie was there. Bernie saw him . . ."

She was studying Sam's face as she spoke, but as always, it remained inscrutable.

"Bernie knows what Marco looks like," she continued. "Maybe he didn't go to April's house at all."

Her mind was speeding now, but Sam rose from his chair. "You promised to have coffee with me and I'm going to make you keep your date. You're going off half-cocked saying things you know nothing about and I can't take any more of it on an empty stomach." Sam grabbed for the charts.

"I'm not done," Rae said.

He carried them and handed them to one of the file clerks, and then said to Rae, "These aren't going anywhere, but you and I are."

"But I've got to check on Bernie," Rae protested.

"Just where do you think I'm taking you for coffee?" Sam asked.

Perhaps nowhere in the building was there greater evidence of Walker Stuart's vision for what his hospital should look like in the twenty-first century than in the operating suite. The layout and the technology were even more sophisticated than in Rae's maternity unit. Each room was big enough to handle two cases simultaneously. Lasers, operating microscopes, video equipment—no expense had been spared. Even the location of the fifteen-room unit had been carefully chosen by Walker. To protect it from the usual stampede of visitors that invaded the rest of the floors, he moved it from the fourth floor to the safety of the basement.

They had changed into surgical scrubs suits and donned caps and masks. Rae walked alongside Sam as they made their way down the shiny white-tiled floors. They passed the nursing station, which had a TV monitor linked to every room.

"She's in room one," the nurse said.

"What's the word?" Sam asked, but the nurse only shook her head and returned to her phone conversation.

Rae hastened her pace. "I hope no news is good news."

"Room one," Sam said. "My territory."

"I wish you hadn't said that," Rae said. "Only the really tough cases go there."

"I'd say a subdural hematoma and a ruptured spleen qualify."

Rae shivered at his impersonal tone. Doctors—and she was guilty of this all the time—usually referred to their patients as body parts. It was their way of dealing with illness and dying. It provided enough space to work with. But to hear Sam talk about Bernie as if she were no more than a collection of organs did not seem appropriate just then, even to Rae, who *was* a doctor.

Each operating room was some fifty by fifty feet. The clear glass walls made for easy viewing but afforded absolutely no privacy for the patient. How many times had Rae passed by operating rooms and seen a woman's legs spread wide open during a hysterectomy, or an old man with a catheter stuck up his penis? She had not thought much about it until now. Then and there she decided that in the future, she would ask for the blinds to be drawn—for every case.

Room 1 was located at the far end of the corridor. Rae saw a team of doctors and nurses all huddled like a football team around the operating table. There were so many people that she couldn't even see Bernie.

"Ready?" Sam asked as he placed his hand on the door.

Rae took a deep breath and followed him into the room. The first thing she noticed was the unmistakable odor of fresh blood. She knew that smell better than any in the world.

The second thing Rae noticed was the quiet. Another bad sign, she thought. Doctors and nurses kidded around when a surgery was going well. Who was dating whom, who had a golf handicap under four, who bought which latest car—all of these were common topics during an operation.

But silence: only when something was terribly wrong did the members of the operating team keep their mouths shut. Rae would have preferred it if they yelled and screamed for instruments, as she had done when they tried to save Nola's baby boy. Silence meant each doctor had all the instruments he needed and was concentrating so hard on a delicate part of the operation that he couldn't even afford the distraction of his own voice.

Sam must have been thinking the same thing, Rae thought, for he didn't say a word as she moved closer to the table. She passed by the instrument stand. Her eye caught a softball-size purple mass with a one-inch crater break in its skin, lying in a basin. Bernie's spleen, Rae realized, her stomach lurching.

As she approached the table, she saw that there were two teams working on Bernie. One worked at the head of the table and another worked in the middle.

On another tray Rae saw instruments that she never used during her surgery. There was a saw and a drill for cutting through the bone of Bernie's skull. Blood stained the silver like melted red licorice. In another bucket on the floor were strands of silver hair. The hair bothered Rae much more than the blood on the drill did. The hair belonged to Bernie. It was part of Bernie the person, not Bernie the patient.

Blood was pouring through multiple IV lines that ran into Bernie's body. Hoping to see that the general surgeons had gotten control of the bleeding, Rae walked still closer to the table. As she had predicted, Bernie had been sliced open along the entire length of her belly. A four-point metal retractor—another piece of hardware more suited to a home garage tool box than to a person's body—held her open like an open fish.

Sam walked up to her just then. "Get me out of here," she said queasily and headed out of the operating room.

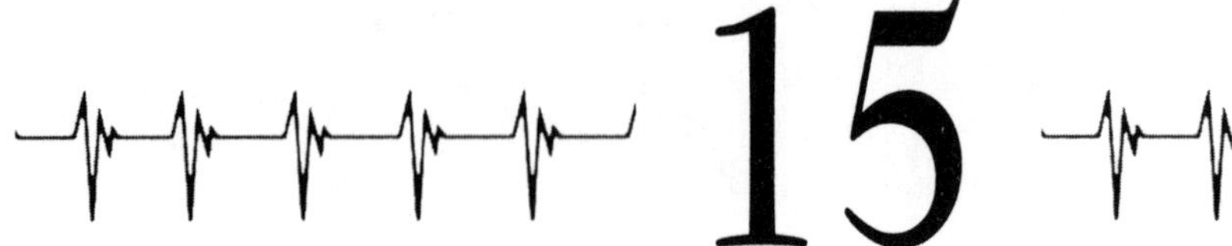

# 15

OUTSIDE THE HOSPITAL, SAM OFFERED RAE A RIDE IN HIS NAVY-blue Mercedes. She was too numb to protest. They drove in silence as she tried to erase the images of Bernie's traumatized body from her mind.

To distract herself, she began to tell Sam about the real Bernie, the whole Bernie, the woman she had met when she first came to Berkeley Hills Hospital ten years ago. "We fought in the beginning," Rae said. "We still fight . . ." She wanted to tell Sam how much Bernie meant to her, but the words simply would not come out.

They pulled into Raymond's coffee house on the Berkeley Marina and sat at a comfortable window table. The window was open and Rae was surprised at the warmth of the breeze coming off the bay. There were a few other customers, mostly college students dressed in jeans and T-shirts. The restaurant smelled of freshly baked muffins and strong coffee. Suddenly Rae felt very hungry.

She ordered two scrambled eggs, wheat toast, and a decaf cappuccino.

"A cup of coffee for me," Sam said. "And a really big stack of pancakes."

Then, after the waitress left, he gazed at Rae and smiled. "Isn't this great?" he asked.

"Tell me how you ended up at Berkeley Hills Hospital, Sam," Rae said.

"My wife divorced me," he replied flatly. "Something about her career being more important than mine. I thought we were doing just fine, but I guess she felt differently."

"How long were you married?"

"How long is necessary?"

Rae sighed. Sam had made his point, even if, once again, he was talking around her questions.

"She was a lawyer," Sam went on to say. "Everything had to be answered with either a yes or a no."

Rae detected a hint of sadness in Sam's voice. "Do you still love her?" she asked.

Outside the window, a couple of kids flew kites near the shore.

"She loved her work more than anything," Sam said.

"See, there you go again," Rae said. "I asked you a simple question and you avoided answering it. Anyway, there's nothing wrong with a woman loving her work. Men do it all the time."

"Really?" Sam asked sardonically.

"What's wrong with a woman putting her career first?"

"Then why get married?" Sam said.

"Why did you?" Rae asked.

Sam's face clouded over. "One's life should come before anything," he said. "Like what we're doing now: sitting out here by the bay, watching the sky change colors, feeling the air on our faces and smelling sea air—why else are we here? If we can't enjoy this, what's the point?"

"Maybe you ought to go work for Hollywood," Rae commented wryly. "They love stuff like that. But life is about blood and guts, Sam, about healing and preventing death. And with Bernie on that operating table—" She stopped just long enough to steady her voice. "And with Bernie fighting for her life I'm determined to find out what's going on with those patients at the Birth Center. I feel the need to do that more than smell the sea air."

The waitress returned with the coffees. "Beautiful day, isn't it?" she asked.

"Perfect," Sam said.

"Depends," Rae said.

"You were saying?" Sam asked.

Rae waited until the waitress was out of hearing range and then said, "What good is the view to Bernie now? For that matter, how does the color of the sky matter to Nola's baby? That's what life is about, Sam. A constant struggle against death and dying."

She felt her face flush with emotion and an emptiness in her gut that she knew no amount of breakfast could fill. Or was the emptiness in her heart—still there after twenty-five years, only bigger?

"You seem to be very far away," Sam said.

Please, Rae thought, turning away from him. Don't let Bernie die too.

"Rae?" Sam asked, concerned.

She placed her chin in her hand and stared straight at him. "Now listen to me," she said. "I don't care if my theory is far-fetched. Bernie might die for something I know is connected with the Birth Center—"

Sam started to speak but she waved him off.

"I've got two—less than two weeks to prove it," she continued. "Those eight bad babies, the one who died, the one patient who died, Nola, Meredith, and now Bernie . . ."

She took a deep breath. "These are not coincidences, Sam. And don't try to tell me that they are. For all I know, you might be involved with it, because of Marco, I mean. Those charts were signed out to him."

"Marco?" Sam asked. "You think—"

"I don't know what to think—exactly," Rae said. "But whoever is involved, I'll find out soon enough."

"You'll do anything to keep your department," Sam said with conviction.

Rae slapped her palm on the table. "Damn my department!" she said. "I'm going to prove that something's going on for Bernie's sake and for those babies!"

She rose. "Thank you for breakfast but I've got to get back. If I'm going to do anything I can't sit here all morning being all touchy-feely."

They drove back to the hospital in silence. Just before she got out of the car, Sam gave her his card. "Call me, anytime," he said.

Rae studied the name. Samuel Arthur Hartman, M.D. "I might be pretty busy for the next two weeks," she said.

"Yes, I know," he said dryly.

The three-column statue was directly in front of her. She tilted her head and felt the warm rays of sun against her cheeks. Was that what Sam had meant? she thought as she entered the lobby. Perhaps the sun's rays on her face did feel good, but was it enough? Using the nearest phone, she called the operating room. Bernie was still on the table.

"They're closing now, though," the nurse said. "You might want to wait for her in ICU."

Rae gave a loud sigh of relief. "Thank God she made it through the operation," she said.

"Now all she has to do is wake up," the nurse muttered.

Rae rarely had a patient admitted to the intensive care unit. The whole place made her uncomfortable because it housed the patients who had the greatest chance of dying. She much preferred her third-floor maternity ward, where life began hour after hour, seven days a week.

She also always found it oddly incongruous that the sickest patients had the most beautiful views. Most patients were comatose or very heavily sedated. They didn't know if it was night or day so the magnificent vistas were wasted on them. On the other hand, for those lucky patients who woke up and could actually see outside their windows, what better invitation back to life than the view of the sun and the sea? Rae recalled her conversation with Sam. Perhaps he did have a point. But then she saw Bernie, and felt once again the absurdity of his words.

Bernie lay on a bed in a cubicle in the middle of the unit. Her head was wrapped in layers of sterile gauze. A clear plastic endotracheal tube sprang from her mouth. Attached to her arms and chest were monitors that measured her blood pressure and the pressures in her pulmonary artery and right atrium. EKG leads tracked her heartbeat. Her urine trickled out of her bladder, down a plastic Foley catheter, and finally into a white collecting bag.

"Terrible, terrible thing," murmured a nurse who came to stand at Rae's side.

Rae nodded. A thin sheet had slipped off Bernie's body and her small breasts were bare. A huge white surgical dressing covered Bernie's abdomen from her chest to her pubic bone.

Rae drew the sheet over Bernie's shoulders and gently touched her forehead. "Has she woken up at all?" Rae asked.

"We take one thing at a time in this unit," the nurse answered, shaking her head.

Next to the bed was a director's chair. Rae sat down and took Bernie's hand. She took heart in the fact that her skin felt dry but warm. At least her pressure was normal. She sat there with Bernie until she saw the sailboats returning to their berths as dusk prepared to descend upon the bay.

Finally she rose. Her muscles felt stiff and her eyes weary. "I'll be back tomorrow, Bernie. You just hang in there," she said in parting.

Minutes later, she drove slowly down the steep descent of Marin Avenue. She passed the fountain and on I-80 kept the speedometer at fifty-five. To her right, billowy clouds hovered overhead. Yet in the middle of the white mass was a gap through which the sun laid a path of shimmering gold light across the calm waters. That was exactly what she needed, Rae thought. Some light to shine through the jumbled and murky thinking that had plagued her for the past two days.

Leopold greeted her at the door. Rae patted his head distractedly and then fed him. Next she changed out of her jeans and turtleneck and into a white blouse and baggy shorts.

Her dinner would consist of leftover pesto pasta and a slice of stale French bread. She poured herself a glass of red wine and then went into her study and spread out the seven pages of yellow legal paper on her desk. She wanted to compare the thoughts she had while sitting next to Bernie with the notes she had taken from her chart reviews.

About halfway through dinner, she rose and began to pace the floor. Leopold watched. Normally his undemanding presence comforted her. But now it simply reminded her that time was running out.

"I can't believe that everything is just a coincidence, Leopold," she said out loud. She lifted the papers from the desk and took them over to her big chair. Leopold followed her and placed his head on the armrest. "Nola and Meredith got transported over on the same day," she said. "Nola's baby had a triple nuchal cord. Meredith had a shoulder dystocia. The other babies—herpes, breech, hypertension, prodromal labor . . . but they all had fetal distress by the time they got here."

Leopold's ears had perked up as if Rae had finally captured his full attention. "I spoke with Jenny and Freda," she explained to her dog. "But they said neither Nola's nor Meredith's baby had signs of distress at the Birth Center. Even inside the ambulance, the babies, according to the twins at least, had normal heart rates during the transport. But when they arrived at labor and delivery, all the babies were in trouble. So does that mean something happened between the time the patients left the ambulance and when they arrived upstairs? And if so, what could have happened in that short amount of time? And how?"

She thought again of Bernie. How she wished she had her friend to discuss things with. Bernie would help her come up with an answer. Bernie would—

But Bernie had helped out too much already. And look where that had gotten her.

Rae rested her hand on her chin. There was no one else she could talk to, she thought. Her life had been spent in the hospital or in her office. That kind of existence afforded her little time to establish relationships with anybody else.

Even with a child of her own, she told herself.

She shook her head miserably. She'd have to cope with those feelings of loss at another time.

On the other hand, she thought hopefully, she could always call Walker. He was as much a mentor as a friend. She could tell him anything and he would listen. He'd listen to everything she had to say and most likely not call it far-fetched. Besides, he needed to know. If someone was out to hurt the babies, Walker would want to help Rae put an end to it.

Then she saw Sam's card on the table. He had offered to help. But what help could he give when he didn't even answer her simple questions directly?

Still, she lifted the card and studied the number. One thing he could do was to finally answer her questions concerning Marco and himself. Marco checked out those charts. At least, the charts were signed out to him. In any event, she knew Sam Hartman knew more than he was letting on. And this time she wasn't going to let him weasel out of it.

Yes, she'd call Sam before she called Walker, she decided as she lifted the phone. Even if she had to lock him inside her condo, he wasn't leaving until she was satisfied he had told her what she needed to know.

An hour later, Mack the doorman called to let Rae know that Sam was on his way up. When the doorbell rang, Leopold barked furiously. Rae rarely received visitors at her condo. Besides, Harvey always knocked. Bo used to have a key and would let himself in.

She opened the door and Sam stood there smiling. He wore a white dress shirt, charcoal pants, and a blue blazer. Actually, he looked rather dashing on such short notice, she thought reluctantly.

"That's some elevator ride," he said. "Wow, aren't you friendly," he said to Leopold, who was eagerly sniffing his hand.

"Don't flatter yourself," Rae said. "Leopold likes everybody."

She escorted Sam into the living room. The sun had set and the clouds were rimmed in shades of red and orange. Traffic was backed up thirty stories below along I-80.

"Pretty place," Sam said.

"Anything to drink?" she asked.

"Just water."

She fetched a glass, filled it with ice and Perrier, and then joined Sam in the living room. He had made himself comfortable in a wingback chair that looked directly out onto the bay. She sat in a matching chair next to him so that although they were sitting side by side, they did not have to look directly at one another.

"Ah, thank you," Sam said after downing half of the glass. "So, you said you needed my help?"

"Just don't say anything until I'm finished," she warned him. "Sam, I want you to tell me once and for all what you know about Marco and that proposed cardiac center. Why don't you tell me the truth about it? Where do Marco's loyalties lie? Where do yours?"

She paused to watch Sam's reaction. If he raised his eyebrow the wrong way, or if some signal went off inside those lake-blue eyes, she'd know that not only did he believe that she was on to something but that somehow he was involved.

"Is it safe for me to speak now?" Sam asked.

"Maybe," Rae said. "If you'll answer my question."

Sam crossed one knee over the other. "Which question was that—exactly?"

Rae smiled ruefully. "Uh-uh, not this time. I asked you to tell me about Marco and Howard Marvin and what they plan for Bo's Birth Center."

"You wonder if Marco's trying to set up the Birth Center—is that the question, Rae?"

Rae studied Sam's face, just as he studied hers. His seemed neither perplexed nor incredulous. His gaze remained direct, his chin slightly lifted, as if he would weigh her upcoming answer and decide if it were true.

"Just tell me what you know," she said evenly. She was not going to let him turn the tables on her this time.

His eyes narrowed and he said, "But you delivered the last two patients that got sent over from the Birth Center, Rae. From how I understand things, you want the Birth Center shut down as much as Marco does. Shouldn't I be asking what you know about a scheme to discredit the Birth Center?"

"You answer my question first and then you can ask any damn thing you please," she said. Although she kept her voice calm, she had to fight the rush of anger that Sam's provocative comment instinctively aroused.

"Marco can answer any questions you have for him," Sam said.

"Marco wants Bo to sell it to Howard Marvin," Rae said. "You heard Bo at dinner last night."

"I said you can ask him—"

"But I'm asking you, Sam! I need to know!"

She had not meant to raise her voice, but there was something about him that made her lose control of her feelings. The problem was, she knew it had nothing to do with the issue of the Birth Center. She turned away, and then looked back at him. In a quieter and calmer voice she said, "Please, just tell me what you know."

Sam smiled. "I'm flattered by your interest in me," he said.

"Come on, Sam, just answer my question."

"Okay, okay," Sam said. He turned to face her directly. "Rae, Marco's not crazy. Sure, he may want a piece of the action if Howard plans to open up some fancy heart center. But whatever role Marco's playing in all of this, he wouldn't do anything illegal, and he certainly wouldn't do anything to hurt any women or babies. So if you think he's involved with some sinister plot—"

"That's exactly what I think," Rae interrupted.

"But that's simply ridiculous," Sam said in exasperation.

Rae didn't answer. Instead, she held his gaze and let the silence lengthen. "Well?" she finally asked.

"It's too far-fetched," Sam said flatly.

"No it isn't!" Rae said. She had jumped out of her chair and stood up in front of Sam. "Eight bad babies in two months, Sam," she said. "I don't know what's acceptable where you came from, but at my hospital we question statistics like that. At least I do."

"Maybe you ought to talk to Bo."

"Bo has no reason to make himself look bad," Rae said. She had never imagined she'd wind up defending Bo to Sam. "Believe me, he loves that Birth Center more than anything. But something's going on that we need to pay attention to. For all I know, Marco could be involved."

"And you think I'm involved too, is that it?"

"Well, are you?" Rae asked.

There, she had said it, she thought. And now that she had, she might as well get on with it.

"I mean, those charts were signed out to Marco and somehow they mysteriously showed up. You came back to the hospital the night Bernie was attacked."

"So?"

"Maybe you put them back for Marco. Maybe you're involved in some other way. I mean, look, the ambulance drivers didn't want to talk to me when I started asking them questions. On the other hand, I saw you talking to them like you were old friends."

"So now you're bringing the ambulance company into this?"

"That's exactly what I'm trying to tell you, Sam," Rae said. "I don't know about you, or Marco, or anybody else, but think—I know—those drivers are involved."

Sam arched an eyebrow but Rae persisted. "Those babies were fine in the Birth Center. They were not fine in our delivery suite. Maybe something happened to them inside our emergency room, but I don't think so because Sylvia knows that Meredith's baby's heart rate had already bottomed out before Meredith hit the door."

"But the ambulance reports said that the heart rates were normal on the ride to the hospital," Sam interrupted.

"I don't care what those reports said!" Rae cried. She took a second or two to settle down and then said, "I've talked to those twins. They lied to me then and I know they lied on those reports."

"How do you know?"

"Because I called Hillstar and found out that they are new to the company—"

"And?"

"And, well, they wouldn't tell me anything else."

"So how do you know they're involved?" he persisted.

"Because that's the only damn explanation that makes sense!"

She waited for her words to sink in, not for Sam's sake, but for her own. He was watching her again with a scientific air, as if he were weighing the merit of her conclusion as well.

"It's the only thing that makes sense," she repeated so quietly that she could barely hear her own voice.

She sat down, rested her hands in her lap and waited for Sam to say something. He gazed at her with such an intensity that it felt as if he were trying to see straight through her and into a place she didn't even know existed.

Finally he said, "And why would a couple of ambulance drivers want to kill babies? Why would they want to see the Birth Center shut down? For Christ sakes, Rae, they make their living driving between the Birth Center and the hospital. The way you're talking, you'll probably tell me next that they're somehow connected to Howard Marvin's plan to buy the center from Bo and turn it into that heart center."

"That's exactly what I was about to tell you!" She hadn't meant to blurt out her conclusion, but with so much going on, she found it nearly impossible to remain calm.

Sam looked at her incredulously. "You're kidding, right?"

"I am not," she said. "Think about it."

"No," he said. "The whole thing's preposterous. I don't buy it. I mean, I want to buy it because I know what all this means to you. But it's ludicrous! It's incredible! It's insane."

"Okay! Okay!" Rae shouted. "So I don't have all of the answers! That doesn't mean I'm not right! But tell me I'm not right about the fact that ten women got transferred by the same two ambulance attendants and we wound up with ten bad babies on our maternity ward!"

"Maybe something happened to them when they hit the door of the hospital," Sam said.

"You're not listening, Sam. There's no indication of that at all."

Rae paused and then said, "Look, Sam, I've known for some time how high the stakes are surrounding Bo's Birth Center. I just didn't know the extent of it until yesterday. You were at the board meeting, Sam. You were also there at Marco's party. I can't help but believe that all of this has something to do with what Marco said about Perfect Health Plan."

"Oh, so now the insurers are in on the conspiracy?" Sam asked. "And just how is that—exactly?"

"Since Bo refuses to sell it, maybe someone at Perfect Health Plan wants to see a few bad babies come out of his place. If the Birth Center looks bad, Bo will be forced to sell. Now I know Marco's your buddy, but he could be involved. Sure, he denied it last night but because he denied it so vehemently, I wonder if he hasn't already cut some deal. At least Bo thinks he has."

"Or maybe you have?" Sam said.

"Don't be silly," Rae said.

"A case could be made," Sam countered, "that since you want to see your department survive, you'd be the main person wishing the Birth Center to go out of business. Or if Perfect Health Plan wants to buy the Birth Center, perhaps it's you who wants a few bad babies coming out of there."

"But I just delivered Nola and Meredith this morning!" Rae protested. "Why would I do such a thing?"

"It makes perfect sense to me."

"Now *that's* ridiculous!" Rae said. "Maybe you're involved as deeply as Marco is. You know, these cases didn't start until you got here. Marco would love nothing more than for Berkeley Hills to stop delivering babies so that his program could expand. Now I see what he's really after. He wants my department out *and* he wants the Birth Center. He wants it all, damn it!"

Sam rose and grabbed her wrist. He stood so close she could practically feel the anger radiating from his body.

"I'll tell you why I came to Berkeley Hills Hospital, damn it!" Sam said. "Marco told me about a beautiful, unattached, female obstetrician who needed this."

And then he kissed her, hard and deep. To her surprise, she kissed him back and pressed her body closer to his. They had spent the last ten minutes fighting over Bo's Birth Center, but as she stood on tiptoe in his arms she realized that it was also the center that had brought Sam and her together. As much as she didn't want to admit it, somewhere along the line, she had fallen for Sam—perhaps even the first time she had seen him, when he saved Nola's baby.

Finally he released her and gazed down upon her face. "Do you want me to stop?" he asked.

"I wish I did," she answered him fervently, her breath coming in ragged gasps.

This time she was the one who wrapped her arms around Sam, and hung on to him as he lowered her to the floor. Walls and windows that were so familiar to her were now a blur. She felt her heart pounding.

"Should I be worried?" she asked.

"Should I?" he murmured as he sucked on her throat.

He made love to her as if she had the body of a goddess. Slowly, deliberately, always waiting for her response. Her clothes came off—how, she did not know. She only knew that no part of her body was off limits to him. And against the backdrop of the last two days, where babies and their mothers were at mortal risk and Bernie was about as close to death as a person could get, Rae wanted to keep a firm hold on life forever.

So she clung to Sam as he pushed inside of her and let the act of love hold the shadows at bay, if only for the moment.

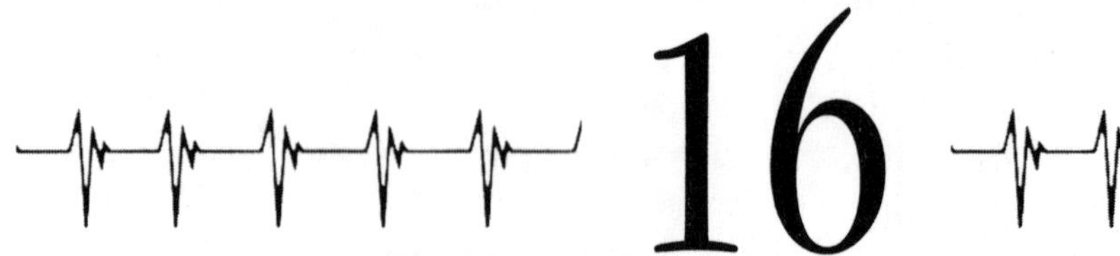

# 16

"You know that what we just did doesn't really mean anything," Rae said as she stared past Sam's bare shoulder and caressed the curve of his back. His skin felt moist and warm. He smelled of sweat, and aftershave.

"Not a thing," Sam said with mock seriousness.

"Hey, did Marco really say that about me?"

Sam turned to face her. "Did he say what?" he asked, reaching up to stroke her ear.

"You know, about me and why you came to Berkeley."

"Nope."

"Oh, so just what *did* he say?" Rae asked with a smile.

"He said you were very stubborn and *very* short."

"Good old Marco." Rae laughed.

Sam pushed himself up onto his elbows and gazed down at her, and she stared back as if seeing him for the first time. It was an intelligent face, full of intensity, but the curve of his mouth hinted at an irreverent nature. She had certainly seen evidence of that! As he bent down to kiss her again, she thought his eyes held more mystery now than when she had first met him.

A stranger, Rae thought in wonderment. She had just made love with a complete stranger.

Why now? she asked herself as he intertwined his fingers with hers, and stretched her arms at right angles to their bodies. She imagined that from above, they now formed the sign of the cross.

Had she believed in God, she thought, she would have found the image lovely. Absolutely lovely.

And why *had* she made love with Sam Hartman? she asked herself next. Why with the same man she had confronted just minutes ago about his possible role in the Birth Center disasters? Was it because she had been so needy? Or was it because there was something very special about Sam Hartman?

The phone rang and Rae pulled on the cord until the mouthpiece dropped from the desktop. "Bernie's nurse said she's coming out of her coma," said a ward clerk from the hospital's intensive care unit. "You wanted us to call you if anything changed."

"Sam, Sam!" Rae said excitedly. She tapped him on his back with the receiver. "I've got to go. Bernie's waking up!"

Sam sat up immediately. "I'll drive," he said.

He rose and stood completely naked in front of her, yet he seemed as comfortable as if he were wearing a full-length coat. She had expected a moment of awkwardness.

"You look lovely," Sam said as he stared down at her.

Her first impulse was to cover herself with her hands. But watching Sam watching her, she realized she didn't feel embarrassed at all. In fact, she felt very comfortable with him—too comfortable.

"I hope you don't expect to drive me to the hospital dressed like that," she said abruptly. She jerked her head to her right. "The shower's that way."

The man strolled across the room like he was taking a walk in the park, she thought with a flash of irritation. Once he disappeared, she picked their clothes off the floor. Enough of Sam Hartman, she told herself. She couldn't wait to see Bernie! Bernie was going to be all right.

The splash of running water startled her as she walked into her bedroom. How strange it was to hear that sound when she wasn't the one in the shower stall. She hoped her last words to him had not sounded too curt. It was just, she told herself, that Sam stirred up feelings inside of her she preferred not to have.

On the one hand, he seemed to care for her. And how she wanted someone to care! On the other hand, even after making love to him, she still suspected him of knowing more than he admitted.

Besides, he had made love to her just when she thought she had backed him into a corner. Was that because he wanted to distract her from Marco? Was he using her as part of some plan to satisfy his needs? Wasn't that where love always led—to someone else's destruction?

"Next, please!" she heard Sam yell from the bedroom.

She had lain his clothes out on the bed for him. Now she stroked the soft wool blazer. What was she going to do next, she thought? And how?

It took only fifteen minutes for Rae to shower, change into jeans and sweater, and lead Sam out the door of her condominium.

"This thing about the paramedics," Sam began as his Mercedes purred up the steep hill to the hospital. "Now, I'm not saying I believe you, but if what you think is true, have you figured out exactly what they're doing to the patients?"

"I don't need you to believe me," Rae said impatiently. "And no, I haven't. All I know is that they must be working for somebody—"

"Don't start in on Marco again, okay, Rae?"

"Marco, Howard Marvin, a disgruntled nurse worried about her job—"

"Know of any unhappy nurses around here?" Sam interrupted.

"Know of any happy ones?" Rae countered. Suddenly, she paused. She recalled Donna Wilson, the nurse who had been a staunch opponent of the Birth Center but who was now working there. Rae had thought that odd when she first ran into her. Now she felt worried.

"What?" Sam asked.

"Well, there is one nurse who used to work for us, but now works for Bo."

"Just one?"

Rae furrowed her brow. "I mean, there's one who hated the Birth Center, and now she works there. I mean, she *really* hated the Birth Center."

"Any other suspects before you start investigating her background?"

Rae shook her head. "Well, there are the people on the board of trustees."

"Or even Leopold perhaps, Dr. Duprey?" Sam said. He turned to smile at her. "Maybe he's not man's best friend after all."

Rae was in no mood for joking. "Don't leave yourself off the list, Dr. Hartman," she fired back.

Sam chuckled. Rae sighed and folded her arms across her chest.

The car pulled into the parking lot. "Listen, Rae," he said, "I'm joking of course, but other people won't be. You need to be prepared for people accusing you of all sorts of things. I have this feeling I'm not going to be the only one you tell this to—"

"I don't care what people think about me," Rae snapped.

"That's what worries me."

Rae cut her eyes to Sam's face, but he stared straight ahead as he set the brake.

"Things might heat up more than you can imagine," Sam said.

Rae walked alongside Sam into the busy lobby.

"Just be careful," he warned as he punched the elevator button.

Rae let out a big sigh. As long as she suspected Marco, she knew she couldn't completely trust Sam even though he did seem concerned about her and even though she had slept with him, she thought ruefully as they rode up the elevator to the seventh-floor intensive care unit.

The first person she saw as she stepped inside the room was Mona Stair, whose angular features made her look more like a runway model than an ICU nurse.

"I hear Bernie's coming around," Rae said cheerily as she looked past Mona toward Bernie's side of the room. The drape had been drawn around her bed—a good sign, Rae thought. A comatose patient needed little privacy. Bernie, on the other hand, was waking up.

But Mona wasn't smiling. "What?" Rae asked. Please, no more bad news, she thought.

"I'm *really* sorry, Dr. Duprey," Mona said. "There was a communication problem . . . I mean, I told Bella—the ward clerk—to get you up here because Bernie's getting worse, not better."

Rae froze. Afraid to ask, she waited for Mona's explanation.

"We've got her on a dopamine drip to raise her pressure," Mona continued. "Her most recent chest X ray is consistent with ARDS. Her serum creatinine's up—the renal guys are talking about starting dialysis tonight and—hey, are you okay, Dr. Duprey?"

Rae had stopped listening. Bernie had adult respiratory distress syndrome, a lung condition from which few people recovered. Add to that, kidney failure. Dialysis might help, but even that might not be enough . . .

"Rae?" Sam asked.

"Get me out of here, Sam," Rae said. "Now, please."

Above the roof garden, the sky was an ever-changing canvas of blues and blacks and purples. It was hard for Rae to see where the sky ended and the earth began. To the right the skyline of San Francisco sat under the mercy of the thickening clouds. Rae thought she could feel the threat of rain in the air but she wasn't sure.

She pulled at the collar of her turtleneck sweater. Sam stood next to her and also studied the sky. "Bernie and I were just up here yesterday," she said sadly.

Sam didn't respond. To Rae, his silence said more than if he had spoken a thousand words. After all, there really was no explanation for the suffering of innocent people.

"What made you become a doctor, Rae?" Sam asked suddenly.

No one had asked her that question in years, she realized with surprise.

Down below, she could see the parking lots of the hospital and of the Birth Center. Why couldn't things have been different between the two institutions? she mused. Perhaps when she became department chief—

She thought again. How could she be chief if there was no department? How could she stay a doctor if her license was taken away? Why would she want to be either if Bernie was not around?

"Well?" Sam asked.

"Well what?"

"What made you decide to become a doctor?"

Rae sighed and clasped her fingers together. "Oh, the usual stuff. I wanted to help sick people—you know."

"Who was the first sick person you wanted to help?"

Rae thought about her mother. "What's with the fifty questions? I thought we came up here to forget about medicine for a minute."

"I doubt if you ever can," Sam said. He paused and crossed his hands together against the four-foot-high cement railing. "I admire that," he added.

Rae cocked her head and studied his face. He looked tired but at peace—at peace with himself and with the world. Rae envied *that,* she thought, and the feeling surprised her.

"My mother died when I was thirteen years old," Rae said. "In the back of an ambulance, giving birth. I rode with her. She abrupted and bled out. I had this little yellow sweater and I tried to wipe up the mess—like that would save her. I guess she was the first really sick person I had ever known. So sick she died."

Sam kept staring ahead. "And she lives on in you," he said.

His words touched a spot in her heart that she didn't know still existed, the spot where all the happy feelings in a person's life are stored. Feelings that one can only experience as a child; feelings that cannot be bought or bartered. This place, or at least the gateway to this place in Rae's heart, had not been visited by herself, or anyone else, in years. Her father had seen to that at her mother's funeral.

She stared across the bay. The dark clouds were growing more ominous. They resembled a huge black cloak hovering over the city, ready to fall and smother everything. Life was like that, Rae thought. Smothering. Suffocating. Bad turned to worse. Like Bernie's prognosis.

"I've been meaning to tell you something," Sam said, "ever since I saw you—this little woman with such tiny hands—operating on Nola. You gave your heart and soul to save her child. An earthquake could have leveled that operating room and you wouldn't have noticed.

"Anyway, when you say you became a doctor to help people, I believe it. That's why I'm thinking I've got to believe you enough to at least consider the possibility that Nola's situation was no coincidence or an act of bad luck."

Rae slowly turned to Sam.

"And there's one other thing that I guess I really don't expect you to believe."

Rae waited. Sam took a deep breath. "I think I'm falling in love with you," he said simply.

Rae turned to look back at the city. How good it felt to hear those words! Of course, she couldn't take them seriously. But to hear him say them, for him to say he felt that way after seeing her do what she had dedicated her life to, gave the statement a different meaning. He was saying that he had fallen in love with the side of her that other men in the past—including Bo—had always resented, if not rejected outright. She closed her eyes tightly for a moment to fully soak up the sentiment of his declaration. But in the end, they *were* just words, weren't they?

"Love only leads to grief," Rae said finally. Didn't it? she thought.

"So?" Sam said. "Life leads to death but people go on living."

Rae had no answer for him. He had a point, one she had never thought about.

"I'm ready to go back inside," she said. "And thank you. I do feel better."

She walked him to the elevator. "I'll catch a cab home," she said. "I want to go and spend more time with Bernie."

"Don't forget to spend some time with Rae," Sam said gently. He entered the elevator and waved good-bye. She pondered his advice as the silver doors closed between them.

Rae felt a hand nudging her awake. She opened her eyes and saw Mona smiling at her. Then she felt a pain in her neck, and heard an old woman cry out, "Stop it! Stop it!" Suddenly she realized she had fallen asleep at Bernie's bedside in the ICU.

"What time is it?" she asked, rubbing her neck.

"It's coming up on ten o'clock," Mona said.

Rae bolted up. "How's Bernie?"

Mona smiled. "She's still here."

Rae rose, walked over to the bed, and smoothed Bernie's forehead. A tinge of blood covered the gauze dressing over the spot where the neurosurgeons had drilled the hole in her skull. "I'm going to find the person who did this," she whispered fiercely. "Hold on to life, Bernie. Hold on to life!"

She rode the elevator down to the first floor. The lobby was empty except for a few pregnant women and their partners carrying pillows. Obviously a birthing class had just ended. In the preceding year the crowd would have been bigger—instead of five couples to a class there would have been ten to fifteen. But not anymore, Rae thought. Not with everybody wanting to deliver at the Birth Center.

She passed the door to medical records. It was open and inside she saw Marco sitting at a desk and reviewing a stack of charts.

There were few signs left of the morning's destruction. Even the police tape had been removed.

Curious about what Marco was up to at such a late hour, Rae entered the room. "Marcella kick you out again?" she asked.

Marco jumped. "Jesus, why didn't you announce yourself?" he asked. He closed the top chart and pushed it away from him with an air of nonchalance.

Rae recognized the name on the chart. "Weren't those in my box, Marco?" she asked. She thumbed through the other seven. The charts were the same ones she had reviewed.

She looked up at him. "Since when do you care about our OB patients?"

"Since when do you start spreading rumors that I'm trying to knock off a few babies?" he asked.

"I didn't say—"

"Sammy says you did," Marco said.

"He what?" she asked angrily. How could Sam have betrayed her like that?

Marco sat back in the chair and with a smug look on his tanned face said, "And I've got to tell you, Rae, I agree with the old boy. I've checked out these charts and in my estimation, each patient had a pregnancy complication. That's what caused a few gorked-out babies—not some loonies running around doing bad things to pregnant women. And just what *are* these bad things you think they're doing?"

Rae snatched the charts from him. "Go to hell," she said. "And take Sam with you. We're talking babies here—innocent little babies whose only mistakes were being born on the wrong day. Okay, let's say you're not involved. But even you've got to admit something's off here. Or don't you want to admit it, Marco? Is your precious little department that important to you?"

"Isn't yours?" he responded sarcastically.

Rae looked through the charts. She wanted to make sure everything was in place. Now that Sam had spoken to Marco—and to think, she had slept with that rat—she knew anything was possible. She was on her own on this one.

Marco rose. "I was on your side until tonight, Rae," he said. "See you at the hearing."

"Hey!" she said as he started for the door.

"Yes?" he asked with mock sweetness.

"Where are the ambulance reports? The ambulance reports are missing."

"I was wondering the same thing," he said.

Rae charged over to him. "You have them. Give them back to me."

Marco patted Rae's head like one would pat a child's. "You're cute when you're angry, did you know that?"

Rae swatted his hand away. "No more games, Marco. Just give me the reports."

Marco's face filled with dark anger. "I said I don't have them. And don't let me hear you dragging my name through the mud to anybody else," he warned. "I've got the board of trustees in my back pocket and it won't take much for me to have them yank your chain. Oh, yeah, I know all about that little deal you made with Heidi. She told me last night. Just be happy you get two weeks. I wouldn't have given you two hours. You're crazy if you think you can keep delivering babies here. But then, like I told Sammy, you're stubborn. I can respect that. Just keep my name out of it, okay? Or would you prefer me to make a few phone calls and get the board to call for the vote on Monday?"

Marco had her, Rae thought. He had her just where he wanted her. Even though saving her department was no longer her primary motivation for investigating the baby cases, she still needed time to get to the bottom of it. And she didn't believe that Marco was innocent. He talked a good game but she wasn't buying.

She handed him back the charts. "Somehow I get the feeling those reports will be back in their proper places before you leave this hospital."

"You're pushing it, Rae," Marco said menacingly.

"I didn't say *you* would put them back, now did I?" Rae asked innocently. She reached up and patted Marco on the head. "Tell April I said hello."

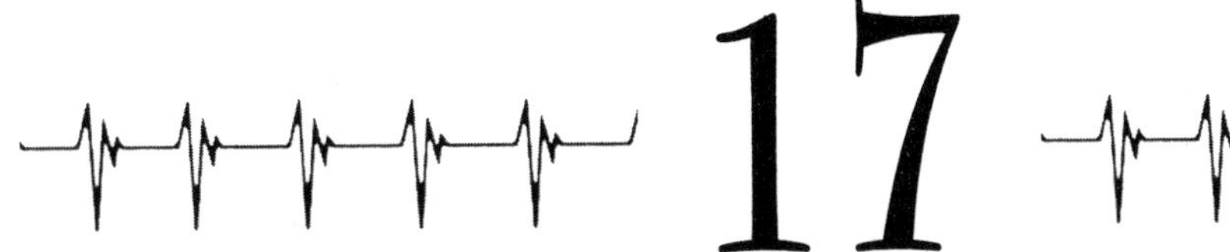

# 17

RAE WAS SEETHING AS SHE LEFT MEDICAL RECORDS. SOMEONE had stolen the ambulance reports from the charts. But who? Sam had told Marco that Rae suspected him of trying to kill the babies. Worse, Sam probably told Marco how he and Rae had spent the evening. Had they had a good laugh over that? And Heidi had told Marco about Rae's plan to bring back the obstetricians who'd gone over to the Birth Center in just two weeks.

When, she thought furiously, was all the double-dealing and double-crossing going to end?

What bothered her the most was that Marco had asked a question that burned through to her very core: Exactly *what* was being done to the babies that led to such low Apgar scores? If she could figure out the answer to that question, she should be able to confirm the who, and finally, the when, how, and why.

When she got to the nearest house phone she called Sam's number. No answer. Next she called his answering service and to her chagrin was informed that Dr. Hartman was in surgery. She'd deal with Sam spilling his guts to Marco later, she thought as she hung up the phone. Meanwhile, she would—

*''Any obstetrician, stat! Labor and delivery! Any obstetrician, stat! Labor and delivery!''*

The distress call that was suddenly barked over the PA system came from the hospital operator. Rae forgot all about Sam and Marco as she sped down the stairs to the third floor.

"Whacha got?" she asked as she ran toward the nursing station.

Looking up, a nurse answered, "Patient in room two—her baby's on the perineum and coming down fast!"

"Where's her doctor?"

"Dr. Henshaw's on her way. But at eight months pregnant, she's moving kind of slow these days! Glad you could make it!" she called after Rae as she ran by.

At least it wasn't Bo's patient, Rae thought gratefully as she sped around the corner. And most likely the patient had not been transferred from the Birth Center because Dr. Mattie Henshaw rarely delivered her patients there.

Inside room two, ten people stood around the bed. In Berkeley, crowds often showed up for a friend's delivery. Eva, the same nurse who had fainted at Nola's surgery, stood between the patient's legs. The baby's head was about a quarter of the way out.

"Everybody relax, the doctor's here now," Eva said with obvious relief.

"Ow, the baby's coming!" the patient cried out.

There was no time to review the woman's chart, although Rae did glance at the name Irene Butler stamped on the delivery record lying on the countertop.

"Any problems indicated in the chart, Eva?" Rae asked, as she snapped on a pair of gloves from the instrument tray and quickly slipped on a white paper jumpsuit that Eva had made available to her.

Irene was young, probably no more than twenty, with a Mohawk haircut and, despite her advanced labor, still wearing bright red lipstick. In fact, all of the other people in the room were young and were dressed in leather coats or vests. Bikers, Rae concluded.

"She's preeclamptic," Eva said. "Blood pressure's one-sixty over one-oh-two. Two-plus protein."

Rae took Eva's place and watched for the next contraction. "I'm Dr. Duprey, Mrs. Butler," she said. "You're doing just fine." Then to Eva, she said, "Is she on magnesium sulfate?"

"It's running at two grams an hour," Eva replied.

The magnesium sulfate would help prevent the grand mal seizures that preeclampsia could bring on, especially in labor. The problem was, magnesium sulfate also relaxed the uterine muscle, especially after delivery, and that increased a woman's risk of postpartum bleeding.

"Will it be much longer now?" one of the young men asked.

"Hey, what do you think, Bozo?" a young woman quipped, slapping the back of the man's head.

"Just one more push," Rae said. She looked into Irene's brown eyes and drew her into her world. She kept her voice even, and when she knew she had her full attention, she said, "Now."

Irene took a deep breath, like a kid at the side of a pool who's about to jump into the water. She bore down hard, and the baby's head slid out, slowly and beautifully—just the way it was supposed to, Rae thought.

"Now for the shoulders . . ."

Irene pushed again. The baby's shoulder dropped under the pubic arch and the rest of the body immediately followed. The baby howled and so did everyone else in the room.

"Congratulations," Rae said with a broad grin as she handed the pink, wiggling baby boy to Irene.

For a few seconds, Rae allowed herself to enjoy the beauty of a natural birth. So simple, she thought, as if giving birth was the easiest thing in the world. She glanced up and saw the smiling faces of everyone around the bed. For a few seconds, she felt happy too and let herself appreciate the pure joy of new life and the promise that it brings. There was nothing like the innocent wail of a newborn, and the look of astonished love on a mother's face, and how that look affected everybody, sometimes forever, but always for a few seconds . . . always.

Rae then handed the Mayo scissors to a man she assumed was the baby's father, but he pointed to another man who looked, she thought, barely out of his teens. Patiently, Rae guided his trembling hand to the gelatinous white and blue tissue between the clamps. When he snipped the cord, blood sprayed briefly from the cut ends onto the front of her jumpsuit.

Next Rae tugged on the umbilical cord. The placenta slid out all shiny and purple under the lights. She checked Irene for lacerations, and finding none, she turned to the instrument tray for another gauze pad.

And then she heard it, and smelled it, and felt it splash against her legs.

She spun around. A four-foot-diameter puddle of bright-red blood covered the floor directly under Irene's legs. More blood soaked the part of the plastic gown that covered Rae's feet. Even the side of her jumpsuit looked as if a bucketful of red paint had been splashed across it.

She swiftly pushed her fist elbow-deep into Irene's vagina. She knew just how fast a postpartum uterus could bleed out. Like opening a half-gallon milk carton all the way across the top, then turning the whole thing upside down.

"How about getting a little oxytocin running, Eva?" she asked calmly.

"This just hasn't been my day," Eva said in her soft voice.

Fortunately, Irene already had an IV line running. By now Rae's fingers had found her marshmallow-soft cervix. She pressed her fist deep into the boggy womb.

"Ow!" Irene cried.

"Okay, everybody into the hallway but the father!" Rae ordered. "I'm sorry, I don't mean to hurt you," she apologized as the bikers hurried out. "Just give me a minute here."

The blood kept coming. It was normal for some blood, about a small bowl's worth, to follow the delivery of a placenta. But there was far more blood than that coming out of Irene's body. The most common cause of postpartum hemorrhage was a boggy uterus. Oxytocin was supposed to help with that problem, but even oxytocin wouldn't work if the uterus was filled with blood clots.

Seconds later, Rae's probing revealed that indeed, the uterus was not only boggy but filled with clots. She began to pull them out by the handful, dropping them into a plastic bag hanging under the bed. She had been massaging Irene's belly with her left hand as she removed the clots with her right. Still the uterus failed to contract.

"Add ten more units of oxytocin to the kitty, Eva," Rae said, massaging the uterus more firmly. Her right hand was still inside Irene. Her left hand was on top of her abdomen. She glanced up at the blood pressure monitor. Still holding, she noted with relief, but not for long if the bleeding didn't stop. In that eventuality, she would have to operate to tie off the hypogastric arteries that carried the blood to the womb; and if that didn't work, then she'd have to perform an emergency hysterectomy, or the woman would bleed to death.

"Here's the oxytocin," Eva said.

The extra oxytocin should make the uterine muscle contract within minutes.

"How about some Methergine?" Eva asked.

"It might raise her blood pressure even higher," Rae said, reminding Eva of Methergine's unwanted side effect. "Let's try the oxytocin first and give it a couple of minutes to work."

If only someone had given her mother oxytocin, or Methergine, Rae thought briefly, she would not have died in the back of that ambulance.

She began to massage Irene's uterus harder and harder, faster and faster, as she watched Eva draw up the oxytocin from a small vial into a syringe. Turning back to Irene she said, "Stay with me, hon. We're giving you something to help make your uterus contract and that will stop this bleed—"

*Help make your uterus contract . . .*

Quickly she turned her attention from Irene back to Eva, who was now injecting the IV bag with the clear liquid. Using the nipple port, Eva inserted the needle tip and advanced the plunger. Because oxytocin was the same color and consistency as the salt water, it didn't look as if anything had been added.

"And stop this bleeding." Rae said slowly, as if in a trance.

Eva then squeezed the bag so as to disperse the liquid evenly throughout the IV solution.

*Oxytocin causes contractions . . .*

Rae's mind was racing now.

Eva opened the stopcock so that the IV solution ran even faster into Irene's peripheral IV line and from there, into her arm.

*The higher the dose of the oxytocin, the stronger the contractions . . .*

"Eva, stop!" Rae blurted.

Eva looked at Rae incredulously. "You don't want it?" she asked.

"The oxytocin," Rae said excitedly. "That's what's they've been using—"

"What are you talking about, Dr. Duprey?" Eva asked, obviously alarmed.

Rae forced herself back to the present. Irene was still bleeding and she had to get it to stop before she could analyze her brainstorm concerning the rash of bad babies.

"You okay, Dr. Duprey?" Eva asked. "Don't tell me you're going to get back at me for fainting on you?" she joked tentatively.

"I think *I'm* going to faint," the patient's husband said.

"I'm fine, Eva, just get him on the couch, now," Rae ordered.

As Eva escorted Irene's husband to the other side of the room, Rae noted that the stronger dose of oxytocin had finally kicked in. The warm muscle of the uterus was now clamped down around her cramped fingers and the blood had stopped pouring out of Irene's womb.

"Another save, Dr. Duprey," Eva said when she got back to the table, giving Rae the thumbs-up sign.

"And it's a good thing too."

Rae turned and saw that the person who had spoken was Dr. Mattie Henshaw. Mattie's face was flushed pink against her jet-black bob cut. "Sorry about the delay. That run from the parking lot to the elevator is a killer," Mattie complained.

"She's all yours now," Rae responded with a smile. She congratulated the new parents and then unzipped her bloody jumpsuit. Her hands shook even though she tried her best to still them.

Outside the room, she leaned against the door. No wonder Nola Payne's baby showed severe fetal distress, she thought miserably. The powerful uterine contractions stimulated by oxytocin were meant to start labor, make an ongoing labor stronger, or stop a woman's bleeding after birth. But if given in high enough doses, it could also cause the uterus to contract so severely that the oxygen to the baby could get cut off. A normal labor contraction cut off fifty percent of the baby's oxygen. A very strong contraction could essentially cut it off completely.

She stared down at the floor in concentration. How she hoped she was wrong. But she wasn't. Oxytocin had caused severe contractions in the women coming out of the Birth Center and the contractions had led to the fetal distress. There was no doubt in her mind. None whatsoever.

Her thoughts sped ahead. There were other things that she would have to explain if she was right about the oxytocin. If the paramedics were the ones injecting the oxytocin and they did not inject it in the ambulance, when and where *did* they inject it? Surely the drug company that supplied the IV bags did not do the injecting. If it had, there would be dead babies everywhere. If the paramedics didn't inject the bags inside the ambulance, did they do it at the warehouse where the bags were stored? Did that mean other paramedics were involved? Was Rae willing to believe that the conspiracy reached that far?

What about her theory that someone was paying the twins for their services? Certainly an ambulance company would not want to see the Birth Center closed, so it couldn't be them. How about Marco? It seemed to Rae that even he wouldn't be so stupid as to get too many other people involved.

Maybe she was wrong about the oxytocin. Her theory seemed to raise more questions than it answered. On the other hand, suppose she was right on the mark? Another patient could be coming over from the Birth Center at any moment. Another victim. No, make that *two* innocent victims. There were always two lives involved when it came to OB.

She thought about calling Sam, but the operator had just said he was in the operating room. She could call Walker, but frankly, without proof, she would only appear desperate enough to say just about anything. Bo? No, she didn't want to call him. But she had to. Only he could direct his patients back to her hospital at least until the mystery was solved.

She'd have to be very careful when she spoke with him, though. He no longer seemed to care about his patients. It was obvious he didn't care about her. Her watch said eleven o'clock. Even though it had been a year since she last called him at home, she remembered the number as if it were her own.

"Hello, this is Bo. Please leave a message at the sound of the beep."

Rae's heart sank upon hearing his answering machine. Time was running out. She cupped her hand to the phone and tried to decide whether to leave a message or not. Finally, she took a deep breath and said, "Bo, this is Rae. I need to talk to you—right away. I know it's late, but it's extremely important—"

"Hi," Bo said. "I was in the shower."

"Can we meet?"

"Gee, Rae, it's pretty late," he said coolly.

Rae took another deep breath and said, "I wouldn't call unless it was important." She paused and waited for him to say something.

With her free hand she rubbed her tired eyes. "Please, Bo, I need to talk to you."

She was groveling now, she thought. He had her just where he liked her, begging him for something.

"Fine, I'll be waiting for you here," he said finally.

Bo lived in the hills above the Claremont Hotel in a custom-built home. As Rae set the brake of her Porsche, she studied its angular lines and the multiple windows that looked out onto the bay. This house had once been a place of refuge. But soon the refuge became a prison. The terra cotta walls had seemed to close down around her as their relationship deteriorated. The house contained three thousand square feet of living space, but even that eventually proved too small for Bo's mood swings and Rae's ever-increasing intolerance of them. She had told Bernie that Bo had left her over the miscarriage. The truth was that her relationship with Bo was over long before that.

He greeted her at the door.

"Thanks for agreeing to see me," Rae said, walking quickly into the room. She wanted the meeting over as quickly as possible. "I need to talk to you about the Birth Center again," Rae said.

Bo frowned and sat down on the couch. "Bo," Rae said, "this is very hard for me to say. But the way I see it, something bad is happening to your patients."

"Rae, you've already made it clear what you think about me and the center," Bo said with exasperation.

"It's the babies, Bo," Rae continued in a rush of words. "Somebody's after them. Someone is spiking the patients' IV bags with oxytocin. That's why there are so many cases of fetal distress."

Bo rolled his eyes as he crossed his arms over his chest. "Oh, for God's sake! You're going to have to do better than that, Rae."

It did sound ridiculous, but she was deadly serious. "I mean it, Bo. It's the only possibility that makes sense. Nola leaves the center with a normal fetal heart rate. She arrives at our place with a bradycardia. Meredith spends two hours trying to push out her baby in the Birth Center. By the time she gets over here, the baby's head comes flying out. And you had eight other cases, Bo, where babies had normal heart rates in the Birth Center but displayed fetal distress by the time they got to our unit. And your patient who died two weeks ago—her uterus ruptured, Bo."

She kept expecting Bo to interrupt her. But he listened in silence.

"Until we can prove this *isn't* happening," she pleaded, "I want—no, I'm begging you—to shut down the Birth Center."

There, she had said it. She had played her trump card and now it was up to Bo.

"Why in the world would somebody go through all that trouble?" he asked skeptically.

"To make the Birth Center look bad," she replied. "To put you out of business. Look, if you were telling me this stuff, I would probably think you were crazy too. But I wouldn't leave it at that, Bo. Not when we're talking about little babies."

"We've talked about little babies before. Your level of sympathy has obviously reached a new high point."

"Fine," Rae said, "but I know you're a good doctor, Bo. You always put the patients first. At least look at the charts again."

"You think I haven't?" Bo shouted at her. "I've reviewed those damn charts at least a hundred times. I have never had a maternal death in my whole career, Rae. Do you know how that feels—to see a woman bleed to death in front of your eyes? Do you know how hard it is to look at yourself in the mirror the next day—and the day after that? She was gone by the time we got her on the table, but I opened her up anyway because I had to do something! Hell, her uterus had exploded like someone had stuck a grenade into her. But even so, Rae, I'm not going to let you sit here and tell me she died because some crazy person wants to put me out of business!"

Rae had no idea he had taken his patient's death so hard. "But that's just my point, Bo," she said. "I reviewed that case yesterday and an overdose of oxytocin could have done it. Oxytocin is something that wouldn't show up on an autopsy. It only stays in the bloodstream for a minute or two."

"Oxytocin my ass!" Bo said. "Her uterus ruptured because she had a myomectomy! Everybody knows you don't let a woman labor after fibroids have been removed from the uterine cavity! The problem was that she never told me. When I asked her about that scar on her belly, she told me it was from an ovarian cyst she had removed when she was twelve years old. The records had long been destroyed so I had only her word to go by. How was I supposed to know that delivering at the Birth Center meant that much to her?

She never gave me reason to tell her that a woman who had that kind of fibroid surgery must deliver all her babies by cesarean section! But I still feel responsible, Rae. I feel like I killed her, not some damn oxytocin!"

Rae wanted to reach out and comfort Bo, but she knew how dangerous that would be. He might interpret her compassion as desire. Part of her longed to tell him that she understood exactly what it feels like to see a woman bleed to death and not be able to do a damn thing.

It dawned on her that in her seven years with Bo, she had never told him about her mother's death. But she had told Sam all about it within a couple of days of meeting him. Had Sam blabbed about that to Marco as well?

"Believe me," Bo said, "until you know what it's like to watch a patient die like that, you don't know the first thing about what it means to be an obstetrician. Of course I've reviewed those charts. What do you think I was doing in medical records the other day? Why do you think I was so upset about the four missing ones? I can't sleep at night, Rae. I'm afraid to sleep because all I do is dream about that nightmare in the operating room!"

He slumped down on the couch and placed his head in his hands. Rae started to speak but stopped when Bo waved her off. "I told you to leave my Birth Center alone, Rae," he said. "Now I want you to leave me alone too."

"Bo," Rae began.

"Good-bye, Rae."

Rae found Sam waiting for her in the lobby of her condominium. "You're about the last person I want to see right now," she said coldly. She glanced at her watch. It was a minute before midnight.

"Can I come up—just for five minutes?" Sam asked. He had taken off his navy blazer and held it across his arm.

Rae had had enough arguments for one evening. "I'll give you two so you better know what you want to say."

They rode the elevator in silence. Leopold was not there so Rae knew Harvey had him. As she placed her key in the door, she asked, "Why'd you tell Marco, Sam?"

"Because he's my friend," Sam said. "And because I wanted some answers, too."

"Well, you sure do know how to pick 'em," Rae said sarcastically.

She turned around when she heard footsteps and the panting of a dog behind her.

"Are you missing a dog?" Harvey asked. "He's certainly missing you."

Leopold sniffed and then licked Sam's left hand. "This is Sam Hartman, Harvey," Rae said. "Sam, this is Harvey Polk, my violin instructor."

Sam shook Harvey's hand as Rae patted Leopold's head. "I forgot Rae played the violin," Sam said.

"That makes two of us," Harvey said sardonically as he headed back across the hall to his unit.

She didn't invite Sam into the living room but stood in the foyer with her arms crossed. "Well?" she asked.

"So, yes, I ran what you said by Marco," Sam said. "He thinks it's all conjecture, I'm afraid."

"I don't care what Marco thinks," Rae said. "Or you."

"I see," Sam said. "Anyway, I came to tell you about Donna Wilson."

Rae was taken aback. "You spoke to Donna?"

"Can we go into the living room?" Sam asked.

Inside, Rae pointed to the two chairs that they had sat in earlier. How quickly things changed, she thought wryly.

"I knew you planned to talk to Donna," Sam explained once they were seated. "But your little theory has really gotten under my skin. So I went over to the Birth Center and asked her a few questions myself."

"Oh?"

"I asked her if she had worked yesterday. She said no. Then I asked her if she knew the twins, and she said she knew *of* the twins, but what precisely did I want to know about them? Then a nurse named Freda showed up, and well, I guess things sort of got out of hand. They didn't exactly throw me out, but let's just say I had overstayed my welcome. I don't think Donna's involved in any way though. She certainly seemed up front and I double-checked. She really wasn't on duty yesterday morning."

Rae drummed her fingertips along the armrest. She wasn't sure what to think.

"You know, Sam, it would be so much easier if I knew whose side you were on," she said.

"I thought that after this evening, it was obvious," he said quietly.

"Do you mean after we slept together, or after you betrayed my confidence?" she retorted sharply.

Sam rose without responding. "My two minutes are up," he said.

Rae walked him to the door. She felt guilty about her outburst. Maybe he really was just trying to help. "Thank you for the information on Donna," she said in a more conciliatory tone. "You were right. I need to speak with a lot of people about a lot of things. The problem is, there's so much to do and so little time."

Sam nodded. "I know what you mean. Oh, I left my coat on the chair."

Rae turned and walked back into the living room. As she swept up the blazer, a group of folded papers slid out of the inside pocket. She stooped down to retrieve them but then stopped short. At the top of each page were the words *Ambulance Report.* Her heart froze. Quickly she pushed them under the chair and returned to the foyer.

Sam's eyes narrowed when he saw her. "Are you okay? You seem upset."

She faked a smile. "I'm fine," she said as she handed over his jacket. "Just a little tired."

Rae wanted to get him out before she aroused any more suspicion. Nervously she said, "Hey, why don't I call you tomorrow?"

Sam nodded. "I guess that will have to do. May I?"

He smiled and then leaned down to kiss her. She closed her eyes, the brush of his soft lips reminding her bitterly of the passion of their lovemaking only a few hours ago. But feelings of the heart often caused one to do foolish things. Sam was somehow involved—and Rae had been a fool.

No wonder he was being so helpful! He and Marco probably had everything planned from the beginning. Slowly, she closed the door behind him. And she had fallen in love with him, she thought miserably.

She retrieved the ambulance reports and brought them to her study. Actually, they weren't originals but photocopies. She recognized the names at the top of the reports. They belonged to the four patients whose charts were missing.

Sam seemed to have written on them. There were check marks

by the dates of the transports. The times of the transports were underlined. Dots had been placed in front of the fetal heart rates, and at the bottom Sam had circled in red the signature of the ambulance driver.

Rae placed the papers on her desk and rubbed her eyes. God, she was tired! It was almost one o'clock in the morning. She sighed and then studied the papers again. Why had Sam gone over them in such obvious detail?

She had a sudden thought. Sam could have asked Yvonne to make copies for him *before* the originals were stolen. Maybe he had asked for them for another reason, a good reason.

She rose and headed for her bedroom. Perhaps things would be clearer in the morning, especially since she planned to pay another visit to the paramedics.

And put a call in to Donna Wilson, she thought, just before falling into a deep sleep.

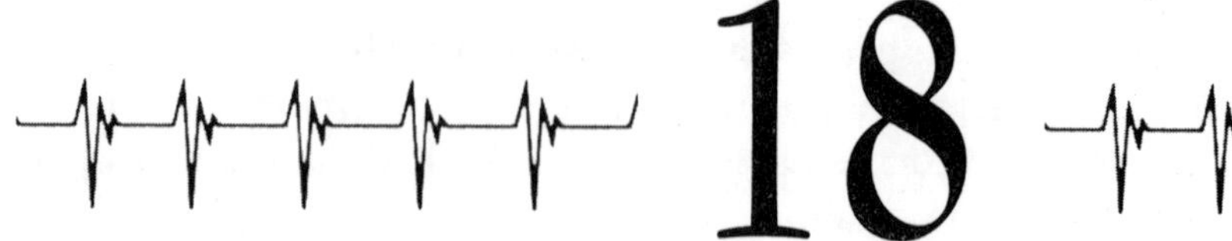

# 18

Sunday mornings were Rae's favorite. Most people slept in, and she and Leopold often had the Emeryville Marina to themselves. Except for the seagulls, of course, who always sailed overhead.

As Rae strolled along the concrete path, the bay lapped against the rocks and the private sailboats rocked to and fro in their berths. She thought about what Sam had said about the sun and the sky and the water, and all about life and how it should be lived. How she wanted to reach out and hold on to that belief forever.

But nothing was forever, she thought. This lesson she had learned at an early age. So why try to reach for it at all?

"Come on, boy!" she called out to Leopold, who had been enjoying himself chasing down seagulls.

They returned to her condo. She scooped out chunks of dried dog food from a bag that was as big as she was and filled Leopold's bowl. While he ate she made a quick breakfast of cold cereal and an apple, orange juice, and coffee. About midway through their meals, Harvey showed up.

"You walked him *and* you fed him?" Harvey asked in amazement as he helped himself to a bowl of cereal.

"He *is* my dog," Rae said.

Harvey arched a thick gray eyebrow. Rae rolled her eyes. "What did you think of Sam?" she asked.

"Nice enough fellow," Harvey said. "He's quite smitten with you, I can tell that much."

"Hmm," Rae said.

"Will you be home most of the day?" Harvey asked as he poured himself a cup of coffee.

"Harvey," Rae said, "what do you do when you want to trust somebody but you can't?"

"Oh, that's easy," Harvey said. "You trust yourself."

They finished their breakfast in silence. The only one making any noise was Leopold, who was eating with his usual enthusiasm.

Thirty minutes later she pulled her Porsche into the hospital's parking lot and walked across the street to the emergency room. Clouds tumbled down along the eastern hills behind the hospital and blocked out the sun that she and Leopold had enjoyed only an hour earlier.

The Hillstar ambulance sat parked in front of the emergency room and the twins were coming out of the emergency room doors. Each held a plastic coffee cup in his hand. It was amazing how much they looked alike, except one seemed much bulkier.

She had forgotten who was who, so she had to wait until they got close enough to read their name tags. It occurred to her that they might not recognize her either, because when she had spoken to them the first time she was more appropriately dressed. Now she wore blue jeans, a blue and white striped shirt, and black flats.

"Good morning," she said cheerily to the larger twin, who turned out to be Leonard. Rae remembered he was the driver and the less friendly of the two.

She waited until a wave of recognition crossed his face. It did and was followed by a look of displeasure. "Yes?" he asked gruffly.

"It takes a while for my brother to warm up to the human race in the morning," interjected a smiling Theodore McHenry. "How's that kid's arm?"

"I was just going to check on her," Rae said.

"I thought you did a fine job," Theodore said. "That nurse—jeez! I thought we were going to wind up trying to resuscitate *her*."

"What do you want, doctor?" Leonard said.

"Nothing really," Rae answered with what she hoped was a nonchalant air. She knew she had to be careful if she wanted to get the twins to level with her. "It's just that, well, I'm going to see the mother of that little baby and she said something yesterday that I think she's unclear on. You probably don't know it but she's an

L and D nurse at City Hospital. She was just wondering why you changed her IV bag on the way over from the Birth Center."

"She's lying," Leonard snapped.

"Well, *lying* is probably not quite the word for it. She felt that you gave her excellent care," Rae said placatingly as she watched their faces. They looked at each other in that secret way reserved for twins. "I told her she must be mistaken. But she's adamant about it. I mean, you guys never change IV bags in the rig, right?"

"That's right," said Theodore cheerily.

"Okay, that's all I wanted to know," Rae said.

"Good," Leonard said as he moved to open up the back doors.

Rae stepped aside as Theodore went around to the front. She looked into the back of the ambulance, and seeing the gurney fixed to a hook on the floor, immediately felt her legs weaken as memories of her mother's death came flooding back.

"I thought we were finished here," Leonard said impatiently.

"Do you give tours of these things?" she asked.

"Sure do!" Theodore said from the front seat. "Any time!"

"How about now?" Rae asked nervously.

Leonard shot his brother a warning glance. "Come on, Theodore. Not now."

"Climb aboard!" Theodore said, as if Leonard hadn't spoken at all.

For most people, getting into an ambulance would have been no big deal. For Rae it seemed as daunting as boarding a paratrooper's plane. But she had to find the courage to overcome her fear. The babies were depending on her. She was puzzled because she thought Theodore, since he was the one who had signed the reports, must also be the one spiking the patients' IV bags with the oxytocin. So why was he so nice? Wouldn't he try to dissuade her from looking at anything? Maybe it was Leonard who was the guilty one. He was certainly acting suspicious.

"Well, come on if you're coming," Leonard said.

Now even Leonard was inviting her in. What was going on here? Rae asked herself. She swallowed hard. She had no choice but to go through with it.

Slowly she climbed into the ambulance. Theodore had come into the back and pulled her up by grabbing her hand. His grip was strong and she thought he could easily lift a woman as big as Nola. As soon as she was inside, she felt her respiratory rate double. Sweat trickled down her back. It was crazy, but she almost expected to see blood everywhere, just as she had twenty-five years ago.

"What's the matter, Doc?" Theodore asked. "You look like you could use a little $O_2$."

"I can't stay long," Rae said shakily as she peered around the small cabin. She wiped the sweat from her forehead.

The cabin looked like a hybrid of a miniature hospital supply room and an operating room. Packaged instruments, wall oxygen, blood pressure cuff, and a gurney for a bed were neatly placed along the walls. To her right was a long gray mattress covering what could have been a window seat. The gurney—the same one that had brought over Nola and Meredith—was immediately in front of her. The back of the cabin was separated by two high-back seats—one for the driver and one for a passenger. The space between them was barely large enough for a small child to pass through.

"Everything has its place, doesn't it?" Rae observed, wiping her brow again.

"Are you sure you're all right?" Theodore asked.

"Fine, fine," she reassured him.

"If you say so. Well, any questions?"

Rae caught sight of an IV bag hanging from a hook next to the wall oxygen. The wrapping was off and she knew that would be the bag used on the next patient transferred from the Birth Center. If only she could get hold of it and have it tested for oxytocin, she thought. It was certainly possible that the reason Meredith didn't see Theodore inject anything into the IV bag was because he had injected it *before* he hooked it up to her IV catheter.

But how was she going to get her hands on that bag when the twins had already refused to give it to her?

"Can I see that?" she asked, pointing to the bag.

"Sure," Theodore said.

She held it in her hands, which, to her embarrassment, were still trembling. The longer she remained inside the ambulance, the more claustrophobic she felt. She turned the bag over and over. Nothing appeared suspicious about it, and the thought dismayed her.

"Well, I guess I'll be going," she said, handing it back to Theodore. There must be some way she could get that bag and herself out of the ambulance, she thought.

Theodore hung the bag on the hook. "Too bad you can't stay longer," he said.

"Thank you," she said. "Hey, can I see how you work your radio?" she asked.

"Now that's the best part," Theodore said, and he squeezed back between the two seats.

That was when Rae snatched the bag from the hook.

"Hey!" Leonard yelled after her. But by then she had jumped out of the ambulance and was streaking toward the parking lot. She lost herself in the sea of cars and when she saw that the twins had not chased her, she opened her car door and threw the IV bag in the back.

She was never, ever going back inside an ambulance, she promised herself as she slid into the driver's seat. For a few minutes she gripped the steering wheel and waited for her breathing to slow down. Her hairline was soaked, her muscles still trembling. From the glove compartment she removed a tissue and used it to wipe her face and neck.

And now, she thought, for her next trick, she needed to get hold of a lab to run the oxytocin level for her. Her cellular phone had been installed behind the stick shift. She dialed the hospital's operator and asked for special chemistry.

The voice that answered in the laboratory seemed young but energetic. After giving her name, Rae asked, "Can you tell me where I can get an oxytocin level run?" The clerk told Rae to hold on a minute and then returned and informed her that the hospital didn't run oxytocin levels. "I know that," Rae said irritably. "That's why I'm asking you who does."

She waited again and rapped her fingernails on the dashboard. The clerk came back on the phone and informed Rae that no one in the lab knew where such testing could be done. In fact, she checked their laboratory manual and the test wasn't even listed.

Rae knew that oxytocin levels were rarely measured except maybe in research projects. But it had been worth a shot. She grudgingly thanked the clerk and hung up the phone. She had a bag but no testing center. "Great," she said out loud. Across the street stood the Birth Center, and Rae pulled into the parking lot on the other side of a van. The Hillstar ambulance was still parked across the street, but the twins were not in sight.

She found Donna Wilson exiting the lobby's elevator.

"Can you spare any IV bags, Donna?" Rae asked.

Donna frowned. "Boy, you all must really be hard up over at Berkeley Hills," she said, "if you have to come here for medical supplies."

Rae chuckled. She wished it were that simple.

Donna returned with an IV bag. "Any chance of your coming back to work with us?" Rae asked casually as she looked the bag over. Everything about the bag appeared normal, she thought.

"As soon as this dump closes," Donna said.

Rae tried to keep her face impassive. "Oh?"

"I told you, I'm here because I have to be, not because I want to be," Donna said.

"That reminds me," Rae said slowly. She had to be careful. She didn't want to upset Donna as Sam had. "Have you heard any rumors about Bo selling this place and it being turned into a cardiac surgery center?"

Donna cast her eyes downward. "No," she said after a few seconds.

"Are you sure?" Rae asked.

"As long as I get my job back at Berkeley Hills, they could turn this place into a beauty parlor, for all I care." She looked at Rae. "But that doesn't mean I'm doing anything to expedite the sale," she said slowly. "I don't care what Dr. Hartman thinks."

Rae nodded. She believed Donna.

"Well, thanks for the bag," she said. "Hopefully we'll see you back at the hospital soon."

So Sam had told the truth, Rae thought.

With two bags in her car trunk, Rae sped up I-80. Now all she had to do was find a lab that could test them for oxytocin before her hearing.

Inside her study half an hour later, Rae reached for the phone. Harvey had Leopold over at his place so she had no distractions. In front of her was a list of numbers belonging to labs throughout the state of California, as well as a listing for New York and Washington, D.C. But before she could pick up the receiver, the phone rang.

It was Sam. "I've got something to show you," he said.

"Can't it wait until tomorrow?" Rae asked. The next day was

Monday, and as far as she was concerned, he could either go to her office or meet her on the maternity ward. She certainly didn't want him back in her home.

"You'll definitely want to see this."

He sounded very serious. What did she have to lose? she thought. It wasn't as if she were fooled by him anymore. "Okay, Sam," she said, "but I'm very busy."

While waiting for Sam, Rae called the labs. Not one could help her out, according to the lab techs. She had reached the bottom of her California list and was just about to switch to the out-of-state labs when the tech for a lab in San Diego said she could run the tests for Rae.

"And how long will it take?" she asked as she eagerly wrote down the information.

"Hold on, please," the tech said. "Let me check."

Rae could barely hear a muffled conversation between the tech and someone in the background. Finally the tech came back on. "From the time we get the bags here and the report back to you in the mail, it will take about two weeks."

"Two weeks!" Rae cried. "Sorry. Look, I need those results now."

But the tech had hung up before Rae finished her sentence.

"Damn it!" she said as she slammed the receiver into the cradle.

Then the doorbell rang. She had forgotten all about Sam. What in the world did he want to show her that was so important?

He stood there with a medical journal in his hand. "For you," he said as he handed it to her.

They sat in the living room. Rae felt her mood was gloomy enough; and now here was Sam, giving her some reading material and smiling at her as if it were the Sunday funnies.

"I've been doing some homework of my own," he said. "I've marked page fifty-two for you. It's a half-page article about a midwestern hospital called Rushing River, where a bunch of maternity nurses got canned due to cutbacks. Next thing you know, you've got labor patients going unattended."

Rae flipped through the pages until she found Sam's folded corner on page fifty-two.

Sam rose and began to pace in front of the window. "What happened next," he said, "was that their cesarean section rate shot through the ceiling."

"Do you want me to read it or not?" Rae asked.

"I'm saving you the trouble," Sam said.

Rae leaned back in her chair and spread the article across her lap. "Then you could have told me this on the phone," she said.

"Anyway," Sam said, ignoring her comment, "everyone wondered what the hell was going on. They looked at the C-section rate and found out that most sections were being done for fetal distress—not because women were trying to deliver babies as big as Nola's."

Rae couldn't help but be interested in what Sam was saying. Sitting up in her chair she said, "Go on."

"Well, what happened," Sam said, "was that the few nurses who were left were trying to juggle their patient load as best as possible. But they have a lot of babies at Rushing River, and at least half of them are born to first-time moms. We all know that seventy percent of first-time moms wind up with oxytocin to move things along. The problem was the nurse would get the oxytocin started in one room and then get it going in another room and after a while she'd have four or five oxytocin drips going at the same time. And bang! Everybody was getting hyperstimulated and the babies' heart rates were bottoming out."

"All they had to do was turn off the oxytocin," Rae said, unimpressed with Sam's story.

"By the time they got back to some of the mothers it was too late for that," Sam said. "They whipped those patients down to the section room and got them delivered. If you look at the article, you'll see that the number of low-Apgar-score babies increased, as did the number of nursery ICU admissions."

Rae studied the report. "One woman died from a ruptured uterus?" she asked incredulously as she looked upon Sam's face.

"So did her baby when that happened," Sam said. "Just like Bo's patient."

Rae read the whole article for herself and then closed the journal. Outside, a soft patter of rain hit the window.

"Where'd you get this?" she asked.

"From the hospital librarian," he said. "I asked her to do a MEDLINE search on fetal distress for me. This was the only article that got my attention."

Sam was watching as he waited for her answer. Was he just

pretending to care? Had the librarian really given him the article or had he found it some time ago and used it to devise his own plan with Marco and the ambulance drivers? And what about the photocopies of the ambulance reports—why hadn't he told her about them?

What made Rae most suspicious was the fact that she had not told Sam that she suspected the paramedics were using oxytocin. That thought had not occurred to her until she herself used oxytocin to stop Mattie Henshaw's patient from bleeding to death. So had he come up with the same theory after talking to a librarian? Or, more likely, was he afraid that Rae was eventually going to put two and two together and discover what he already knew—already knew because he was involved?

"So, what's your next step?" he asked. He had risen again, his eyes scanning the carpet.

"Looking for something?" she asked.

"No, not really," he answered nonchalantly.

Rae wanted to confront him about the ambulance reports. Or did she? She had essentially stolen the copies from him. Was a thief any better than a liar? she thought.

"Is there anything else?" she asked.

"Yes. Can I take you to dinner tonight?"

She rose and handed him back the journal. "I've got some calls to make and some things to think through," she said. "You asked me what my next step is, and unfortunately it doesn't involve a lot of socializing."

Rae saw Sam's hurt look and knew she was being meaner than she had to be. In fact, she was being downright rude. She had made love to the man only the day before. Now here she was essentially throwing him out of her condo—again.

Still, she couldn't tell him about her plans to go to the ambulance warehouse. She'd just have to make something else up until she could fully trust him. She needed a bag from the warehouse because if the paramedics were spiking the bags, they were most likely doing it there. If she could just show that the warehouse supply was clear, she could prove that the paramedics were in on the killings.

She walked him to the door. "Oh, I almost forgot," he said. "The twin named Theodore. I heard you paid him a little visit today. Did you notice anything about his eyes? I saw it today, just like I think I saw it the first time I spoke with him in the cafeteria."

"Was that really your first time, Sam?"

He stared hard at her for a second time and then said, "I'll let you answer that one for yourself, Rae. Anyway, Theodore's pupils are very small, much smaller than his brother's. It's nice having a natural comparison."

Rae glanced at her watch. It was coming up on five in the evening.

"And he's leaner than his brother. I think—no, I'd bet you money he's on something," Sam said.

Now what was Sam up too? Trying to throw her another ringer?

"Theodore could be on a number of things," Sam began. "But it's the weight loss, the long sleeves, and the small pupils that make me suspect IV narcotics. You can be on that stuff for years without getting caught. It's the long sleeves that let me know he's shooting up. Have you ever seen the twins in short sleeves?"

"Their uniforms have long sleeves, Sam," Rae said dismissively.

"Everybody knows about the street junkies—the ones hiding in the alleys with no other place to go, not knowing if each fix will be their last or not. But most heroin addicts—"

"Heroin?" Rae interrupted incredulously.

"Most heroin addicts," Sam continued, "hold down steady jobs, for a while, at least. All they have to do—besides wear long sleeves summer and winter—is get to a bathroom alone three or four times during the workday."

Although Rae didn't believe Sam, she recalled something that Bernie had said: the twins didn't stay in one place for too long.

"A junkie ambulance driver?" Rae said with disbelief. "I suppose there are doctors running around shooting up too? You wear long sleeves a lot, Sam. I have on long sleeves and I go to the bathroom at least every four hours."

Sam rose and took a chair right next to Rae. He patted her on the head like a child. "How you manage to do what you do *and* be so naive is beyond me," Sam said. Then his face took on a more serious expression. "Heroin doesn't choose a profession," he said. "My brother shot up ten to twelve times a day. He was an anesthesiologist in Boston too."

Rae's eyes widened. "Your brother?"

"At first it was morphine—Theodore could have easily started off on that. Of course my brother had no problem getting hold of syringes and needles. And neither would Theodore. I was once naive like you, Rae. I saw him every day and I didn't know he had a problem until the day he overdosed on that stuff and one of the nurses found him stone dead in the locker room."

Touched by Sam's story, Rae gently touched his cheek. "I'm so sorry," she said.

"Me too," he said with a sad laugh. "But the reason I'm telling you is not for your sympathy. I think it's a real possibility in Theodore's case. Which ups the ante. Addicts can be extremely dangerous. So be careful, okay?"

"We could get him tested, I guess," Rae suggested. "But I can't believe we might have to worry about a strung-out ambulance driver on top of everything else."

"Testing will not be exactly easy," Sam said. "But I want to know *how* Theodore is paying for his habit. That's always the question with a heroin addict."

"That's it! He's being paid!" Rae said excitedly.

"Paid? By whom?"

Rae took a seat next to Sam. "Look," she said, "I don't know if he's on heroin or not. I've got to find that out first. But let's say he is. This whole time I've been trying to figure out why a paramedic would do this thing to the patients at the Birth Center. Well, if he's acting as a henchman for the person who's giving him money for his dope, then he doesn't really need a logical reason. All he has to do is spike the bags like he's told. There's nothing like an addiction to motivate you."

"Heroin's the worst," Sam said grimly.

"Now I see how somebody who's supposed to help save lives might wind up trying to kill those he's hired to save. Heroin costs a lot of money—more than a paramedic can make."

"So someone's paying Theodore just enough to get him through each day, and all Theodore has to do is spike a few bags at the warehouse and load them onto his truck. Somebody with some money. And with a high enough stake to see the Birth Center shut down."

"It's a possibility," Sam admitted. "I wonder who?"

They were staring at each other now as if searching for answers to entirely different questions. The rain beat down upon the window even harder and a bolt of lightning broke across the sky. "Maybe we can compare notes over dinner?" Sam said.

"Well, I . . ." Rae stammered. She had already told him she had things to do that did not involve socializing with him. On the other hand she wanted to—had to!—confront him about the copies of the ambulance reports if she was ever going to feel comfortable around him. And oh how she wanted to feel comfortable around him.

"I have connections at Chez Panisse," he said temptingly.

"But Chez Panisse isn't open on Sundays," Rae replied.

"There's a chef visiting from Florence," Sam explained. "Alice is making an exception."

"For someone who's only been in Berkeley a couple of months, you get around," Rae said with admiration.

"I like to eat," Sam said simply. "Can you meet me in an hour?"

Rae nodded. She'd have to confront him about the reports sooner or later. "Sam," she said, "there is something I need to talk to you about. But if you aren't straight with me . . ."

Sam arched an eyebrow and then opened the door. "Chez Panisse, in an hour. I'll answer any and all questions you have."

# 19

AFTER SAM LEFT, RAE CALCULATED THAT SHE HAD JUST ENOUGH time for a visit to the ambulance company before meeting him for dinner. Minutes later, freshly groomed and dressed to kill—or be killed, she thought wryly—she used her car cellular phone to call information for the number of the Hillstar Ambulance Company. The rain pelted against the windshield as she turned off I-80 at the Richmond Street exit. She had just passed Raymond's on her right. Who, she mused, was paying off Theodore McHenry? And what excuse would she give the receptionist for wanting a liter of lactated Ringer's? She still hadn't answered either question by the time she pulled into the parking lot.

The first thing she noted was the tight security. The parking lot was enclosed by a wire fence, and she had to ring up on the intercom to get in. She parked her car among Firebirds and Camaros—guy cars, she thought. Behind the main building, which looked like a miniature-size college campus, were parked at least thirty ambulances in marked stalls. Rae tried not to look at them as she walked past. One ambulance was bad enough. But a whole army?

Inside the front office, she presented herself to a young woman dressed in a tight-fitting black tube dress. "Are you the one who just called?" asked the woman. She looked bored as she twisted a short red curl above her ear.

Rae introduced herself. She had expected to see dispatch equipment, but the room looked like any other generic reception area for a business. The exception was the paramedics and EMTs passing through, mostly good-looking, buffed young men who called out greetings to the young receptionist.

"Nice place," Rae commented, wondering where the IV bags were stored.

"Not my idea of a way to spend a Sunday evening, but to each his own," the woman replied. She yawned loudly. "So, what's cookin', Doc? I'm sure we both have better things to do than just standing here looking at each other."

Rae hadn't exactly figured out how to ask a stranger for an IV bag. Stealing one from an ambulance was one thing, but from a warehouse was something entirely different. "Well, I was wondering . . ." she began.

She reached into her purse, pulled out her wallet, and placed a fifty-dollar bill on the counter. "Would that cover a liter of lactated Ringer's?" she asked.

The young woman's eyes lit right up. She looked at the bill and then at Rae. Finally, she took the money and stuffed it down the front of her dress. "My evening might not be wasted after all," she said with satisfaction. "I'll get one from the box."

She went into a back room and brought out the bag Rae requested. "Would you mind if I didn't give you a receipt?" she asked, as she handed Rae the plastic-wrapped liter of fluid. Rae had brought a grocery store bag to carry it in.

"It'll be our little secret," Rae said. She was about to place her wallet back in her purse but then asked, "Tell me something. Are your drivers ever tested for drugs?"

The young woman's eyes narrowed suspiciously. "Hey, are you a cop?" she asked as she reached back into the top of her dress.

Rae flipped another fifty-dollar bill on the counter. "I won't ask for a receipt for this little favor either," she promised.

The woman took it. Her eyes darted left and right and then she said, "No, thank goodness they don't test any—"

"May I help you?"

Rae turned and saw a gentle-looking, gray-haired woman staring at her. "I was just leaving," Rae said.

The older woman took a seat behind the counter. "My granddaughter," she said. "Now what would I do without her?"

The young woman winked at Rae. "I don't work here. I just help granny out."

Rae nodded. "You'll go far in this world," she said. "Just don't spend our little secret in one place."

Inside her car, Rae pulled out a magnifying lens and studied the IV bag. She searched every inch of the plastic wrapping for a needle puncture. But night had descended, made even darker by the rain, and it was hard to see much of anything.

She checked the time on the clock. Her dinner date with Sam was supposed to start in five minutes. If she hurried, she had just enough time to call the lab that would run the test on the first IV bag. She wanted to let them know she'd be sending them a total of three bags immediately.

So with the rain beating down on her windshield and the roof of her car, and using the overhead light to shine against a small notepad upon which she had written the number, she called the San Diego lab. A different tech answered the phone this time and he said the results could be out in five days. As long as Rae was willing to pay the extra fee there should be no problem.

"All it takes is money," Rae thought to herself as she hung up.

Feeling more optimistic, Rae gunned the engine back down I-80 and exited on University. She took the frontage road to Cedar and headed east. Due to the rain, the streets were deserted for the most part. She wondered where Nola lived and how she had come to have her baby at the Birth Center.

The restaurant was located on Shattuck Avenue and was world renowned for it emphasis on fresh, high-quality food. In front was a wooden archway lined with wisteria, but otherwise it was an unassuming, two-story wooden structure. Yet some of Berkeley's most affluent people ate there, especially those who lived nearby in the half-million- to one-million-dollar homes in the hills surrounding Rae's hospital. But the best thing was that you could come dressed as you liked there—from after-five dresses to a form-fitting, short black skirt and jacket, as Rae now wore.

She ran up the narrow wooden staircase to the cafe. The prix fixe dining room occupied the first floor.

"Rae, I haven't seen you in ages!" cried Alex, the maître d'.

"Hello. How's little George?" Rae asked.

"I want my money back," Alex said with a grimace. "I told you to put him back the minute he got here."

"Gee, there seems to be a conspiracy against two-year-olds," Rae laughed.

"So what brings you here tonight?"

Before Rae could answer, a male waiter walked up to Alex and said, "Your wife's on the phone. Something about your son and the VCR."

"See what I mean!" cried Alex as he threw up his hands and rolled his eyes.

As Alex left, a waiter approached Rae. "Can I help you?" he asked.

"I'm supposed to meet Sam Hartman," Rae said.

"Ah, here's his name," the waiter said as he pointed at the reservation book. "I guess he hasn't come in yet—oh, oh, that's right. I took the call. He said he will be a little late. He's a doctor, right?"

Rae nodded and thanked him for the information. "I'll wait over—"

Just then she saw Walker Stuart coming up the staircase. "Well, well," he said beaming. "I'm waiting for Denise. Hopefully she'll be late as usual and that'll give me time to get caught up with you."

Rae was happy to see Walker. She had a million things to tell him. But exactly how, she wondered as the waiter led them to a table for two, did one tell the CEO of the hospital that somebody was running around trying to bump off pregnant women and their babies?

"I'm glad I ran into you tonight," Walker said after they were seated. He was dressed in a black blazer, charcoal pants, and an ecru-white silk and linen shirt, the latter accentuating the white of his neatly cropped beard. On the table sat a bottle of Billecart-Salmon Brut, which Walker had ordered after Rae explained that she was waiting for Sam.

"Me too," Rae said. "Saves me a visit to your office tomorrow."

"Listen, Rae," he said, "I was in my office today. Sometimes even CEOs have to catch up with the paperwork on a Sunday. Anyway, I received a copy of a complaint against you from Arnie Driver. It said he's scheduled a hearing to have you thrown off the staff."

Rae nodded unhappily, but before she could speak, Walker continued. "When you get home tonight, you'll find a message on your machine from me. I called your place right before I came here. If there is anything I can do, you tell me, okay? Unfortunately, I can't call Arnie and give him hell. The medical staff bylaws say I need to be notified about such hearings but they don't allow me to participate."

"I know that, Walker," Rae said. "But there are more important things than my hearing I want to talk to you about."

"Don't say that, Rae. What can be more important than your position on our staff? We're talking about your livelihood here. And I don't want to lose the best obstetrician this hospital has ever had."

"Walker, I promise you, I'm taking this very seriously. But I think it's all connected—the bad babies, the hearing, the assault on Bernie . . ."

"Did you know her well?" Walker asked.

"Bernie Brown is my best friend," Rae said.

"You're kidding! The nurse, you mean—the one . . . I'm sorry, Rae. I had no idea. I would have asked you about her first if I knew she was a friend of yours."

"She doesn't have an enemy in the world, Walker," Rae said.

Walker sighed and gazed around the room as if lost for words. Finally he said, "And you were the one who found her."

"Any word from the police?" Rae asked. She sipped her champagne, but suddenly it had no taste.

Walker shook his head. "But our security people are giving the police whatever they need: log books, computer printouts, employee records—the works."

They were silent for a few moments and then Rae said, "It gets worse, Walker."

"Tell me," he said.

Rae told him about her oxytocin theory and the role she suspected the Hillstar ambulance drivers played. Walker listened intently, nodding his head occasionally or running his fingertip thoughtfully up and down the stem of his glass. "And," Rae concluded, "I think whoever wants bad babies coming out of the Birth Center is most likely the person who attacked Bernie."

She sipped her champagne again and waited for Walker to say something.

"Seems to me, based upon what you said," Walker replied, "that Berkeley Hills Hospital looks like the villain here. The babies may have come out of the Birth Center in trouble, but they delivered in our hospital. That means our delivery records will show that the problem is ours, not theirs. I hope you haven't told this story to too many people?"

"But what do *you* think, Walker? Just tell me I'm not crazy."

"You're not, but I think your story is," he said flatly.

"But it could happen—"

Walker leaned toward her. "Look, Rae, I want to believe your story. No one wants that damn Birth Center shut down more than I do. But—well, for instance, if what you say is true, why not just measure the level of oxytocin in each patient's blood?"

Rae leaned forward and patted Walker's hand. "That, Walker, is why *you're* the administrator and *I'm* the doctor. Oxytocin is the perfect drug for someone who wants to kill pregnant women and babies. Nobody measures it—for one thing, it only stays in the bloodstream for a minute or two. It's a clear fluid that looks like water, so a person could spike an IV bag and no one would know."

Rae paused to show Walker the fifth finger of her right hand. "The vials are shorter than my pinkie," she explained. "That makes them easy to steal and then hide. They're all over labor and delivery, and in the OR—even a cleaning lady could slip a few in her pocket if she wanted."

Walker stroked his beard. "Well, for everyone's sake, Rae, let's hope to God you're wrong."

"You still don't believe me, do you?" Rae asked curtly.

"If I believed you, I would have to go to the police," he said. "But they would want hard evidence—proof—that what you say is true." He paused to shake his head. "You're the finest obstetrician we have, Rae. You know my personal feelings and the respect and admiration I have for you. But what you just told me, well, frankly, it gives me great concern. I'm worried about you. You're overworked, you've got some asshole trying to throw you off the staff, and if that happens, you'll be reported to the state medical board and they'd really go after you for these crackpot suspicions."

Rae leaned forward. "In medicine, Walker, a doctor often has to use her intuition. For example, a patient who had a cesarean section two days ago might have normal vital signs, but an anxious look on her face and a little shortness of breath would make me wonder if she has a pulmonary embolus from a blood clot in her leg. Now unless that thought occurs to me, I wouldn't order a set of blood gases that could show a low blood oxygen level. A low blood oxygen would make me order a ventilation-perfusion scan that would confirm the diagnosis of a pulmonary embolus. An embolus can kill, Walker, so we would place that patient on heparin and eventually the clot would dissolve. But unless I had followed my gut instinct, and ordered that first set of blood gases, the embolus would have killed her."

Rae paused to see if her words were getting through to Walker.

"I don't know, Rae," he said slowly. "Instincts are one thing. Wrongheadedness is another."

"Walker, do you know Howard Marvin?" Rae asked.

"Now there's a wily son of a bitch," Walker said, still obviously distracted by Rae's oxytocin theory.

"Yes, so I've heard. Do you know if he's interested in buying off Bo and turning the Birth Center into some kind of mini-heart-hospital?"

"What?"

"Has he talked to you—I mean, has he tried to get the hospital to go in with him? That's what Bo said. And according to Bo, Marco's supposed to run the thing."

"No, Howard Marvin has never discussed that idea."

"But would you consider it if he did call you, Walker? Even after what I've told you, would you put Marco's program over mine?"

Walker placed his glass on his table. "If the opportunity presented itself, and OB was still losing money, why yes I would, Rae. But you've posed a hypothetical question. We have something much more concrete to worry about, don't you think? Bad babies and your hearing, and a maniac who beat up your best friend. So let's focus on what's in front of us, okay? Rae, are you listening?"

"Yeah," Rae said. "But I also wanted to tell you I think Howard's somehow involved in this oxytocin thing."

Walker heaved a loud sigh. Then, dropping his voice, he said, "I said Howard Marvin is a son of a bitch, Rae, but that's with his business dealings. You're accusing him of being a murderer, can't you see that? Now look, for the last time, you keep talking about a murder conspiracy and somebody's likely to lock you up.

"There have been bad babies for sure, but the way I see it, it's because the Birth Center delivered bad care. Isn't that what you told Heidi? Isn't that the way you planned to get the doctors back to Berkeley Hills? Stick to your original plan, Rae. Expose the Birth Center for offering third-rate medicine. Don't make up theories that make my hospital, and you most of all, look bad."

"This isn't about how we look, Walker."

"Please, Rae, be smart about this. And for God's sake, don't tell this to anybody at your hearing! I told you I don't believe it and I'm on your side! Imagine what Arnie Driver and the rest of the docs on the committee will think."

He paused to wave his hand over his head. Rae looked up and saw Walker's wife, Denise, dressed in a St. John knit suit, standing next to Alex.

"Promise me?" Walker said again.

"I can't," Rae said, slumping back against her chair. Suddenly she felt more like a petulant child than the vice-head of obstetrics. This father figure thing was a two-way street, she thought ruefully.

Walker swallowed his last sip of champagne and rose from the table. "I'm not done with you yet," he admonished. "We'll talk again. In the meantime, I'm going to wrack my brain to figure out a way I can talk some sense into Arnie Driver. I don't want my best obstetrician thrown off the staff for trying to save babies. But please, Rae, no more talk about ambulance drivers and a baby murder conspiracy!"

She had desperately hoped Walker would believe her. Now she had to ask herself a tough question: If he didn't, how in the hell was she going to get her colleagues to?

"I hope you got my message," Sam said five minutes later as he slipped into the seat across from Rae. "Marco called and asked me to get a case started until the first-call guy got done with an aortic valve."

The waiter had not yet come by to remove the champagne glasses since Walker's departure from the table five minutes earlier. Now Sam glanced at the empty glass in front of him and the near-full one in front of Rae and raised one eyebrow quizzically. She couldn't help but notice that he had that pumped-up look most doctors get after coming out of the OR. It came from the exhilaration of being involved with saving a life, mixed with gratitude that it was someone else who had come close to death and not yourself.

Unfortunately, Rae thought, as Sam picked up the menu, she did not share his exhilaration. Walker's admonishment had left her as flat as the half-hour-old champagne still in her glass.

"Walker was just here," Rae said. "I told him about my theory and he started drinking."

"I'm surprised *your* glass is still full," Sam said.

Rae frowned. "Very funny."

"Look, Rae, you can't expect people to buy into it the first time they hear it."

"Oh, yes I can," Rae said, staring at him defiantly. She sat back and crossed her arms over her chest. "I expect them to and I'm going to make sure they do. Walker just doesn't want to believe it—like you once said you didn't want to believe it until you saw that article."

"You don't give up, do you?"

She picked up her menu. "So you're late because Marco asked you to do him a favor?" Rae asked. "I thought you were the one who said a doctor should fit medicine into his life—not the other way around."

She gazed up from her menu to catch Sam's expression. He pursed his lips together as if pondering the question of the century. "Touché," he said finally.

They placed their orders: a half dozen Hog Island oysters followed by squid risotto for Rae and a porcini mushroom salad followed by roasted quail and creamy polenta for Sam.

"And a bottle of Dolcetto," Sam said to the waiter. He turned back to Rae. "Anyway, about last night," he began. "I drove home thinking that you seemed nervous—upset, really, right before I left. I kept thinking that it might have been my fault. Did I say or do something?"

Rae thought about the ambulance reports. "You're always saying and doing things to upset me," she said lightly, trying to decide how best to confront him.

Sam frowned. "But last night was different. Usually when you have something to say to me, you say it. I admire that quality in you, Rae. It allows me to be myself. There's no guessing . . . my marriage was based on trying to read my wife's mind."

Rae reached for her purse and pulled out the copies of the ambulance reports. She placed them on the table and then watched Sam's face.

He reached out slowly for them. He flipped through each page and by the time he reached the last one, he was no longer looking at the pages but directly at her. She had never seen him angry before, but she knew he was angry now. She didn't care, she told herself firmly—she needed an explanation.

"I've been looking all over for these," he said quietly.

The waiter came with the first course. Sam folded the papers and placed them into the front pocket of his blazer. Then he picked up his fork and began eating the mushrooms. "Excellent," he said.

"Well?" Rae asked.

"How're the Hoggies?" Sam inquired.

"I found the copies on the floor of my living room," Rae said.

"Umm-hmm," Sam said.

"So, why do you have them?" Rae asked.

"What took you so long to give them to me?" Sam asked. He had stopped chewing and was staring at her. "And why haven't you said anything about the other night? In your condo, remember?"

Rae picked up the cut lemon and squeezed the juice across the oysters. Using a small fork, she freed the first one from its shell and dipped it into the mignonette sauce. Two could play this game. "Why haven't you?" she asked.

"Because I've been trying to be patient with this baby thing!" Sam yelled.

People sitting at nearby tables turned toward them. One man called out, "A baby? Don't do it, man! Your life will be over!" The room erupted in laughter.

Ignoring the crowd, Rae said, "What were you doing with the reports, Sam? They're the same ones Marco—or somebody—stole from the patients' charts!"

"You think I stole these?" Sam asked, pointing at his breast pocket incredulously.

"No, but . . ."

"Okay, here it is," Sam said. "I'm only going to tell you once, so pay attention."

"I am," Rae said.

"I was there at Nola's section," Sam said, "remember? But you weren't there when the paramedics first brought her into the room.

She was screaming her head off about the pain. Then this gorked-out kid gets delivered. Later, I see the twins piling French fries on their lunch trays. Of course I was nice to them: I wanted to ask them what happened. That's when I noticed that Theodore's pupils were as small as pinheads. I knew he was on something. His size, compared to his brother, confirmed it for me . . .

"I make it my business to follow up on my patients, Rae. I heard about Meredith—no, not from you, from Marco, believe it or not. I decided I had to see for myself why two bad cases—back to back—had happened in less than two hours in the number one baby hospital in the state.

"Then you came to me with your theories about a conspiracy and pointed your finger at me, at Marco, and at Howard Marvin. I should be angry, but I know not to take things personally when you care so much about those babies. That stuff was crazy, but your suspicions about the ambulance drivers—well, hell, Rae, maybe you are on to something. The problem is that, based upon the facts, I can't figure out how they could have gotten oxytocin or anything else into the bags when you have a veteran maternity nurse as a witness saying that they didn't."

Rae couldn't believe what she was hearing. Sam had not only been listening to her all along, but had been thinking, really thinking, about all of it. Now, as she stared across the table at his face—filled with frustration and concern—she knew he was telling the truth. And she believed him—finally.

"Okay, that's right, the one thing that Meredith Bey was most certain of was that the twins never injected her line with anything," Rae explained eagerly. "But Nola Payne went off when she saw Betty, the recovery room nurse, changing her IV bag. It was still wrapped in plastic."

"That's the contradiction that makes this whole thing so damn confusing," he interrupted.

"Sam, if you think about it, it wouldn't take much for somebody to draw up the oxytocin into a syringe and then attach the syringe to a spinal needle and stick the spinal needle through the plastic the bag is wrapped in."

For a few seconds Sam stared at her, and then finally said with dawning realization, "And straight through the rubber nipple port."

"That's right," Rae said.

Sam sat back in his chair. "Incredible."

"Is it?" Rae asked.

"And the hole would be so tiny nobody would notice," Sam added.

"Not without a magnifying lens," Rae said. "That's why I went to the ambulance warehouse to check things out for myself."

"You went there? Alone?"

"And there were no holes in their bags."

They sat in silence as Rae's words sunk in. Sam obviously accepted her theory as a good possibility to explain what had been happening to the patients at the Birth Center. But Rae had more questions and decided she might as well ask them all.

"Sam, I asked you earlier about Marco and Howard Marvin. I want to know all you know."

Sam sighed. "Marco has not told me *who* is behind the idea of a freestanding cardiac center. I do know that he has big plans to expand his heart program because he wants me to be in charge of insuring quality outcomes if the venture ever takes off."

"So he *has* been talking to Howard Marvin?"

"You're not listening, Rae," Sam said. "Did you hear me bring up Howard's name? I couldn't say one way or the other if Marco's interested in teaming up with Perfect Health. But what difference does it make? I didn't even know until the board meeting Friday morning that his heart program's expansion was linked to the closure of yours, okay?"

Rae nodded numbly. "And the reports?" she asked.

Sam sighed. "Yvonne copied them for me so that I could review them at my leisure. But don't tell anybody. I promised her I wouldn't tell a soul."

The waiter returned to clear away the empty plates. During their main course, Rae found herself relaxing. Unlike Bo, Sam was placing no demands on her for entering into a relationship. Yet somehow, they seemed to be in one. In many ways, he was a bad risk. He was a doctor, and she could certainly vouch for the fact that doctors made problematic partners. Plus he was white.

Yet, he was a man before his color. In the long run, what else mattered more than that? A man of bone and muscle and flesh just like everyone else. He had a brain and a heart and a soul. And of all the men—of all the people—Rae had ever met, Sam most seemed to have his soul in the right place.

"Sam," she said, "let's go home. I don't want dessert. I want you."

Back at Rae's place, they spent the next two hours making love. This time, Rae knew it was not out of neediness but out of compassion and understanding. Her heart spoke to his, and his to hers. As it should be, she thought happily.

"Do you always treat your suspects this well?" Sam asked with a smile, rolling her over and interrupting her thoughts.

"You have the right to remain silent," Rae teased as she leaned over to kiss him. "You have the right to remain attractive at all times . . ."

The rest of her words were lost in his embrace. The reason why she had decided to trust Sam Hartman, she thought with sudden amazement, was that she had finally come to trust herself.

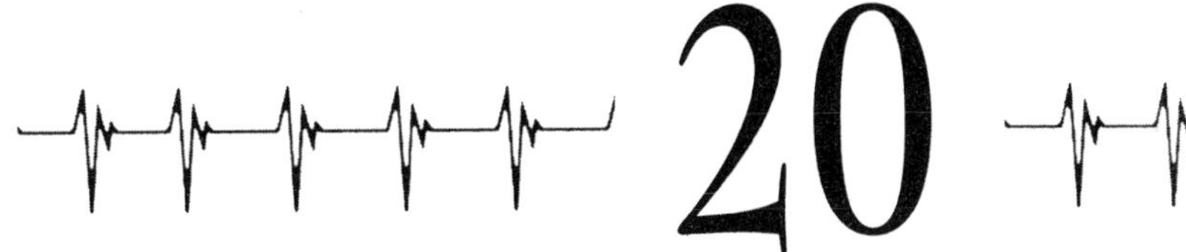

# 20

For the next several days, Rae tried to adhere to her regular schedule while waiting for the oxytocin report to come back from the special lab. She had mailed all three bags simultaneously: the one from the Birth Center, the unwrapped one from the ambulance, and the one she had bribed from the warehouse receptionist. But somehow the hospital seemed a less friendly place to Rae. There were fewer cheerful greetings in the hallways, nurses and doctors had begun to look at her with more than a trace of suspicion, and sometimes Rae thought she even heard whispers after she walked past.

She knew exactly what they were talking about.

According to Jessica, the nurse attending to Baby Jesus in the neonatal ICU, Arnie Driver had spent the week telling everybody that Rae had deliberately taken her time in delivering Nola's baby and had made the delivery of Meredith's baby as complicated as possible.

The day before, Rae had just finished seeing her last patient for the morning when her desk phone rang. Bobbie, her office manager, told Rae that Dr. Hartman was on the line—again.

Rae smiled and picked up the phone. Rae had seen him often during the past week, responding gladly to his frequent invitations. True to form, Sam asked her if she was free for the afternoon.

"Not today. I've been trying all week to talk to the paramedics again. They've been off for a few days but they're back. My hearing's tomorrow. I've had my office manager call down to the lab. So far I haven't heard anything."

"Mind if I come along?" Sam asked.

"Meet me in front of the emergency room in half an hour," Rae said.

She hung up the phone and completed her paperwork. Bobbie poked her head into the room. "Sorry," she said. "Results still aren't ready."

"We've got a few more days," Rae said, then gathered up her things and headed for the emergency room.

The afternoon was bright and brisk, perfect for a college football game, Rae thought. But this was no game she was playing. This was as real as it got. She saw Sam standing by the Hillstar ambulance and he waved Rae over. He was still dressed in surgical scrubs and gown. "Leonard's by himself right now," Sam said.

She walked over to the ambulance. The back door was open and inside, Leonard was fiddling with an IV bag. "Hi, remember me?" Rae asked. Enough of Dr. Nice, Rae had told herself. The twins were lying and she wasn't going to let them off the hook this time.

Leonard dropped the bag. Quickly he stooped to pick it up. "What do *you* want? Did you come to steal another IV bag?" he asked nastily.

Rae thought about climbing into the back cabin with him. But she remembered her previous reaction and decided to stay put. Sam stood next to her with his arms crossed.

"I want to know why your brother said he didn't change Meredith's IV bag when I know and you know he did," Rae said.

"Get lost," Leonard said.

"Meredith's an L and D nurse—I told you that, remember?"

"You told me a lot of things," Leonard said.

"She's not going to let this drop," Rae said. "Her husband's an attorney."

Rae cut her eyes to Sam to warn him to keep his trap shut. So what if she was lying?

"So?" Leonard said. He tore the wrapping off the bag and hung it on the same hook from which Rae had stolen the bag the week before.

"A medical *malpractice* attorney," Rae said. "He believes his wife, not your brother."

Leonard jumped to the ground and leaned against the rig. "Okay, fine," he said. He wiped his thick neck. "So what if my brother changes an IV bag every now and then? That's in our job description, you know. Don't come to us just because you fucked up. Oh yeah," he said, when he saw the look on her face, "I heard all about it, *Doc.*"

Leonard leaned against the ambulance. "Any more questions?" he asked.

"So why did he change it?" Rae asked. Despite her best efforts, she felt fury building inside her. Obviously Arnie had spoken to the drivers too. He certainly was building a case against her. Well, she thought, Arnie didn't know who he was messing with.

"How the hell do I know?" Leonard asked. "He changed it, okay? What's a bag of salt water got to do with a bad baby anyway?"

To her surprise, Rae believed for the first time since she met the paramedics that Leonard was on the level. He may have lied about what his brother did or did not do, but he seemed not to know about the damage the IV bag had caused. In fact, he stared at Rae as if he depended on her to tell him what she was so worried about.

"Maybe there was more than salt water in that bag," she said.

Leonard's big hands balled into fists the size of cantaloupes. He turned to Sam. "You better get her out of here," he said menacingly.

Sam held up his own hands in protest. "Hey, I'm scared of her too," he said.

"Look, Leonard," Rae said as she took a step closer. Leonard was some six feet tall so she had to tilt her head back to face him. "I stole that bag and I sent it to the lab. Anytime now I'll find out what else was in it besides salt water. So quit trying to defend your brother. You know he's done something and you know the answer's in that bag."

"I don't know anything," Leonard snapped.

"So prove it," Rae said. She looked into the back cabin. "Let me look at those bags."

Leonard moved his bulk so he blocked her way. "What's the name of that lab?" he asked.

"Get out of my way!" Rae said. She tried to push him aside but he grabbed her. Sam jumped in and pulled Leonard's arm away.

"Okay, okay," said Leonard, his hands in the air. "But how do I know *you* didn't put something in that bag and then ship it, huh?

How do I know you don't want to get your hands on some more, spike them with whatever the hell you think my brother used, and then send them to the lab just to save your own hide?"

"Just where is your brother?" Sam asked.

"Far away, I hope," Leonard said. He turned his back to Rae and Sam and started to climb back into the ambulance.

"Oh, he's far away, all right," Sam said. "Shooting up gets you in la-la land in a hurry."

"Fuck off," Leonard said, but Rae saw that Sam's words seemed to cause Leonard's hands to slip as he tried to pull himself into the cabin.

"Where's he getting the money, huh, baby brother?" Sam asked. "Just how much heroin can you buy on a paramedic's salary?"

"Leave me alone," Leonard snarled.

"He's always sneaking off, right? He goes for a pee more times in one day than you go all week, wouldn't you say? It's also why he's so much smaller than you, isn't that right? And his eyes, Leonard. The eyes always give it away."

Leonard had finally made it into the back cabin. Before either Rae or Sam could say another word, he had grabbed both doors from inside and slammed them shut.

After the ugly confrontation with Leonard, Rae checked up on a few of her patients in the maternity ward and then headed for the nearest phone. She punched in the number of the lab in San Diego. After going through the voice mail system, she finally found the tech who could identify the bags Rae had sent.

"But why are you calling?" the tech asked. "You canceled the order."

Rae's hand clutched the phone. "What do you mean I canceled—?" She lowered her voice as patients stared at her as they walked by. "Who said I canceled the order?"

"You *are* Dr. Duprey?"

"Yes! But I didn't cancel any damn order!"

She could not believe what she was hearing.

"Look, I don't care who called you," she said furiously. "Find those bags and run the damn levels! You've had all week!"

The tech informed Rae that the bags had indeed been received days earlier but wound up in the wrong place for several days. They were just about to run the tests when the call to cancel the order came in. The tech was not sure now where the bags were, but they were most likely on their way to the dump. Rae wanted to jump through the phone and strangle the woman on the other end.

"I'll do my best to find them," she pronounced finally. "But I can't promise anything."

Rae hung up the phone. The person she was maddest at was herself. How could she have been so stupid as to tell Leonard what she had done with the bags? It had been at least an hour since their confrontation. An hour would have been plenty of time to find the lab she was using, given the fact that it was the only one in the state.

On the other hand, she thought suddenly as she made her way to the parking lot, she *hadn't* told Leonard what she suspected was in the bag. So how could he have known what lab to look for if he didn't suspect oxytocin himself? He must have looked at the bags after she left and found something to confirm his suspicions. That was why he had canceled the order—to protect himself until he found out what the hell was going on.

There was only one thing to do now: follow Bo's suggestion and go to the police.

She had to call information for the address, but after that it took her no time at all to find the Berkeley Police Station. It was an old white building located on Milvia Avenue, and had it not been for the ten or so blue squad cars in the side parking lot, Rae would have missed it completely.

She parked her Porsche across the street and entered the front door. Two winding stone stairwells led up to the second-floor business level; Rae took the one on the left.

The first thing she noticed by the reception window was a directory with listings for Homicide, Narcotics, and other departments. Just seeing the words made her uncomfortable. But then, perhaps patients felt the same way when they passed by hospital doors with names like Coronary Care Unit and Blood Bank on them. Still, she had to settle down and keep her mind focused on why she was there.

A friendly woman with extension braids greeted her. "I'd like to file a report," Rae said. She wasn't sure how one went about filing a report—she wasn't even sure if that was the description of what she needed to do.

"What kind of report?" the woman asked.

"The kind you need when somebody's trying to kill pregnant women."

The woman gave Rae a skeptical look. "I'm a doctor at the hospital," Rae insisted. "I'm serious."

Slowly the woman handed Rae a form. She didn't seem friendly anymore. "Sure you are, honey," she said. "Just take this over there and write down your story."

Rae sat down and filled in her name and address. She looked up when a policeman approached her. "Hey, you're Dr. Duprey," the man said. He held out his hand. "I'm Sergeant Lane, remember?"

Rae rose. "Sergeant Lane," she said and shook his hand eagerly. What a bit of luck, she thought. He had been the sympathetic one after Bernie was attacked.

"I'm trying to file a report about some suspicious happenings at the hospital," Rae said. "Can I skip the forms and speak to you instead for a minute?"

"My office is just overhead," the sergeant said, pointing his thumb at the ceiling.

As they made their way upstairs, he asked how Bernie was faring. Rae explained that the dialysis had started; they would just have to wait and see. He told her their investigative trail was lukewarm at the moment and that they were trying to hunt down Bernie's ex-husband.

"But Bernie hasn't heard from him in years," Rae said as she took her seat across from a small desk. She looked around the scantily furnished room. "This is your office?" she asked.

"This is where we talk to people," Sergeant Lane said.

There was a knock on the door just then. "Ah, Mailer. Come on in and take notes."

Rae did not shake the young cop's hand nor did he offer his to her. She remembered how he had accused her of being involved in Bernie's attack. The less she said to him, she figured, the better.

"So, let's have it," Sergeant Lane said.

It took Rae all of ten minutes to lay out her story. "Anything else?" the sergeant asked.

"Yeah. What do we do now?" Rae asked.

The young cop snickered.

"Knock it off, Mailer," the sergeant said sternly.

"You don't believe me," Rae said flatly.

"Well, it's not for us to believe—" the sergeant began.

"Hell no, we don't believe any of it," Mailer said. He sat on the edge of the desk. "Naturally, after you gave your statement at the hospital, we snooped around a bit. You're the vice-chair of OB."

Rae nodded.

"Well, there seems to be a little dispute between your hospital and the Birth Center."

Rae's eyes narrowed suspiciously. She knew what was coming.

"But—" she began.

"Hear him out," Sergeant Lane said in an avuncular tone. "You know how impatient these young people are."

"And we also found out that you don't like the Birth Center, Dr. Duprey."

"Okay, okay," Rae said. She stood up. "May I have that form back? I'd still like to file my report."

There was no point in continuing the discussion. But if she filed a formal report, the police would be at least be obligated to check things out.

"We want to help you," Sergeant Lane said. "But since this is a medical complaint, why don't you take it to the health department?"

"Because I'm pretty sure the health department doesn't have a homicide division," Rae retorted sharply.

She quickly filled out all of the boxes and scribbled a summary of what she had just said. "Here you go," she said as she handed the report to Mailer. Then she gathered up her things and headed for the door. "Nice talking to you, officers."

"We need proof, not grudges," Mailer shouted after her.

"That's what the city hires *you* for!" Rae shouted back.

# 21

FRUSTRATED AS SHE WAS AT RECEIVING NO HELP FROM THE POlice, Rae couldn't really blame them. Trying to describe the biochemical effects of oxytocin on the uterus and abnormal neonatal blood gases to men who dealt with murderers and drug addicts on a daily basis had not been easy. In fact, the more she tried to make them understand, the crazier she must have looked to them. Sam, Marco, Walker—they had all warned her what people's reactions to her theories might be.

Now it was time to confront Leonard about having canceled the lab order. She also wanted to know if he had found holes in the bags, as she suspected. But first she wanted to see if Sam was almost done with his case; after all, it wouldn't hurt having him around.

Inside the hospital's lobby, three pregnant women and their mates had gathered in front of the reception desk for a tour of the maternity suite. Rae noticed how nervous and excited they seemed to be. In a few weeks they would be holding their babies and fussing over who had whose eyes and noses.

"It's good to see you smiling again," a deep male voice said behind her.

She half-turned to face Walker. "Got a minute?" she asked.

They sat on one of the leather couches in the lobby. She wanted to tell him about her little jaunt to the police station but then recalled guiltily that he had asked her to keep her story to herself.

Not wanting to provoke more criticism, she simply told Walker about her suspicion that Leonard had canceled the oxytocin order.

"Wait a minute. Slow down!" Walker said. "Exactly what order are you talking about?"

"Oh, I forgot to tell you," Rae said. Quickly she explained what had happened.

Walker shook his head. "And you told the paramedic you sent the bags off—oh, never mind," Walker said, visibly trying to control his irritation. Rae noted with relief that he did not seem interested in berating her over her mistake.

"So," he said calmly but sternly, "in terms of your hearing, which I seem to be more concerned about than you are, what kind of case do you have without those test results?"

"None," Rae said.

"Exactly," Walker said. "My point is, Rae, I'm sure your clinical management of those two cases was perfect. Just tell the committee what you did, step by step, and they'll understand. Nobody gets thrown off the staff for being a great doctor."

"There are a few people on that committee who have some personal issues with me, Walker," Rae said. "Arnie did not like how I showed him up at the resuscitation of Nola's baby. Bo, like you said, is trying to make me take the blame to protect the reputation of the Birth Center. Marco happens to be furious at me for accusing him of stealing charts,"

"Stealing charts? Patient charts?"

"That's not important now," Rae interrupted. "Anyway, I asked the lab to find those bags again and run the levels. And they will find them, Walker. I mean, they couldn't have gone far in that short amount of time."

"Always the optimist," Walker said.

"It's called desperation."

Just then her beeper went off. The alphanumeric message was from her answering service. Rae recognized the 619 area code for San Diego and scrolled down as she read the message: "Bags have been found by lab. Tests being done."

"See, Walker?" Rae said as she clipped her pager to her purse. "Now just pray that the results are here in time."

Walker looked at Rae askance. "I thought you didn't believe in prayer," he said.

Rae rose. "I don't," she said. "But that shouldn't stop you."

She winked at him but he kept frowning. "Please, Rae," he said, "your whole career's on the line here. Sometimes I feel like a father to you. I'm giving you the best advice I can give."

Rae patted Walker's shoulder. "I won't disappoint you, pop," she said with a laugh.

"I'm serious, Rae," he said.

"And *I'm* going to the ER," she said. "There are a couple of paramedics I need to visit."

She left him standing in the lobby. Walker, she decided, like all fathers, would just have to settle for her doing what she felt was best.

Before finding the paramedics, Rae first called the OR and inquired about Sam. The OR nurse confirmed that he was still in surgery. Rae hung up the phone and decided to pay another visit to the twins by herself.

She passed Sylvia Height. "Hey, did you hear about that last patient from the Birth Center?" Sylvia asked.

Rae stopped cold. "You mean Meredith—the one with the shoulder—"

"No, the one from today," Sylvia said. "A patient of Dr. Michaels. A ruptured uterus. She's not good and they almost lost the baby."

Rae grabbed Sylvia by the shoulders. "Where's the patient?" Rae asked.

"She's up in ICU," Sylvia said. "She's dying, Dr. Duprey."

Rae called the OR once again and left a message for Sam to meet her in the ICU as soon as he was done. Then she ran up all seven flights of stairs to the unit. It was a clear night and the lights across the bay made San Francisco look like the City of Oz. But there, in the room next to where Bernie lay, was a young woman who Rae knew must be the patient she had come to see.

"It's a shame," said a nurse named Lourdes. "She's only twenty-two and she has a two-year-old at home. Her poor husband—he left a few minutes ago. He couldn't take it." Lourdes shook her head sadly. "I'm six weeks pregnant. That could just as likely happen to me."

Rae walked over to the dying woman. Her face was puffy, probably from all the liters of fluid they must have given her during her surgery. Her eyes were open and glassy. She had an endotracheal tube shooting out from her mouth. From her neck snaked a Swan-

Ganz catheter. Large purple splotches marred her arms and legs from where someone had tried to start more IV lines.

Rae took the patient's swollen hand in hers. It remained limp, even when Rae squeezed it hard. She lay there motionless against the backdrop of the city's shimmering, vibrant beauty.

"She bled out," Lourdes said, joining Rae at the bedside. "At some point her uterus ruptured and she bled out before they got to her. But, from what I hear, they had to do something."

"Where's her chart?" Rae snapped. Lourdes stared at her blankly. "Where's her damn chart?"

Rae hadn't meant to be rude but this woman had suffered from a ruptured uterus—a classic complication of an oxytocin overdose. Damn that Bo! Rae thought as she followed Lourdes's pointing finger toward the central desk.

The patient's name was Allison Border. Just as Rae opened the chart, Sam walked in. "My patient's on bypass," he said. "I have about ten minutes."

"Sit down. Wail till you hear this," Rae said angrily.

She rifled through the chart and found the evidence she needed. "Yep, here it is. Listen, Sam," she said, beginning to read the damning sequence of events out loud to him. The Birth Center reported a normal contraction pattern, but the woman had developed early signs of preeclampsia and was transferred over to the hospital for management. The ambulance report—signed by Theodore McHenry—said that the baby's heartbeat was normal and that the patient was having contractions every two to three minutes. But then there was a notation that just before the patient arrived at the hospital, she began to complain of abdominal pain. There was also a note by Sylvia, the emergency room nurse, stating that the baby's heart rate had dropped precipitously.

"Just like all the others," Rae said.

Finally she read to Sam Bo's scribble noting that the patient had had a spontaneous rupture of the uterus. Next to that he had written the word *etiology* followed by a question mark. "I could kill him," Rae said vehemently.

Sam took the chart from her and read it for himself. "I think there's been enough of that already," he said.

"But I warned him!" Rae cried. That poor woman. Her belly filling up with her own blood. The terror she must have felt. And now she would never see her precious baby. "That's it, Sam. That was the last one, I swear—"

Just then Sam's beeper went off. "It's the OR. I'll call you."

He stood there, obviously torn between Rae and his work. Rae waved him off and walked back to Lourdes's station.

"I didn't mean to yell at you," she apologized.

"I know," Lourdes said. "It's okay."

Bernie's bed was across the room from where Rae and Lourdes stood. "I hope she wakes up soon," Rae said.

"At least her electroencephalogram is normal." Lourdes gestured at the patient Bo had just delivered. "On the other hand, we're still planning to do her EEG tomorrow. It doesn't look good . . ." Her voiced trailed off. "Sometimes, I hate my job," she sighed finally, and then walked over to the bedside.

Rae watched her go about checking the patient as if she expected her to wake up any moment. What a job, Rae thought. What a job all of the ICU staff had when so many of their patients left the unit in body bags while on Rae's third floor, women were escorted in wheelchairs to the first floor lobby with their newborn babies in their arms. Or at least that was how it was supposed to be, Rae thought as she looked miserably upon the dying woman.

Just then the door to the unit opened and in walked Bo in white surgical scrubs.

"How many more women have to die before you believe me, Bo?" Rae demanded without preamble and loudly enough for the rest of the staff to hear.

He kept going, seeming not to hear her, but she saw the tightening of his jaw and knew he had. He walked over to Allison's bed and Rae followed him. Without turning to her he said, "I'm warning you. Don't start with me again." Unlike her, Bo kept his voice low.

Rae moved to stand directly in front of him on the other side of the bed. "How many disasters do you need, Bo? What do you think ruptured your patient's uterus this time?"

"She had preeclampsia, Rae," Bo said calmly. But he wasn't looking at her; it was as if he were talking to himself.

"Preeclampsia doesn't cause the uterus to split open, damn it!" Rae cried.

"You doctors okay?" Lourdes called over.

Rae looked from Bo to Lourdes. "We're just fine," Rae said evenly.

Lourdes hesitated and finally left.

"Well?" Rae demanded.

Bo slowly shook his head and stuffed his hands into his side pockets. "Rae, you're in the process of destroying your own career. But hands off mine. And hands off my Birth Center. You start in on me at the hearing and I'll use it as a personal forum to pin you to the wall!"

"Bo, this isn't about my hearing!"

Bo waved her off. "Now I'm going away for a few minutes," he said, his voice perceptibly shaking with anger. "And when I get back, I don't want you to be here, you got that?"

"You can't let these things keep happening! Don't you get it?"

"Have a nice life, Rae," Bo said. "Let me say this again: My Birth Center is one baby I won't let you destroy."

He turned on his heel and walked out of the room. Rae was left to stare after him with nothing more to show for their conversation than blind rage.

Lourdes returned with a worried look on her face. "When will that EEG be done?" Rae asked.

"They say tomorrow," Lourdes said.

Rae pulled up a chair next to the patient's bed. "Any word from her husband?" she asked. She took the patient's swollen hand into her own.

Lourdes shook her head. "He's really bad off," she said. "He went downstairs to make some phone calls and to get some coffee."

Five minutes later, Rae felt a reassuring hand squeeze her shoulder. She knew Sam's touch without looking up. "We're still on bypass," he said.

"Bo was just here," Rae said.

"Anything I need to know?" Sam asked.

Just then Rae's beeper went off. She let go of Allison's hand and read the message. "Well, the good news, which you missed earlier, is that the lab has found the bags and is running the levels."

Sam waited for her to finish.

"The bad news is that the results won't be ready until two o'clock tomorrow."

"Why's that the bad news?" Sam asked.

"Because Bo plans to crucify me at noon," she answered.

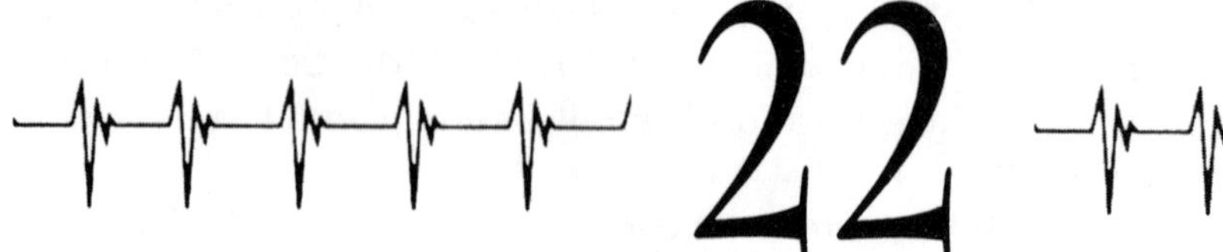

# 22

RAE SLEPT FITFULLY THAT NIGHT AND AWOKE THE NEXT MORNING with a terrible headache. "Well, it ain't over till it's over, Leopold," she said, popping two aspirins into her mouth. She showered quickly and dressed in a smart black suit and white silk blouse.

She had an office full of patients to see before her hearing. It took all she had to concentrate on their health concerns instead of the fact that her entire future in medicine was on the line. But she managed to listen to the histories, perform the pelvic exams, and order the appropriate tests. After seeing her last patient, she headed for the bathroom to reapply her lipstick.

"Rae," Bobbie said just before Rae closed the door.

Rae turned. In Bobby's hand was a signed request for a patient's chart. Rae looked at the name. "Anna Johnson?" she asked. "She's transferring to the Birth Center?"

Rae removed the paper from Bobby's hand. "But she's due any day now," Rae said. "I delivered her last two children." She looked questioningly at Bobby.

"At first she didn't tell me why," Bobby explained. "Finally, I got her to admit she's heard rumors about you mishandling a couple of deliveries on your patients. She was too embarrassed to ask you about them, so she felt it was easier to leave."

Rae pulled her lipstick out of her purse and went into the bathroom. Bobby stood at the open door. Rae's hand shook with anger. "Damn it!" she said as she dropped the lipstick on the floor.

"I wish Anna had given me a chance to speak to her," Rae said. "I suppose if I'd heard the rumors that have been going around about me I'd think about finding another doctor too. But if I could have just spoken to her for a minute, I might have been able to convince her that the best place to deliver is at the hospital, not at the Birth Center. If she has some kind of emergency over there, Bobby, and winds up being transferred over . . ."

She didn't want to think about the possibilities. Anna Johnson was one of her favorite patients: close to her own age and one of the few black women professional photographers in the country; two daughters, Kim, age seven, and Lisa, age six; coach of the girls' T-ball team.

"Don't worry," Bobby comforted her. "Anna was made to have babies. You just concentrate on taking care of yourself. Knock them dead at the hearing."

Rae retrieved her lipstick and slipped it back inside her purse. Forget how she looked. "Is your resume ready, Bobby?" Rae asked as she walked past her. From her office she retrieved a black portfolio that contained her notes for the hearing. "This might be our last day together."

"If they throw you off the staff, Rae, I'm going back to school to become a plumber," Bobby said. "I wouldn't want to stay in medicine if they get rid of their best docs."

Rae looked up from the desk. Bobbie gave her the thumbs-up sign. "So, you're not worried?" she asked.

"They're the ones who need to worry," Bobbie said.

Buoyed by Bobbie's confidence, Rae returned her thumbs-up sign and headed out of the office. The time was five minutes to twelve. Rae hurried across the street.

Surprisingly, by the time she reached the other side, she felt out of breath. Her legs felt heavy as she rushed past the tall columns of sculpture in front of her hospital. Perhaps it was because she knew there was at least a fifty-fifty chance that this might be the last time in a long time she could enter the hospital as a member of the medical staff. If she lost her case, she could be summarily suspended at the end of the meeting. Only after winning a formal appeal—and that could take weeks—months even, would she have a chance at being reinstated.

But how many more babies and mothers would have suffered by

then? she thought as she entered the lobby. Would she have a practice to return to, even if she won the appeal? And what about her dream of becoming the department's first black woman chair? Certainly they would have found someone else by then, and she would have missed her opportunity.

It was the thought of Nola, Meredith, Allison, and now her new worries for Anna Jones that spurred Rae on. In fact, she felt all of her energy returning by the time she stood before the tall, silver doors of the board room. The hallway was quiet. Rae guessed her colleagues—no, her jurors—were already inside. What did they have in store for her? she thought. Would they give her a fair trial? Her left palm was sweaty against the leather portfolio. Finally, taking a deep breath, she grabbed the doorknob and turned it. She kept her back straight, her shoulders high, and her chin lifted as she entered the board room.

"Ah, Dr. Duprey has arrived," Arnie said. He sat at the head of the table and pointed to an empty chair several seats away. Rae assessed the situation quickly as she walked to her chair and sat down.

Her jury consisted of nine doctors and, of course, she knew them all. There was Arnie, who was staring at her challengingly, a pathologist, a radiologist, an internist, and a general surgeon. There were three obstetricians who delivered most of their patients at the Birth Center. And, naturally, there was Bo.

The mood was solemn. Rae had served on other ad hoc committees but never as the accused. She knew how doctors hated to judge one another openly. Of course, behind closed doors, doctors were just like everybody else. Petty jealousies, hoping the worst for the other person—the dark side of human nature did not confine itself to any particular profession. But in a group setting, doctors usually tried to give a colleague the benefit of the doubt. A doctor knew that sometimes no matter how hard one tried, bad things sometimes just happened to patients.

It was just her luck, Rae thought, as she scanned the room and tried to figure out who might be on her side and who had already decided to stick with Arnie, that she would have to defend herself by saying that bad things were not just "happening" to the Birth Center's patients but that somebody was actually trying to bump them off.

Arnie called the meeting to order. He explained to the group that he had called the ad hoc committee to decide if Rae should keep her privileges to practice obstetrics and gynecology at Berkeley Hills Hospital. He gave his version of what had happened at Nola's surgery. "She couldn't even tell a hand from a foot," Arnie said. "She needed more room in the uterus but even when a nurse suggested that she T the incision, she refused to do it. The original scrub nurse tried to tell her she was feeling poorly—as it turns out that nurse was pregnant—but Dr. Duprey didn't care about her either and she started screaming at the staff when she passed out."

Rae's colleagues began to fidget in their chairs. Nobody looked in her direction except for Bo. Next Arnie went on to explain how Rae had tried to deliver Meredith's baby on a moving gurney instead of waiting until she got into a delivery room. According to Arnie, Rae lost control of the situation completely when she deliberately broke the baby's clavicle. "Nobody I've talked to has ever tried to reduce a shoulder dystocia on a moving gurney before. The mother was very upset. She's an L and D nurse and she's worried sick—"

"Quit lying," Rae interrupted.

"You'll get your turn," Arnie said.

Rae glared at him. She most certainly would, she thought.

The general surgeon spoke up. "So what's your point, Arnie?" he asked. "She got both babies out, didn't she?"

"That's not really the point," Arnie said.

"Perhaps I can explain," Bo said. Arnie nodded in Bo's direction as Bo rose from his seat. "We're not talking about an error in judgment here. What you all don't know is that Rae promised the board that she would do anything—and I mean *anything*—to discredit my Birth Center in order to save her department. She made a deal with the board's chairman—and get this, in two weeks no less—to prove that not having a C-section room on our premises is a bad thing for our patients. She's trying to prove that bad things happen to women during the transports. If she can do that, then all the obstetricians will bring their patients back here and force me to shut the Birth Center down. She's even asked—no, *demanded*—several times that I close it."

"Is this true, Rae?" asked the surgeon, looking at his watch.

"Which part?" Rae asked.

A murmur rippled around the room.

"But you see," Bo went on to say, "Rae couldn't find anything wrong with the transport of the patients. Not having a C-section room on site has never been a problem for us. Why, she even came to the Birth Center to interrogate two of my best nurses to get them to admit that something was wrong. But what did she find? Absolutely nothing.

"Now I'm sure when Rae speaks to you—"

"Hey, quit trying to sound like Perry Mason," the pathologist said. "Just get on with it."

Rae mouthed "thank you" to him and settled back into her chair. The thought of someone on her side made her feel better.

"Let him finish," Arnie protested.

"So, what she does next, you see, is make it look like the transports are dangerous. Instead of operating quickly on Nola's baby, she takes her sweet time—just so the kid can get into some real trouble—and finally she pulls out a baby who doesn't have a prayer for making it through the end of the week."

Bo's prediction for Nola's baby hit Rae like a brick. Nothing he had said up to this point had bothered her much; she knew he was lying and she had yet to present her defense. But she had been so busy with everything that she hadn't checked on Baby Jesus in the last couple of days. Had he taken a turn for the worse? Poor baby, she thought. Poor, poor baby . . .

She dropped her eyes to the table but then looked up quickly as Bo continued to speak. He had paused to look around the room and to make sure his words were having the desired effect on the listeners. Apparently satisfied that they were, he spread his fingertips on the glass table and leaned forward.

"But I can assure you that a Birth Center that is backed up by a hospital for cesareans is perfectly legitimate. I think—I know—Rae thinks so too. So then why, you're probably asking yourself, does it matter to her whether the Birth Center stays open or not?"

Another ripple of concern spread around the table.

Bo looked directly at Rae. "Because you see, Dr. Rae Duprey's lifelong ambition has been to become head of the obstetrical department of a major hospital. This hospital, to be exact. This is the number one hospital in the state of California. She's slated to become the chairman at the beginning of the year. But if she doesn't get the obstetricians to bring their patients back here, the hospital's board of trustees will have to shut down Rae's obstetrical unit. So how can Dr. Duprey, who wants to do nothing else with her life, be the department's next chairman if there's no department?"

"You bastard!" Rae shouted as she sprang from her chair. "How can you stand there and say that!" But Bo was looking at her like the cat who ate the canary. He had her just where he wanted her.

Bo looked around the room and then smiled grimly. "I move that the medical staff privileges for Dr. Rae Duprey be summarily suspended."

"Not just yet," Rae said. She didn't wait for Bo's words to sink in this time. She stood up and spread her handwritten notes and photocopies from the patients' charts out on the table in front of her.

Bo sat down and leaned back in his chair as if waiting to be entertained. Well, just watch this, mister, Rae thought as she looked around the room at all of the faces. Unfortunately, they were now staring back at her quite demandingly. In the beginning of the meeting they had looked like people who were in a hurry to get back to their offices or to the operating room. Now they looked like a real jury and one who had pretty much decided the accused had some explaining to do.

Rae straightened her back and began.

It took her all of fifteen minutes to go through the details of Nola's surgery and Meredith's delivery. Next she reviewed the eight recent low-Apgar-score babies born to women at the Birth Center. All the frightening similarities between the cases were emphasized. The last case she discussed was that of the woman who was now dying in the unit, the patient with the ruptured uterus.

"She's not dying," Bo said.

Rae ignored him and explained that had these patients labored in her hospital from the beginning, all of these things could have been prevented.

The internist, a doctor in his sixties who wore a bow tie and who had tufts of white hair sticking out from the sides of his head like matted cotton, raised his hand. "What you're telling us," he said in a raspy voice, "is that something happened to these patients on the way over here?"

Rae nodded her head.

"Well, that sounds kind of fishy."

"Complications of pregnancy do happen," Bo said.

"Well, I suppose," the internist said.

"So, what else could it be?" the surgeon asked. "Come on, Rae, if you've got something to say, get it on the table." He glanced at his watch again.

"Yes, why don't you tell them, Rae?" Bo asked. "Go ahead. I'm sure they'll all find it very entertaining."

They were all looking at her now. Their eyes were full of the expectation—no, real hope—that Rae would say something to disprove Bo's accusations. It was one thing for a doctor to use bad judgment. But to deliberately harm a patient for personal gain was egregious—criminal even—and had to be punished swiftly and completely. Rae took a deep breath. She felt as if she was about to jump off of a fifty-foot-high diving board. Walker had warned her not to bring up the oxytocin theory; and without the test results, she didn't know how she was going to land in the water.

But she did know that she couldn't live with herself if she didn't place the patients' welfare above everything else. After all, she was a doctor. *Save the life!* As a doctor, that was all she knew how to do. "All right, ladies and gentlemen. You want answers? I've got answers," she said, taking another deep breath.

Rae spent the next five minutes explaining what she thought was behind the disasters coming out of the Birth Center. She kept her voice as calm as possible, fully aware that what she had to say sounded bizarre, if not insane. At the best of times, several of the men in the crowd had a hard time taking any woman seriously, even if that woman was another physician. And a short black woman? Rae knew she was already pushing it before she opened her mouth to speak.

She got through her presentation in a very methodical manner, despite the outrage she felt every time she spoke about what was happening. Even Walker, she thought, would have been proud of how she kept her cool, not going off half-cocked, as he said she was wont to do.

"What is *not* happening here," she said in conclusion, "are normal complications of pregnancy. Somebody is doing something to those women—and believe me, it's not Mother Nature."

The room fell completely silent and then, like a sudden birth, it erupted into a free-for-all.

"Preposterous!"

"I think she's onto something!"

"She's crazy!"

"I knew something sounded fishy!"

"Just what the hell is going on over there, Bo!"

"Over there? Over *here!*"

Arnie rose, pounded his fist on the table, and called for order. But nobody paid any attention to him. Then Bo rose and shouted above the fracas, "Hey, come on, let's get real here," he demanded. "Rae only concocted this—this conspiracy theory—to save her department. And if I know her, she'll use whatever power comes with running that department to push me out in the street! Some diabolical plot my ass! If anyone has a reason to knock off a few babies by spiking any IV bags, you're looking at her!"

"Why don't you tell them where *you* were, Bo?" Rae shouted back. Now she was leaning on her fingertips. "And you, Arnie? Why, I wouldn't let you stick a pacifier in a baby, let alone another endotracheal tube!"

"Call for the vote, damn it! I want her out!" Bo said to the room at large.

Arnie pounded his fist on the table. "Is there a motion?"

"So moved!"

"Is there a second?"

"Second!"

"Any discussion?"

The room finally fell silent. Rae and Bo glared at one another. "I warned you," Bo said through clenched teeth.

Slowly she sank back into her chair. Everything had been said. There was nothing to add. "Call for the damn vote," she said.

"Would you please leave the room?" Arnie asked.

Rae rose and went to the door. But before stepping into the hallway she turned and faced her colleagues. "Vote how you want about me," she said, "but whatever you do, don't vote against the lives of innocent babies."

Outside the door, Rae paced the floor nervously. How had she gotten into the position of letting someone else choose her fate? How many allies did she have in that room? How many had she gained—or lost?

She looked at her watch after fifteen minutes had passed. The longer things took, the better she felt. If they were against her they would not need much time to decide. Or was it the other way around?

Finally the door opened and Arnie said, "Come in. We've made our decision."

His face gave away nothing. Nor did the faces of the other eight people who sat around her.

"Well?" she asked.

"The vote was six to three," Arnie said. Rae waited. She could have strangled him for stretching out the suspense.

"Six to three against you, Rae," he said finally.

"But what about the babies!" Rae shouted. "What about the patients—that woman upstairs who's dying because somebody tried to kill her! How many more women have to die for you people to do something?"

"This meeting is adjourned," Arnie said with finality.

"Like hell it is!" Rae shouted. "You can't do this."

"We just did," Bo said smugly.

Arnie stood up and towered over Rae. All of the other doctors except for Bo now rose from their chairs and scurried out of the room like mice.

"You can make a formal appeal if you insist," Arnie said.

"But the babies . . ."

"Can it, Rae," Bo said. "This isn't about any damn babies. Not that you would really care anyway."

"We'll assign another obstetrician to your patients," Arnie said. "Of course you'll be reported to the state medical board—"

"Report me to the governor, you asshole," Rae said. "But it doesn't end here."

"Give my best to Dr. Hartman," Bo said. He slapped Arnie on the back and the two of them walked out of the room.

"Why don't you give your best to your patients!" Rae shouted after him, as she felt her inner world collapse.

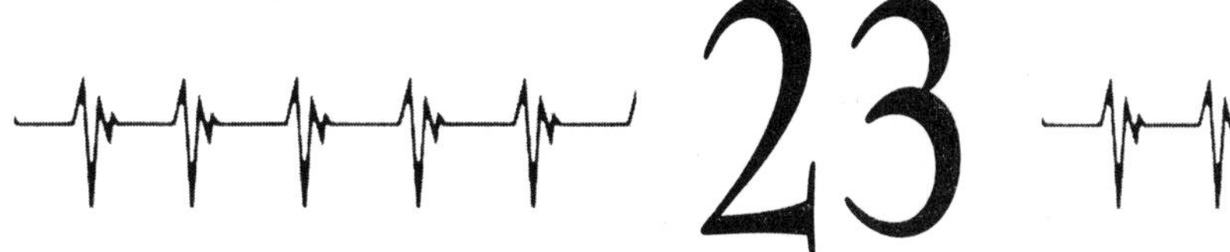

# 23

"PRACTICING MEDICINE IS MY WHOLE LIFE," RAE SAID TO SAM. "And I'm not going to stop."

Sam had joined her in the cafeteria. A spoon sat in an opened carton of lemon yogurt next to an apple with one bite taken out of the middle.

"Worst of all, as long as the Birth Center stays open, those killers aren't going to stop." She paused as Sam picked up her apple and handed it to her. She took another bite. Delicious. "If only I had those lab results," she said. "Oh, and Bo told me to tell you hi."

"For some reason," Sam said, handing Rae her yogurt carton, "I get the feeling that this little setback hasn't slowed you down much."

Rae placed another spoonful of the creamy lemon yogurt into her mouth. Then she finished it off with gusto. Just the fact that Sam had confidence in her helped tremendously. Even a woman as independent as she prided herself in being didn't mind having another person in her corner. "You got that right," she said as she wiped her mouth with her napkin. "It's going to take a hell of a lot more than suspending my privileges to keep me out of this joint."

"How did I know that?" Sam asked.

Just then Rae's beeper went off. She read the message: the lab results were in. "Oh, just in time," she said sarcastically. "I have to call the lab."

She was back in two minutes. Sam had finished eating the rest of her apple. After sliding back into her chair she said, "The bags from the Birth Center were clean. So was the one from the warehouse I paid fifty bucks to get."

"Fifty bucks? Jeez. And the one from the ambulance?" he asked.

"What do you think?" Rae asked.

"Full of oxytocin?" Sam asked.

"Enough to put a cow into labor," Rae said. She shook her head wearily. "And they didn't believe me," she muttered. Then she looked up at Sam. "I've got to find Bo. The lab is faxing me a copy of their report. He's got to believe me now."

"Don't be so sure," Sam warned.

"Oh, come on, Sam," Rae said. "What choice will he—"

But Rae stopped at the sight of Marco approaching their table. "Hey, sorry about the way things turned out," Marco said.

"Yeah, I can see how disappointed you are," Rae said.

"I mean it, Rae," Marco said. "Don't I, Sammy?" He slipped into the chair next to Sam's.

"You could volunteer to be on the appeal committee," Sam said.

"Yeah, Marco," Rae said. "And while you're at it, why don't you volunteer to chair the whole thing? With your clout around here, I'm sure you can convince the others to reinstate me. That way, I can do what I have to do to keep my department open. Is that a deal?"

Marco pursed his lips, sat back in his chair, and crossed his arms. "Hey, Sammy," he said finally, "didn't you tell the little lady not to go shooting her mouth off at the hearing?"

Sam grabbed Marco's shoulder. "We've been friends a long time, Marco," he said, "but one more crack like that and you'll be looking up at me from the floor."

The two of them stood staring at each other. Rae rose from her chair. "There's a killer still on the loose," she said, and started to walk away.

"Hey, Rae!" Sam said.

Rae waited for him to catch up with her. "Where are you headed?"

"I'm going over to the Birth Center," she said, "to slug it out with Bo."

Sam lifted her chin in his hand and looked down at her. "Rae, that's probably a very bad idea."

"You may be right, but it's the only thing to do. So wish me luck," she said as she turned to walk away again.

Suddenly she stopped. Walking directly in front of her was a hugely round, short woman with a blond beehive hairdo. She was dressed in a polka dot bathrobe and had some kind of fuzzy leopard-skin slippers on her feet. Nola Payne must have been discharged some days ago and was obviously feeling a bit better.

It occurred to her that Nola was walking in the direction away from the elevators that would take her to the nursery. She turned right and disappeared into a door. Rae walked up to the spot. In front of her was the door to the hospital's chapel. Had it always been there and she had just never noticed it?

Inside, Rae saw Nola sitting in one of the ten or so sleek, sky-blue chairs. She was staring at a piece of stained glass, illuminated by a light. The glass depicted a picture of a lovely garden at an ocean shore. A small wooden bridge crossed the waters to the horizon; above the bridge billowy clouds broke in the center and exposed the sun. Rae, who had not been inside a church since her mother's funeral, sat down on a chair in the back.

Everything in the room was so quiet. It was hard for her to believe that just on the other side of the wall was the frenetic world of the hospital. Nola's head was bent forward, and Rae knew that she was praying for her child.

Despite Nola's outlandish appearance and behavior, she seemed to possess an inner serenity. A dignity even, Rae thought, the kind that no worldly possessions could ever confer.

How Rae wished for that same serenity! But her mother's premature death had taught her that nothing in life could be trusted. Life was about chaos. Life was about anything and everything that made people question over and over: Was there really a God?

Suddenly, Rae brought her hands together. "Oh, God, please be there and please give me strength," she whispered.

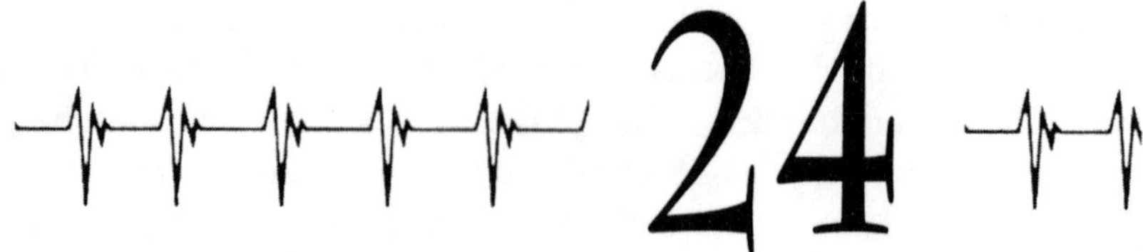

# 24

At the Birth Center, Rae waited inside Bo's office, which was located down the hall from the triage room. It was furnished like his home: sleek pieces of glass and leather and chrome furniture. What a stark contrast, Rae thought, it made to the rest of the Birth Center.

"He won't be much longer," said Jenny, the short nurse with the braces who had taken care of Nola Payne. "He wants you to wait—can I get you some tea?"

"How long did he say he'd be?" Rae asked.

"We have mint and chamomile," Jenny said instead of answering her.

Rae shrugged her shoulders. Her beef was not with Jenny. "I'll take the mint, thank you."

"Dr. Duprey?" Jenny asked. She hadn't moved from her place at the door. "Maybe you can get a job with us at City Hospital?"

So the word was already out, Rae mused. She forced a smile. "And could you put a little honey in it, Jenny?" she asked.

Rae had finished two cups of tea by the time Bo showed up. He was dressed in the lime-green scrubs of the Birth Center. There was a splotch of dried blood on his neck where the mask hadn't protected him.

He pulled up a chair next to Rae and sat with his knees wide apart. "Need a job?" he asked.

Rat sat her cup on his desk and pulled out the faxed report. "I sent three IV bags to the lab," she said. "One from here, which came back negative. The other was from the ambulance warehouse, which also came back negative." She paused to point to the middle of the page. "But the one from the ambulance—your Hillstar ambulance—had enough oxytocin in it to get every baby in America delivered in sixty seconds."

Bo read the report as casually as if she had given him the sports page of the *Chronicle.* "So what?" he said. He handed the page back to her.

"So we've got an ambulance driver who has more on his mind than getting your patients from here to my hospital."

"*Your* hospital doesn't want you anymore," Bo said.

"And I think somebody's paying him to do it," Rae continued as if Bo had not spoken.

"To do what?" Bo snapped.

Rae started to get out of her chair but she sat back down. She had to stay calm, no matter what. "Look, Bo," she said, "it's not about me and you anymore. You've got to close down, at least long enough to find out who's doing this."

Bo began to laugh, an unpleasant laugh that made her blood boil. "You're too much, you know that, Rae? But you're certainly original. Only you would come up with the idea to spike the bag yourself and then send it to the lab—ingenious!"

He threw his head back and slapped his knee, but then just as fast, his face clouded over with what Rae saw was something close to hatred. He snatched the report back from her. She held on a second too long and the edge cut the skin between the first two fingers of her right hand. With her left hand she pressed the spot to stop the bleeding.

"The only one who filled that bag with oxytocin was you, Rae," Bo said. "Nobody else is desperate enough to do something like that."

"Bo, will you listen to me?" Rae said. She did feel desperate. But she had to keep her cool if she was going to talk some sense into him.

"I mean it, Rae," he said. "You'd do it in a minute to get what you want. So unless you've got something else to show me . . ."

She tapped her fingertip against the paper. Drops of blood hit the spot she wanted Bo to see. "I'm showing you what you need to see!" she said.

"Enough!" he shouted. He stood up and crumpled the paper in his hand. "I've reviewed all the cases, damn it. I've talked to the patients and I've talked to the drivers and all of the nurses around here. And nobody seems to know anything about any oxytocin overdoses. Not to mention you just had your turn to present your side. But did anybody believe you?"

"Three people did."

"Bullshit!" Bo said. "They didn't believe you—they pitied you!"

Bo's words stung Rae as if he had just slapped her with the back of his hand. "Pitied me?" she asked.

"You looked ridiculous," Bo said.

Rae narrowed her eyes. Nothing she could say would change Bo's mind.

"Then more women will die, Bo," she said bitterly.

"The Birth Center stays open," Bo snapped.

"But—"

"You may leave now, Rae," Bo said.

His voice was ice cold. He walked over to the door and opened it. "Get the hell out of my office," he said.

Slowly Rae picked up the lab report and stuffed it into her purse. Without another word, she walked out the door.

When Rae got back to the hospital, she ran into Sam in the elevator. By the time the elevator doors opened, Rae had explained to Sam that Bo had read the lab report but still refused to close down the Birth Center.

"Are you okay?" Sam asked as they made their way toward the ICU. Rae was on her way to check in on the patient who had ruptured her uterus.

"I'm just fine," she said.

Sam looked at her sideways. "Then I guess that's all that matters," he said.

The coronary care unit was down the hall from the ICU. "I'll join you in a minute," Sam said.

Inside the ICU, Rae stopped off at Bernie's bed first. A nurse was giving her a sponge bath. She stopped to inform Rae that Bernie's dialysis treatments were going well. "Any signs of waking up?" Rae asked.

The nurse shook her head. "At least *she's* still alive," the nurse said.

Rae followed the nurse's glance to Bo's patient across the room. An elderly woman, dressed in a light pink shawl and an ankle-length yellow skirt, sat in a chair next to the bed. Twisted around her fingers was what appeared to be a string of beads, which Rae quickly realized was a rosary. The woman had obviously been weeping.

Rae turned back to the nurse. "Her mother," the nurse said. "She's just been told that her daughter's EEG results are back. It's bad news."

Rae walked over to the elderly woman. Lourdes, the nurse from the day before, was adjusting the monitors. There were tears in her eyes. "It's always harder to do when they're young," she said.

"Harder to do what?" Rae whispered. Surely Lourdes did not mean what Rae feared she meant. She glanced at the old woman's face, but she was in a world of her own.

"To turn off the respirator," Lourdes whispered back.

Rae's eyes widened. Although she was a doctor, she had never been confronted with deliberately ending another person's life. It felt antithetical to everything she stood for.

"At least wait for her husband to return," she said.

"He's already said his good-byes," Lourdes answered.

Rae slumped down into the chair on the other side of Allison's bed and took her hand. It was still warm and it was hard for Rae to imagine that this woman had a heart that was still pumping but none of the brain activity that was so necessary to function as a normal human being.

"Mrs. Taylor," Lourdes asked Allison's mother quietly, "are you ready now?"

"Does Dr. Michaels know about this?" Rae asked. "Doesn't a doctor have to be here?"

"Her primary care doctor gave the order. We've been trying to reach Dr. Michaels but the Birth Center said he's out for the afternoon and can't be reached. And no, the doctors don't have to be present for this. They can give a phone order. It happens all the time."

"She's my baby," Mrs. Taylor said, looking up at them both with stricken eyes, "how could I ever possibly be ready?"

"Mrs. Taylor," Rae said gently, "you brought her into the world. You need to help her leave now. You have a new grandson downstairs. I think Allison would want you to go to him."

Sobbing, Allison's mother smoothed her daughter's hair one last time. "I love you, honey. Be brave," she said, kissing her closed eyes before turning to leave the room.

Lourdes leaned over and slowly pulled the plug out of the outlet.

Rae held on to Allison's hand. Could it really be that easy? she wondered. In front of her was the window. The sun was setting behind Mt. Tam, softly and quietly, like a baby easing into sleep.

But Allison's breathing was labored. Seconds passed between each rise of her chest. It was as if she were sighing instead of breathing. The sighs grew further and further apart until finally, just as the sun dipped below the horizon, her chest rose, and fell, for the very last time.

As Rae was getting up from her chair to leave, she heard someone behind her. She turned around, expecting Lourdes to have returned. Instead she saw Bo.

"Get away from my patient," he snarled.

Still holding her hand Rae said, "She's gone, Bo."

"Let go of her hand. I'm warning, you, Rae."

Rae squeezed Allison's hand one last time. She certainly didn't want to make a scene at the bedside.

"You're the boss, Bo," she said. But before she left, she pulled the white sheet over Allison's face. Then, taking a deep breath, she headed for the door.

After her confrontation with Bo in the ICU, Rae tracked down Sam to tell him about Allison and to let him in on her newest plan. "The boys at the police station told me to come back when I had some evidence—not just a grudge—to show them," she said. She patted her purse, thinking about the lab report inside. Sam took the elevator down with her to the lobby.

"I hate to tell you this, Rae," he said, "but the police might not buy your 'evidence' either. I mean, they might say that you're the one who spiked the bags."

Rae frowned. Bo had accused her of the same thing. "Then I'll just have to make them believe me," she said with conviction.

An hour later, Rae sat across from Sergeant Lane in his office. She had shown Lane the lab report and he had studied it with patient interest. On the other hand, Officer Mailer had eyed it suspiciously and then asked for the number to the lab. Lane had told Sam and Rae to hold on while he made a phone call to the hospital's medical staff president.

Rae rapped her fingernails on the side of the wooden chair as she listened to Lane's conversation with Arnie. Of course Arnie would tell the sergeant about her suspension, but she didn't care. In her mind they were dealing with murder—something outside the hospital's jurisdiction.

"Okay, well, thanks so much for your time, Dr. Driver," Lane said. "Yeah, I've got my money on the Raiders too." He hung up the phone and then looked at Rae. "Seems we have a problem here, Doctor," he said.

He explained Rae's suspension to Mailer and the younger man's eyes lit up. Rae crossed her arms over her chest and said, "I didn't come here to talk about me, I came here to find out who's killing the patients!"

"Yes, well," Lane said, "Dr. Driver said a pregnant woman just died of blood loss from some kind of obstetrical complication."

"Her uterus ruptured! That's what she died from!" Rae snatched the lab report from Mailer and threw it on Lane's desk. "She got a big whopping dose of oxytocin while she was in the ambulance and now she's in a body bag!"

Mailer sat back in his chair. "I have no murder, I have no case, Dr. Duprey," he said calmly.

"No murder?" Rae asked.

Mailer strolled over and sat on the end of the desk next to Rae. He lifted the lab report and folded it in half. "We do follow up on the complaints of our citizens," he said. "When we heard about that young pregnant woman who died this evening—"

"You've heard?" Rae asked. "So then why the runaround?"

"Our coroner is a swell guy," Mailer said slowly, and he was obviously enjoying himself as he spoke. "He got the official cause of death from the patient's doctor—"

"The patient's doctor?" Rae asked incredulously.

"And the person Sarge just spoke to gave the same cause of

death—hemorrhage from a surgical complication.'' He handed the paper back to her, stood up, and left the room.

''I would like to help you, Dr. Duprey,'' Lane said. ''I really would.''

Rae placed the report in her purse. ''I'm not the one who needs the help,'' she said. ''Unfortunately, the ones who do don't even know it.''

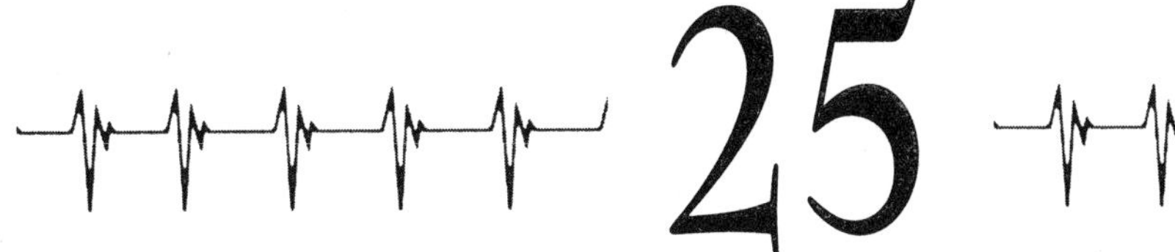

# 25

RAE SAT ON THE WING CHAIR IN HER STUDY, WITH ONE LEG DANGLING over the armrest. In her left hand she held a glass of wine. She had been staring out the window for at least half an hour. Or had it been an hour? She wasn't sure. She had never felt so defeated. Even after her mother died, she had emerged at least with a determination to become an obstetrician, to save the lives of pregnant women and their unborn children. Yet she had failed to save Bo's last patient. The way things stood now, without hospital privileges, she wasn't even an obstetrician anymore.

How had she screwed up things so badly? she wondered. If she had tried she couldn't have done a better job at making people think she was the one who had lost her mind. Bo refused to close down the Birth Center. The obstetricians would keep delivering their patients over there and exposing them to what could turn out to be a fatal ambulance ride. The police—well, she believed sergeant Lane wanted to help her, but even she had to admit she had given him little to go on. She needed more proof—something that no one could say she had fabricated.

"Where do I get that kind of proof?" she asked Leopold, who was lying on the floor in front of her.

A knock on the door sounded and Harvey used his key to let himself in. "I felt weird vibrations coming from over here," he said. In one hand he carried his bow and violin. "Since you won't come to me, I thought I'd come to you."

"No time," Rae said as she took another sip of wine. But Harvey went into her bedroom and came back with her violin case. He opened it and handed the violin to her.

"Oh, put that glass down," Harvey said. When she didn't move, he took it from her hand himself and handed her the instrument. As Harvey tuned his strings, she tuned hers—out of habit, not because she had any interest in playing, she told herself.

Just how long had it been since she had last played? she wondered as she fingered the violin's neck. Then she recalled it was the night she had delivered Nola's baby.

"Rae, sometimes our hearts speak to us through our music," he said as he sat down on the sofa.

"It's my heart that's gotten me into all this trouble," Rae said.

"No troubles, only music," Harvey murmured.

He began to play Chopin's "Nocturne in E-flat Major." His thick fingertips barely moved against the strings. Yet beautiful, rich music poured forth from the simple wooden instrument.

About halfway through the song, she joined him. Her fingers felt a little rusty and without the sheet music in front of her, she had to concentrate to keep up. But soon the condo was filled with the glorious vibrations of what Rae's mother had always told her were the sounds of heaven. Music, she had said, was God's voice on earth.

They finished the piece. Rae's violin vibrated with the resonance of her last note. "Feeling better?" Harvey asked.

"What do you do when nobody believes you?" she asked. She told Harvey about the outcome of her hearing, of the patient Lourdes had pulled the plug on, and of the reaction from Lane and Mailer. Harvey listened with detached patience, but Rae knew he had heard her every word.

"I've got to convince somebody before another patient or another baby gets killed," she said finally.

"You've convinced me," Harvey said.

"Oh yeah, so where were you this afternoon?" asked Rae, recalling the ad hoc's committee six to three vote.

She rose and gazed out the window. The moon was full against an otherwise black sky. Staring at it, she felt close to despair. "They say more babies are born when the moon's full than at any other time," she said to Harvey.

"Then I guess you'd better get going," Harvey said. "You won't save anybody sitting around here."

He smiled at her and she smiled back. Harvey was right. Wallowing in self-pity would get her nowhere.

She walked him to the door. "What would I do without you around?" she asked.

"At my age," he said with a laugh as he kissed her cheek goodbye, "I never ask myself that particular question."

She closed the door and leaned against it. "Leopold," she said, "I'm going back out. There are a couple of ambulance drivers I need to talk to."

Speeding down I-80, she called Sam on her car phone and asked him to meet her in the hospital's lobby. He arrived a minute after she did. "The ambulance is parked outside," she said.

As they made their way through the lobby, she told him about her visit to the police station. "Just don't say I told you so," she said as they passed through the emergency room.

"So what are your plans for the twins tonight?" Sam asked.

"Well," Rae said, "I may have been naive to think a heroin addict couldn't drive an ambulance, but they don't need to know that."

She found Leonard sitting in the front seat of the ambulance. "Oh, for God's sake. What now?" he asked.

"Could you step outside?" she asked.

Leonard groaned. "Can't it wait?"

"This won't take long," Sam said.

Leonard climbed out of the ambulance. Rae let him have it right away. "So you killed another one?" she said. "How does it feel, exactly, to murder a woman?"

Leonard cut his gray eyes from Rae to Sam and back to Rae. "What woman?" he asked.

"Did you see her?" Rae continued. "I mean, right before she died. She looked pretty good, didn't she? All blown up like that, tubes coming and going every which way."

Leonard's eyes widened. "What are you talking about? I didn't kill anybody."

"Oh no? So what do you call it when you fill an IV bag with so much oxytocin the patient's uterus explodes by the time she hits the emergency room?" She spit the words out like lemon seeds.

"Her uterus ruptured?" Leonard asked, paling visibly. "She died?"

"Wasn't that what you wanted to happen?" Rae asked. She could see that Leonard was starting to sweat. "Isn't that part of the deal? Didn't your brother explain all of this to you?"

Leonard began to pace back and forth in front of the ambulance. "She didn't die—she couldn't have died—"

"By now she's stuffed in a body bag and in a drawer in our morgue," Rae said.

"No . . . what happened—"

"A person can be a heroin addict, Leonard, but *you* don't have to kill to feed the habit. Don't you see, Leonard, he's made a murderer out of you."

"I'm no murderer!" Leonard shouted. He stopped pacing and glared at Rae. "I don't know what you're talking about! My brother's done nothing wrong. He hasn't put anything anywhere. You want to check our bags?"

Leonard rushed to the back of the ambulance and threw open the doors. "Fine, take a look. Take some home if you want."

Rae walked around to the doors. The thought of going back into an ambulance turned her blood to ice.

"Sam, please," she said, reaching out to him.

Sam jumped into the ambulance for her. "Just tell me what you want me to do."

Rae ignored Leonard's stare and said, "Check the bin where the bags are stored."

She could hear Sam walking around the back cabin. Leonard kept staring at her so she turned away and called out to Sam again. "And could you pass me some of the bags please?"

"Here," he said, jumping down to the ground and holding three bags in his arms.

All of them were still encased in their plastic wrapping. "I need a light," she said.

Sam reached for a penlight in his coat pocket and handed it to her. She inspected the bag carefully and then tossed it at Leonard. He caught it in one of his massive hands.

Next she threw Leonard the penlight. "Look over the nipple port," she instructed.

Leonard turned the bag this way and that. "I don't see anything."

"You don't see that hole? You don't see the hole that Theodore made when he injected the oxytocin?"

"Okay! Okay! I see it," Leonard yelled. Then he dropped his voice and said, "But that proves nothing about my brother. He wouldn't kill anybody."

"So who put the holes in the bag, Leonard?" Sam asked calmly. "If it wasn't your brother, I suppose it had to be you?"

Leonard looked confused.

"Just where is your brother now?" Rae asked.

"He's on a break."

"To shoot up," Rae said. "A break to shoot up."

"Leave me alone!" Leonard raged.

"He didn't leave that patient alone," Rae said. "You should have heard her last breaths, Leonard. Long painful breaths, like there was no air in the room! All she wanted to be was a mother. Now she'll never see her baby. Do you have children, Leonard?"

"Okay! Okay!" Leonard cried as he held his head in his hands and fell against the side of the ambulance.

"I didn't know what was happening," he said. "I swear I didn't." He handed Rae the bag. "And I know my brother doesn't know who's doing this either. We hang the bags, Dr. Duprey, that's all. We don't put anything in them. Those bad babies . . . those patients—me and my brother have been freaking out trying to figure out what's been happening. But I would never try to kill a baby. My brother—he has three kids. He wouldn't do such a thing. Just tell me what we have to do to prove it to you."

"Stop protecting him!" Sam said sharply. "I know what it's like having a brother on drugs. So tell me who he's working for. Tell me who's paying Thodore to spike the bags!"

"We work for Hillstar!" Leonard yelled back. "We get paid for driving ambulances!"

"Quit lying!" Rae said. "First you lied about Meredith. You said you never changed her bag. Then you pretend like nothing's been going on with the patients. Now you're lying about your brother!"

"I was afraid!" Leonard said. "We were new. I didn't want to lose my job! I didn't know what was going on with those patients, but I sure the hell wasn't going to take the blame—"

"But your brother's on drugs, Leonard," Sam said in a placating voice. "A heroin addict is a desperate man. Maybe you didn't know anything."

"I didn't do anything," Leonard pleaded.

"But desperate people do desperate things," Rae said. "Addiction makes everybody desperate."

"Desperate enough to kill little babies?" Leonard asked in a pitiful voice.

"Desperate enough to kill anybody," Sam said. "Even the addict himself."

Leonard shook his head. "And he had promised me when we took this job he was clean," he said.

Sam touched Leonard's shoulder. "They always say that," he said.

Leonard looked from Sam to Rae. "But," he said, "my brother was always just as scared as I was whenever he heard a low heartbeat."

"Maybe he's being paid to look scared," Rae offered.

Leonard wiped his eyes. Such a pitiful sight, Rae thought. "So, what can I do?" he asked.

"Just come down to the police station with me," Rae said.

"But my brother?" he asked hesitantly. "I've got to talk with him first."

"You can talk with him later," Sam said.

"No," Leonard said vehemently. "I'm not going to turn him in like that. He's my brother—my twin brother . . . we do everything together."

Rae sighed. "Fine, talk to him first."

"But what will I say? Suppose you're wrong?"

"I'm not wrong."

"Then you come with me. Just tell him that you found some holes in the bags and you want to ask him some questions. Then, if he looks guilty to me, I'll believe you and talk him into going to the station. I mean, they'll want to clean him up, right? They'll be more interested in the person who's paying him to spike the bags—"

"Okay, okay," Rae said. "But let's just get on with it."

"No, Rae," Sam interrupted.

"I don't have a choice!" Rae snapped.

"Then I'm coming with you," Sam said firmly.

"Where should I meet you guys?" Rae asked.

"At my house, in an hour," Leonard said. "Theo's supposed to come over to pick up some CDs."

"You can meet her at the hospital," Sam said.

"No, my house or—"

"Fine."

"No, Rae."

"Sam, I said we don't have a choice!"

Rae jotted down Leonard's address. As they walked back into the hospital, Sam's beeper went off suddenly. A patient was crashing in the cath lab and needed emergency surgery.

"Don't go over there without me," Sam warned.

"But you'll be hours," Rae protested.

"Then we'll hook up with them tomorrow," he said.

"Tomorrow might be too late," she replied.

A look of exasperation crossed Sam's face. "Sometimes you have to put yourself first, Rae. I hope you figure that out before it's too late." Then he leaned down to kiss her before catching the elevator to the basement.

Rae checked the address that Leonard had given her. His house was in West Berkeley, ten minutes away. She had forty-five minutes to kill, so she headed for the vending machines to get a Coke. A sense of hope buoyed her—something was finally giving!

To get to the vending machines she had to pass through the cafeteria. There, in a far corner, she spotted Marco and Walker sitting across from each other at a table. By the time Rae's paper cup was full, Marco was standing and pointing his finger angrily at Walker before turning to leave the room.

"This might be the last case I do in this fucking hospital," Marco said to her as he stormed by.

"That would be fine with me," she retorted, recalling the suspension of her medical staff privileges. She headed toward Walker. Whatever Marco had argued with Walker about was not her concern. She had enough on her mind to worry about without dealing with Marco's problems. Besides, what could he possibly have to argue with Walker over? It was her department that was in jeopardy, not his. And now that the medical staff had decided she was responsible for the outcomes of Nola's and Meredith's babies, the Birth Center would stay open and her maternity unit would close.

Marco suddenly grabbed her elbow from behind.

"What?" she demanded, jerking her arm away.

"Walker's your good buddy, Rae," he said. "You better talk some sense into him. Mr. CEO may have lost his shirt on that MRI scanner in Kentucky, but that doesn't mean he can't make good on his promises to me. I told him not to mess around. He'll pay for this and he'll pay big."

Rae had no idea what Marco was talking about.

"I want to talk to Walker now, not you," Rae said, stepping back.

"That fool is letting the opportunity of a lifetime slip through his greedy fingers," Marco said. He grabbed her elbow again and gazed at her with narrowed eyes. "Just give him my message," he said.

"What on earth are you talking about, Marco?" Rae asked. She yanked her arm free again and left without waiting for an answer to her question.

Walker was finishing up a cup of black coffee. "You might as well be an obstetrician if you're going to keep these kind of hours," Rae joked as she slipped into a chair across from him.

She could tell that he was just as upset as Marco had been. Now what had Marco said? Something about Walker losing money on an MRI scanner—in Kentucky, of all damn places. Well, she thought, Walker had never said anything to her about an MRI scanner. If he wanted to discuss his investments with her, she'd have to wait until he brought it up. She urgently wanted to talk to him about the paramedics.

"I suppose you're wondering what that little scene was all about between me and the Great One," Walker said.

Yes, she was curious, Rae thought, but that could wait. "Marco's always making a scene," Rae said. "But listen, I've got to talk to you . . ."

Rae stopped when she saw that Walker was staring up at the ceiling and studying it as if some message were written there. Obviously, he was distracted.

"Okay, fine," said Rae, sitting back in her chair resignedly. "What did you and Marco fight about?"

Walker leaned forward and crossed his hands together. "Will you keep this in strict confidence?" he asked.

Rae nodded her head.

"Well, Howard Marvin, the CEO of Perfect Health, called me. He wants to discuss that freestanding heart hospital you asked me about the other day."

Rae leaned forward in her chair. "When did he call?" she asked.

"This afternoon."

Rae drummed her short fingernails on the tabletop and waited for Walker to continue. When he didn't, she said, "So what did you say?"

"I told him that the owner of the Birth Center is not selling," Walker said. "Of course, he was well aware of that. But Marco wants me to meet with him anyway. Supposedly Marco has been working on a plan to force Bo to sell the Birth Center."

Her eyes narrowed. "What kind of plan?" she asked suspiciously.

"Now, Rae," Walker said, "don't go off half-cocked again. We're not talking about that conspiracy theory of yours, okay?"

"So what kind of plan *are* you talking about, Walker?" she asked. Her fears that Marco was somehow involved in the bad baby cases all came rushing back with a vengeance. He had motive and he had money. Those four missing charts had been signed out to him. . . . And if Marco was involved—no, she had already decided that Sam was not a part of it.

"Marco wouldn't tell me what his plan is."

"So then how do you know he's not the one hurting the mothers and babies?"

"Because that theory of yours is a bunch of baloney, Rae!" Walker said angrily. "But the point is that Marco is threatening to take his patients to City Hospital if I don't meet with Howard Marvin. If Marco goes, our whole heart program goes. Hell, our whole hospital goes down the toilet."

"Then why not meet with Howard anyway?" Rae asked. "What do you have to lose?"

"Nothing, except my job," Walker said. "The board has specifically ordered me not to meet with Howard Marvin unless Bo first agrees to sell the Birth Center. At this point, it's only a fallback possibility. As you know, the plan is to close your department. I want to make the politics crystal clear. Anyway, Bo has threatened to go public and blame our hospital for mismanaging cases he transfers over here. And you, Rae, will be the first person he pulls through the mud. I told Marco I will not let this happen. You mean too much to me."

"Tell me, Walker," she said, "would Marco make more money running an expanded program over here or heading up the freestanding heart center for Howard?"

Walker sighed and rubbed his beard. "Well, let's see." He appeared to mentally calculate some figures and said, "Why, I believe he'd double his income by working at the new heart center. He's already approaching seven figures." Walker let out a long whistle. "Jesus, no wonder he's threatening to leave . . .

"Anyway, he can come to me when Bo's willing to sell. The way things are going around here, I may be looking for a nice little two-bedroom on Maui for early retirement."

Rae recalled Marco's statement about Walker having lost money on an MRI scanner in Kentucky. "I hope Maui will be more profitable than Kentucky," she said.

Walker smiled wanly. "I see Marco has a big mouth," he said. "But at least Perfect Health Plan hasn't made it across the Pacific."

Rae could see that Walker did not want to follow that line of conversation. They rarely discussed their financial situations and she didn't feel that it was appropriate to discuss it then. "Perfect Health Plan," she said in a disgusted tone, as if she had just tasted the bitter remains of Walker's coffee. "Everybody's a puppet to them. So far they've managed to come into Berkeley and get doctor fighting against doctor, doctor against administrator, and doctor against the board of trustees."

"Speaking of which," Walker said, "I'm going to do what I can to reverse the outcome of your hearing. The first thing I plan to do is to find Bo and beat the shit out of him myself."

"But my test results came in," Rae interrupted. "They showed oxytocin was found in the bag from the ambulance—but not from the Birth Center or from the warehouse."

"You're kidding?" he asked. "Are you sure?" He looked at her, eyes wide with disbelief.

"Hey," she said, "I told you from the beginning what was happening. Oh, come on, Walker, you're starting to sound like Bo."

Walker ran his hands through his neat white beard. "Sorry," he said. "It's just that, well, I'm surprised, that's all."

"So do you believe me now?" she asked.

"Does Bo know about the results?" he asked.

"I told him personally, in his office," she said.

"I can't believe he still has the place open!" Walker said. "I mean, it's one thing to have no proof to support such a ridiculous theory—"

"I never said it was ridiculous—"

"But you have proof, and he still has the place open."

"That's what I want to talk to you about," Rae said. "I'm about to meet with the two paramedics. Leonard has seen the holes in the bags and has practically admitted that Theodore is a heroin addict. Someone is paying for Theodore's habit and it's the same person who wants Theodore to spike the bags with oxytocin. So I'm going over to Leonard's house and he's going to get his brother to talk. Then we're all going down to the station and I'll prove—"

"We have a heroin addict driving one of our rigs?" Walker asked, his voice teetering again on the edge of disbelief.

"It's possible," she confirmed.

"And he's running around killing babies?"

"And pregnant women."

"That's impossible!" Walker cried, rising suddenly.

"Now look, Walker," Rae said. She wasn't about to let him refuse to believe her now. So much was at stake and she was running out of options. Walker simply had to believe her.

Walker sat down in his chair. "No, you look, Rae," he said. "You're not going to see any paramedics. You say one of them is an addict and they're both involved in doing this thing with the oxytocin. So what makes you think they won't do something to you? They're setting a trap for you, Rae. Going to meet them will be way too dangerous."

Rae recalled that Sam had said the same thing. "So then you come with me," she suggested.

"I'm not going and neither are you. But I'll call their boss and insist on a meeting right away. That's how it's done, you know."

"We don't have time for all that!" Rae said, her voice rising. She rose from the table.

"Sit down," Walker said.

Rae walked around to Walker and gave him a hug from behind. "I don't mean to yell at you," she said, "but I'm not that little girl from medical school anymore. Sam told me the same thing."

"Sam who?" Walker asked.

"Sam Hartman," Rae said. She let go of Walker and leaned against the table. "You know, the new anesthesiologist."

"The one recruited by Marco?" asked Walker as he raised an eyebrow.

A shadow of somehting—doubt? suspicion?—crossed his face. Rae nodded and Walker said carefully, "What's Sam got to do with you?"

Rae crossed her arms. "He offered to go with me. But he was called away for an emergency heart—"

"How convenient."

"I was there when he got the page," Rae said defensively.

"Just be careful, Rae," Walker said. "I wouldn't trust Marco right now and from what I saw at the board meeting, Marco and Sam look like they go way back. There's more there than meets the eye."

"I've already thought about that, Walker," she said, with more confidence than she felt. "I trust him now, at least enough to—"

Now Walker rose from the table. "Just be careful who you trust," he said. "Love blinds one to the truth."

"Who said anything about love?" Rae asked, feeling the blood rush to her face.

Walker shook his head and then said, "What did you say were the names of the paramedics? I'll have no junkies in my ambulances."

Rae gave him the twins' names and then asked, "Marco says since you lost your shirt on some MRI scanner in Kentucky, you're afraid to go in on the heart center with Howard Marvin. What I'm getting at, Walker, is, well, if you weren't so gun-shy over that, would you have partnered up with him?"

"It's late," Walker said, rubbing his eyes.

"Tell me, Walker, I need to know," Rae said.

"Marco has it all wrong, Rae. I'd invest in a minute with Howard Marvin if I thought it was a good thing for this hospital. But the bottom line is that he wants us to ante up five million dollars. You were at the last board meeting. We don't have that kind of money just lying around. Five million dollars? If he could get it down to two we might have a chance. And as far as that MRI scanner is concerned—well, you win some, you lose some. There'll be other investment opportunities for me. What's important is who comes out on top in the end."

"What's important is who's coming out of that Birth Center," Rae said, checking her watch. "And that's why I'm going to Leonard's. I can't let any more bad babies come out of there."

"Let me handle this, Rae," Walker warned again.

"I'll talk to you tomorrow," Rae said as she strode away.

Yet, as she left, she wondered whether she was bothered more by Walker's warning that the twins might be setting a trap for her or by his veiled suspicions about Sam—suspicions that she had dropped days ago.

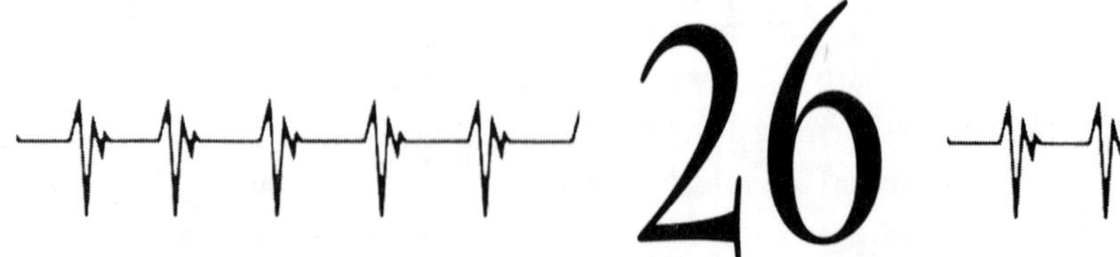

# 26

As usual, Rae decided to take the emergency room exit since it was closest to the parking lot. The time was coming up on nine o'clock. The emergency room itself was eerily quiet. Most of the nurses were busy catching up on their paperwork, and the emergency physician, Everett Lyon, dressed in his trademark battle fatigues, hovered over a patient on a gurney in the corner.

As she was walking toward the exit, Rae heard the siren of an ambulance. It grew louder and louder, until yellow and red lights began to flash across the glass doors. "Is that the Code Three we were waiting for?" Everett asked.

"No, it's the ambulance from the Birth Center!" the clerk said in surprise.

Rae walked faster. An ambulance from the Birth Center should not need its siren unless . . .

She broke into a run. Trailing her was Everett and a couple of female nurses. They got outside just as the back doors of the ambulance burst open. Rae gasped.

Lying there, on the gurney, was Rae's patient Anna Johnson. Her face was ashen, her forehead covered with sweat. She clawed at her neck, gasping for air.

"What the hell happened this time?" demanded Everett as Rae helped the paramedics and the emergency room nurses lower Anna's gurney to the ground.

Please, Rae prayed, as she noted the bluish color of Anna's skin, don't let it be what she thought it was. Blue skin meant that Anna was not getting adequate oxygen. A sudden lack of oxygen meant that something besides air was filling Anna's lungs. Worse, Anna's neck veins were distended like ropes, a sign of right-sided heart failure.

"She was fine a minute ago!" the young woman paramedic said.

"I can't breathe," Anna gasped. Suddenly her face turned as dusky as the night and she fell back against the gurney.

"Hey, step back!" shouted the nurse at Rae. "You just got suspended. You have no right to be here. Either get out or I'm calling security."

Rae ignored the nurse, ran to the head of the gurney, and helped push it inside the emergency room. "Who the hell around here can get her intubated?" she demanded. Fortunately, another nurse was rolling the red crash cart toward the door. Rae's mind sped through the list of possibilities for what had happened to Anna. It could only be one of three things: a heart attack, a pulmonary embolus, or—

"I'm calling security, Dr. Duprey!" the nurse yelled, gesturing at the security guard.

"She's had an amniotic fluid embolus, damn it!" Rae yelled. She did not have to remind herself that an amniotic fluid embolus was the most dreaded complication in obstetrics. It carried close to a 100 percent mortality rate. The old theory was that oxytocin caused the uterus to contract so violently that the amniotic fluid was forced out of the water bag and into the veins of the womb. From there the fluid got into the patient's bloodstream and caused a complete collapse of the heart and lungs.

The new theory was that the victim had a severe allergic reaction to chemicals introduced into her bloodstream during labor. No one knew where the chemicals came from or exactly how they worked; but the reaction would be similar to anaphylactic shock in someone allergic to penicillin. But old theory or new, Rae thought, the results were the same.

Everett slipped an endotracheal tube down Anna's throat and started to force oxygen into her lungs with a breathing bag. One of the nurses checked for the carotid pulse. Rae snatched a Doppler from the front counter and listened to her belly for the baby's heart rate. "It's still alive!" she shouted. "Our only chance is to get her to the operating room!"

Despite Everett's efforts, Anna's blue color did not improve. Her neck veins were dilated and even more distended. Rae was convinced of her diagnosis.

"Martin!" the nurse screamed.

Rae ran to the foot of the gurney and started to pull it toward the hall. "Her name's Anna Johnson! We've got to get her to the operating room and get her on bypass!" Rae barked. She had done so much research on oxytocin by now that she was prepared to recognize every one of its complications, proven or unproven.

"Dr. Lyon!" the nurse insisted. "Dr. Duprey was suspended today."

"She's in failure, can't you see that!" Rae said desperately as she pushed the nurse out of her way.

A young black man in a hospital security uniform grabbed Rae's shoulder. "Dr. Duprey, you've got to go—"

Rae clutched the gurney even tighter. "You let them fuss around here anymore and you'll have a dead woman on your hands," she hissed. "We've got to get her on a heart-lung machine. Look at her! She's dying right in front of you."

Everett felt the patient's neck for the carotid pulse. "Holy shit," he said.

"What did you expect?" Rae said as she pushed the nurse out of the way. "She's in right heart failure!"

Rae jerked herself away from the security guard, but the nurse blocked her path. With a mighty heave, Rae thrust the gurney forward and knocked the nurse out of her way. *Save the life! Save the life!* Nothing else mattered.

"Dr. Everett, do something!" the nurse yelled.

"I'm calling the OR, damn it!" he said.

"Well, just don't stand there!" cried another nurse to the nurse Rae had just run over. "Give me a hand with this, will you?"

"Hurry!" Rae shouted to the team. "I'll meet you downstairs in the OR!"

She tore down the hallway. Her heart pounded so loudly she thought the sound bounced off the walls. If they hurried, Rae thought, Anna would be on bypass in ten minutes or less. That would mean Anna and her baby would have a chance. And she'd do everything she could to give them that chance.

At the bottom of the stairs was a set of double doors. Through the glass, she spotted Sam wheeling in the heart patient.

"Sam, wait!" she shouted as she entered the operating suite, the same suite where they had operated on Bernie.

"Rae? What—" Sam started to ask.

"I need your bypass machine!" Rae said. "A patient's coming down from the ER," she went on, trying to catch her breath. "She's another patient from the Birth Center, Sam. She just had an amniotic fluid embolus. Unless we put her on bypass she's going to die. She's going to die, do you understand?"

The doors to the suite burst open and Everett Lyon rolled the gurney in. The same nurse who had given Rae such a hard time was now kneeling on top of the gurney and giving the patient's chest external cardiac massage.

"Which room?" Everett asked.

Rae looked at the male patient on Sam's gurney and then at Sam. "She's going to die, Sam," she pleaded. "Bypass is her only chance. I read about a case just like this . . . a case report—the woman died anyway, but the baby—the baby made it, Sam, please."

Sam gazed down on the face of his patient, who appeared oblivious to what was going on.

"Diana!" Sam yelled to a nurse behind the counter. "Call in the second team to attend to Mr. Billings here! Dr. Duprey has a patient who needs the pump first—and call Dr. Donavelli! Stat!"

"But Dr. Duprey has been suspended," the nurse called out uncertainly.

"I'm going to the locker room to change!" Rae said.

It took her all of thirty seconds to tear off her clothes and don the white surgical top and trousers. She left her jeans, jacket, and shoes strewn about as she headed back to the operating room.

Inside, at least ten people were preparing for action. Sam had disconnected the patient's endotracheal tube from the Ambu bag and connected it to the anesthesia ventilator instead. Still Anna remained as blue as before. Her neck veins were even more dilated. The lime-green gown from the Birth Center had been removed and her pregnant belly and large breasts had been splashed with brown-gold Betadine antiseptic.

Rae gloved herself. Fortunately, the heart-lung machine had already been primed for Mr. Billings—Marco's heart patient—Rae thought. The staff rushed to get everything ready in the room, which was stocked with enough equipment to do three surgeries at one time.

"We don't know anything about babies," said one of the nurses nervously as she pulled the drape over Anna.

Rae stepped up on a lift. "Where the hell is Marco?" she shouted.

"I see him coming in now," Sam answered.

"What's Mr. Billings doing out in the hallway?" Marco asked indignantly as he entered the room.

Rae started to speak but Sam beat her to it. "We need this patient on bypass now. She's in right heart failure."

Marco held out his arms so that the nurse could slip on his gown. "I didn't know I had a woman on the schedule," he said.

"She's not on the schedule and she's pregnant," Sam said.

"Pregnant? How far—shit, never mind, just tell me her pressure, Sammy."

"Who knows for sure? All we've got is a peripheral IV. Otherwise, we're flying blind. Oh, and as soon as we're done, Rae needs to section her."

Without another word, Marco rushed to the table and stood directly across from Rae. To his right was the scrub tech. Rae saw Marco use his gloved finger to feel from the top of the breastplate to the sternal notch while at the same time, he studied a video monitor next to Rae.

"Is that her heart?" he asked incredulously.

"Just be glad it's not yours," Sam said.

Even Rae, who was not used to looking at ultrasound pictures of an adult heart, could tell that the heart on Sam's monitor was way too big and too floppy to keep a person alive.

"Knife!" Marco barked, and then with the silver blade, he sliced open Anna's skin down the middle of her chest.

Rae was about to wipe away the small amount of blood that oozed up from the cut edges but decided to wait for instructions from Marco. She didn't know anything about cracking open a patient's chest. The oxygen-deprived blood was almost the color of grape jam, not the bright strawberry red it should have been.

"Saw!" Marco called out.

The scrub nurse handed Marco what looked to Rae like a huge silver staple gun, the kind that used air pressure to drill staples into a wall. On the end of it was a small hook and a two-inch serrated edge.

"Lungs down, Sam," Marco said. Then he slipped the hook under the top of the sternum and in less than five seconds had split the sternum in two. The sound mimicked a buzz saw cutting wood. There was little bleeding from the bones but the room filled with the smell of charred flesh.

"Got that heparin going, Sammy?" Marco called out. He used both of his hands to pull the chest even further apart, like opening a doctor's bag as wide as possible.

"Heparin's going in!"

As Marco and the scrub nurse placed a huge silver retractor along the edges of the cut sternum, Rae removed a pair of scissors from the instrument table and cut a hole in the lower portion of the drape over Anna's womb. Even though she didn't know if Anna or her baby would make it—if either of them was still alive even now!—she did know that as soon as Marco got Anna on bypass, she had to be ready to cut the baby out.

Marco, hurry! she thought as she glanced back into Anna's chest cavity. He had already cut through the thin pericardial lining. He exposed the thick white wall of the aorta, which sprang like a two-inch-wide white pipe from the left ventricle of the heart.

A heart that should be beating, Rae thought as she felt her body fill with anger. Not the pitiful quivering thing below her that was characteristic of heart failure. It was covered by a layer of yellow fat through which protruded a red piece of tissue resembling a little dog's ear. Looking at the mass, Rae realized how close a person always was to death. Just a heartbeat away. Just an ambulance ride away . . .

"Is she heparinized?" Marco asked.

"She's all yours," Sam answered.

Rae stole a quick glance at the clock. Three minutes had passed since they entered the room. Still Anna was as blue as ever. And her baby—was her baby still alive?

She wanted to tell Marco to hurry, but she knew how fast he was already moving. Until then, she had never seen him operate, but watching him now, seeing his hands move with smooth expertise, she couldn't help but feel new respect for the man.

"Suture," he said, and within thirty seconds he had sewn a small purse-string suture into the ascending aorta. Rae knew that if he went too deep with the needle he'd have blood shooting up to the ceiling. She worked with blood all the time. A woman could exsanguinate in ten to fifteen minutes from uterine hemorrhage, but it only took thirty seconds to bleed to death from a hole in the body's biggest artery.

Next Marco cut a window in the middle of his purse string. Next he punched the tapered tip of clear plastic tube about an inch in diameter through the aortic wall. "Hold this here and don't move," he said to Rae.

"Not a muscle," she promised as he handed her the clear plastic tube whose clear, watery solution was being pushed toward the distal end by the patient's blood. Just when the blood reached the end of the tube, Marco placed a clamp across it to stop the flow.

"Is that really you, Dr. Duprey?" Marco asked without looking up.

"I've been waiting to do something," Rae said.

Next Marco grabbed the little dog-ear piece of tissue. "When was the last time you saw the appendage of the right atrium?" he asked. But before she had time to tell him she hadn't seen a heart since anatomy class in her first year of medical school, Marco asked, "How long since she arrested?"

"Too long—at least five minutes," Rae said, struggling to keep her voice calm.

"And remember, we still have a baby to deliver, Marco," Sam said.

"Who could forget?"

"As soon as you get her on the pump," Rae added.

Marco sewed in a second purse-string suture even faster than the first. He used a scalpel to cut the opening. By now Rae had caught on to the operation. As the blood poured out of the right side of the heart, she stuck in the second tube that would be hooked up to the heart-lung machine.

"Come to me, Henry," Marco instructed the pump tech as Rae tapped the line to clear the bubbles.

"No need," Marco said. "That line goes to the machine."

The nurse informed Marco that four minutes had elapsed since the patient had entered the room.

The pump tech approached the table. Marco attached his two

tubes to the ones Henry held in his hands. When Marco freed the clamps, Rae saw the blood seep down the tubes toward the bypass machine. Blood would travel from the right side of the patient's heart and into the machine, where it would receive oxygen, and then get pumped back into the ascending aorta and from there, throughout the woman's organs.

Marco peered at Rae over his surgical loops. "What happened to her?" he asked.

"A misunderstanding," Rae said as she turned away from Marco and watched Henry turn on the machine. It was a sophisticated-looking piece of technology. A rectangular glass and silver base, about the size of a child's toy box, contained spinning disks that resembled movie reels lying flat.

"Dr. Duprey thinks this patient had an amniotic fluid embolus," Sam said.

"I *know* she had one," Rae said, still staring at the machine. Besides, she was too afraid to look back at Anna. If the machine didn't work, if Anna's blood could not be oxygenated . . .

"An embolus!" Marco bellowed. "I cracked her open for—"

"Her $O_2$ sats are coming up!" Sam announced.

Rae peered over the drape. All she could see was the top of Anna's head. But that was enough, she thought, as she pictured the newly oxygenated blood crossing the membrane between Anna's uterus and the placenta. For the small portion of her forehead exposed by the drape was turning from blue to pink, from death to life.

Marco had already cinched down the arterial and venous cannulas with more sutures. "We'll talk about the treatment of an amniotic fluid embolus later," Rae said. "It's definitely—"

"How about a femoral line for a real blood pressure, Sammy?" asked Marco, cutting Rae off.

"Why, I'd appreciate that very much, Dr. Donavelli," Sam said. "Like I said, I'm flying blind."

"How about we get this baby out?" Rae said.

Not even waiting for their answer, she sliced open Anna's abdomen. Twenty seconds later, she had opened the womb. "Push down here," she told Marco as she lifted the baby's head out of the pelvis. She could tell by the color of the blood that the pump was working.

And sure enough, five seconds later, she had delivered a screaming baby boy.

She wanted to jump for joy, but instead, she only smiled as she suctioned out the baby's nose and mouth with a blue syringe.

"Noisy little thing," Marco observed as Rae handed the baby to the nurse.

"Yeah, ain't it great?" Rae said with a laugh. In another five minutes she had Anna's abdomen closed.

"Don't let word get out that the obstetricians and cardiac surgeons are working together," Sam joked. "Might get you both thrown off the staff—oops, sorry, Rae."

"How do you know when it's time to take her off of bypass?" the scrub nurse asked.

"I think she's ready to come off it now actually," Sam said. He was staring at the monitor, and Rae saw that the heart had returned to its normal size. Rae watched as the pump tech flicked a few buttons. Anna's heart began to beat on its own.

"Sammy, old boy, you're a genius," Marco said.

"You didn't do too badly yourself, Marco."

"So how do you close her chest?" Rae asked Marco. After all, they still had a case to finish, and Rae still had a murderer to find.

Marco answered Rae's question by driving a thick needle between the patient's ribs and pulling through a piece of stainless steel wire suture. He placed at least five or six of them and then brought the two sides of the patient's sternum together.

Sam leaned over the drape. "Doctors," he said, "you've saved another life." In the background the baby cried lustily. "Excuse me, make that *two* lives," he said.

Rae tore off her gown and snapped off her gloves. Marco was doing the same thing. "Thanks, Marco," she said as they moved Anna to the gurney.

Marco frowned. "You owe me one, Rae," he said crisply. "I just hope you left that baby with a mother who'll be able to teach him to tie his own shoelaces."

The same thought had already crossed Rae's mind. Anna's heart was beating on its own, but how much brain damage had she suffered prior to the bypass? Would she even wake up? If she did wake up, would she be able to mother her child?

"Her husband's waiting outside," the nurse said. "Which of you plans to speak to him?"

Marco stepped to the side. "You're on, Doctor," he said. "I still have to work on Mr. Billings."

"Now for the really hard part," Rae said, and headed for the door.

"When will I be able to see her, Rae?" asked Tim Johnson, Anna's husband. He had accepted the news of Anna's surgery quietly and calmly. But Rae did not fail to see the slight shaking of his hands as he held them in his lap. Nor did she miss the tears welling up in the corners of his eyes.

"She'll be moved directly to the ICU," Rae explained. "You'll be able to visit her there. But Tim, we don't know how she'll be when she wakes up."

"If she wakes up," Tim interrupted.

Rae nodded. "I'm so sorry."

"How did something like happen?" he asked. "What in the world went wrong?"

Rae stood up. "That's what I'm trying to find out," she said. She placed her hand on his shoulder. "Why don't you go on up to the nursery to check on your son now. As soon as I find out, I'll let you know."

Rae stepped back into the operating room and wrote orders inside Anna's chart. She felt a little shaky. She could only imagine how Tim Johnson must have felt. Anna had come so close to dying. In fact, with no pulse or spontaneous respiration, she had been, at least until they got her on bypass, clinically dead.

The surgery had taken them only thirty minutes, and with any luck at all she would be only a few minutes late for her meeting with the twins. It occurred to her then that the last patient had been transferred over under the care of two other paramedics. She felt certain that they must have innocently used a contaminated bag.

"Will you sign these postop orders for me?" she asked Sam as she rubbed her eyes. "I forgot. I no longer have privileges here."

"How did you know she had an AFE?" Sam asked curiously.

"Because she came over from the Birth Center. That was about all she could have had—if you believe she got overdosed with oxytocin, that is."

"What, you don't like my handwriting?" he asked when he caught her staring at him.

She sat up in her chair. "I've still got a date to make."

Sam placed his hand over hers. "Tomorrow," he said. "Please don't go tonight."

"If they've got something they want to tell me, it has to be tonight," Rae said. "Don't you see what just happened here, Sam? We haven't had any bad babies coming out of the Birth Center since last week. But we've had two in the last two days. The way I see it, whoever wants to shut down the Birth Center is getting more desperate. I can't afford to wait until tomorrow, Sam."

"But you can't go by yourself," Sam said stubbornly.

"Can you walk me to my car at least?" she asked.

Sam made a call to the front desk. "I have ten minutes," he said.

As they made their way back toward the emergency room, Rae thought of what questions she would ask once she got to Leonard's house. "So will you call me when you get there?" Sam asked. "And when you leave?"

"Hey, Doc!" a male voice called out to Rae.

Rae looked up and saw Martin, the security guard, approaching her. "How did everbody do?"

"Everybody's okay. Thanks for not throwing me out of the building," she smiled. Martin extended his hand and she shook it.

"She was in pretty bad shape, that's all I know," he said.

Rae started to answer him, but was suddenly distracted by the sight of the young paramedic who had brought over the last patient from the Birth Center removing IV bags from the hospital's bin.

"One moment, Martin," she said as she headed to the back of the room.

Sam followed her.

"Excuse me, Miss?" Rae said.

The paramedic smiled. "Hey, good call. I heard you saved her life. I really don't know what the hell happened. One minute she was fine, the next minute—"

Rae placed her hand on the bag. "What are you doing with these?" she asked. "I thought you got your bags from the warehouse over on Elmwood Street."

"That's where I get all the other ones," the woman said, "but not the ones for the Birth Center." She stopped to point to ten-inch letters on the top of the cart. "BC," she read out loud. "All of the IVs we use in the Birth Center rig are stored here."

Rae looked at Sam. "Who told me the bags for the Birth Center ambulance were kept at the warehouse?" she asked.

"Nobody would have told you that," the paramedic said. "There's a special contract between our ambulance service and the hospital. All IVs used on Birth Center patients are stored here. For convenience, or at least that's what I heard."

Rae grabbed the paramedic by her shoulders. The woman was at least six inches taller than Rae. "Are you sure?" she asked fiercely. "Are you absolutely sure?"

Wide-eyed, the woman simply nodded her head. "Yeah, Doc, I'm sure. I'm just doing my job."

Rae felt Sam pulling her back. "Sorry," she said as the paramedic scurried away. Just before the woman made it out the door, Rae shouted after her, *"No!"*

She ran over to the door and snatched the IV bags back. "Please," she said urgently, "would you give me these and stock your rig with the bags from our general supply bins instead?"

"No, I can't do that, Doc," the paramedic said. "My orders are to—"

"Who gave you those orders?" Rae asked. Whoever had ordered the paramedic to use the BC bin bags might very well be the same person who had paid Theodore to spike the bags with oxytocin in the first place.

"Hey, what did I do?" the paramedic asked, bewildered.

"Nothing," Sam reassured her. "But nonetheless, please—just this once—get a bag from the bin over there?"

Rae followed her gaze to the general IV supply bins for the emergency room. She turned back to them and shrugged her shoulders. "I suppose so," she said. "As long as it's lactated Ringer's, to me, a bag is a bag."

Once the paramedic had left, Rae said, "I can't believe I was so stupid. I was the one who assumed the bags for the Birth Center ambulance were stored in their warehouse. So who in this emergency room is paying off Theodore, Sam?"

"Who says it's somebody in our emergency room?" He had taken a bag from her and was studying it for needle holes. "Hey, look at this," he said.

Rae leaned over his IV bag. "Damn it!" she said when she saw the puncture. The small aperture was barely perceptible, and no one would notice it unless she was looking for it. Together they found the holes in five other bags as well, pierced right through the plastic.

"We've got to get rid of these things," Rae said.

Sam looked at the bin and so did Rae. In total, there were about twenty bags on the cart. "Why don't you keep them in your locker?" Sam suggested.

Rae frowned. "I don't have the time," she said. "I'm going to be late for my meeting with the twins. Besides, I'm not even sure I have a locker here anymore. But Sam, you can store them in *your* locker. You have another five minutes before your case."

"It's going to take me more than five minutes to get all these over there," Sam said.

Rae went over to another supply bin and removed a roll of one-inch-wide white tape. It took her a minute to string the tape in a crisscross fashion across the bin. Then she took her pen and wrote "Contaminated: Do Not Use" across the tape. "Okay, this should work for now. Then you can store the bags when you're done, Sam," she said.

"Actually, I just remembered. I don't have room," he replied. "They promised me my own locker soon, but right now, I'm sharing one with Marco."

"Fine, fine," she said distractedly, as she stuffed her pen back into her purse. They could decide how to dispose of the bags later.

"A lot of people use this emergency room," Sam said.

"But every day?" Rae asked. "Or as many days as necessary to kill off a few babies?"

"Even every day it could be one of a hundred people," Sam said.

"Then we better find that one person—or persons—soon. Two cases in two days—how many tomorrow?"

But instead of walking on, she stopped to ponder an idea that had just occurred to her. Suddenly she began to pull the tape she had so carefully placed across the cart.

"Maybe," she said, "the person doing all of this is not the person stocking the bin. Maybe all the killer's doing is injecting the bags once they're here. That would explain why only six bags—and not all twenty—have been tampered with. There would only be so much time to spike them. So let's replace these bags with new ones—I mean, ones without holes. Then let's hang around and see who shows up to inject them."

Now that she had removed all of the tape, she began to pull the contaminated bags out of the bin, stuffing them behind the cart. Then she replaced them with new bags from the main supply bin, after first checking to make sure that there were no holes in them. Luckily the bin was located in a back alcove, so no one, other than Sam, could see her.

"And you think that person's coming back tonight?"

"Can you say he isn't?" Rae asked.

"Who's going to act as your lookout man?"

Rae remembered she had a couple of paramedics to talk to, and Sam still had a case to do. "I'll ask one of the nurses," she improvised.

"I don't think they'll believe your oxytocin theory," Sam said. "And of course, the word's out about your suspension."

Rae frowned as she placed the last new bag in the bin. "You're on my side, remember?" she said testily.

"I'm just trying to get you to understand what you're up against. Sure, they know you were right about the amniotic fluid embolus, but a maniac on the loose is another thing altogether."

"Go do your case, Sam," Rae said. "Right now, I don't need you or anybody putting up more hurdles. I'll find somebody, okay?"

Sam bent down to kiss her. "Just be careful," he said, staring into her eyes. "You don't know who you're up against."

After Sam left, Rae had to decide between keeping her appointment with the twins and staking out the IV bin. The emergency room was now in full swing. Several incoming patients were dressed in costumes and Rae suddenly remembered that it was Halloween. Sighing impatiently, she checked her watch. She should have been at Leonard's house twenty minutes ago!

"There she is!"

Immediately Rae recognized the deep voice of Arnie Driver. Walking with Arnie was Martin, the security guard.

"I could have you arrested for assault and battery," Arnie said.

"Leave me alone, Arnie." As she tried to push her way past him though, she felt a gentle yet firm hand on her shoulder. She looked up and saw Martin staring at her. "I hate to do this to you, Dr. Duprey," he said apologetically.

"Well, I sure as hell don't," Arnie said. "You had no right to operate on that patient. You don't have privileges here anymore, remember? So either leave on your own or I'll have Martin throw you out. And if he doesn't, I'll throw you out myself!"

Arnie's face had turned bright red. What a fool he was! Even the near-death experience of the Birth Center's last patient had not been enough to raise his suspicions that Rae's oxytocin theory might have some merit.

Rae extended her elbow to Martin like a bride offering her arm to the groom. "I'd be honored to have you escort me away from this jackass," she said sweetly.

"And if I see you back here," Arnie shouted after her, "I *will* call the police."

"I'm sorry about all this," Martin said once Rae was outside the door.

"You were just doing your job, Martin. And now I've got to go and do mine."

"I mean it, Dr. Duprey," Martin said. "I saw that last patient come in here. I thought she was going to die on us. If it hadn't been for you—well, I'm no doctor, but I've been here long enough to know that she didn't have a chance in hell if you hadn't made the diagnosis."

Rae was touched by Martin's sincerity. "Thank you," she said.

"If there's anything—and I mean anything—I can do for you, Dr. Duprey, you just let me know."

"Actually, there is something you can do, Martin. Keep an eye on the Birth Center's IV bin." She narrowed her eyes as she stared at the bin. "Jot down for me the names of any and all people who stop by there."

Martin's face became one big question mark, but he kept his thoughts to himself.

"I'll be back later tonight," Rae continued. "Remember, if anybody even nods his head in that direction, I want to know about it, okay?"

"You got it, Doctor," Martin said. He smiled and Rae thanked him again, then got in her car and sped to West Berkeley.

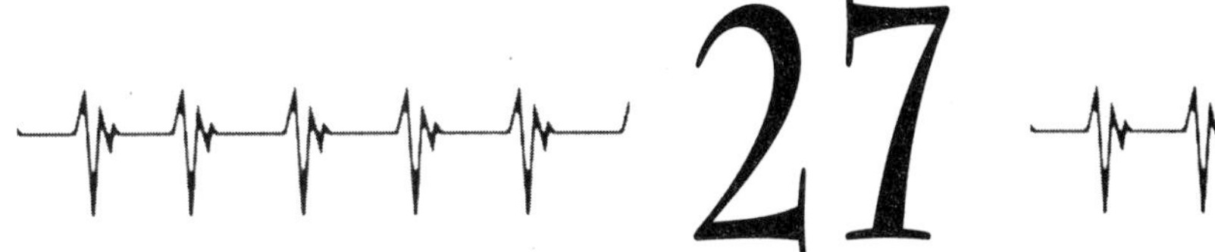

# 27

RAE SPED DOWN MARIN AVENUE AND MADE A LEFT ON SAN Pablo. The houses got smaller and smaller, and even in the darkness she could also see that the gardens got drabber and the cars parked along the street had more dents and scrapes than those in the hills. She rechecked the address. At Ellis Street she made a right and parked in front of the second house from the corner.

There were no cars parked in front of Leonard's brown-shingled house. She did see a motorcycle in the open garage. A hammock swung from two posts on a wooden porch. Under the hammock was a set of free weights.

Before knocking, she looked around her. She may not have taken Sam's advice by coming but at least she could be as careful as possible. The lights throughout the house were on, which she thought was a good sign.

Suddenly she heard a soft thud on the porch to her right. She jumped away from the door as her heart lurched inside her chest. But she settled down when a brown and white cat walked up to her and rubbed against her leg. "Damn it," she said as she reached down to stroke the soft fur between his ears, "don't do that again."

When she knocked on the door it opened a few inches. She listened for sounds coming from the house, but there were none. She knocked again. Still no answer. "Leonard, it's me, Rae Duprey," she called out through the partially opened door.

When he didn't answer, Rae pushed open the door a few more

inches. The door squeaked on its hinges and the cat rubbed against her leg. "Leonard?" she called out again, but more tentatively. "Anybody home?"

Taking a deep breath, she entered the house and walked across the living room. Perhaps the twins had already come and gone, she thought, glancing around the interior of what was obviously the home of a bachelor: sparse wooden furniture, a thirty-two-inch TV screen, a dying plant in flowerpot, and a few sports magazines scattered here and there.

To her right was an open door, through which she could see an old refrigerator. She kept walking in the direction of what she thought would be the bedroom. On her left was a bathroom with a few blue towels hanging from a rack. An open closet was just across from it. Further down the hall was another room with enough exercise equipment to rival a small gym.

Rae poked her head inside. There was also a small table near the door with a fourteen-inch framed picture of the twins dressed in black shorts and nothing else. They looked ten years younger, and Rae couldn't tell one from the other. Both had massive muscles, the kind that teenage boys assumed they were supposed to have.

There was only one door left in the house, at the end of the hall, and it was closed. Rae knocked, but again there was no answer. She knocked louder, thinking that Leonard may have fallen asleep. "I'm coming in," she warned, "so you better be dressed."

She pushed open the door. The first thing she noticed was the trail of blood on the floor in front of her. Her eyes followed the trail to the bed, and there, lying flat on his back, was Leonard. Only his bulky size distinguished him from his brother. That, and the fact that presumably Theodore was still alive.

Quickly she looked around the room. Was the person who had done this still here? She walked gingerly over to him, taking great care not to step in the blood. After seeing how the crime team went over the file room in medical records, she knew it was best not to disturb anything.

Even though her mind continued to click forward rationally, Rae felt a paralyzing wave of terror begin to rise within her. Her hands shook. Her heart raced. The closer she got to the body, the more terrified she became.

He was shirtless, just like in the picture, but now his chest was a bloody, gaping wound with no signs of spontaneous respiration. Without touching anything else, she knelt down to feel his carotid artery. No pulse, yet his skin was still warm. Whoever killed him had done so recently. Rae stood up quickly. She could be next.

On the night stand was a phone. Hands still trembling, she picked it up. But before she could punch in the first number, she heard the siren of a police car.

She ran into the living room and out the front door. The car screeched to a halt behind her Porsche and an officer came out of the car with his pistol drawn. Immediately Rae recognized Officer Mailer, the young cop who had given her a hard time after Bernie's assault.

"Put that thing away," Rae yelled out to him.

"Get your hands up!" Mailer shouted back.

Another squad car pulled up just as Rae raised her arms.

"What's going on here, Dr. Duprey?" he asked as his backup approached them.

She definitely didn't want to piss off Mailer. He was just stupid enough to shoot her head off. But the whole scene seemed surreal. Why did she have a policeman pointing a gun at her when there was obviously at least one murderer loose in the area?

The new cop, whose badge read DAVID NUNN, pointed his gun at Rae and looked at Mailer for an explanation. "A neighbor claimed she heard shots fired, sarge," he said. "I found Dr. Duprey rushing out of this house."

"I had an appointment with the paramedics," Rae explained quickly. "When I got here, one of them was dead."

The sergeant looked from Rae to the Mailer. "Hold her here," he said. "I'll go inside."

He returned within minutes. "I'll get the boys to come down for evidence," he said. "Mailer, why don't you take the good doctor on in."

"In where?" Rae asked as the sergeant walked to his car. Certainly not to jail!

Mailer pulled out a set of handcuffs. Rae's eyes widened as she looked at them. "You're kidding, right?" she asked nervously.

"Turn around," he said.

She didn't move. "Hey, I said I came here to visit him. He was dead when I knocked on the door."

Mailer grabbed Rae's right hand and cocked her thumb back. Pain shot thorugh her arm and she thought she would throw up. He slapped the handcuffs on her and cinched them down until the metal dug into her skin.

"Hey, Mailer," the sergeant called out. "Take those things off of her. She's a witness, not a suspect."

"We don't know that, sarge," Mailer yelled back.

"Well I do!" Rae said as she turned her back to the officer. "So take these damn things off!"

Mailer groaned and unhooked them. He applied as much force taking them off as he did putting them on.

Massaging her wrists with her fingers, Rae asked bitterly, "What did I ever do to you?"

"Just get in the car, Doctor," Mailer snapped as he held open the door for her.

Rae looked inside the car at the backseat. Even without handcuffs on, she was still going to feel like a criminal if she climbed in.

"I said get in," Mailer repeated gruffly, then placed his hand on the top of her head and kept it there until she was inside.

The seat was made of some sort of black plastic. There was no fabric covering any of it, and it was perfectly smooth except for two small grooves cut in the back.

"Are my hips supposed to fit in there?" Rae asked sarcastically.

"One of these days I'm going to put those cuffs back on you and keep them on," he answered.

More squad cars arrived and Mailer finally got into the front seat and drove Rae to the Berkeley station. Once inside, she followed his instructions to sit down in a chair next to a conference room.

"How long do I have to be here?" she demanded, but when Mailer walked away without answering, she shouted after him, "I have to make a phone call!"

Rae leaned over and put her head in her hands. What the hell was she going to do now? She had thought that the next time she came down to the station, she would be accompanied by the twins, who would tell everybody about the holes in the IV bags. Now here she was, a "witness," Sergeant Nunn had called her. And it seemed certain that Officer Mailer would try to convince the sergeant that she was the prime suspect for the murder of the paramedic.

She raised her head when she heard a familiar male voice booming out of the conference room. When she had first sat down, she noticed that a meeting of some sort was in progress inside the room. But she had been too preoccupied to pay any attention to what was being discussed.

"So ladies," the voice continued. It was Sergeant Lane, the cop she had met in medical records shortly after Bernie had been beaten. "If you should ever have the misfortune to find yourself in a hostage situation, and somebody's holding you with a weapon pointed to your head—like this—"

Rae couldn't see inside the room, but pictured Sergeant Lane demonstrating on some giggling volunteer.

"Remember," he said, "you can always blink at the officers who are present. The officers should recognize your signal. Wait for them to give you the return signal—and then pretend to faint dead away."

Rae heard a muffled thud, and then a round of nervous titters from the women in the room.

"The perpetrator will be startled and his gun will tend to move away from your face—like you just saw—long enough for one of the officers to grab him."

"What happens if the officer misses?" a woman asked.

"Next question," the sergeant said, and Rae heard the room erupt in laughter.

"Yeah, right," Rae said out loud, rolling her eyes to herself. Distracted, she looked down the hall for Mailer's return.

The class broke up and about thirty women piled out. A few looked at Rae and she gave them all a half smile. Finally the sergeant came out of the room. In his hand he carried a large gun, which he tucked back into his holster.

Rae stood up. "Sergeant, there's been a terrible mistake and I've got to talk to you," she said.

"Dr. Duprey?" he asked, surprised.

"I've been waiting for you, sarge," Mailer said, walking up stiffly.

"And I need to make a phone call," Rae said.

"Perhaps we should find a quieter place," Lane said.

They took Rae to the same room where she had filed her report about the Birth Center. Mailer asked her how she knew the paramedics and why she had gone over there. She told him about her last conversation with Leonard, and how even Leonard had seen the holes in the bags inside his ambulance.

"And I just know that whoever killed him had something to do with the deaths coming out of the Birth Center," she concluded.

The two policemen were staring at her in total disbelief. This was getting a little old, she thought. She had now told them everything she knew; but clearly it was not enough to convince them. There would be little more she could do in the police station.

"Am I under arrest?" she asked finally, looking from one dumbfounded face to the other.

"I really do want to believe your story, Dr. Duprey," Lane said, "but, well, it still sounds incredible."

"It's ridiculous," Mailer said flatly.

Rae stood up. "Then I'm out of here," she said. "I have to get back to my emergency room and hunt down the real killer."

After picking up her purse, she turned and walked down the hall. "Just don't leave town!" Mailer shouted after her as she turned the corner.

Twenty minutes later, Rae heard her beeper go off just as she down-shifted to begin her ascent up Marin Avenue. She hoped that Martin, the security guard, was still in the ER. Better yet, she hoped that he had made a list of the visitors to the IV bin, as she had requested.

In the darkness she pressed the side button on her beeper to illuminate the display panel. The alphanumeric message was that Mr. Theodore McHenry had just found out about his brother and wanted to see her. There was a phone number listed, which Rae immediately dialed on her cell phone.

"Dr. Duprey?" Theodore said. His voice sounded strangled, desperate. "Thank God I found you! I just heard—Leonard's dead, Dr. Duprey. Somebody shot him!"

"Where are you now?" Rae asked. "We need to talk."

"I can't believe he's dead. I was just talking to him—on the phone. He told me what you said. But I swear to you, I don't know anything about any holes in those bags."

"But Leonard saw them!" said Rae, shouting into the speaker. She forced herself to calm down, reminding herself that the man just lost his brother.

"I can show you the holes myself," she explained quickly. "The same ones that Leonard saw. Just promise me, promise me when you see them you'll go to the police station with me."

"I'm scared, Dr. Duprey," Theodore said shakily, and Rae could tell that he was crying.

"Listen, Theodore," Rae said. She was pulling into the parking garage. "Can you meet me at the hospital?"

"I'm too afraid to go anywhere!"

"Twenty minutes." Rae said as she pulled the brake.

"Maybe whoever killed Leo is going to kill me next!"

"You'll be safe in the ambulance. I'll meet you in front of the emergency room."

"I can't—"

"Yes, you can! Twenty minutes—now hurry!"

The phone clicked dead.

Rae wasn't sure what to think. She knew Theodore was involved, yet he denied knowing anything. Most likely someone was paying him to hang the bags, not spike them. All Theodore wanted was money to support his habit. For that he could hang a contaminated IV bag—no questions asked.

But the important thing was that he was willing to help her. The person responsible for the killings was more desperate than ever, she thought. He wasn't limiting himself to helpless women and babies anymore. Everybody was now fair game. The only question was, who would be next?

By the time her foot hit the pavement, she had her answer. Nobody, she told herself. Not if she had anything to do with it. Holding on to her purse, she ran from the parking lot to the hospital.

Across the street Rae saw the Hillstar ambulance parked in front of the emergency room entrance. Theodore would soon be waiting for her, but she had to speak to Martin before he left. Again Sam's warning to take care of herself crept into her thoughts. Getting backup wouldn't hurt. For all she knew Theodore could have killed his brother.

Inside the lobby, she used the house phone to put in a call to Sam. The nurse who answered said that he was still tied up with the heart case. "Tell him to meet me in front of the emergency room when he's done," Rae asked.

"It's extremely important," she added, but the nurse had already hung up the phone. She wondered if the woman had taken down the message at all.

Next she called Walker's office. He rarely worked so late, but she had seen him meeting with Marco only a couple of hours ago, so maybe there was hope. After the fourth ring, he answered. "Rae, I'm on my way home," he said.

"I need to see you now," she persisted. He wearily agreed to see her.

When she entered his office, Walker was sitting at his desk. Computer printouts were spread out in front of him. "I've been trying to figure out a way to keep Marco happy," he said without looking up. He was obviously still fuming from his earlier conversation with the heart surgeon.

Rae plopped down in the chair in front of him. She waited for him to look up from his note pad. "One of the twins is dead," she said flatly.

"What twins?" Walker asked, putting down his pen.

"The paramedics." Rae recounted everything that happened: how she had found Leonard's body, the blood on the bedroom floor, her trip to the police station, and her conversation on her cell phone with the surviving twin.

"He called you?" Walker asked.

"He's waiting for me now," Rae said.

Walker stood up and closed the door to his office. "What? Are you crazy? You're going to see him?"

"He's waiting for me in front of the ER," she explained, understanding Walker's point. "But first I've got to check with one of our security guards. I came here to ask you to go with me, not to argue about whether I should go at all."

"What's the security guard have to do with this?" Walker asked, confused. He rose and walked around to sit on the end of his desk in front of Rae.

Rae explained to Walker her plan with Martin. "That's why I really came back here, Walker. If I have to stake out the ER all night, I'm going to do it, damn it. But I'll catch the person who's doing this. Believe me, the next time I talk to Mailer and Lane, I'll make them believe me."

"Rae, slow down," he cautioned, waving both hands in front of her. "Let's think this thing through first."

He rose and began to pace to and fro in front of the windows, his arms folded across his chest. "Jesus Christ, Rae," he finally said, "I must remind you that the last thing we need is for our reputation to be trashed on the front pages of *The Oakland Tribune.*"

"But this isn't about how we look, Walker!"

"The way I see it, it could even be that damn Birth Center that's behind this. Or City Hospital, for all we know. But whoever it is, I'm not going to let this hospital be dragged through the mud for something we didn't do."

"I don't care if we get written up in *The Wall Street Journal!*" Rae cried.

"But you've got to care, Rae!" Walker snapped back. "You bring down this hospital's reputation, you'll be delivering babies in your office instead of on the third floor!"

"That's about the only place I can deliver them now," Rae said sarcastically.

She drummed her fingertips on the armrest. "I'm meeting with Theodore with or without you. So are you coming or not?" she asked icily.

"Of course I'm coming," Walker said. "But hold on a minute, okay? You've got to give me time to digest this. It's unbelievable, unthinkable . . ."

Rae stood up. Outside the window she could see the lights of the Birth Center glowing innocently in front of her.

"I don't know any other way to convince you, Walker," she said. "If I did, I would have done it days ago."

"All right, Rae," he said. "If you really believe this, then I'll stand by you. But Lord help us all if what you say is true."

"Thank you, Walker," Rae said, rising. Had she had the time she would have hugged him. Instead, she watched as he leaned across his desk and picked up the phone.

"Go ahead. I'll be right there. But first, I've got to call the police," he said. "Just promise that you'll call me from the ER if the paramedic shows up before I do."

"He better show up," Rae said as she walked toward the door. "Otherwise, we'll go to him."

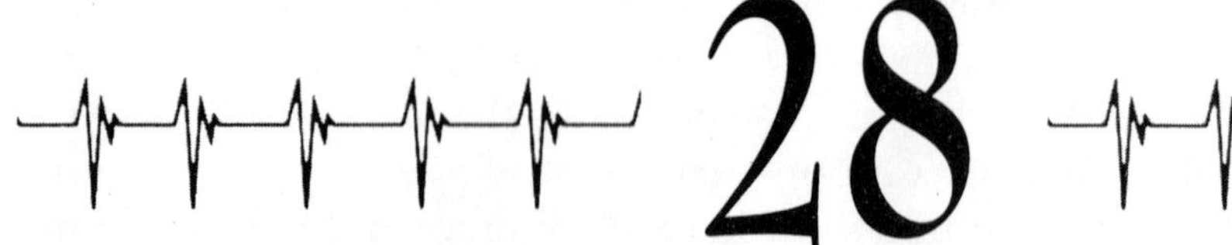

# 28

As Rae made her way through the emergency room, she realized she had not given much thought to how this whole affair would play out—even if she did catch the killer, it could potentially backfire and end up ruining the hospital's name. Then who would want to deliver there? No wonder Walker had a hard time accepting her suspicion that someone at Berkeley Hills was spiking the bags.

"Have you seen Martin?" she asked the ward clerk, a young woman with blood red lips and a witch's hat on. Rae did a double take when she saw that all of the nurses wore the same hats.

"Where's *your* Halloween costume, Dr. Duprey?" the receptionist asked.

"I need to find Martin," Rae said urgently. "Is he on break?"

"Martin's not wearing a costume either," the receptionist teased. "I told him—"

"Never mind all that," Rae said, her eyes searching the room.

"He'd look real cute dressed as a bunny rab—"

"Just tell me where the hell he is!" Rae barked.

A few other nurses behind the desk looked in Rae's direction. "He's on break," the young woman said, pouting.

Rae grumbled a thank-you and walked away. She felt the young woman's angry stare follow her down the hall. For the next ten minutes the sliding glass doors to the emergency room opened and closed, but Martin never showed. Just how long a break did he get? Rae asked herself. Outside the doors Rae saw the white shape of the Hillstar ambulance. She checked her watch again. Her twenty minutes were up. Theodore was waiting.

Back at the nursing station, Rae said to the young receptionist, "When Martin does show up, tell him not to leave until I get back."

"Whatever you say," the receptionist replied coldly. Rae left but as she passed through the sliding glass doors, she wondered if the receptionist would tell Martin anything at all.

It was a perfect night for Halloween. The temperature was brisk enough to make one comfortable in a heavy costume, and the moon was so full that street lights were barely needed. She walked up to the ambulance and stood on her tiptoes to look inside the driver's window.

It appeared empty. Either Theodore hadn't shown up yet or he had already come and gone. "Damn it!" she cried as she slammed her fist against the door.

She turned around and started to head back to the emergency room. Her only chance now to save the babies was to talk to Martin and hope his list pointed to the killer. But suddenly the doors to the emergency room slid open again and coming through them was Theodore.

She let out a deep breath and said, "Whew! I thought I'd missed you."

"Get in," Theodore said shortly.

Rae cocked her head at his curt tone.

"Look, Theodore . . ." she began.

He came up to the door and pulled it open. "After you, Doctor," he said.

Rae stood her ground. Something was off. Theodore sounded nothing like the grief-stricken man she had spoken to earlier on the phone.

She started to back away. "I just remembered I have to go—"

"Inside," Theodore commanded. He grabbed for her elbow.

But Rae was too fast. She jerked her arm away from him and started to move toward the hospital. Terror surged through her body. He caught her before she could take a step and dug the gun so deeply under her rib cage that she could barely breathe.

"Okay, okay," she gasped.

She was terrified of Theodore, but she was also terrified of getting inside the ambulance.

She took one step backward. Her legs felt as if they would collapse. Another step. Her breathing grew more shallow. One more step. Now it was her heart. Pounding. Pounding. Pounding hard enough to rip open her chest. Finally, fearing she was on the verge of collapse, she reached the door of the ambulance.

"Climb in," Theodore said.

But she couldn't climb in. She couldn't even move. Her mouth was so dry she couldn't swallow. Theodore came up to her and jammed the end of the gun barrel into her ribs again. The pain was unbearable.

"I said climb in, bitch," he said.

She winced in pain and grabbed for the inside handle. Her hands slipped and she grabbed it again. Somehow she raised her right foot and pulled herself into the driver's seat.

Theodore climbed in after her and slammed shut the door. "Move over," he said.

Between the seats was a huge console with radio equipment and speakers. Rae slid across as best she could. She could feel her pulse galloping through her veins. Her breathing came in ragged gasps.

Why hadn't she listened to Sam? Or Walker? Where were they now?

"What do you want?" she asked, trying to keep her voice steady.

He didn't answer; in fact, he almost didn't seem to hear her. In the fluorescent glare of the emergency dock, she had noticed that his pupils were mere pinpricks. He must have shot up recently. Worse, she could also smell the rancid fumes of cheap liquor on his breath.

Theodore sandwiched the gun between the steering wheel and his left thumb and used his right hand to turned the key in the ignition. Rae looked out the window, hoping to signal somebody that she was in trouble. But at that moment no one was walking toward the emergency room. Even if someone had, he would most likely think Rae was enjoying a ride-along on Halloween night.

The ambulance lurched forward. Immediately the night was filled with the sound of the siren and the flashing lights. No one would suspect that she was being kidnapped inside an ambulance, Rae thought. Just as no one believed that anything had gone wrong inside the ambulance for the past two months.

The car made a sharp right turn at the end of the driveway, but instead of turning left into the Birth Center it headed straight for Marin Avenue. Rae's mind sped through her options. Theodore gunned the engine and they headed for the hill's descent. Where were they going? Rae asked herself. How was she going to get away from Theodore? And what about the babies? Without Leonard to corroborate her story, she had no case.

The ambulance ran through the first stop sign. "Buckle up, Doctor. I wouldn't want you to get hurt," he said with mock concern. But strapping herself into a seat next to a lunatic was something that Rae could not do.

Suddenly Theodore's hand slapped her mouth so hard she tasted blood. "I tried to ask you nicely," he said coldly.

Fumbling, she found the seat belt and strapped herself in. The ambulance picked up more speed. Somehow, she told herself, she had to keep her wits about her.

"Where are we going?" she asked, eyeing the gun in Theodore's left hand. He was using only his right hand to steer the wheel.

"No more questions!" Theodore barked.

Rae took her eyes from the wheel and looked ahead. "Watch out!" she shouted as soon as she saw a car door open on the passenger side of the street.

But her warning was too late. The ambulance picked off the door of the car and the sound of the impact exploded in Rae's ears.

"Bastard!" Theodore shouted out the window and Rae heard the metal crash onto the concrete behind them.

Rae clutched the sides of the seat. She eyed the handle of the passenger door. No, she told herself. If she tried to escape, she'd wind up dead on the pavement.

"Please, Theodore," she said, deciding that her only option was to reason with him. "You can get help. I talked to our CEO—he wants to help you."

Theodore laughed—a wild man's laugh, full of insanity, devoid of feeling. "So now everybody wants to help poor little Theodore."

"I mean it, Theodore."

"Shut up!" Theodore bellowed. Rae saw his hand swing out at her again.

She raised her hands to protect herself but Theodore's blow was so powerful it knocked them away and again the back of his hand slammed against her mouth. She felt her teeth bite down on her lip, and again she tasted a gush of hot, salty blood inside her mouth. She thought of Bernie and wondered if her friend's attacker had begun his assault on her in the same way.

The ambulance was about halfway down the hill. With her right hand, Rae wiped the blood from her mouth. Again she eyed the door handle. Better the pavement than another minute with this maniac. If only she could get it open before Theodore could grab her. But that meant she'd have to unbuckle the seat belt, and do it in a way that Theodore couldn't see.

Taking a chance, she let her fingers slide slowly to the buckle. But just when she thought she had it unfastened, Theodore grabbed her arm viciously. Again she could not fight him off as he dug his fingers into her flesh so hard she cried out in pain.

"That's the same sound that nurse made," Theodore said. "No, it was a little louder."

Rae's eyes widened. "You tried to kill Bernie?" she asked.

"Yeah, that was her name," Theodore muttered.

Filled with sudden rage at the thought of Bernie fighting to hang on to life in the ICU, Rae lunged for the steering wheel, but this time he hit her in the face with the butt of his gun. Pain exploded in her head and she fell back against the inside of the door.

"I told her to mind her own business!" Theodore said. "But she started asking me all kinds of questions. Just like you keep doing."

Never before in her life had Rae wanted to be a man, but she did now. A large man, big enough to slowly crush Theodore to death.

"I don't see why your brother bothered worrying about you," Rae said, her voice filled with contempt.

"My brother loved me!" Theodore screamed. He swung wildly at her again but missed.

"He didn't love you," Rae taunted. "He wanted to turn you in. That's what he told me."

"Shut up!" Theodore shouted. "He didn't tell you a damn thing!"

"Why do you think he asked me to meet you tonight?" Rae asked. "He knew what you've been doing—the holes in the bags—"

"You lying bitch!" Theodore yelled.

"He was going to tell everybody that you killed those women, those babies."

She had to speak quickly, she thought. She didn't want to give Theodore any time to think.

"All the drugs, all the times he had to cover for you. Well, he said he was sick of it, and sick of you."

"He wanted me to come clean, that's all he cared about!" Theodore retorted, his voice shaking. "But he didn't understand what it's like. I need my stuff. Every three hours, like a baby needs a tit. I told him, but he didn't understand."

He paused to wipe the sweat from his forehead. "But no way was I going to do time."

"Who's your boss, Theodore?" Rae asked. "Who's been paying you?"

"It's hard enough getting my stuff on the street," Theodore said. "I tried to make a deal with Leo. I told him we should just move on—like we always move on. I told him tonight . . .

"But all he did was to yammer on and on about you and those damn babies."

Another wave of fear swept over Rae. "*You* killed him?" she asked.

"Why didn't you just leave us alone, Dr. Duprey? Why couldn't you just let things be?"

Theodore rocked back and forth against the steering wheel. He had slowed down the ambulance as he spoke.

"But Leonard was your brother!"

"All I did was change a few IV bags on the way to the hospital," Theodore said. He was sobbing now. "What's the big deal about that? But Leonard wouldn't listen to me. He kept accusing me of killing those women . . . those babies. But I didn't kill anybody, Dr. Duprey. I just changed the bags."

"So who injcted them with oxytocin, Theodore?" Rae pressed.

"I tell you I don't know anything about any damn oxytocin! Just like I told Leonard, I was only supposed to change the bags when he asked me."

"Who?" Rae asked excitedly. "Who told you to change them?"

"I had no choice but to shoot him," Theodore whispered, and then he stepped on the gas and the ambulance lurched forward.

"Who put the oxytocin in the bags that killed those women and babies?" Rae demanded.

But Theodore had retreated into his own world, muttering incoherently to himself under his breath as they sped down the dark streets. Rae tried desperately to think of another way to reach him.

The honking of a car interrupted her thoughts. She looked up and saw a Volvo coming directly at them.

Rae grabbed for the steering wheel again. Theodore pushed her away. Her eyes were frozen on the scene in front of them. Surely the ambulance would hit the Volvo head on.

At the last possible second Theodore swerved to his right, avoiding the collision. Yet no sooner had he done so than a van came shooting out of a side street to Rae's right.

"Look out!" Rae screamed.

But it was too late. The ambulance hit the front third of the van with a sickening thud, spinning it around like a toy and toppling it over. Rae held on to the seat as the ambulance almost flipped over onto its side.

"Whoa, Nellie!" Theodore sang out as he straightened out the wheel. "I loved my brother, Dr. Duprey. I loved him more than anything!"

"Your brother is dead and you killed him!" Rae yelled.

"I didn't kill him—*you* made me kill him!" he screamed.

Theodore wiped his nose on the back of the hand gripping the gun. "It's all your fault . . . your fault, Dr. Duprey," Theodore said. "But it doesn't matter anymore, does it? He's waiting for us—for both of us. I told you I loved him."

Theodore gunned the engine and turned up the sirens. Rae saw the speedometer edge up toward sixty miles per hour. At each intersection the ambulance left the ground and fell back to earth with a thundering explosion, almost hurling her to the ceiling.

Rae saw the fountain directly in front of them. Surely Theodore saw it too!

"You're going to kill us both, you fool!" she shouted.

The speedometer had now reached seventy-five. Theodore's left hand gripped the wheel, his right hand gripped around the gun. His profile was set in stone, his eyes focused on the fountain in front of him.

"So whose life are you going to try to save this time, Dr. Duprey?" Theodore shouted as the ambulance zeroed in on the fountain like a magnet.

"Mine, you crazy fuck!" Rae said, and this time, she unbuckled her seat belt and with all her might hurled her entire body against Theodore's.

The gun went off as she crashed into him. The windshield shattered and she instinctively ducked. Glass splashed against her back like hail. Theodore cried out in pain and she knew it had hit him full in the face.

He let go of the steering wheel. She hung on and turned it to the left as sharply as she could. The rig flipped over, and then hit the road, metal screeching across the concrete like the world coming to an end.

*I'm going to die,* she thought with sudden certainty.

The sound went on and on while she held on to the steering wheel desperately. Her only hope was that the ambulance would come to a halt before it careened into the fountain. She heard the back of the rig tearing open. The ambulance changed direction and she knew that it had hit the fountain after all.

All at once, everything was quiet. The ambulance had stopped moving. Slowly she pushed herself up. Her head bumped against the steering wheel and she winced in pain. Pieces of glass slid off her back and onto the seat. She looked up and where the roof should have been was the passenger window. It was stuck, so she climbed through the shattered windshield.

A crowd of children dressed as ghosts and superheroes had gathered about twenty feet from the ambulance. Rae saw Theodore's body on the pavement. His face was turned toward her and under the light of the full moon Rae could see that in death his eyes were wide open.

She climbed down from the ambulance and began walking away quickly. "Hey!" she heard one of the children call out to her. But she had no time to stop. All she needed was for the cops to come and find another dead paramedic in connection with her.

First she limped into the backyard of one of the houses whose lights were out. The foliage was thick and she hid as a couple of squad cars and another ambulance pulled up to the scene. Several streets paralleled Marin Avenue, and Rae took one of them up the hill.

What had Theodore said that was nagging at her? Something about only changing the IV bags. Yes, she recalled, that was it. According to him, someone else had spiked them. Who, she thought?

The pounding in her head made thinking nearly impossible. She heard the siren of a police car and, turning, saw search lights scanning the yards a half a block behind her. She quickly squatted behind a bush. The squad car passed, and she pushed on. The hospital was half a mile away and she needed to get there as fast as she could.

Her last chance at finding the killer, Rae decided as she approached the hospital twenty minutes later, was to stake out the emergency room all night. But how? She no longer had privileges. She couldn't afford to be seen. Her life was probably still in danger. She had to be invisible, she told herself.

Behind the hospital was the loading dock. Next to that was a special elevator used for transporting dead bodies from the hospital's morgue to the hearses from the funeral homes or the coroner's office. If only there was more cloud cover, she thought desperately, staring at the brightly iulluminated scene.

As she stood there, a coroner's hearse pulled up to the service elevator. A man dressed in a black suit pushed a gurney out of the back and waited for the elevator to arrive. Once the door opened, he pushed the gurney inside, and just before the doors closed, Rae rushed in.

"Hey, you can't come in here," the man protested.

"I already am," Rae replied.

"But—"

"Look, Rae said, "I'm late for work, okay? I don't want my boss seeing me sneaking in again. I can't afford to get fired. I need another way in."

The man looked her up and down and then said, "I bet the stiff waiting for me looks better than you. What happened?"

As the doors of the elevator opened directly into the morgue, they were greeted by the unmistakable odor of formalin.

"Thanks for the ride," she said, stepping out of the elevator and into the back hallway.

She walked quietly down the corridor, just some fifty feet from the left turn that led to labor and delivery. How ironic, she thought, that the hospital's morgue was so close to the place where life began. But then, she herself had come so close to death only minutes before. Perhaps that was how life and death were, sepearated from each other by nothing more than five or six heartbeats, a single good deed or a single evil one. Had her mother known that just before her death? Had theodore known that just before he was ejected through the windshield? Certainly the person spiking the IV bags knew it well.

She reached the door to the janitor's locker room toward the end of the hallway. Once inside, she made her way to the sink and quickly washed the dried blood from her hands and neck. Then she donned a pair of white surgical scrubs. From a closet she pulled a bucket and mop and filled the bucket with soapy water. She stuffed her clothes into a bin and then looked at herself in the mirror.

What better way, she thought wryly, to move about without anybody recognizing her? Berkeley Hills Hospital was predominantly white. Pretending to be a black cleaning lady should be easy to pull off. She'd be invisible.

And sure enough, as she mopped her way to the emergency room, no one paid any attention to her. She kept her head low—she had watched Claudia so many times pretending to see nothing, to hear nothing, but in fact, soaking up everything like a sponge.

Inside the emergency room, she cleaned the same spot on the floor for the next hour as she waited for someone to approach the IV bags in the Birth Center bin. Ambulances came and went, patients checked in and out, doctors and nurses did their best to keep the customers happy. But the bin marked BC for Birth Center received no visitors.

As the minutes passed like hours, Rae felt the need for sleep slowly descend upon her like a death shroud. The spot on the floor that she had mopped over and over now seemed like a blurry white haze. What she needed was to go to the call room and get some rest. But what if the killer showed up while she was sleeping? Perhaps he was lurking somewhere waiting for her—the cleaning lady—to get out of the way.

She stole a glance at the clock. Five A.M. Sleep was out of the question. She would go outside and get some fresh air instead. Once she exited the hospital, she placed her mop on the cart and leaned against the wall. She closed her eyes and inhaled deeply. In two hours the sun would be up and her cover would be blown.

"Hey, Dr. Duprey!"

Rae almost jumped out of her skin when she heard the male voice calling out to her. But then she reminded herself that she wasn't Dr. Duprey: she was the cleaning lady.

So instead of looking up to see who was calling her, she looked down at her cart and started to push it back into the emergency room.

"Nice costume, Dr. Duprey."

This time Rae had to look up. Standing there was Martin, the security guard. So much for camouflage.

"Where have you been?" she asked. She kept her voice low, even though they were outside. "Did you make the list?"

Martin shrugged and stuffed his hands in his pockets. "No need to make one really," he said. "No one came near that bin that had no business being there."

"The person I'm looking for would think he has every reason in the world to pay a visit to that bin," she said. "So I want to know everybody you saw—everybody."

From his right side pocket Martin pulled out a crumpled piece of paper and handed it to her. "Most people just passed by, Dr. Duprey. I mean, it's on the way to the rest rooms. But I did what you said."

On Martin's list were several names scrawled in blue ink. Rae read the names quickly. All in all there were ten of them, including the name of the emergency room physician and the head nurse.

"Is this everybody?" she asked.

"There's more on the other side," Martin said.

Rae flipped the paper over. Only one name was written down.

She stared at Martin. "Are you sure you saw Dr. Hartman?" she asked as she read the name again.

Martin leaned over and read the name. "He's the new guy, right? I had to ask him. I've never seen him before. He's the only one who really stopped at the bin."

Rae didn't want to believe it. "Are you sure it was him?"

Martin stood up straighter and pumped out his chest. "As sure as I am that you're no cleaning lady," he said.

"What did you see him do with the bags?" she whispered.

"I was about to ask him," Martin said. "But he saw me coming and took off. I figured he got paged, or something. You doctors are always getting paged—hey, are you okay?"

But Rae had grabbed her mop and bucket and was heading back into the emergency room.

No, not Sam, she told herself. Not Sam.

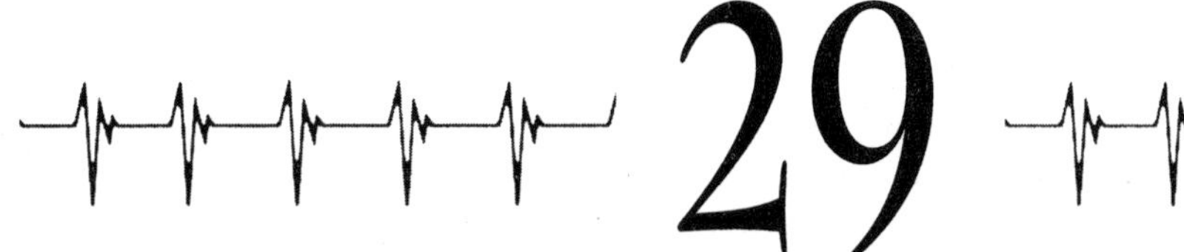

# 29

BACK INSIDE THE EMERGENCY ROOM, RAE TRIED TO CONVINCE herself that Sam Hartman was no baby killer. How could he be? He had been in surgery the whole time. It was one thing for Rae to pretend to be a cleaning lady, but for Sam to be two places at once? Impossible.

To prove it, she rose and used the nearby phone to call the OR. She pretended to be a nurse in the emergency room who wanted to know if Dr. Hartman was still in surgery. The nurse who answered the phone told Rae that Dr. Hartman should be done in about an hour.

"Thank you," Rae said as a huge wave of relief swept over her. "I don't know how they stay in surgery for so long."

"Oh, Dr. Hartman always gets a break once the patient goes on bypass," the nurse volunteered cheerily.

"You mean he's been able to leave the OR?"

"For at least thirty minutes," the nurse said.

Weakly, Rae hung up the phone and turned back to the bin. She examined the top bag and saw that it had been tampered with. Quickly she examined the other ten. Each had a hole over the nipple port.

"Hey, did you find what you were looking for?" Martin asked. Rae had not seen him approach her.

"He was right in front of me the whole time," Rae said as she picked up her mop. "I guess we only see what we want to see, Martin. We only believe what we want to believe."

And then she walked away, towards Walker's office. He was the CEO of the hospital. Walker would know what to do.

In a trance of grief and worry, and still dressed in her cleaning lady's outfit, Rae made her way through the hospital corridors somehow, and walked through Walker's open door and into his office. The room was dark, so she clicked on the light. Walker wouldn't arrive for another two hours, but she couldn't wait. She had to tell him about Sam immediately, while he was still in the operating room.

She wondered if Walker had called the police and convinced them of her suspicions. Did he know about Theodore's death by now? Would the cops call him in the middle of the night just because an ambulance driver got killed in a crash?

She picked up the phone. Even the fact that she loved Sam could not prevent her from turning him in. With fingers that felt like lead, she dialed Walker's home number. She got a busy signal so she tried again. Still busy. Now who could Walker be talking to at five in the morning? Then she remembered that his daughter had moved to New York, and often called Walker at eight o'clock Eastern Standard Time. Rae hung up the phone. She'd try in another few minutes.

She collapsed in Walker's chair, remembering suddenly what it felt like to kiss Sam, and how his hands warmed her as they moved over her body. Were those truly the same hands that had spiked liters of lactated Ringer's with lethal doses of oxytocin? It seemed impossible. But Martin had written down Sam's name. Sam had motive and opportunity.

But did Rae *believe* that he did it? Isn't that what Sam had said love was all about? Was believing in the word of another person more important than the facts in front of her face?

She looked at the phone again. This time she found that she could not bring herself to call Walker. Besides, what exactly did she plan to tell him? So far he didn't believe anything she had said. At least Sam believed her oxytocin theory. Or he said he did. Was that to throw her off the track too? Would he have lied so consistently just to shut down the Birth Center? Did he want it that badly, more than anybody—

A knock on the door startled her. Her breathing stopped. Who knew she was there? Had she been followed?

The door clicked opened. She leapt out of her seat and ran for her mop. She kept her head down, too afraid to look up.

"Is somebody in here?" asked a hesitant female voice.

It sounded familiar to Rae, but she was too scared to place it.

"I've got to clean up now."

It was Claudia! Rae walked over to the door and flung it open. She smiled at Claudia's startled expression.

"Who are you?" Claudia asked.

"It's me, Claudia," Rae said. "Managed care has put such a dent in my income that I had to take on a second job."

"Dr. Duprey?" Claudia asked, her eyes blinking.

"It *is* Halloween," Rae said.

She stepped out of the way but Claudia didn't budge. "What are you doing here this time of night, honey?"

Rae sighed. "I've got to talk to Walker, Claudia," she said. "I thought I'd call him from here."

"Don't you have a phone at home?" Claudia asked, concerned.

Rae laughed. "I'm going to wait a few more minutes before I make my call. Come on in and clean up if you want to."

"I could come back—"

"No, I'd love the company, really," Rae reassured her.

Claudia blinked one more time. "That *is* you, Dr. Duprey. Child, you really had me going." She pushed her vacuum cleaner in and whistled as she went about cleaning the office.

Rae dialed Walker's home number, then frowned when she heard the busy signal again.

"Well, well, well, looks like Mr. Stuart left this open. He never does that."

Rae looked up and saw Claudia standing in front of the glass cabinet. "Want to hear a little music, Claudia?" she asked, walking over.

Claudia chuckled. "You sound like you've got man problems, sugar," she said.

Rae thought of her upcoming conversation with Walker. She shrugged her shoulders and sighed. "Why do we always wind up hurting the ones we love, Claudia?" she asked.

"You never hurt your true love. The Lord makes sure of that, one way or the other."

How Rae wanted to believe her!

"Well, I'm all done here, sugar," Claudia said. "Mr. Stuart is very neat. I always get this place cleaned in no time."

"Sure you don't want to listen to some music?" Rae asked as she stood in front of the cabinet. The glass door was indeed slightly ajar.

"No time," Claudia said as she backed out the door with her vacuum cleaner. "I don't even have time to do the job they're paying me for."

After she left, Rae opened the cabinet and retrieved the cradle. Walker would make everything okay again and if the board of trustees agreed to keep Rae's department open, Walker would be dedicated to making sure it remained the number one maternity unit in the state.

The soft satin felt good against Rae's fingertips. She opened the cradle and found that the secret compartment, too, was unlocked. A lullaby would be just the thing.

Opening the tiny door she reached in to turn the knob. But instead, her fingertips grazed what seemed to be several small medicine vials. Rae pulled out one of them. It sat in her fingers as if frozen to her skin. She stared at it in sheer disbelief. It was a vial of oxytocin.

Quickly she pulled out the others. In total there were ten. Ten clear vials that looked like Christmas tree lights. But these vials were no presents. Her pulse roared in her ears. Walker—not Sam—was the baby killer!

Quickly she placed the vials back into the cradle, and then the cradle back on the shelf. She ran to the phone and picked up the receiver, but just as quickly put it down again. How did she know Walker put those oxytocin vials in the cradle? How did she know that he had anything to do with anything?

Because she *believed* he did, she realized. *Desperate people do desperate things.* Walker's words echoed in her mind. She had not known it at the time, but he had spoken from the heart.

Again she lifted the phone and dialed the operating room. But before the nurse answered, Rae heard the doorknob turning. She slipped the receiver back into place and grabbed her mop. With her head down, she began pushing the cart out of the room.

She never looked up. But her heart stopped when she noticed Walker's shoes. No one else in the hospital wore such shiny wing tips. The shoes stopped to let her by. She could only hope that he had not recognized her.

Soapy water sloshed out of the bucket as she rushed down the hall to the service elevator. She kept looking over her shoulder, expecting to see Walker trailing her. But the hallway remained empty. When the doors opened, she banged the bucket against the frame. Water drenched the hem of her pants and the noise seemed loud enough to wake the dead. Inhaling deeply, she told herself to stay calm.

She left the bucket and mop outside the female physicians' locker room, but when she opened the door another bleary-eyed doctor stood in front of her. Immediately Rae cast her eyes downward and pretended to ready the room for vacuuming while she waited for the doctor to leave. Everyone knew that Rae had been suspended. She couldn't afford for the obstetrician to call security.

Finally the woman left without so much as giving Rae a second glance. She hurried to the wall phone that was just on her left. "Damn it!" she said after calling the operating room and getting a busy signal. She had to talk to Sam! She dialed again. Still busy.

The clock read 5:25 A.M. Sam should finish the case in half an hour. Her only choice was to go down to the operating room. First she had to change her wet clothes. Only clean scrubs were allowed downstairs.

Nervously she turned the dial of her locker's combination. But her shaking fingers overshot the last turn and she had to dial it again. That was when she heard the door to the locker room click open. She looked up, prepared to explain to the person entering that she was just cleaning out her locker. But her words froze in her throat. Standing there, holding the red satin cradle, was Walker.

Rae removed her hand from the lock. Her pulse was racing out of control. Did Walker know that she knew?

Jerking her thumb over her shoulder, she said with a forced smile, "The boys' locker room is down the hall, Walker."

He didn't smile.

"I told you I would take care of things," he said. He threw the cradle to the floor. Brahms's Lullaby played for a few notes, and then everything was silent.

"Walker, listen—" Rae began, but stopped when she saw his hand reach into his suit pocket and pull out a gun. Her eyes widened.

The silver caught the light from the ceiling as he pointed the gun directly at her chest.

"Never trust a junkie," he said. "Perhaps I should thank you for getting rid of him for me."

Rae remembered the sight of Theodore's dead body splayed out on the pavement. "I don't know what you mean, Walker," she said hoarsely.

"Maybe if you hadn't left that case open," he said, "I might not have put two and two together. Your disguise—it almost worked. But I saw Claudia leave my office earlier. And besides, you don't walk like a janitor. Not even close."

Rae laughed unsteadily as she finished turning the combination and opened her locker. "You've got this all wrong, Walker."

"Get away from there!" he shouted suddenly.

She stopped. She felt her heart would too. Walker had killed so many people. He'd kill her, of that she had no doubt. But there had to be a way, she thought. It couldn't end like this.

"I mean it, Walker, you don't understand."

He took a step closer. "I said, get away from there."

The Dictaphone was resting on top of a pile of clothes in her locker. As she turned to face Walker fully she picked it up lightly and slipped it into the right-hand pocket of her baggy scrub pants. She could only hope her body had shielded the action from him.

"You should have listened to me," Walker said.

Her heart leapt to her throat. He had seen her! Think, Rae, think! she pushed herself as she closed the locker door with shaking hands.

"Please, Walker," she began, "there's been enough killing."

She stopped talking when he pointed the gun to her head. Would she hear the gun go off just before the bullet burrowed through her brain? Would it hurt? Was there life after death? Would Sam ever know that she loved him?

She squeezed her eyes shut. There was nothing else to do.

"Now, let's get going," Walker said.

Startled, Rae opened her eyes again. He stood at the open door, his gun still pointed in her direction. Confused, and afraid, she remained where she was.

"Remember, say anything—do anything—and you wind up like the others. Oh, and don't worry about your outfit. Nobody bothers the cleaning lady, right? Now move. Take your bucket and mop with you."

"Where are we going?" she asked as he grabbed her by the elbow and shoved her into the empty hallway. If only someone would come by! she thought frantically.

"Why, we're going to spike a few bags of salt water," Walker said with feigned sweetness.

The emergency room! Rae thought. Perhaps she would have a chance to escape.

Walker shoved the gun into her side. She winced at the pain.

"I know what you're thinking, but forget it," he said. "We're in this together, just like always."

# 30

THE BACK HALLWAYS WERE AS QUIET AS DEATH. RAE WALKED alongside Walker and he stared straight ahead. She wondered how many times he had walked to the emergency room knowing that his actions would kill innocent women and their babies. Time, she needed time, she decided. Somehow, she was going to get away from Walker. Or die trying, she thought.

After riding the service elevator, they walked through the back hallway that led to the emergency room. Rae stopped before they went in and asked, "Shouldn't we go in the back door?"

"Why would we do that?" Walker asked. "I'm the CEO. You're the cleaning lady. Who cares what either of us does around here?"

Inside, the emergency room was total pandemonium. Halloween had obviously conferred more tricks than treats on Berkeley's citizens. It looked as if there was one big party going on with people in costumes, green and red hair, and dark makeup that made them look like cadavers. For a second Rae thought of breaking away, or running into the crowd. But Walker might shoot at her, she thought. She couldn't chance him hitting her or an innocent bystander.

"This way," he said, tapping Rae's shoulder.

She followed him down another hallway that led directly to the IV storage bin marked BC. Her pace slowed and she crashed the cart into the wall.

"Why so nervous?" asked Walker, as he patted her shoulder like an old chum. "These early morning hours are the best. Usually there aren't many people around, and those who do walk by are so sleepy they don't pay much attention."

"There's quite an audience tonight," Rae said.

"They don't care what we do, Rae. It's Halloween night—you're supposed to look scared."

"But the CEO—people will wonder why you're here," she tried.

"Not when you're known for keeping late and early hours." He smiled and for the first time Rae could see the arrogance on his face. How had she misinterpreted it for so many years? But as Sam had said, people believe what they want to believe.

Sam, she thought. How she wanted Sam!

Walker stopped in front of the bin. Rae looked around and just as he had said, there was no one in sight. The voices of patients and staff seemed far away here.

"The CEO of the hospital is above suspicion," Walker said as he opened his coat pocket and removed six syringes with five-inch spinal needles already attached. Rae could see that the syringes were prefilled with the oxytocin—the clear fluid that was meant to enhance labor, not hurl patients to their deaths.

Proudly he held up the syringes. "Lovely," he said. "So simple. As you can see, I've come prepared. I'd say I've gotten this down to a science."

Just like an executioner, Rae thought, as she recalled her conversation with Walker in Chez Panisse. Then he had pretended to know nothing about the chemistry of oxytocin. She felt like kicking herself. Why had she trusted him? Why hadn't she remembered that he had been a chemistry major, of all things? He had the greatest motive, the best access—

"As you seem to have guessed," he said, still looking at the syringes as adoringly as a parent looks at a newborn, "I've simply been popping these babies into the bags and then placing my call to Theodore. First I only spiked the bags when Bo was on call for the Birth Center. I thought he would, after a few bad babies, shut the damn thing down and bring his business back here."

"But he didn't," Rae said sadly.

"No, he didn't. He could have shut it down . . . he should have shut it down when he had the chance and sold the thing to Howard Marvin."

"Howard Marvin?" Rae asked incredulously.

"Damn it, Rae, quit being so naive," Walker said. They had been speaking in hushed voices, but Walker's voice had risen and he looked down at her like a father scolding a child.

"Why do you think I've been doing all of this?" he asked. "It's not just for the good of our patients. I get something out of it too. You heard Marco. Yes, I invested in that MRI scanner in Louisville. It was the last—and I'm afraid, the worst—in a string of rather unfortunate investments I've made recently. My daughter's tuition for law school, our savings, my pension plan—everything and anything I could find to throw at the deal of a lifetime, I was told. Of course, Denise didn't know. She would never have approved. But women—hell, what's life if you don't take chances?"

Rae watched Walker's face. He didn't even resemble the man she had known and respected for so many years. His expression was hard as flint and cruel, as if in his heart there was no longer room for compassion or empathy of any kind. Rae felt sick with the knowledge that she had trusted him with the lives so many people. But she'd have to deal with those feelings later. Right now she had future lives to save.

"So what happened?" she asked.

"Damn thing went belly up," he said. "Howard lost money on it too, but what's two hundred fifty grand when you've got millions? One day he called me. Expressed his condolences and all. He made me a deal. I accepted. All I had to do was persuade Bo to sell Howard the Birth Center so that Howard could turn it into that freestanding heart center Marco told you about, and he'd give me back the two hundred fifty thousand I put in—a bonus, if you will. Everything would be hunky-dory again. In fact, better. You'd keep your department open, Marco would be happy, the board would be smiling at all the new revenues coming in from our split with the heart center—"

"Just one big happy family," said Rae, trying to keep the misery out of her voice.

"Exactly," Walker said.

"So Howard Marvin's the one who's really been killing the babies?" Rae asked.

"Hell no," Walker said with a terrible grin. "I take full credit. The board tells me to keep this hospital in the black—not *how* to do it.

The only one who knew anything was that junkie. Howard didn't care how I got Bo to sell. He's an insurance man, Rae. Pure and simple. All he cares about is money."

"Sounds like a guy I'd like to have dinner with," Rae said bitterly.

"Anyway," Walker said, "after Bo refused to sell his precious little Birth Center, I figured maybe the other docs who delivered over there would get the message. So I had Theodore change the IV bags the day that Nola Payne came over."

"Why Nola?" Rae asked. Trying to keep a lid on her mounting anger was becoming impossible.

"I didn't care what patient came over," Walker said. "It was a crap shoot—since I never really knew on any given night if anyone would come over from the Birth Center at all." He paused to smile at her. "I knew you were on duty that night. I took the chance that if someone did come over you'd at least be the person to assist the Birth Center doctor if you didn't wind up doing the delivery yourself. You were my last resort, Rae. I knew you would want to find out why a woman could leave the Birth Center with a good fetal heartbeat and have a next-to-dead baby by the time she came over here."

"You set me up?" Rae whispered. Her mind sped back to that morning. Her eyes narrowed. So all of this had been planned and executed with military precision, she thought. And she had been the first lieutenant.

"The same with Meredith's baby," Walker said proudly. "When that happened, I knew two bad babies back to back would definitely get your attention."

"And Bernie?" Rae asked. "Did you try to kill her too?"

Walker frowned. "That damn junkie," he said. "All he was supposed to do was put the charts back. I had to review them, to make sure Bo hadn't changed anything to cover his ass. I never trusted him, Rae. I don't know what you ever saw in the man.

"Anyway, I told Theodore not to worry. No one would be hanging out in medical records at that time of the morning. But Bernie was there—"

"Trying to help me out," Rae said.

"I thought so," Walker said. "Theodore must have seen her and lost it."

"You used Marco's name to get the charts," she said.

"Hey, how did you know that?" Walker asked, clearly impressed.

"Just a wild guess," Rae said.

Walker patted Rae on the head. She felt like slapping it away. But she had a plan, and no matter what, she was determined to carry it out. If only she could buy some time.

"Well," Walker said, "let's get going. Since Theodore's no longer with us, we'll just have to wait for the new paramedic to use these bags on the next patients. Let's see—I have six syringes. That should get at least three patients in trouble, don't you think? I noticed, after reviewing the charts, that this stuff works better on women who have had at least one baby. That patient who ruptured her uterus the other day had had three."

He handed Rae one of the syringes. "Why don't you do the honor?" he asked sweetly.

Rae stared at the syringe.

"I . . . I think I should watch how you do it first," Rae said nervously.

She knew now that Walker was crazy. Whether it was the pressure of his job, or family, or an investment deal gone sour that had caused his insanity—Rae didn't care. Whatever it was, he had lost touch with reality. She was dealing with a lunatic, a madman.

Walker patted his jacket pocket, the one Rae knew contained the gun. "Come on, Rae. Even a novice could do it," he said.

"But I don't think I can get the needle in the right place."

"There is a silencer attached to this gun," Walker said deliberately, as if speaking to an extremely stupid child. She could hear the undercurrent of anger in his voice. "I don't have to tell you how much I need Bo to sell that Birth Center. Do it. Now."

Walker thrust the six syringes in front of Rae's face. Slowly she removed them from his hand and placed five in the top pocket of her scrub suit. Images of dead babies and dead mothers filled her brain. Could she stab Walker with the needles, she thought? He would shoot her first. Oxytocin would cause him no harm. She had to go along with him and pray that someone showed up.

Walker handed her a bag. He turned it so that she could see the rubber nipple port through the plastic wrapping.

"Like stealing candy from a baby," he said.

"But these already have holes in them," Rae said.

"Ah, so they do," Walker said. "I forgot that I just put them in.

Right after I saw Dr. Hartman leave the area. Oh, and right after Martin went on his break.''

No wonder Martin had not jotted Walker's name down on his list, she thought ruefully. She paused again and then plunged the needle through the plastic and into the nipple port.

''Now squeeze,'' he said, and she pushed the plunger. The oxytocin went in quickly, disappearing into the watery solution with deadly speed.

Suddenly, Rae heard a commotion. She looked up and saw Officer Mailer standing farther down the hall. Next to him stood Sergeant Lane. Both had their guns drawn. Two nurses and Dr. Everett Lloyd also looked on. Rae stared at Walker, then at the bag, and then at the empty syringe in her hand.

''Oh, I forgot to tell you,'' Walker whispered, ''I called these representatives of Berkeley's finest before I came to your locker room.'' Then he stepped away and in an authoritative voice said, ''Perfect timing, gentlemen. May I introduce you to your baby killer, Dr. Rae Duprey.''

''No, he's—'' Rae started to say.

''Move away from him!'' Officer Mailer called out.

''But—''

''I said move away!''

Rae dropped the bag and the syringe. With her right hand she reached into her pocket.

''Get your hands up!'' Mailer cried shrilly.

Unable to speak, all she could do was raise her hands slowly and show the Dictaphone as clearly as she could.

''Don't make me have to use this thing,'' Mailer said.

''Not so fast, gentlemen. I think I have something you might want to hear.''

''This is your final warning, *Doctor,*'' Mailer said coldly.

''She's bluffing!'' Walker said, even as he stared at her with disbelief.

Rae knew she had to hurry before he regained his composure.

''Oh, really?'' she asked. She started to press the button to rewind the tape. ''On here,'' she shouted to the crowd in front of her, ''is Walker's confession. He's the one who spiked the bags. He's the one who's killed the babies. I have it all here.''

''She has nothing!'' Walker shouted.

"Then listen to this!"

But before Rae could turn on the machine, Walker knocked the Dictaphone out of her hand and sent it flying. She tried to make a run for it, but he grabbed her and pulled her against his chest. His gun was out and pressed to the side of her head.

"I'll shoot her, I swear I'll blow her brains out!" he shouted.

"Everybody back!" Officer Lane called out.

To Rae's horror, the two policemen and the emergency room staff disappeared around the corner. Walker held her there for a few seconds. She was too terrified to move, too terrified to breathe. "Move it!" Walker said.

He pushed her toward the end of the hallway. "Let us out of here!" Walker shouted.

"Drop your gun, Mr. Stuart!" Sergeant Lane called out. "Then just let her go and nobody gets hurt."

They had reached the spot where the officers had been. Walker had shoved the gun so deeply against her throat that swallowing was painful. "Damn you, Rae!" he said, his voice cracking.

Rae forced herself to stay alert. Walker's arm was around her neck like a vice so it was difficult to see to her left or right. Finally, as they rounded the corner, the entire emergency room came into view. Straining to turn her head, she could just see the officers positioned behind a bin, and to the right of them a crowd of patients and medical staff looking on.

"I want these people out of here!" Walker said.

Then, from within the crowd, a commotion started and Rae saw a man dressed as a beetle push his way through. "Hey!" he shouted in a drunken voice, "Who's the Jimmy Cagney over there—"

The blast from Walker's gun almost burst Rae's eardrums. Obviously he had lied about the silencer. Rae watched the man's body drop to the ground. Immediately Walker's gun was pressed against her head.

"I mean it!" Walker said. "Now you put *your* guns down or I'll kill the doctor!"

No one moved.

"I said put your guns down!" Walker screamed out again.

What had Sergeant Lane said about being in a hostage situation? she thought desperately. Something about distracting the hostage taker, but how? Walker was holding her so tightly she could barely breathe, let alone think.

It came to her suddenly, in a rush. Blink at the officer. Lane had said to blink at the officer. But did they have a good view of her face? she thought, panicking. She turned her head a fraction to the right, in the officer's direction. The barrel of Walker's gun dug deeper and more painfully into her skull.

She had hoped Lane was closest to her, but as it turned out Mailer had the best view of her face. Locking her eyes onto his as best she could, she blinked once. When he didn't respond, she blinked again.

She saw him stare uncomprehendingly back at her. Damn it! she thought. She blinked for a third time. Now, what had the sergeant said? Blink, and when the officer gave the signal, she was supposed to faint? But what was the signal? She had never found out.

"You son of a bitch!" she said to Walker. "Go ahead and shoot me. Then they'll shoot *you,* and that's all that counts."

Walker shoved the gun in harder. At the same time, Rae saw two nurses approach in the opposite direction.

"Hey!" one of them called out.

"Get back!" Mailer cried.

Walker's gun went off twice. Screaming, the two nurses threw themselves to the floor as bullets sprayed against the wall behind them.

"I mean it!" Walker shouted.

Then, to Rae's added horror, Sam entered the room. His eyes locked onto hers. "No!" he shouted and started toward her.

"Sam, stop!" Rae said. She struggled against Walker, but again his gun went off. "Mailer!" she called out. He turned to look at her and she blinked her eyes slowly. Would it work this time?

He stared at her for a second and then nodded. He reached up and scratched his nose. Was he giving her the signal? She could only guess. Either way, she could be a dead woman.

Now! she told herself. She let her body go limp against Walker's. She heard the sound of a different gun go off. Suddenly she was free, and falling to the floor . . .

But Walker's body did not fall next to her.

"He's on the move!" shouted Sergeant Lane as Walker ran toward the crowd. People screamed. Turning her head, Rae watched him disappear. The officers couldn't shoot. They would only hurt innocent people.

Rae rose and rushed to Sam, as did several of the ER personnel. Wincing, he tried to push himself up with his left hand. Blood poured out of his right shoulder and onto his white surgical gown.

"Can't you give him something, Everett?" she begged the emergency physician as she helped Sam onto the gurney.

"Are you all right?" Rae asked as she cradled Sam's head in her hands.

"Am I all right?" Sam said with a pained smile. "You're the doctor. What do you think?"

Rae bent down and kissed his forehead. "I'll tell you later," she said. "I've gotta go."

"Rae!" Sam yelled out after her, but she was already running down the hallway. She had a murderer to catch.

Walker C. Stuart.

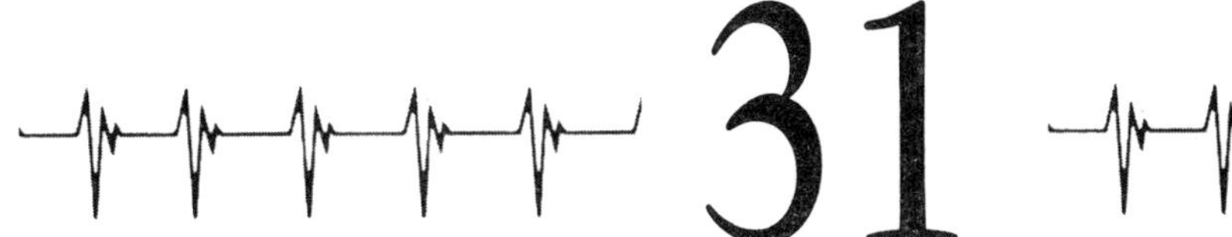

# 31

IMMEDIATELY OUTSIDE THE EMERGENCY ROOM RAE FELT A strong hand grabbing her shoulder. She turned in fear, expecting to find Walker and his gun. But it was only Sergeant Lane. He held her tight while he spoke in a cool voice into a wall phone.

"Let me go," Rae said as she tried to jerk free.

"You're staying with me," the sergeant said to her, then into the phone he said, "Okay, got it. Mailer's on his tail. He has a radio. We'll get him. You just get your team here."

When he hung up he looked at Rae. "We might get lucky," he said. "The SWAT team was already assembled—in the middle of a special training session in West Berkeley. Otherwise they'd all have to come in from wherever the hell they were." He paused to look at his watch. "ETA is ten minutes."

"We don't have ten minutes," Rae hissed, and this time she successfully freed herself from Lane's grasp.

Suddenly his radio blared scratchily and Rae could just make out Officer Mailer's voice. "He's up here—they've got some kind of garden—"

"He's on the seventh floor!" Rae said, and she darted toward the stairs.

Sergeant Lane caught up with her and grabbed the back of her shirt. "Now listen," he said. "He's armed and dangerous. You stay down here."

"He may be on the roof now, but he won't stay there," Rae said.

She had turned to face the sergeant. "Just how well do you know this hospital?" she asked.

"This isn't my first time here if that's what you mean," he said defensively.

"Please," she said, suddenly deciding to change her approach. "He killed those women, those babies . . . he almost killed my best friend. I can't stay here—nobody knows this hospital better than I do. I can show you the shortcuts. We've got to catch him."

The sergeant frowned, but Rae saw a glint of understanding in his eyes, the same look she saw when a patient was given a treatment option bound to be painful, but nevertheless, likely to cure. "Okay, just stay where I can see you," he warned.

Rae ran up the seven flights of stairs with Lane close on her heels. There were only two doors that led onto the garden. A crowd of nurses had gathered at the west doorway, so Rae knew it must be the one Walker had taken.

"Move it!" the sergeant said as he pushed his way through the throng of people. Rae followed him out into the night.

At first all looked quiet. Suddenly, Officer Mailer stood up from behind one of the planters lining the path. In both hands he held his gun, crouching low as he walked. Sergeant Lane pulled his gun out and told Rae to stay back.

He scampered to one of the planters and crouched down. Rae looked out from behind a pole to see if she could see Walker. Across the garden was the other exit door, still closed. It was in easy view. If Walker had escaped from the roof garden, Mailer would have seen him.

Walker could be in any number of places. What was a beautiful garden by day was now a haven for a fugitive by night, Rae thought. And Walker Stuart was a fugitive. The man who was trusted by the hospital's board of trustees to run the hospital was now on the run himself.

Mailer moved closer to the far edge of the garden. He advanced stealthily, always checking his back, crouching lower and lower, hands steady on his gun.

When he was a couple of inches away, he leaned over as if expecting to find Walker hanging down from the ledge. Suddenly Rae saw a hazy figure dart toward him. "Mailer!" she shouted.

But her warning came too late. Walker had come out of the

shadows and ran at Mailer from his blind side. In what appeared like slow motion, Walker crouched down and pushed his shoulder into Mailer's back. Mailer's gun exploded, the sound piercing the night air like the explosion of a truck tire.

Mailer's body hit the concrete ledge and his feet flipped over his head. His death-scream filled the night. Sergeant Lane's gun exploded next, but Walker's shadowy figure disappeared behind another planter.

Rae closed her eyes as she imagined Mailer hitting the pavement, seven stories below.

"Stay down!" Sergeant Lane shouted in Rae's direction as he crawled from one planter to the next. Then the far door opened, and Walker's shadow slipped inside.

"Where's that door lead to?" he shouted to Rae, who had already run out to meet him.

"Down the back stairway—"

"Come on!" Lane said. He entered first, telling Rae to hold back until he made certain Walker was not waiting for them. With her back against the concrete wall, she waited for Lane to let her know it was safe to enter.

"When's the SWAT team getting here?" she whispered.

"Little good they'll do until we have him cornered," Lane hissed back.

Suddenly from someplace in the distance Rae could hear the sound of sirens. There was also the harsh honking of a fire truck. "Stay close," Lane said to her as he waved her in.

Rae nodded as she followed the sergeant down the stairs. At each landing he went ahead of her. Every door they passed was closed. The sergeant stopped, hesitated, and then moved on.

When they reached the third floor—the maternity ward—she saw that the door had been left open. Lane stopped and told Rae to stand all the way back. He peered carefully around the other side. Rae expected to hear the sound of Walker's gun exploding in the stairwell. But there was only silence.

"He'll need another hostage," Lane said. "His best chance is another woman."

They were now standing inside the maternity unit, in the stark white hallway that was like a second home to Rae. "But the nurses will see him," Rae said.

"He's got that gun, remember?" Lane said. "It's a powerful negotiator."

And sure enough, Rae heard screaming coming from the direction of the labor deck. Lane took off to the right.

"No!" Rae shouted after him. "He's going left!"

The sergeant stopped cold. "Look, I know where the maternity unit is."

Rae's mind raced. She had a hunch, and the more she thought about it the more certain she felt. "You said he needed a hostage. I think Walker's going somewhere where it's real easy to get one."

"Which is?"

"The nursery!" Rae cried. "He's headed for the babies!"

"Holy Jesus!" Sergeant Lane said. "Are you sure?"

"Come on!" Rae called as she ran in the direction of the nursery.

"Hey, I said to stick with me!"

But Rae was already racing down the hallway, leaving Lane behind. The back of her throat felt raw and burned. Breathing was getting more and more difficult. Not because she was out of shape, but because a tremendous fear now filled her heart. Fear for the lives of the babies in the nursery. The innocent, smooth-skinned, flat-nosed babies she loved more than her own life.

Taking a little-used back hallway to the nursery, Rae cautiously made her way to a storage room that led to it. The room was separated from the nursery by a door with a small window. A smudge clouded the glass. Rae rubbed it with the heel of her hand. Sure enough, there stood Walker, his back to her.

In front of Walker stood two nursery nurses, with stunned expressions on their faces. Walker turned slightly, and Rae saw that he held a naked newborn in the crook of his left arm. Against the side of the baby's head was the barrel of Walker's gun.

It took all of Rae's willpower not to rush blindly at him and grab the baby. The *little baby!* She had to save him!

Rae looked around the storage room. What could she use as a weapon? If only she could sneak up behind him and hit him on the head, or distract him long enough for Sergeant Lane to shoot him. She glanced back through the window. Where the hell *was* Sergeant Lane? she thought. And the SWAT team? How much more containment did they need?

Running her hands through her hair, she turned and studied the contents of the room. There were only surgical gowns and a few IV bags, a sink and a paper towel dispenser. Rae looked back into the nursery. Maybe she could pick up something along the way. Something big and heavy that would take care of Walker with one blow. But not so heavy that she couldn't lift it, and swing it hard . . .

Out of the corner of her eye she saw, across the room to her left, a shadowy figure enter a doorway. It must be a member of the SWAT team! The man held a rifle and it was pointed directly at Walker.

Why doesn't he shoot? Rae thought frantically. But how could he shoot with all the babies everywhere? Even from Rae's position on the opposite side of the door she could hear the chorus of newborns crying from their bassinets, as if they knew Walker was in the nursery and holding a gun to one of their own.

She couldn't just stand there, she agonized. And where were the other members of the SWAT team? Where was Sergeant Lane? What was wrong with these people? Why didn't they move in?

The phone in the nursery rang and Rae jumped. She watched as Walker kept the gun pointed at the baby and nodded at one of the nurses to answer the phone. It was Jessica, she noted with dismay. Jessica picked it up, then held it out to Walker.

"Tell them I want to talk to my wife!" Walker shouted, his voice cracking. "I want to talk to Denise!"

Jessica spoke into the receiver. "They'll find your wife—but they need time."

"Three minutes!"

"They said it'll take fifteen minutes to get her here!" Jessica cried. Her hands shook perceptibly, and even Rae could see the tears in her eyes.

"Tell that to this baby!" Walker snapped. "Three minutes!"

Rae saw the second hand beating past the numbers on the clock. Her own heart beat much faster. Three minutes to live! The baby looked no more than two hours old. Two hours and three minutes of time on this earth—no way, Rae told herself. No way in hell.

Again she looked around the room for something to use against Walker. Maybe if she simply barged out and rammed into him, she wouldn't need to hit him.

The phone rang for a third time. "She's coming, she's on her way!" Jessica shouted frantically.

"Two minutes!" Walker shouted.

What had Walker also said about desperate people? Desperate people do desperate things. He had not been speaking of quiet desperation, the way so many people lived out their lives. No, he meant the kind of desperation that was defined by one's actions, not one's thoughts or desires or dreams.

"Please, Mr. Stuart," Rae heard another nurse plead. "Let the babies go. You have us."

"Shut up!" Walker said. "Just shut the hell up and get me my wife!"

The nurse fell silent, but the babies screamed louder.

"I know you're out there!" he said. "I know what you're thinking!"

At first Rae thought Walker was hearing voices, or seeing things. She scanned the windows that surrounded the nursery. She saw no one, and then she understood what Walker meant: the rest of the SWAT team had them surrounded but were staying out of sight. But what exactly were they waiting for?

Then Rae saw another figure slip into the shadow next to the SWAT team officer she had seen earlier. It was Bo! He saw her too, and put his finger to his lips.

"Walker!" he shouted. "It's me, Bo! Please, put your gun down. I'll sell the Birth Center—hell, I'll shut it down right now! But let the baby go, Walker. Let all the people go!"

"Too late!" Walker yelled out. He was crying now.

"Rae!" Walker called out. "I know you're out there, too. Tell them, Rae! Tell them I want to talk to Denise!"

Ring phone, ring! Rae thought. Surely the SWAT team wasn't foolish enough to think Walker was bluffing? Surely they were not waiting for Walker's self-imposed time limit to elapse just to see what he would do.

"Talk to them, Rae!" Walker was sobbing outright now. "Tell them they have a choice. They can waste some more time out there or they can get Denise here and save this kid! She's all I have left, Rae. You know that. Who do you want to save now, Rae? Tell them they want to save this baby! Tell them for me—you're the only one who can!"

Hearing Walker speak directly to her was like a cold slap in the face. He was right! Rae thought in amazement.

*Save the life! Save the life!* She knew just how to save hers and those of the babies she had dedicated her life to. Now her thoughts were clear, her plan as precise as the blade of her favorite scalpel.

Slowly she crouched down on her hands and knees. The tile felt cool to her palms. She pushed open the door cautiously, hoping the movement would go unnoticed. The only person who had a good view of it was the SWAT team member in the little alcove on the other side of the room.

Her heart hammered against her chest as she crawled into the nursery. She held on to the door as it closed. Listening for a gasp from one of the nurses, or a shout of reognition from Walker, she waited on her hands and knees. But the only sounds were the increasingly frantic cries of the babies.

She looked up slowly as she made her way across the floor. The hard surface hurt her knees and she wondered briefly how babies ever made crawling their primary mode of transportation. She could see Walker's profile. His usually neatly combed hair was now sticking out wildly from his head. His tie was loosened. The gun was now against the baby's cheek, and Rae's heart went out to the tiny creature even more when she saw it opening its mouth toward the gun's tip in a nursing reflex.

Now she was hidden behind a counter, out of view of everyone in the room. To her right was another door, and standing there she saw four members of the SWAT team with their rifles drawn.

She rounded the counter and four feet in front of her she saw the back of Walker's legs. When she looked up, she could see the baby that Walker held in his hand still rooting toward the barrel of the gun. Overhead the second hand clicked down to thirty seconds. It was now or never.

Rae sprang up from the floor. In her hand were the five syringes Walker had given her earlier, protective sheaths off. She clasped them within her palm and drew her hand back. She heard a nurse gasp.

Walker turned, but before he could redirect his gun, she plunged all five needles into the left side of his neck. Save the baby! That was what she had been trained to do. She felt the needles dig deep into his flesh, and she kept pushing, hoping to hit the brachial plexus, the set of nerves that runs from the brain to the arm.

Walker gave a terrible, ferocious scream, and, as if in slow motion,

Rae saw the baby begin to drop to the ground. She dove for the floor, her body slamming onto the cold tile just before the baby's, who landed instead in her outstreatched arms.

Rae heard the sound of gunfire overhead. Turning her head up, she saw Walker's body falling toward her, blocking out the light in an explosion of blood and noise, and she ducked her head back down and cradled the baby to her chest tightly. The breath whooshed out of her lungs from the force of Walker's body landing on her, but she held on to the baby as if it were the last thing she had to do.

The sound of heavy boots rushing into the nursery finally made her look up. The SWAT team surrounded her, guns drawn. Somebody pulled Walker off of her, and she looked down at the baby, who was staring back at her with questioning eyes. A boy, she thought dazedly. It was a beautiful baby boy.

"Are you okay, Dr. Duprey?"

The voice belonged to Sergeant Lane. He reached down to take the baby from her. But she held on for a few more minutes, and only after having satisfied herself that he was fine, did she hand him to the policeman.

As she pulled herself to her feet, she looked over at Walker. His suit coat was open and his chest was riddled with bullet holes. His face was unmarked. How peaceful it seemed, she thought. He looked like the Walker she had first met, a man filled with a dream for the world's greatest hospital.

There was a pool of blood spreading on the floor beneath him. Rae reached up and felt more blood from Walker's body on her neck. She stared at her fingers and then looked over at the baby.

"Clean as a whistle," the sergeant said, reading her mind.

"I've got to go back to the emergency room," she told Lane.

"Rae."

She turned. Standing there was Bo.

"I'm so sorry," he said. "I never thought—"

"None of us did," she said.

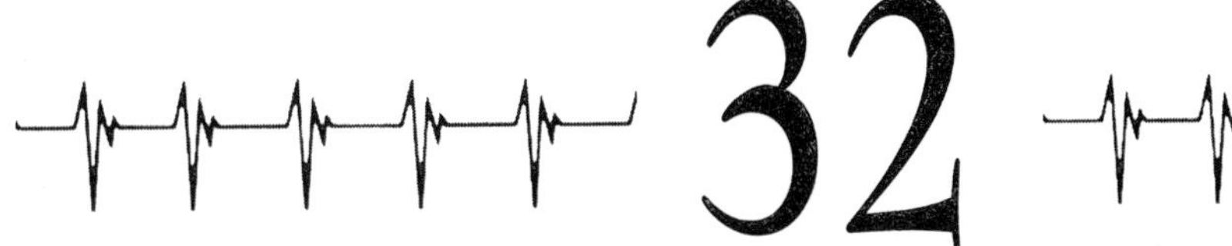

# 32

"It only hurts when I laugh," Sam told Rae as the emergency room doctor finished bandaging up his arm. She had showered and changed back into her street clothes.

"Come back in five days and I'll take out those stitches," Dr. Lloyd said. He scribbled a prescription on a pad.

Sam smiled and thanked him, then turned to Rae and said, "Maybe he ought to write a sleeping pill for you."

But before Rae could answer, she saw a couple of ambulance attendants walking by. They were pushing a gurney covered by a sheet. Tenting the sheet was the outline of a human figure.

"He was my friend," Rae said as it rolled past. "One of my very best friends."

Sam rose and took her hand. "No he wasn't, Rae. Let's go see a real friend."

Inside the intensive care unit, Rae stood next to Sam at Bernie's bedside.

"Why don't I give you two a moment alone," Sam said.

She pulled up a chair next to Bernie's bed. Outside the window, the sun was coming up on the San Francisco skyline. The bay waters were still—not a whitecap in sight. The horizon under the Golden Gate Bridge was as sharp as a pencil line. Rae took Bernie's long, tapered fingers into her own. They were warm and alive and to Rae, that was all that mattered for now. She gazed out the window again and thought what a nice view Bernie would have when she woke up.

"We found the person who did this to you, Bernie," she said. "You can wake up now because you'll never have to worry about him again."

She squeezed her friend's hand harder, and waited for her words to sink in—not just into Bernie's mind, but into her own heart, where they were sorely needed.

"I hear she's doing better," Sam said, joining her at the bedside.

"She's going to be just fine, Sam," Rae said, rising.

At the elevator, with Sam at her side, Rae pressed the button for the third floor.

"What now? Don't you think you ought to be heading home?" Sam asked.

"Almost," Rae answered.

When the doors opened, Rae led Sam to the nursery. The baby who had been held hostage by Walker was now swaddled in a warm blanket and nursing contentedly at his mother's breast while she spoke to two of the staff pediatricians. The other babies in the room were now quiet, a rare thing indeed. *"Now,* I can go home," Rae said with a satisfied smile.

About halfway down the hallway, Rae saw Nola Payne coming toward her, and walking next to her, holding a huge newborn baby—Baby Jesus!—was a nurse. The last time they had met, Nola didn't recognize her. Still, the sight of her with her baby filled Rae with pride.

"Baby Jesus," Nola said. She stopped and the nurse stopped too. Rae studied the baby, who stared back at her with big, slate-blue eyes. Then he smiled. Just let anyone try to convince her it was gas!

"Baby Jesus," Nola repeated.

But Rae didn't need to be told whose baby this was, or that by some miracle he had risen from what was as near to death as one could get. As she gazed upon him, his little dimples and his triple-rolled chin, she felt overcome with an emotion long suppressed.

A tear slid down her right cheek and stopped at the corner of her lip. She tasted its saltiness with wonder; it had been so many years since she had cried that she had forgotten tears had any taste at all.

"Hey, don't cry! He's going to be all right," the nurse said cheerfully.

"I know, I know," Rae said smiling, and when the second tear came, she didn't bother to wipe that one away either. The first tear had been for Nola's baby. This one was for her mother, almost twenty-five years late.

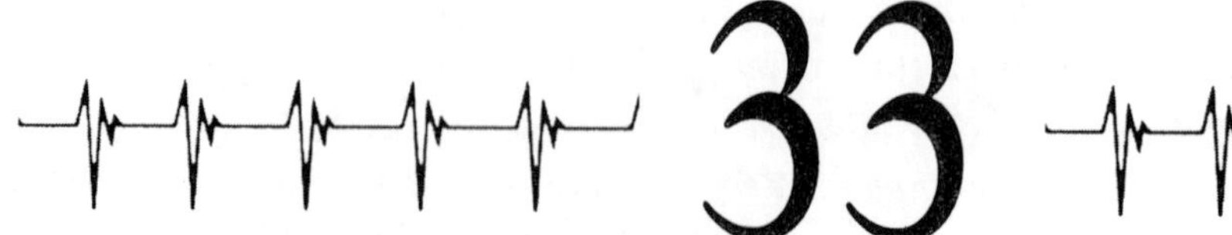

# 33

WITH SAM AT HER SIDE, RAE WALKED BACK THROUGH THE emergency room. It would be so good to get home, she thought wearily. It would be so good to fall asleep in Sam's arms.

At the exit, she and Sam ran into Bo.

"Could I speak to you for a minute, in private?" he asked.

"Excuse us, Sam," she said.

"Not a problem."

She followed Bo to the far corner. "You might be interested to know that I've come to a decision," Bo said. "I'm not going to close the Birth Center—"

Rae waited for the rest of the bad news.

"—but I am," Bo continued, "going to turn it into an outpatient, prenatal clinic. No more deliveries there, Rae. And I'm bringing all my patients back here. So is everyone else."

Rae stared at him, dumbfounded.

"Well, what do you think?" he asked.

Slowly, a smile spread across her face.

"And best of luck to you, Rae. No one deserves, or is more qualified, to run our department next year." He extended his right hand.

Rae extended hers. "There's still that little problem with my suspension," she said.

"What suspension?" Bo asked.

Bo let go of her hand and their eyes locked in gentle understanding. Then he left, and Rae felt as if she had just said good-bye to a stranger and hello to a new friend.

"Dr. Duprey! Dr. Duprey!"

It was Sylvia, the emergency room nurse.

"You dropped this, remember?" Sylvia asked. "I suppose the cops will be coming back soon to take it into custody."

In Sylvia's hand was Rae's Dictaphone. Rae took it and turned it on. "And some steak bones for Leopold," the machine said.

Rae laughed.

"What?" Sam asked.

She handed the Dictaphone back to Sylvia and slipped her hand through Sam's good arm. "I'll tell you later," she said.

Outside, the air was brisk and she could smell the salty scent of the bay. The wind had whipped up and she turned her face toward it. In front of her, reporters with cameras and microphones gathered around Heidi O'Neil, who, as usual, was tugging on the jacket of her red, two-piece suit.

"So, where to now?" Sam asked.

"Well, if you must know," she said, holding on to his good arm and snuggling closer to him, "all I want to do is to go home, get something to eat, take a hot shower, and get some sleep. But you had better stick around because when I wake up there's going to be some wild and passionate lovemaking going on. Now how's that for fitting medicine into my life and not the other way around?"

Sam wrapped his arm around her shoulder. "Sounds like a prescription not to be missed," he said. "After all, you're the doctor."

Rae smiled, and after a few thoughtful seconds said, "That I am, Dr. Hartman. That I most certainly am."